Maya
and the
Book of
Everything

Maya
and the
Book of
Everything

Laurie Graves

This book is published by
Hinterlands Press, Winthrop, Maine
hinterlandspress.com

ISBN: 978-0-9978453-0-3

Library of Congress Control Number: 2016913860

Chapter opener and incidental graphics: openclipart.org
Castle Graphic based on Château de Chaumont by Wladyslaw
Sojka at the German language Wikipedia

Cover design by James T. Egan of Bookfly Design

v 1.4

To Deirdre Graves, whose generosity and careful editing
helped make this book a reality.

To Shannon & Mike Mulkeen, for their close reading and
invaluable suggestions.

And to Clif Graves, who put it all together.

1: The Man Who Didn't Smile

The first time Maya Hammond saw the man who didn't smile, she and her mother, Lily Turcotte, were on a train going from New York to Boston. They had just passed the stretch that went by the seashore—Maya's favorite part of the ride—when she noticed him sitting two seats in front of her. The man was mostly bald, and he had glasses and a smooth, pale face. He wore khakis and a red-striped shirt. Really, there was nothing to set him apart from other men his age.

"But there was something about him," Maya would say later.

For one thing, he had a book in his lap and seemed to be reading, but every so often he would glance up at a woman who was sitting two seats down from him on the other side of the aisle. If Maya leaned just a little in her seat, then she could see the woman's profile—younger than her mother, curly brown hair, and a beautiful, clear complexion. "And afraid," Maya thought.

The woman gripped the arm of her seat, and every so often she would glance back at the man, as though she was checking to see if he was still there. But the woman never caught the man staring at her. Each time, the man appeared to be reading his book. But as soon as she turned away, he looked directly from his book to the woman.

The man who didn't smile must have sensed that Maya was watching him because he turned around so fast that Maya thought he was going to spring from his seat. Maya caught her breath as he considered her, his eyes the palest blue she had ever seen. He stopped frowning, but he didn't smile, and this was when Maya got the impression that here was a man who never smiled. Not ever. Twisting back in his seat, he immediately checked to see if the woman who was afraid was still there—she was—and then he gazed down at his book, pretending to read.

Maya's heart was beating fast and hard, and she looked at her mother to see if she had noticed the man. But Lily was asleep, her head tipped back, her mouth slightly open, and her arms folded across her chest as though she were holding herself close. A few strands of blonde hair brushed across her mother's cheek, and the rest was pulled back in a French twist that, depending on Maya's mood, sometimes seemed elegant and sometimes seemed irritatingly old-fashioned.

When had Maya realized her mother was different from most other mothers? Preschool, Maya had decided quite a while ago. Even when she was four, Maya had noticed the easy, chatty way the other mothers had with their children. Lily, on the other hand, hardly said a word when she brought Maya to school. There was just a fluttery kiss on the top of Maya's head or on her cheek, followed by a squeeze of the hand. And then Lily was gone.

"Thinking about colors and shapes," Maya thought.

As Maya got older, she discovered that her mother hated shopping even more than she disliked small talk. All of Maya's clothes came from catalogs, and Maya eventually realized that her clothes were more expensive than most of her friends' clothes.

"Your mother has never been stingy," Maya's father would point out when he still lived with them. Even so, Maya often thought that it would have been nice to go school shopping with her mother and to have lunch at a little restaurant that served tea, small sandwiches, and cookies.

Then there was her mother's fear of flying, which was so intense that Lily would throw up before getting on a plane. Long before Maya was born, Lily had given up flying, which was why they were on a train with the man who didn't smile and the woman who was afraid.

Slowly, so as not to attract attention, Maya glanced at the man who didn't smile. He was alert now, not even pretending to read his book, and Maya could see that the woman who was afraid was fidgeting as though she couldn't make up her mind whether to stay in her seat or to leave. The woman looked back, first at the man who didn't smile and then very briefly at Maya before quickly turning around in her seat.

But with that brief look, both considering and desperate, Maya was certain that the woman needed help, that something bad was going to happen to her. Maya felt it the way she always did, with a sudden knowing flash that was completely independent of what Maya hoped for or even wanted. So far, she had never been wrong, not even on the day her father had left her and her mother. For some time now, Maya had realized that she could see things that other people couldn't see. "Not cheesy things like ghosts," Maya might have said. Instead, she caught flashes of traits, motivations, and yearnings that people normally took great pains to hide. Sometimes, Maya even had premonitions.

How did these things come to her? Maya didn't know. They just came. But from an early age, Maya had figured out that most people didn't have these flashes, and even though Maya loved to talk, she had learned, over the years, not to mention them. Whenever she did, people would stare at Maya as though there was something a little odd about her. "You have a sixth sense," her grandmother—Mémère Celine—sometimes said, but Maya didn't like having this sixth sense, which made her different from everyone else.

As she watched the woman fidget, Maya knew that somehow she was going to help her. "But what can I do?" Maya asked herself, and then came the unbidden thought: Get up and walk toward the woman.

A family with three small, noisy children and equally noisy parents was heading her way down the aisle. They had chips and sandwiches and soda. Grabbing her messenger bag, Maya stood up, sliding the strap on her shoulder so the open pocket on the back faced outward. Maya decided to head to the snack bar to get a Coke. The first child, a girl, was almost by Maya's seat, and the second child, a boy, was by the man who didn't smile. As she slipped by the little girl, Maya pretended to stumble, tripping the little boy. His orange soda flew from his hand, landing in the lap of the man who didn't smile, and the boy fell with a thud.

"I'm sorry," Maya said truthfully, but the boy was howling with such volume that nobody heard Maya, and his parents rushed to his side, blocking the man who didn't smile.

Maya heard a snarl, and she knew just where it was coming from. But she didn't look back. Maya just kept walking, and when she passed the woman, Maya felt her slip something into the open pocket of her bag.

"Don't look down," Maya thought. "Keep walking." And that is exactly what she did, all the way to the car with the snack bar, where with trembling hands, Maya opened her bag and reached for her wallet. She allowed herself to glance at the outer pocket, but whatever was in there was tucked so far down that Maya couldn't see what it was.

"Later," Maya thought, as she grabbed the cold can of Coke from the man behind the counter and drank half of the soda so fast that she burped a mighty belch. The man laughed, and Maya, who was usually never at a loss for words, was so embarrassed that she couldn't even say, "Excuse me."

Moving quickly to an empty seat by a window, Maya finished her Coke just as the train pulled into the station in Providence. Reluctantly, Maya made her way back to her car, and as soon as she entered, she noticed two empty seats. Both the man who didn't smile and the woman who was afraid were gone.

"Please don't let them come back," Maya thought as she sat next to her mother, who was awake. Lily didn't say anything. She just smiled and patted Maya on the shoulder. Usually, Maya pulled away when her mother did this. What had been a sweet gesture when Maya was six or seven was embarrassing now that she was fifteen. Maya had explained this many times to her mother, but although Lily nodded and smiled sadly, she always seemed to forget, especially when they were in public.

However, today Maya didn't mind. All the while she watched the two seats, but they remained empty as the train left the station. Nevertheless, Maya didn't relax until a half hour had gone by, and there was still no sign of either the man or the woman.

Maya sighed. Lily frowned at Maya, giving her another pat on the shoulder.

2: Going North

As soon as Maya and her mother got off the train in Boston, Lily said, "Let's grab something to eat before we get on the bus for Maine." She headed for the food court, and Maya followed her, but her stomach felt queasy and her mouth dry. Lately, she hadn't had much of an appetite, and the incident on the train took away what little appetite she had.

"I just want something to drink," Maya said. "A strawberry smoothie, maybe."

"A smoothie? But you haven't eaten since morning. And then not that much."

"Mom, that's what I want. I'm not hungry."

Nodding, Lily left Maya and their bags at an empty table, and for once Maya was grateful that her mother wasn't much of a talker. If Maya had been traveling with her father, he would have pestered and cajoled her until she finally gave in.

Not that it was likely she would be traveling with her father anytime soon. He was in North Carolina with Inga Peterson, "that redhead," as Mémère Celine called her. With "that redhead" were her children—Tom, who was about Maya's age, and Caitlin, who was a little younger. Nowadays, Maya's father was taking Tom and Caitlin to the movies and to donut shops and to plays. At night, he would be reading to them in that thrilling voice he had, a voice that could be listened to for hours, as Maya and her mother had often done. He would be writing silly limericks for Tom and Caitlin and talking to them about school and their friends and Shakespeare and movies. Maya hated Inga, but she hated Tom and Caitlin more, even though she had never met them. And Maya didn't want to, either.

"Come down and visit us," Maya's father had said a few months ago when he called. "I miss you."

"No," Maya had answered. "I'm too busy with school. And there's the play."

"Wish I could be there to see you as Ariel in *The Tempest*, but you're too far away."

"Whose fault is that?" Maya asked, knowing she shouldn't have said it, knowing it would make him angry.

But her father just sighed. "I'm going to ignore that. I'd really like you to come and spend the summer with us."

"The whole summer?" Maya had asked. "We always go to Maine for a month."

"For one summer, you can skip going to Maine. Come on, Maya, I really do miss you." And he said it like he meant it.

"Well, maybe," Maya said, softening, but right after the call she changed her mind. "I just can't go down there," she said to her mother. "Not yet. Please don't make me."

Lily replied, "He's your father, Maya. You should go visit him."

"Why should I visit him? He left us, Mom. He left us for that redhead and her kids." Maya started to cry until she was crying so hard that she had the hiccups, and her mother had to give her warm milk and pat her on the back.

Lily finally said, "I'll see what I can do."

That night, after Maya went to bed, her mother made two phone calls—first to Maine and then to North Carolina. "Mom,"

Maya heard Lily say, "I don't know what to do with her. The two of them were so close. Now that Giles is gone, Maya cries over the smallest things. She hardly eats. She's just pining." There was silence as Lily listened. "Could we? For the whole summer? Are you sure it's not too much?" Another silence. "I know, Mom. I shouldn't ask such a question. But still." Lily's voice trailed off. "All right. Thanks, Mom."

Then the other call. "Giles, she just doesn't want to come down." A very long silence. "I know you have rights as her father. I've explained this to her." An even longer silence. "You shouldn't force her. She's old enough to decide where she wants to be. If you do, you'll just make it worse. And Maya's right. It's your own fault, Giles. Remember, you left us."

In the end, her father had given in, but not without a lot of fuming and complaining. "Nobody can go on like your father," Lily said later to Maya. She might have added, "Except you," but she didn't. Lily was not that kind of mother.

And so Maya and her mother were heading north, to Maine, to East Vassalboro, not for a month the way they usually did, but instead for the whole summer. They were carrying what they could. Books, extra clothes, paint, brushes, and easels had been packed and shipped and were waiting for them in East Vassalboro.

Never had Maya been so eager to leave New York City, which she loved, and their brick house, which seemed quiet and dull now that her father was gone. She didn't even mind leaving her best friends, Leah and Danielle, who would be going away with their own parents and wouldn't be back for a while. Leah would be in Maine, too, but on the coast, on Mount Desert Island, many miles away from East Vassalboro.

"I'm so glad to be going to Maine," Maya thought, watching her mother make her way between the tightly packed tables. An older man with gray hair stared at Maya's mother, but Lily ignored him and focused on the tray she was carrying.

"Oh, God," Maya thought. "That man thinks Mom is cute." And even though there was no resemblance between the two men, this man in the food court made Maya think of the man who didn't smile. Then came the awful thought: What if he had somehow followed her here? Maya looked around the food court, but she didn't see either a red-striped shirt or those pale blue eyes.

Just what was in her bag, anyway? Lily had almost reached the table, but Maya slid her hand into the outer pocket of her bag. She felt a roll of Life Savers, a nail file, some change, and something smooth, hard, and rectangular.

"A book," Maya thought, removing her hand from the pocket. She would take it out only in East Vassalboro, when she was alone in her room. It seemed too risky to look at it in public.

Maya's mother set the tray on the table. She had bought a salad, a bottle of water, a smoothie, and a muffin. "Who is the muffin for?" Maya asked as her mother sat down.

"You. I thought you might like one. I know how much you love them."

"I said I wasn't hungry." But then, perversely, Maya was hungry. Not only did Maya drink the smoothie and eat the muffin, but she also helped her mother eat her salad.

"It's nice to see you eat again," Lily said with a smile. "I'd buy more food, but we have to catch our bus."

Her stomach full for the first time in months, Maya fell asleep before the bus even left Boston. She leaned against her mother, and Lily sat very still, not wanting to disturb her. A light rain fell over the busy highway, over the cars and the trucks that passed them, and it tapped gently against the bus's cool windows.

When Maya woke up, they were nearly in Maine, almost at the big bridge that separated Maine from New Hampshire. This was her favorite part of the bus trip. The bridge made it seem as if they were leaving the mainland—the United States—and crossing to an island—Maine. A silly thought, Maya knew, but she loved imagining it anyway.

"We're going home," Lily murmured, shifting her stiff shoulder.

"Home," Maya thought. Normally, New York felt like home, but Maya had to agree with her mother. It felt like they were going home.

At the same time Maya and her mother crossed into Maine, a man with a red-striped shirt and pale blue eyes entered the food court at South Station in Boston. It was full of people, and the man circled patiently, searching the crowd. Reaching for something in his pocket, he held on to it but didn't take it out.

The man scowled fiercely, and a woman who was walking by veered sharply away from him. But he didn't notice the woman. She wasn't important. What he wanted was gone, and he was almost certain it had headed north, but other than that, he didn't have an idea where it was.

Something kept nagging at the edge of his memory. A teenage girl, dark haired and thin, with an impudent face, staring at him when he was on the train. But she couldn't be involved. They would never allow it. She was too young. Then the man re-membered the squalling boy and the explosion of orange soda. Grimacing, the man looked down at his stained pants. Had the girl slipped by during that awful commotion, when his hands had twitched, but he knew he couldn't do anything? The man stood very still. Of course she had. That's when it had happened. He swore softly and terribly, and although it was too low for anybody to hear, everyone passed by him in a wide circle, not wanting to be near him.

"I'll get you," he muttered. "Yes, I will. And this time, you won't slip away."

3: What Maya Found

When most people think of Maine, if they think of it at all, they picture the rocky coast, the little seaside towns, blueberries, and lobster. But to Maya, Maine wasn't the sparkling ocean or the salt-scented air or the waving sea grass. Instead, it was the hills, forests, and farms of inland Maine—bright green in the summer; brilliant red, orange, and yellow in early fall; austere brown in November; and glittering white in deep winter. It was the Kennebec River, which rushed through Waterville, the small city where Mémère Celine and Pépère Roland had been born, and flowed through Augusta, the state's tiny capital. Maya saw the great factories made of brick and steel, which either had been abandoned or had passed on to other uses—apartments, offices, stores, and warehouses.

Mostly, however, Maya thought of East Vassalboro, a country village, that felt even older than Mémère Celine and Pépère Roland. It was a town with a corner store that smelled of oiled floors; a grange hall, freshly painted inside and out, where there were public suppers, plays, and book sales; a small brick library, surprisingly new—the old one, a converted cottage, had burnt down years ago; a historical society housed in what had once been a school; and a big lake that sometimes turned green with algae in the summer.

In the end, though, East Vassalboro was really the farmhouse, more than 150 years old, where Mémère and Pépère lived and where Lily had grown up. Within walking distance of the village, the sprawling house sat beside a road that twisted around and went slightly uphill so that it overlooked the lumber yard, its stream, and the grange hall that were all on the main street. The house, painted white, had everything that Maya loved—a shed, a barn, a front porch, a big kitchen with a round oak table, an even bigger living room, lots of bedrooms, and an attic.

"How can I love both East Vassalboro and New York City?" Maya had once asked. "They're so different."

"I don't know," Maya's mother had answered. "But I feel the same way."

Mémère always made her special ginger cookies when Maya came to visit, cookies that were rolled in sugar and cracked on the top when they baked. They were Maya's favorite cookies, and they were Maya's father's favorite cookies, too.

Mémère brought a small tin with her when she and Pépère came to pick up Maya and her mother at the bus station in Portland. "A little snack for the way back," Mémère said as they drove out of Portland. After the tin had been passed, Maya held it on her lap and ate four cookies as fast as she could.

From the front seat, Mémère had been watching Maya. "You seem to have your appetite back."

"Yes," Maya answered, feeling her bag against her leg. She reluctantly passed the tin to Mémère. "But I think I've had enough."

"Right." Mémère took the tin. "You don't want to overdo."

All the way to East Vassalboro, Pépère and Lily were quiet, as they usually were, but every so often Pépère would look into the rearview mirror and smile at Maya in the backseat. Mémère, on the other hand, had to find out about school, Maya's friends, and what Maya was reading. Mémère spoke about the summer play the town's librarian, Anne Hunter, was directing at the grange, and how Maya should try out for a part. She talked about all the fun things they would do together—go swimming, pick berries, make pies, and go shopping at the stores in Augusta. Mémère did not mention Maya's father. This was the first summer he had not come with Maya and her mother to East Vassalboro, and Maya could tell that Mémère missed him, too.

The ride to East Vassalboro took over an hour, and the closer they got, the more eager Maya was to see exactly what was in her bag. It was a book, she knew, but what kind of book? Why had the man who didn't smile wanted it so much? And why did the woman who was afraid have the book? For that matter, why did the woman slip it into her bag? Fortunately, talking came naturally to Maya, and she could answer Mémère's questions and wonder about the book at the same time.

By the time Pépère drove the car into the driveway of the old farmhouse, it was all Maya could do to stop herself from bolting from the car and racing to her little bedroom beneath the eaves. But Maya knew better than to do that. If there was one thing no kid ever wanted to do, especially a teenager, it was to make parents and grandparents suspicious. So Maya carried her suitcase and bag up to her room and left them by the tall, dark desk that stood between the two windows that looked out into the rustling green leaves of a maple tree. Maya dutifully went downstairs to the kitchen to eat the snack Mémère had prepared for them—cheese, crackers, grapes, and dip. Only when the sun had finally set, and the sky was a deep blue but not yet black did Maya allow herself to yawn.

"Are you tired?" Mémère asked, and Maya nodded. "Why don't you go on up to bed? It's been a long day."

"I think I will." Maya rose from the round oak table.

"I guess I'll go watch the news," Pépère said. "And see what's happening in the big world."

Lily and Mémère stayed at the table, and Maya knew that as soon as she and Pépère left, there would be a discussion of all that had gone on during the past few months. "Good," Maya thought. "Let them talk."

As Pépère settled into his chair at one end of the long living room, Maya ran lightly up the stairs and into her room. Closing the door, she went to her bag, grabbed it, and sat on her bed. Maya reached for the book and then hesitated. Did she hear a noise in the hall? "Mom?" Maya called. "Mémère?" There was no answer. Maya knew she could lock the door, but now she was on edge, and she decided to go downstairs to get a drink of water, just to be sure everyone was where they should be.

Back down the stairs Maya went and was on her way to the kitchen when something from the living room caught her attention. A reporter's voice said, "Today, in Providence, Rhode Island, a young woman was found shot dead not far from the train station. Her name was Mary Parsons, and she was from Augusta, Maine, where she worked as a librarian at the State Library. She was thirty-three years old."

Standing in the doorway, Maya watched as a picture of Mary Parsons, with her soft brown hair and creamy skin, came onto the screen. Maya went into the living room and sat down slowly in a chair next to Pépère.

"I know her," he said.

"So do I," Maya thought. "Except in the picture she doesn't look afraid." Aloud she asked, "You do?"

"Sure. I've seen her many times at the State Library. What a shame! She was so young."

"I saw Mary Parsons on the train today," Maya said suddenly and then immediately wished she hadn't.

"Is that right?" Pépère asked, and Maya just nodded. "Well, you never know, do you? I'm glad you and your mother are here safe and sound in East Vassalboro."

"Me, too." Maya shivered a little, no longer wanting a glass of water.

"I guess I'll go back upstairs." Maya stood, but now she was as reluctant to look at the book as she had been eager to see it just a few minutes ago.

"Sleep tight, Maya."

The news had turned from Mary Parsons to the upcoming presidential vacation trip to Mt. Desert Island, and Maya walked slowly up the stairs. She was certain that the man who didn't smile had been after the book and that he had killed Mary Parsons. "What kind of book would someone want so much that he would kill for it?" Maya asked herself.

Taking a deep breath, Maya stepped into her room and closed the door. "If I don't like what I see, then I'll throw it into the stream tomorrow, and that will take care of that," Maya thought. The man who didn't smile would never find it then.

Sitting on her bed, Maya reached gingerly into the outer pocket of her bag. As soon as she touched the book, Maya knew that she could no more throw it in the stream than she could throw in a puppy or a kitten.

"All right, all right," Maya muttered. "What do you look like?" She quickly pulled the book from her bag and dropped it onto her bed. Maya stared at it. Then she stared at it some more.

"I was disappointed," she would admit later.

The book was small—Maya had expected that—but the deep blue cover was cloth and it had pink and red flowers on it. It looked like the kind of book you would find in the card section of a bookstore, a book that might be blank or have places for addresses. "The man who didn't smile wanted that?" Maya asked aloud, and if it hadn't been for Mary Parsons, who was certainly dead because of this little flowered book, Maya might have laughed. Instead, frowning, she picked up the book and opened it. "Just what are you, anyway?" Maya asked. On the first page, in the middle, crisp and clear, were the words: The Book of Everything.

"Everything?" Maya asked.

As if in response, the book began to hum, and Maya slowly started to turn the pages. She could see tiny, exquisite handwriting. "They look like entries," Maya thought, and when she looked closer at the glowing words, she saw that she was right. There were entries, in alphabetical order, with definitions so small that they couldn't be read. But if Maya squinted, she could just make out some of the words—*accelerate, adaptation, Addington,* and *Andy,* which had a minuscule picture beside it. Maya shook her head. The book seemed to be like a dictionary, yet what dictionary had *Addington* and *Andy* in it? Confused, Maya flipped faster. The pages went on and on, and Maya became even more confused. How could there be so many pages in this little book? And then images, separate from the little pictures, came to Maya—of plants, animals, and people, some of them long gone; historical events; battles; coronations; murders; births; and, most disturbingly, centuries of pursuit of this book. With so much information, Maya began to feel dizzy, and she had to stop turning the pages. After a little while, she felt better, and when Maya looked down, she saw that she had stopped at the letter *S.*

Maya could make out *secret, seize,* and *serpent,* but *secret* stood out from the other two words. It was so dark that it looked as if it had been bolded. Maya ran her finger across it, and the rest of the words and entries disappeared to be replaced by a definition of *secret* with an added note: "For now, this book must remain a secret." Maya snatched her finger away from the book, and the definition and note faded to be replaced by the previous entries as well as some other words beginning with *Se.*

Closing the book with a snap, Maya sat on the edge of her bed. She sat there for a long time, and her thoughts were so fast and uncomfortable that she didn't know if she would ever be able to get to sleep. But along with being high-strung and emotional, Maya also had a practical streak. "She gets that from us," Mémère might have said. "From the French side of the family."

This was no ordinary book, and Maya knew that she had to hide it. But where? Under the mattress? Of course not, too easy to find. In her bags? In the bureau? Maya shook her head. Then where? Not in the attic, sheds, or barns. Maya wanted to be able to retrieve the book without attracting attention and to look at it again as soon as she felt brave enough to do so. Then

Maya knew where to hide it: in the desk, which was old and had a top that could be flipped down. When the top was up, it could also be locked. Inside were slots to file letters and papers, and there was also a compartment in the middle, with plenty of space to slide in the book. Fortunately, the key to the desk was in a drawer beneath the compartment.

As Maya reached for the book, she had one of her flashes, and Maya knew without doubt that this book was good. What it actually did and where it came from were still a mystery to Maya, but its purpose was not evil. It was the man who didn't smile who had done the harm. And hadn't Maya known, as soon as she saw him, that this man was dangerous and not to be trusted?

Maya placed the book in the desk, locked it, put the key inside her bag in a zippered section, and went to bed. Despite Inga Peterson and Tom and Caitlin, Maya wanted very much to talk to her father about the book. Her cell phone was in her bag. She could get up and call him, and Maya shifted restlessly in bed. She could also call Leah, who with her quick laugh, would make Maya feel better. Or Danielle, whose patience had a calming effect on both Maya and Leah. No, Maya decided. The book had told her to keep its existence a secret, and that's just what she would do.

Strangely, after all that had happened, Maya fell quickly asleep, not dreaming, hardly stirring, not waking up even once.

4: Chet Addington

The man who didn't smile had a name, but he hadn't used it for a long time. His bosses and coworkers knew him as Chet Addington, and he felt that was all they needed to know. There was only one in the Association for the Preservation of Order, or APO, as insiders called it, who knew Chet's real name, and there it would stay. "Never to be revealed," Chet thought.

Chet was in a small, not very clean room in a motel in New Hampshire just off Interstate 95. He could have stayed someplace nicer. APO had told him this many times, but Chet preferred to stay in places where people went when they cheated on their spouses or wanted to be alone when they drank too much or had no other place to go. These people were so caught up with their own lives and with their own miseries that they would never even notice him, a man with no outstanding features, with nothing to set him apart from anyone else. And that's how Chet liked it. Above all, he didn't want to be noticed, and he certainly didn't want to go to a hotel that had a lobby with a bar where he would have to pretend to be pleasant, where there were sharp eyes that might see what shouldn't be seen. Chet had done this when he was younger, and he had learned his lesson.

Chet was still confounded by the girl on the train. How had that happened? Could it have been planned all along? "No," he said, opening a can of Vienna Sausages, "it was just dumb luck." Or something like that. Using a white plastic fork, Chet dug out a sausage and bit into it. He had to admit that the league seemed to have more than its share of luck. Chet gulped down one sausage after another until they were gone. Shaking his head, he reached for a diet Dr. Pepper that was on the wobbly stand by his bed. Why shouldn't the league have good luck? "They have a connection to where it all started," Chet reflected. Setting the empty can of sausages and the fork beside his drink, Chet lay down, resting his head in the palm of his hands, and the man who didn't smile actually did smile, but it was not a pleasant smile. He was thinking about how his side was not without its resources. No, indeed. Chet glanced at a small round device on the night stand. Finally he had something that would be too much even for the league.

And at headquarters, there were people waiting to help Chet. Right now, some of them were checking to see who had bought tickets for the train he had been on. Chet reluctantly acknowledged that he had been so focused on Mary Parsons that he had blocked out almost everything else. But he had felt the girl staring at him, and he should have known there was something different about her. He also cursed Mary Parsons for ditching her cell phone before he got to her. It might have given him useful information.

Chet now realized he shouldn't have been so quick to kill Mary, but he had been sure that she had the book. What was the point of dragging things out? Chet could see now that he had been too eager to get his hands on the book he had been pursuing for many, many years. In Chet's mind, Mary hadn't mattered at all and was simply an inconvenience to be disposed of. In retrospect, Chet understood that Mary had been leading him away from the girl and from the train.

Well, no point in going over and over what couldn't be changed. He would just have to wait, and, among other things,

Chet was very good at waiting. This was why he so often found those he was looking for. He didn't wear himself out frantically tracing false leads that took him miles out of his way. When Chet lost the trail, he simply stopped and waited. Usually something turned up to give him a real lead.

The next day, Chet received the list he was waiting for. It was long, but Chet was prepared. He had a stash of Vienna Sausages and diet Dr. Pepper, and if he ran out, there was a convenience store not far from where he was staying. If all went well, he might even treat himself to some beef jerky. However, right now, the list on his laptop was waiting, and maybe it was just wishful thinking, but the glow of the screen seemed promising to Chet, as though it would eventually guide him to the very name he wanted. Pursing his lips, Chet started at the top of the list and began working his way down.

5: To the South End

When Maya woke up, the sun was shining, and the day was clear with a bright blue sky. "A Vassalboro day," Maya thought As Maya got ready for this Vassalboro day, she regarded the desk. Should she look at the book again, or should she wait? Pulling on her shirt, Maya thought she would have another look, but as she slid into her shorts, she decided she'd better wait. Maya changed her mind again as she put on her sandals and then again as she brushed her hair, pulling it back into a ponytail.

"I'll wait until after breakfast," Maya thought as she headed downstairs to the kitchen. Mémère had been up for a while. Bran muffins were on the table along with a small pitcher of milk, some strawberries, and a bowl of scrambled eggs. Lily had just finished setting the table, and Pépère was already in his chair by the window. Maya sat down next to him.

"What are you going to do today?" he asked, giving her ponytail a flip.

"I don't know," Maya answered, thinking of the book. "It all depends."

Lily and Mémère sat down, and the plates of food were passed. "I want to paint this morning," Lily said. "But I'd be free in the afternoon."

Mémère took a muffin. "I'll make my jam in the morning."

"Mini golf this afternoon? In Waterville?" Pépère asked, and the other three nodded. "Good, I feel a winning streak coming on."

"Ha," Maya said. "You never beat Mom." Lily just smiled.

Pépère winked at Maya. "It's all that painting she does. Eye-hand coordination."

"Maya?" Mémère asked. "Would you go to the library for me after you help me get the berries ready? I have some books that are due."

"Sure," Maya answered. She always looked forward to talking with Anne Hunter, the librarian, who spoke to her in an interested but matter-of-fact way, as though Maya were in college rather than in high school. "If only everyone would speak that way to me," Maya often thought. She also loved the way Anne looked and dressed: her dark hair cut in a bob, her funky black and silver glasses, and her snappy dresses, mostly bought at thrift shops.

After breakfast was over and she had helped Mémère with the berries, Maya gathered the books and headed to the library. Going down the road, she paused to watch her mother, who had set up an easel at the edge of the lawn that bordered on a lush pasture full of long, green grass. A little while later, Maya stopped again to take in East Vassalboro—the old houses, mostly yellow or white, and the dark stream that flowed through the center of the village. Past the store she walked and to the library, but as soon as Maya went in, she could tell that something was wrong.

Anne was not sitting behind her desk, the way she usually did. Instead, Anne was sitting in one of the rocking chairs by the window, and she was staring out, her hands folded in her lap. A slim man with white hair sat across from Anne. Leaning forward, he stared intently at her.

"Anne?" Maya called softly.

Anne turned from the window. "Oh, Maya," she said with a sigh, and her eyes were red. "You're back for the summer?"

"Yes, but what's wrong?"

"I just lost a dear friend."

"Mary Parsons?" Maya asked.

The man spun around to consider Maya, and Anne asked, "That's right, but how did you know?"

Maya set the books on the desk. "It was on the news last night. Pépère said he had often seen her at the State Library."

"Yes, of course." Anne motioned to the man sitting across from her. "This is Jeff Perry. He's a friend, too. He works at the Waterville Library, but he knew Mary very well. Jeff, this is Maya Hammond, who's from New York. Her grandparents are Celine and Roland Turcotte. They live less than a mile from here."

Maya nodded at Jeff, and he nodded absently back, but Maya knew that he wished she wasn't there. "I'm sorry," Maya said, stepping away.

Anne blinked, and Maya could see she was trying not to cry. "I'm going to go look for some books."

Maya headed back toward the teen section, but as soon as Anne and Jeff stopped watching her, she edged closer to them, hiding behind a stack where they couldn't see her but where she could hear them even though they spoke in voices so soft they were nearly whispering. But Maya had such good hearing that Mémère often called her "bat ears."

"How could this have happened?" Anne asked.

"I don't know," Jeff replied. "And where could it be now? You're sure they don't have it?"

"Yes. Mary sent me a text message just before she got off the train. She said she found someone to give it to, but she didn't say who. Too dangerous."

"A last minute change," Jeff murmured.

"A last minute change. And, Jeff, it's as though they knew for sure Mary was going to be on that train. This is the worst it has ever been. We've had some close calls, but nothing like this."

"Will anyone from the league be coming here?"

"I don't know, but I doubt it. Why would they come here? Mary was killed in Rhode Island."

"I thought they might send someone because the book was heading for Maine. And you and Mary were such good friends."

"Well, maybe. But so far I haven't heard."

Maya hardly dared to breathe. She didn't understand all the references, but she knew enough. They were talking about the book, and they were talking about her, even though they didn't know it. Maya longed to tell Anne what had happened on the train, but "for now this book must remain a secret." And so it would.

"What else is in that book?" Maya thought and decided she needed to take another look. Creeping back to the teen section, Maya grabbed *A Wrinkle in Time* and headed for the front desk.

"Just check yourself out," Anne said when she saw that Maya had a book. "You know what to do." Then she added, "I'm sorry, Maya. Tomorrow, I'll be more myself."

"That's all right." Maya did as she was told, and with the book tucked under her arm, she slipped out of the library, leaving Jeff and Anne in the chairs by the window. Maya looked back once, but they were too busy talking to notice her.

Maya raced back to the farmhouse. Lily was still painting, and Pépère was weeding the garden. Mémère was in the kitchen, finishing the jam, and Maya sped by her.

"I'm going upstairs to read," Maya called out.

"Hope it's a good book!" came the cheerful reply.

They were all occupied, but for how long? "This time, I'll lock the door, just in case. I should have done that last night," Maya thought as she went into her room. If her mother, grandmother, or grandfather tried the door and found it locked, then they would just think she was being a moody teenager who wanted to be alone.

With the bedroom door locked, Maya went to the desk, unlocked it, and reached for the book. For a brief moment, it felt smooth and soft, but when Maya pulled it out, it was the same blue cloth-covered book with red and pink flowers.

The book began to hum again, and Maya flipped forward to the letter *S*, to see if the same message was still under the *Secret* entry. However, when Maya stopped at the letter *S*, the word *South End* was bolded, and next to it, in parentheses, was *Waterville, Maine, 1976*

Maya frowned. Why 1976? That was a long time ago. Maya figured there was only one way to find out. If she touched the words, the definition would be expanded, and then she would know. Maya ran her finger over *South End.*

What occurred next was so surprising that even with all that had happened in the past two days, there was no way Maya could have anticipated it. Instead of giving a definition, the booked seemed to swell and grow until it engulfed her, and everything went dark. Maya could hear noises, but they weren't East Vassalboro noises There were the sounds of traffic and babies crying and mothers calling and children playing. An old man with a slurred voice was speaking French. Closing her eyes, Maya screamed, but she couldn't open her mouth, and the scream was only in her head.

Maya felt herself land with a thud, though not a hard one, and she cautiously opened her eyes. She was standing on a sidewalk by a small grocery store, next to some covered stairs that went down a steep hill. Wooden boxes full of fruit were on the sidewalk by the store, and Maya could smell cantaloupe, peaches, and grapes mingled with the scent of wet pavement. Strange looking cars were parked by the sidewalk, and people went in and out of the store, but nobody seemed to think it was odd that Maya was standing there. She even got a smile from an old woman carrying a paper bag full of groceries out of the store.

Then Maya heard a whistle, soft and melodious, coming up the stairs. A teenage boy, tall and slim, walked toward her. His clothes were worn but clean, and when he looked up at her, Maya thought he had the most beautiful blue eyes she had ever seen. He had none of the awkwardness that most boys his age had. Instead, there was something grave, almost elegant, about him.

"Hi," he said when he reached the top of the stairs. "You must be new around here. I don't remember seeing you before."

Maya felt a little shaky. All she could do was nod, and she stumbled slightly when she tried to move.

"Are you O.K.?" he asked.

"I don't know," Maya answered in a soft voice.

"Come on," he said, guiding her to some steps with peeling paint. "My aunt lives here. She won't care if we sit on her steps."

Maya let him lead her to the steps, and she gratefully sat down.

"Do you want something to drink? A soda?"

Maya licked dry lips. "Sure."

As the boy left her and went into the store, Maya's head began to clear. All around were tenement buildings, three stories tall and with open porches in the front. Turning, Maya saw that on the porch behind her sat an enormous woman in a lawn chair. Her dark hair was bunched in pin curls, and she wore a bright, blue sleeveless dress that cascaded in pleats over her knees. The woman said something in French, and Maya shook her head. The woman switched to English. "You look pretty pale. Andy will be back with a drink tout de suite."

Nodding, Maya twisted back around and rubbed her face. The boy—Andy—stepped out of the store, and he carried two orange sodas. "Here," Andy said, handing Maya a can as he sat next to her.

"Thanks." Maya took the can. "You're Andy?"

"I am. And your name?"

"Maya."

"That's an unusual name," Andy said. "But pretty."

"Bonjour, Andy," the woman called from the porch.

"Bonjour, ma tante," Andy called back.

"You and your mom having supper with me tonight?"

"I think so."

"Bon. She should be out of work soon."

Maya thought, "Am I really in Waterville? In 1976?" Aloud Maya asked, "Where does your mother work?"

"At the Hathaway."

"So I am in Waterville," Maya thought. "Before the factory closed and when a lot of people still spoke French." She realized she was clutching something in the hand not holding the can of soda. When Maya opened her hand, she saw it was the blue book, very small now but with the same red and pink flowers. Maya tucked the book in the pocket of her shorts. The last thing she wanted was to lose that book. Maya was beginning to understand why the man who didn't smile wanted it.

Andy was watching her. "Where are you from?"

"New York City," Maya answered.

"New York City," Andy repeated. "I'd love to go there."

"Maybe you will someday. I come to Maine every summer."

"Why?"

"To visit my mémère and pépère."

"Where do they live?"

"On Summer Street," Maya answered quickly. It was where Mémère Celine had really lived before she married Pépère Roland, and Maya knew the street couldn't be far from here. It was on the edge of the South End. But in 1976, Mémère, Pépère, and her mother were in East Vassalboro, about ten miles away, and Maya hadn't even been born yet. It gave her a funny feeling to think about this.

"Tell me about New York City," Andy said.

"Like what?"

"Do you go to museums and plays and movies?"

"Yes."

"Where do you live?"

"In Greenwich Village."

"The Village," Andy said with a sigh.

"In a brick house. There's a studio on the top floor for my mother, who's an artist."

"What about your father?"

"He used to be a professor at NYU, but now he's at Duke University in North Carolina."

"He left you and your mother?" Maya nodded, and Andy shook his head. "My father left us, too."

They sat together in silence for a while, drinking their sodas. Andy frowned at nothing in particular, and Maya scraped at some of the chipped paint on the steps.

"What does your father teach?" Andy asked.

"English literature. But his specialty is Shakespeare."

"Shakespeare?" Andy asked, and his frown was gone.

"What's wrong with that?" Maya asked.

"Nothing's wrong with that. I think it's cool. I just never knew anybody whose father taught Shakespeare in college, that's all. Do you like Shakespeare?"

For the first time since landing in the South End, Maya smiled. "Yes, I do. I even played Ariel in our school play this spring. What about you?"

"He's crazy about Shakespeare," a voice said, and a woman stood not far from them. She was slight and had a shiny black braid that went all the way down her back. The woman's eyes were as dark as her hair, and Maya immediately liked her.

"Mom!" Andy said, starting a little.

His mother laughed. "But God only knows where he gets his love of Shakespeare from."

"You read, Mom."

"But not Shakespeare," his mother said. "I like scary stuff like Stephen King. But never mind that." She turned to Andy. "Who's your friend?"

"This is Maya," Andy said.

"Maya's an unusual name," Andy's mother said. "But pretty."

"I'm from New York," Maya said, knowing that's all she needed to say. "I'm here visiting my mémère."

"New York? That would explain it. I'm Yvette Bolduc, and that's my sister Lucille on the porch."

"They've been talking away," Lucille called. "Seemed like a shame to interrupt them."

"How old are you, Maya?" Yvette asked.

"Fifteen."

"Young," Yvette said, giving Andy a look.

"Mom!" Andy said. "I just met her. We were only talking."

"About Shakespeare," Yvette said.

"About Shakespeare," Andy replied, not looking away.

"Well," said Yvette, smiling just a little at Maya, "you can stay for supper if you want. If it's all right with your mémère."

"Oh, Mémère wouldn't mind," Maya answered, knowing that her grandmother would mind very much if she knew about Maya and the book and the trip back to 1976. But Maya didn't know what else to say. She wasn't even sure how she was going to get back to her own time.

"Shouldn't you give her a call?"

For a moment, Maya thought about really calling her mémère in East Vassalboro, but as soon as she considered it, Maya knew what a ridiculous notion it was. So she came up with yet another lie, one that would take its place among many yet to come. "Mémère's out and won't be back until later. She left supper in the refrigerator." Maya could barely keep a straight face. This was so unlike anything that Mémère would actually do that Maya nearly laughed out loud.

Yvette raised her eyebrows, but all she said was, "All right then." Opening her purse, she handed Andy some money. "Why don't you go to the store and get some ice cream and cookies. Does that sound good, Lucille?"

"Sounds fine to me," Lucille answered. "I'm going to go in and get things started."

As Lucille left the porch, Andy took the money and headed toward the store. Yvette sat next to Maya. "He'll be there a while. As I was going by, I looked through the window and saw Michelle Roy at the checkout. She had just finished her weekly shopping and was unloading her cart. She always buys a lot."

Nodding, Maya glanced sideways at this adult who wasn't much bigger than she was. "How old is Andy?" Maya asked.

"Seventeen. Almost eighteen."

"Seventeen," Maya repeated, thinking about Andy's deep blue eyes.

"That's right," Yvette said firmly, giving Maya a look that needed no words. Maya blushed, and Yvette relented, patting Maya's arm.

"You're a good kid. I could tell right from the start. So, your father teaches Shakespeare?"

"Yes, and you should hear him read." Maya sighed. "He has a wonderful voice. Except now he reads to Tom and Caitlin. Not to me."

"Your father's gone?"

"He left me and my mom for that redhead, Inga Peterson."

"That's tough. Something like that happened to Andy and me. It's funny, when you get married, you think you know how the story is going to end, but you really don't."

"Why do they do it?" Maya asked, trying not to cry.

"I don't know, Maya. If I had the answer, I'd quit sewing shirts at the Hathaway and write a book about why fathers leave. It would be a best seller, and then I'd have enough money to send Andy to college. As it is, by this time next year, I'll hardly have enough for one semester let alone for a whole year. I even quit smoking so that I could save more money. But I just won't have enough."

"Andy should apply anyway. My father always says that colleges have scholarships for families that don't have much money."

"He'd have to get a pretty big scholarship," Yvette said.

"That's how my father got to college," Maya replied.

"He did?" Yvette asked, and Maya nodded. "Maybe there's hope, then. I've always liked to read. Thank God for the Waterville Library. My parents never had any money for books. But Andy is different. He was able to read before he started school. Every Saturday morning, we'd go to the library together and get books for him. He just picked up reading. Then, in school, in the seventh grade, they read *The Merchant of Venice*, and he's been hooked on Shakespeare ever since."

"He should definitely apply to college," Maya said. "What does he have to lose?"

Yvette laughed. "You're an only child, aren't you?"

"How can you tell?"

"By the way you talk. Andy's the same way. All right, Maya from New York. This fall, Andy will apply to colleges, and we'll hope for the best." Yvette stood up. "Here comes Andy with the cookies and ice cream."

Rolling his eyes, Andy handed his mother a bag and the leftover change. "The ice cream's probably melted. I had to wait a long time."

"Oh, well," Yvette said, winking at Maya. "It'll be fine. I'm going to go in and help Lucille. You two can stay here and talk about Shakespeare."

Yvette left, and Andy sat down next to Maya. "My mom's such a pain," he said, and there was a mixture of exasperation and affection in his voice. "Is your mom like my mom?"

"No, but she's a pain in her own way. I think they all are."

Andy grinned. "What did you two talk about?"

"My father and college. He got in on a scholarship. You might be able to get one, too. If you try."

Andy gave Maya an odd look. "My mom and I have been talking a lot about college lately. It's funny you should come right now and tell her about your father."

Feeling the book against her leg, Maya thought, "No, it isn't."

Then, the conversation turned back to Shakespeare. "Your favorite play?" Andy asked.

"*The Tempest.* Yours?"

"The Prince Hal plays. I like Hal, and then there is Falstaff."

"Falstaff!" Maya cried. "That fat thing? He's so pathetic."

"Pathetic!" Andy's face flushed. "He's terrific. He's funny and smart and has a lot of energy."

"You sound just like my father," Maya said. "I don't know why you guys like Falstaff so much."

When Yvette called them in for supper, they were still arguing about Falstaff. All during the meal—hamburgers, canned peas, and fries from a package—Andy and Maya debated Falstaff's merits and flaws. They hardly noticed Yvette and Lucille, who followed the exchange with amusement, bewilderment, and alarm.

"You better watch them," Lucille said to Yvette as they washed and dried dishes. Maya and Andy were sitting on the porch, and they had moved on to *Twelfth Night* and Sir Toby Belch. "He's nothing like Falstaff," Andy maintained firmly. "Oh, yes, he is!" Maya insisted.

Yvette replied, "I probably shouldn't have invited her over for supper, but they were talking about Shakespeare when I came home from work. How often does he get to talk about Shakespeare? Maya's not like anyone he's ever met. Besides, she seems like a good kid. And you know Andy is."

"Oui, oui," Lucille said. "But even good kids can get in trouble."

Lucille was right, but what that trouble would be was far beyond her conception. It was even beyond Maya's conception, and she knew at least a little about what the book could do.

6: And Back Again

When supper was over, Maya knew it was time to leave, but she wasn't sure what she should do. As much as she liked talking with Andy, Maya very much wanted to get back to her own time, to the farmhouse in East Vassalboro. But how? Perhaps the book would give her a hint—Maya was beginning to believe the book could do just about anything—but to look at the book, Maya needed to be alone.

"Well," she said, standing, "I'd better be going."

"I'll walk you home." Andy said quickly.

Maya hadn't counted on that, but what could she say except for "All right"?

"Goodbye, Maya," Yvette said. "It was nice meeting you."

"Come again," Lucille said.

"Thank you," Maya replied, wondering if she ever would.

Andy seemed to know exactly where he was going, and Maya decided that the best thing to do was to follow him. He led her directly to Summer Street, and when they had walked a little ways, Maya recognized where she was. Mémère had often shown Maya where she had lived before moving to East Vassalboro. It was number 10, a two-story apartment building, but nicer than where Lucille lived.

"Here we are," Maya said.

"Here we are," Andy repeated, touching Maya's hand. "Maybe we can get together again and talk about Shakespeare sometime."

"Maybe," Maya replied, not pulling her hand away.

"Maybe we can even read one of the plays."

"*The Tempest*," Maya said quickly.

"*King Henry IV*."

"Part one or part two?"

"Both."

Maya laughed. "What about *Henry V*?"

"If there's time."

Maya pulled her hand away. "I'd better go."

"All right." Andy stood beside her, and it looked as though he wasn't going to leave until she did.

"What am I going to do?" Maya thought. "I can't just go inside." Then she wondered if her great-grandparents still lived there. Before Maya was born, they had both died, but Maya couldn't remember what year that had been.

Slowly, Maya walked toward the house and up the stairs to the first apartment. Turning, Maya saw that Andy was still standing there, and she waved. Andy waved back.

"Man, oh, man," Maya thought as she went across the porch to the door. A light shone from the window, and she peered inside. A stout woman stood by the sink, and this was indeed her great-grandmother. Maya had seen pictures of her at the farmhouse. Maya's great-grandmother glanced up, and she looked so much like Mémère Celine that it made Maya catch her breath.

Maya's great-grandmother came to the door. "Can I help you?"

Later, Maya would marvel at her newfound ability to lie so quickly. However, facing her great-grandmother, whom she had never met, Maya blurted, "I was wondering if Lily was here visiting you."

"Lily? You know Lily? Come in."

Maya stepped into the small, shining kitchen, just as clean as Mémère Celine's. The door closed behind her, and Maya desperately hoped that Andy was on his way home.

"I met Lily at Rummel's, just down the street, when she was visiting you one time. We were both getting an ice cream." Maya spoke so convincingly that she could almost picture meeting the slim, blonde teenager that Lily had been. "We just seemed to get along. I like to talk. Lily likes to listen. We played mini golf, and she got her favorite ice cream, maple walnut. She told me it's what she always gets."

Maya's great-grandmother laughed. "That sounds like Lily. She's a good girl, but she doesn't talk much. She's like her father. But that's all right. My daughter Celine talks enough for the three of them. What's your name?"

"Maya."

"That's an unusual name, but very pretty. Well, Maya, Lily's not here right now. But she'll be coming sometime soon. I'll tell her you stopped by. Does she know where you live?"

"Oh, yes," Maya answered. "She knows just where I live."

"Bon."

Turning to leave, Maya felt her throat get tight and tears come to her eyes. She wanted to give her great-grandmother a kiss on a cheek that was remarkably smooth, just like Mémère Celine's.

"Don't be so stupid," Maya thought crossly.

Maya felt a hand on her shoulder and a pat similar to the one Lily often gave her. "I'll tell Lily you were here."

All Maya could do was nod, and she left quickly so that her great-grandmother wouldn't see that she was crying. Wiping the tears away, Maya paused briefly to see if Andy was still standing there, but he was gone.

"Thank God," Maya said.

Dusk had come. There was still enough light to see, but just barely. Maya walked until she came to a church, and she went around back, where no one would notice her. Sitting on the ground next to the church, Maya took the book, still small, from her pocket. Unsure of what to do, she held it in her hand. Before, the book had seemed to direct her. Maybe it would do the same this time.

Opening the book, Maya slowly began turning the pages. There was that hum, and various images came to her—a forest, a large stone house, a cluster of cottages, a very fat man, a bald man with a squeezebox. When she came to the *H* section, Maya found what she was looking for—the entry *Home* and in parentheses, *East Vassalboro, Maya's present.* The words were bolded, and Maya moved her finger across them.

Now that Maya knew what to expect, she didn't scream, and she didn't feel as dizzy when she landed with that gentle thud. Still, Maya was disoriented, and it took her a few minutes to get her bearings. But there she was, in her own little room beneath the eaves, and the book was the size it had been when Mary Parsons had dropped it into Maya's bag. Someone was knocking on the door. It was Mémère Celine. "Maya? Have you fallen asleep? It's time for lunch. Come on downstairs."

"Lunch?" Maya asked.

"That's right. Your mother's finished painting, and Pépère is done in the garden."

"I'll be down in a minute," Maya said. Into the desk went the book. Hardly any time had passed between when Maya had gone back to 1976 and had come back again. Could it have been just a dream? It felt very real, but Maya began to wonder if maybe she had fallen asleep. But when Mémère had called her, Maya had been standing in the middle of the room. She had not been in bed. Still, it was all so fantastical that Maya couldn't help but think the whole adventure had been unreal.

Before going down to lunch, Maya went to the bathroom, combed her hair, and splashed cold water on her face. When she walked into the kitchen, everything looked just the way it should. Pépère was in his chair, Mémère was bustling around the kitchen, and Lily, with a few paint stains on her hands, was calmly helping her mother. Maya couldn't stop thinking about

Andy, Lucille, Yvette, and her great-grandmother, who all seemed too vivid to be part of a dream.

"Next time," Maya thought, "I'm going to bring something back in my pocket, or maybe take a picture with my cell phone, when no one's looking. Then I'll know for sure."

Satisfied, Maya ate the lunch Mémère had prepared. But Maya felt more than a little full, as though she had had a big meal not that long ago.

Meanwhile, in his shabby motel room in New Hampshire, Chet Addington was going through his list. He had eliminated all the single travelers and had narrowed it down to customers who had bought two or more tickets. Unfortunately, Chet reflected, there had been a lot of travelers that day.

"Summer travelers," Chet said, his mouth pursed primly He didn't approve of vacations, of traveling for the fun of it. In Chet's opinion, traveling should be done for a purpose, for work, and it always made him grumpy to think about how all those silly tourists spread out over the country every summer. He hated seeing their chubby legs in shorts, their stupid hats, and their happy, sun-burnt faces. To make matters worse, they were always taking pictures of themselves. "For God's sake," Chet often muttered. "They already know what they look like. Do they have to take a picture of themselves in every damned place they visit?"

To cheer himself up, Chet thought about APO's recent decision, much debated by the board, that would tip the balance in their favor. For centuries, the league's Book of Everything had invariably slipped away from APO. Then, no matter how much APO tried, no matter how much they mocked, persecuted, or debunked, the league, armed with the book, always won. From Earth being round to the sun being the center of the solar system to germs causing disease, the league pushed with gradually revealed knowledge until such things couldn't be denied. More recently, it had happened with cigarettes. To be sure, APO had had its moments of triumph: the burning of the library at Alexandria, the Visigoths sacking

Rome, the subsequent Dark Ages, and the Inquisition. But the league and the book always overcame them with facts.

Chet got up to stretch his legs. The more people knew, Chet reflected, the more they demanded and the more they questioned. This wasn't good for APO, not for its authority, not for its profits.

"Not for long, you suckers," Chet said, patting his pocket. "Just you wait."

As Mémère, Pépère, Lily, and Maya played mini golf—one of the stupidest games around, Chet often thought—Chet's list of train passengers became shorter and shorter. Then he found what he was looking for.

"Just my luck," Chet muttered. "Her name had to begin with a *T*." But there she was—Lily Turcotte—and even though Chet grumbled to himself about her last name being so far down the alphabet, his preliminary search on the Internet gave him all the information he needed. He would have to go no further.

When Chet googled Lily Turcotte, a long list of *New York Times*'s articles appeared in the search list. Chet clicked on the first piece, and it was about an opening for an art show that had happened the previous fall. There was a picture of Lily, looking blonde and elegant, and beside her stood a man and a young teenager—Giles and Maya Hammond—her husband and daughter. Chet made a snorting sound. It figured that they all wouldn't have the same last name.

"There you are," Chet said, squinting at Maya, her face even more impudent than he had remembered. "You're quite the one, aren't you?" There was an ugly look on Chet's own face. "Well, I'm coming, and there's nothing your precious book can do about it."

APO would help him find where Lily and Maya had gone. And that's exactly what happened. Sometime later, Chet received a call and found out what he needed to know. He would soon be on his way. Chet wasn't sure what he was going to do, but from past experiences he had discovered that threats worked very well. Yes, they most certainly did. And if he had to use his gun, then so be it.

Chet also learned that the book had been used for travel, something that normally didn't happen. APO had been able to pinpoint it to East Vassalboro, Maine, and this information was followed by the question: Do you want backup?

Blinking, Chet wondered why the book would travel with a teenager. At the same time, Chet was convinced that Mary Parsons had chosen this girl for a reason, that she had sensed there was something different about Maya. Nevertheless, Maya was only fifteen, and if he couldn't handle a fifteen year old, then it was time to resign from APO.

"No," Chet had replied. "I don't need backup."

Chet whistled a little tune as he packed what few things he had and checked out of the motel. On his way to the turnpike, Chet stopped at a store and not only bought a six-pack of diet Dr. Pepper but also several packages of beef jerky. He hadn't felt this elated since he had joined APO and had finally found a group that gave him the respect he deserved.

Chet knew that the league would help Maya if they realized she had the book, but he also knew, thanks to one of the calls he had received, that nobody had been sent to East Vassalboro, at least not yet. According to his source, the league still didn't know where the book was.

Oh, things were going his way, and Chet was in such a good mood that he didn't even bother to kick the stray dog that was sniffing around the store. Whistling again, Chet drove out of the parking lot. A fifteen-year-old girl had the book, and there was the disk to shield Chet from the book's notice. How could he fail?

7: The League of Librarians

After playing mini golf, Maya asked Pépère to drive through the South End. "To see where you and Mémère used to go when you were young," Maya said, but really she wanted to find the street where Andy's aunt lived. Pépère did eventually drive down that street. The store was gone, but there was Lucille's apartment building. A large woman with gray hair sat on the porch, and Maya realized with a start that this was Lucille herself, nearly forty years later. Where was Andy? And Yvette?

"What if Lucille sees me and recognizes me?" Maya thought somewhat desperately. However, as Lucille watched their car pass, there was no sign that she recognized Maya.

Later, Maya would be disgusted with herself for even thinking such a thing. "For me, it was this morning. For her, it was a long time ago."

But in the car, Maya had a mixture of feelings. On the one hand, she was glad the whole adventure hadn't been a dream. On the other hand, she felt nervous, apprehensive, even. Where would the book take her next? From her bag came a ringing sound, and Maya jumped.

"It's your phone, Maya," Lily said.

For some reason Maya was disappointed when she answered and found it was her father. "Oh, it's you," Maya said before she could stop herself.

There was a short silence and a half-hearted laugh. "Who were you expecting? Do you have a boyfriend now?"

"Of course not, Dad! Don't be silly."

"Just checking. How are you doing?"

"I'm all right." Maya wished she could tell her father all that had happened. Not here, not in the car, but later. Maya decided she would check with the book when she got home. Maybe the book had changed its mind, or whatever it had. Maybe it would let her tell her father.

"What are you doing?" her father asked.

"We just finished playing mini golf. Mom won, of course. And then we had an ice cream."

"Sounds fun," her father said, and it seemed to Maya that he sounded wistful.

"Well, you have Tom and Caitlin," Maya said, irritated rather than touched. "You can play mini golf with them. I expect they have mini golf in North Carolina, don't they?" Now what had made her say that when only a few minutes ago, she had wanted to tell her father everything?

"Maya!" Her father's voice was sharp. "That was unnecessary."

Beside her, Lily bit her lip to keep from laughing, and up front, Mémère and Pépère were doing the same thing. Oddly enough, this made Maya feel sorry for her father, and by now her feelings were so confused that she knew she had better end the conversation before she started crying.

Maya swallowed. "Look, Dad, I've got to go. I'm in the car right now. I'll call you later."

"Maya, don't forget. We really need to talk."

"I won't."

As soon as Maya hung up, Lily said, "Maya, you shouldn't speak to your father that way."

"I know," Maya said "It just popped out before I could stop it."

"Ha!" Mémère said, twisting around. "I know I shouldn't say this, but he deserves it, leaving you two the way he did."

"Mom," Lily said. "Please. It just makes things worse."

"All right, all right," Mémère muttered. "I won't say another word about it." She would, of course, in a day or two, and Maya remembered what her great-grandmother had said about Mémère Celine and talking.

"I'm the same way," Maya realized. "I have a hard time not talking." Then came another thought. "And Mom has a hard time talking."

When Maya got home, she went to her room, took the book from the desk, and found the letter *S* and the word *Secret*. Maya stared at what the book said, and she read it again several times just to be sure. There was no mention of her father. Instead, the instructions were that the time for secrets was over, and she was to reveal the book's presence to Anne Hunter, the League of Librarians, and afterwards, Andy, in 1976.

Maya could understand why the book would want her to tell Anne, but what was the League of Librarians? And why Andy? Maya shivered a little. She would have to go back again. But in a way she was glad. Ever since she had returned, she had been thinking about Andy and his blue eyes.

After dinner, Maya asked, "Is the library open?"

"Yes, but they will be closing soon," Mémère answered. "Are you thinking of going back?"

Maya nodded. "Anne was busy this morning, and I really didn't get a chance to talk with her." That much was certainly true.

"Go ahead," Lily said. "I know how you two like to chat."

"But don't stay too late," Pépère said. "I was hoping for a game of cribbage tonight."

"I'll be back in time," Maya promised.

Maya wondered if she should bring the book with her. In the end, as she took off her shorts and put on her jeans, she decided to leave the book in the desk. Despite the trip back to 1976, Maya hadn't forgotten Mary Parsons and the man who didn't smile. They were both on her mind, and even though East Vassalboro seemed like the safest place around, Maya felt uneasy. She could sense that something big was about to happen, something dangerous. Although Maya hadn't had the book long, she wanted to protect it. Maya still didn't understand what the book was for or all that it could do, but she was certain that it shouldn't go to the man who didn't smile.

The sun was just beginning to set as Maya headed for the library. In East Vassalboro, this was the time of day that Maya liked best, when the purple shadows came, and everything seemed to slow down, to relax into evening.

When Maya went into the library, she saw that Anne Hunter had more visitors—a tall woman with fair skin and brown hair pulled back into a bun and a compact man with dark red hair and a bushy red beard. This time, they were all sitting around the desk, and as soon as they noticed Maya, they stopped talking. Anne's eyes were no longer red, but her face was grim, and so were the faces of the man and the other woman. Maya could tell that they wished she wasn't there, but Maya suspected that the man and the woman had something to do with the League of Librarians and that they should hear what she had to say.

"Maya," Anne said, "we'll be closing soon. Did you come for something specific?"

"No," Maya answered, peering all around. "Is anybody else here?"

The question surprised Anne. "No, it's just the four of us."

"Are you with the League of Librarians?" Maya asked the man and the woman. She knew this was a blunt question, but she couldn't think of a more discreet way of asking it.

Now all three of them looked surprised, shocked even. "How did you know that?" the woman asked sharply, her voice high and clear.

Again, Maya decided that the direct approach was the best one. "The Book of Everything told me."

Anne gasped, and there was a silence so complete that Maya could hear the chittering songs of the frogs outside. A car went by, and a horn tooted. Maya jumped, and the man said, "Anne, I guess you'd better lock up for the night."

"I guess I'd better."

While Anne locked the front and back doors, the man found a folding chair for Maya and set it by the desk.

"Sit down." He motioned toward the chair, and Maya sat in it, tucking her legs beneath the chair. The three of them had been drinking tea, and the woman asked, "Would you like a cup of tea?" Her face was stern, but Maya sensed that she could trust this woman.

"Yes," Maya said, "I would like a cup of tea."

The woman rose. "We just poured ours, and I expect the water is still hot." She extended her hand to Maya. "My name is Jennifer Morgan, and I'm the head of the northeast division of the League of Librarians. This is David Little. He's the librarian of the Hartland Library, about forty minutes north of here, and is one of the league's historians."

Maya shook hands with both of them. "I'm Maya Hammond, from New York. I'm staying with my grandparents for the summer."

Jennifer left to make tea, and Anne returned from locking the doors. Anne sat down, and there was a look of amazement on her face.

"Maya," she said, "we never would have guessed."

David rubbed his face. "The book always pulls through, doesn't it? There have been close calls before, but never this close. But I had a feeling it would somehow find its way here."

"Yes, you did," Jennifer said, coming back with a steaming mug of tea. "And over the years I've come to trust your intuition, David, which is why I came when you called, even though it was late and at the last minute." Jennifer set the mug of tea on the desk next to Maya. "Be careful. It's hot. Do you take milk or sugar?"

"No," Maya answered. "I drink it black."

Jennifer nodded and then frowned as she sat down. "But I don't know why Mary gave the book to a child. To put her in that kind of danger!"

Maya sat up very straight. "I'm not a child. I'm fifteen years old."

"Mary was desperate," Anne said quickly.

Jennifer sighed. "Yes. Well, then, Maya, I guess you'd better tell us how you got the book."

Maya told them how she and her mother had been traveling together on the train from New York to Boston, how she had spotted the man who didn't smile, and how she could tell there was something not quite right about him.

"That's a good description of him," David said.

"It is," Jennifer agreed. "His name is Chet Addington. At least that's what he calls himself. But go on, Maya."

Maya continued, telling them how she had noticed that Chet was staring at a woman with curly hair—Mary Parsons—how afraid she had seemed, and how Maya had known she had to help.

Jennifer shifted in her seat. "How did you know this?"

Maya shrugged. "I just got the strongest feeling I should do something to help her. So when a family with drinks and food went by, I grabbed my bag, got up, and tripped the little boy as he was going by the man—I mean Chet. The boy's orange soda flew into Chet's lap."

At this, despite themselves, Anne, Jennifer, and David actually laughed. Grinning, Maya went on to explain how, during the ensuing ruckus, she had slipped by Mary, pausing long enough so something could be tucked in Maya's bag. The grin went away. "But I didn't know what Mary had given me. I didn't dare look. It seemed too dangerous."

"It was," Jennifer replied. "Good choice."

"I went to the snack bar and got a Coke. I stayed there while the train stopped in Providence. When I went back to my seat, Mary and Chet were gone. He killed her, didn't he?" Maya turned to Jennifer.

"Yes, he did," Jennifer answered. The room was quiet, and Maya found that her hands were shaking a little. To steady her nerves, Maya reached for the mug of tea and held it for a while, feeling its warmth. Maya took a sip of tea, and then another.

Maya set the mug on the desk. "Why did he kill her?"

"How much do you know about the book?" Jennifer asked.

"Not much," Maya answered. "I know it gives answers and instructions, and it can take you back in time. But when I look through it, what I mostly see are images."

"That's how it is at first," Anne said. "There's so much information. It can be overwhelming."

Jennifer turned to David. "Why don't you explain about the book and the league?"

David leaned forward. "The book has been with us for a very long time. It came to us as soon as we humans developed an alphabet and the written word."

"Where did it come from?" Maya asked.

"From a place called the Great Library, a place that contains every book ever written. And not just on Earth."

"Where is the Great Library?"

"I guess the best way to describe it is that it's in a place that's connected to everything in the universe. We barely understand it ourselves."

"And what is the book for?"

"Very simple," David replied. "To give us knowledge when we're ready for it."

Maya frowned. "I don't understand."

David put his hands together. "Let's take the ancient Greeks. The book couldn't tell them about nuclear physics. It wouldn't have made any sense to them. First, they had to learn geometry and go with that for a while. So that's what the book taught them. And Copernicus wouldn't have known what to do about quantum mechanics. He had to figure out, among other things, that the sun was the center of the solar system."

"Oh," Maya said, beginning to understand, at least a little. "But what is the League of Librarians?"

David continued, "Not long after the Book of Everything came here, another book came, too, from quite another place."

"From hell?" Maya asked.

"Something like that," Jennifer said with a grim smile.

"It's called the Book of Cinnial," David said. "And its job is to stop the Book of Everything from giving people information. So way back, a group was formed to protect the Book of Everything and to give out information when the book felt we were ready. In response, a counter group was formed with the Book of Cinnial at its center. The groups have had different names through the ages, but right now the group with the Book of Everything is called the League of Librarians. And the group with the Book of Cinnial is called the Association for the Preservation of Order, or APO."

"APO," Maya whispered.

David said, "APO has tried its damnedest to get the Book of Everything, to stop the flow of facts. No matter what their name is, they've always wanted to control what's being said, so that they can be in charge and have power. The Book of Cinnial also gives APO valuable information, but it's not as complete as what the Book of Everything gives us. It doesn't have the backing of the Great Library. However, APO does have a powerful weapon that the Book of Everything and the league often can't counter, at least not at first."

"What's that?" Maya asked.

"They have lies," Jennifer replied. "And APO always finds people who have such force of personality that they can make the lies seem more real than the truth. They've done this all through the ages, and they are doing it now."

Anne put her hand on Maya's arm. "But, Maya, facts do matter, and with facts come knowledge. After a while, sometimes a long while, people take notice. So far, even though it's been slow going, the Book of Everything has won. We do know that the sun is the center of the solar system, and not Earth. We know more than we used to."

"But Chet almost got the book," Maya said.

"Yes," Jennifer replied. "He is one of APO's best trackers. There is something about him that often escapes the book's notice, at least for a while. But even with Chet, the book has always caught on in time so that those he is tracking can be warned. The Book of Everything can shield whoever is with the book as well as itself, so APO tries to track it indirectly, by finding out where it has most recently been and then working from there."

Anne said, "They've come pretty close to getting it. The book goes from place to place so that various members of the league can study it and best decide how to use the knowledge it gives us. Mary was taking the book from New York to East Vassalboro, where it would stay for a while before moving on to Hartland with David. We wanted the book to be in the hinterlands, where only a few people would know where it was. We thought it would be safer."

David scratched his chin. "Cinnial's book can also shield itself and whoever is with it. For a long time, we've known that APO has been working on a device that trackers could carry in their pockets, a device that would work like the Book of Cinnial and block them from the Book of Everything's notice. We didn't know how close they were to developing it or where they would use it, but we knew they were working frantically, and that's why we wanted the book in an out-of-the-way place. Well, now we know they have at least one device, and maybe more. Mary sent us a text message when she was on the train. She didn't notice Chet until it was too late, and worse yet, when she turned to the book for advice, it couldn't give her any. It was completely blocked from the Great Library, which is the source of its power."

Maya was silent for a few minutes. "Why did the book send me back in time?"

"The book often has to play defense," David answered. "The way I understand it, not everything is set in time, and this allows the book some wiggle room. It can't change what is fixed, but it can guide and suggest and work with what is not fixed. So far, the book has never been completely wrong. At times, it's been skunked by APO, but that's a different matter. But, when the book travels through time and space, it generates a slight ripple of energy, which leaves it open to being detected by APO. That's why the book mostly travels the old-fashioned way, by train, plane, or car. The book really must have wanted you to go back in time."

"What do we do now?" Anne asked.

"I wish I knew," Jennifer said, shaking her head. "Part of me wants the book so that Maya isn't involved anymore. This is far too dangerous for someone who's fifteen."

"Maya, does the book have more instructions for you?" David asked.

"Yes, it wants me to go back in time again and tell someone else." And even though she trusted these three adults, Maya felt oddly reluctant to reveal Andy's name and that he lived in the South End in 1976.

Jennifer regarded Maya and then sighed. "It was because you were so young that you escaped Chet's notice, although I expect that by now he has figured things out and is heading to Vassalboro. That's what he excels at. But because of your youth and Mary's quick thinking, Chet didn't get the book. We are all in your debt, the whole world included, even though it doesn't know that it is."

Embarrassed, Maya stared at her hands.

"I think we should let Maya carry on with the book's plans," Anne said quietly

"So do I," David said. "Jennifer, I hate to say this, but I think APO got to someone in the league, someone who betrayed us, someone who probably has a device like Chet has."

"Yes," Jennifer replied, "I've thought of that, too. Chet is good, but he knew exactly which train to take so that he would find Mary. And we purposely made a last-minute decision so that APO wouldn't catch wind of our plans."

She turned to Maya. "All right, continue on with the book's plans, but don't tell us where you are going or whom you're going to speak to. There's too much we don't know, and we don't want to inadvertently interfere with the book's plans. Do what the book tells you to do, and if you get confused, go to the entry that says 'Further Instructions.' Let the book guide you.

And whatever happens, don't decide that you know best and do something completely different. Believe me, it's been done before, and the results are never good." She looked at Anne. "Why don't you give her a ride home?"

They all stood, and Jennifer squeezed Maya's hand. "Good luck, Maya. Do what the book wants you to do as soon as you get back home. While you're following the book's instructions, we'll be watching for Chet."

David patted Maya on the back. "That's right, we might be librarians, but we know how to do a few things." He glanced at Anne. "Right?"

"Right," she answered, smiling just a little. "Come on, Maya."

In the gathering dark, Maya followed Anne to the car. On the short ride home, Maya asked Anne a few more questions, and Anne answered them as best she could. Now that Maya knew about the book's history, she felt jumpy, scared even, and Anne put a hand on the girl's thin shoulder.

"Maya," she said, "I can tell you're afraid. But just keep in mind that because of you, the book is safe. You've done exactly the right thing. You seem to have an intuitive sense of what should be done. Just keep listening to that intuition." They were in the driveway of the old farmhouse, and Anne leaned over, giving Maya a kiss on the forehead. "Listen to the book. And call me when you get back." She gave Maya her cell phone number.

When Maya had entered the number into her phone, Anne said, "Good luck, Maya! And remember, we'll be nearby, keeping a watch over the house."

Nodding, Maya bolted from the car. Without looking back, she sprinted into the house.

Anne sat in the driveway for a while, with both hands on the steering wheel. In truth, she was nearly as afraid as Maya. Much of what would happen next would depend on a fifteen-year-old girl. And on the sidelines, waiting, would be the League of Librarians as well as Chet and APO.

Anne drove back to the library, while Maya, mumbling an excuse to Pépère about being too tired to play cribbage, hurried to her room. Maya retrieved the book from the desk, but she just held onto it and asked herself, "What's going to happen next?"

8: Into the Forest, or What You Will

At the library David and Jennifer were still sitting in the chairs by the desk. For several minutes, nobody said anything.

Finally, Jennifer cleared her throat. "Well, here we go."

"I hope we made the right choice," David said quickly.

"So do I. If anything happens to that child, it will be our fault. We could have asked her for the book. She would have given it to us. But..."

"You didn't want to work against the book," David finished.

Jennifer shook her head. "Nothing good ever comes from working against it. Besides, I expect Chet is on Maya's trail, and no matter what our decision, she would be in terrible danger." Jennifer sat up straight. "Mary Parsons, rightly or wrongly, set the course, and now we have to do what we can to protect Maya and her family."

Anne stood by her desk. "And it has to be just the three of us to help Maya. We can't call on anyone else. We don't know who betrayed the league."

There was silence again as Jennifer, David, and Anne considered the situation, and, as subtly as they could, each other.

"You have supplies?" Jennifer asked at last.

"Of course." Anne went to the bookshelf that was on the wall separating the adult area from the children's area. Removing a key chain from her pocket, Anne went through the keys until she found the one she wanted. Then, she removed a book from the second shelf from the top, fitted the key into a lock built into the shelf, and turned the key. The bookshelf swung back. Another key and another lock, and a panel in the wall opened to reveal a small closet stocked with dark clothes, ropes, headsets, and bulletproof vests.

David and Jennifer joined Anne by the secret closet. "Here we go," Jennifer said again, reaching for a black shirt.

Maya stood in the middle of her room, but she still didn't open the book. Maya had never been this scared before. Until the book had come to her, she hadn't been much afraid of anything. One summer after a grange supper, when she had been outside with some of the kids, running around and playing tag in the twilight, Maya had been the one who had faced down the boys when they found a snake by the stream and had started to chase the girls. Maya wouldn't run or scream, not even when they held the frantically twisting snake over her head. She just stood there with her hands folded across her chest. "Put that snake back," Maya had said in a cool voice. The boys, looking sheepish, brought the snake back to where they found it.

Maya was not afraid of dogs, had never been afraid of the dark, didn't mind speaking in front of her class, and loved being on stage. Maya had been upset when her father had left, but what she felt now was completely different. Right from the start, when she saw Chet and Mary on the train, Maya knew that she should be afraid.

"What if I fail?" Maya thought. "What if Chet gets the book?"

Chewing the side of her lip, Maya took her cell phone from her pocket and called her father.

He answered after the second ring. "Maya! You didn't forget."

Momentarily taken aback—Maya had, in fact, forgotten she was supposed to call her father—she said quickly, "No, no, of course not!"

"I'm really glad you didn't forget. I think about you a lot, Mayaroo."

Usually, Maya would have tartly reminded him not to call her by that silly nickname he had used when she was little. But not tonight. "Dad? Can I ask you a question? It's about a story I'm writing, and I need your help. You know how good you are at figuring things out."

"Sure," her father answered cheerfully. "What's the problem?"

"Well, in my story there's a young girl named Nicole who has found a kind of magic book, a Book of Everything, and it's in terrible danger. Some bad guys want it, but if they get it, then they'll be able to stop the human race from progressing."

"Wow!" her father said. "That's quite a book. You have a great imagination, Maya."

"If you only knew," Maya thought, but aloud she said, "Thanks, Dad." She stared at the little flowered book in her hand.

"Not that I'm surprised," her father said. "You always were a precocious child. You were speaking in complete sentences before you were two years old." His voice sounded a little sad, and he asked quietly, "So what happens next?"

"Nicole has to go back in time to do something the book wants her to do. Except she's so afraid that she doesn't know if she can go back."

"Are the bad guys after her? Do they know she has the book?"

"Yes, at least one is. The man who didn't smile."

"Terrific name!" her father said.

"Thanks, Dad. But what should I have Nicole do? Should she go back in time or stay where she is and hope things work out all right?"

"Depending on how you want the story to turn out, you could go either way. If Nicole stays where she is, then she's just a sitting duck, so to speak, and the man who didn't smile will probably get her. Don't you think?"

Maya's mouth was dry, and she thought about Mary Parsons. "Yes, he probably will."

"But if Nicole goes back in time, then chances are she'll be able to discover something that will not only help her but the book as well. Plus, dramatically, going back in time would add interest to the story."

"Yes," Maya said slowly, "you are right. Nicole should go back." Then, quickly—"I love you, Dad."

"Maya, is something wrong?" her father asked.

But Maya had hung up and had stuffed the phone into the pocket of her jeans. Taking a deep breath, Maya opened the book, and soon she was back in the South End. It was still summer, late morning, Maya thought, looking at the sun and the sky. This time, Maya was dizzy for only a few minutes, and she looked around, trying to get her bearings. She wasn't by the store. Instead, she was in a large, tarred yard surrounded by triple-decker apartment buildings. In the middle of the yard, a group of girls was jumping rope, and, off to one side, some small boys were playing with toy trucks and cars.

"Maya!" a voice called, and Maya jumped. Andy was on the porch of the closest apartment building, and he was staring intently at her.

"Andy!" Maya clutched the book.

Andy wasn't smiling. In fact, he was frowning. "Can you come here? I want to talk to you."

Wondering what was wrong, Maya nodded. "I want to talk to you, too. Is this where you live?"

"Yeah."

"Is your mother home?"

"No, she's at work."

"Well, that's good," Maya muttered, going up the steps. Andy's face looked stern, and for a moment, Maya got an impression of him as the adult he would grow up to be—tall, serious, and more than a little intimidating. But Maya didn't look away.

Andy pushed open the screen door. "Come in."

Maya walked into a small but very clean kitchen, and she shook her head. "They must spend all their time cleaning."

"What?" Andy asked, following her.

"Never mind," Maya replied.

Andy motioned to one of four chairs by a chrome-legged table. "Have a seat."

Maya sat down, and Andy sat across from her. Leaning forward a little, he put his hands on the table.

Maya had a feeling she knew why Andy was upset, and she set the book between the two of them. "I think you should go first. I think I know what this is about."

"You do?"

"Yes, you didn't really go home after you dropped me off at Mémère's, did you?" Andy slowly shook his head, and even though Maya knew she had been more than a little dishonest with Andy and his family, she felt irritated. "Andy, that was just plain sneaky."

Andy flushed. "That woman wasn't your mémère. I could tell by the look on her face when she answered the door. She had never seen you before."

"So you followed me to the church, didn't you?"

"Yes, and I saw you take something out of your pocket. It looked like a book." He looked thoughtfully at the book on the table, and Maya nodded. "Then it seemed like you disappeared."

Maya said, "You're right and you're wrong. That woman didn't know me, but she is my grandmother—my great-grandmother." Andy stared at her. "And I did disappear, just the way it looked."

"But how?" Andy asked.

"With the help of this book." Maya put her hand on the cover. "It's the Book of Everything."

"That little flowered book?"

"Go ahead," Maya said. "Take a look."

Andy picked up the book, opened it, and nearly dropped it when it made its high-pitched hum. Then he started turning the pages while Maya fidgeted, knowing he would need some time. After five minutes or so, he looked up, as if in a daze.

"You're from the future?" Maya nodded. Closing the book, Andy rubbed his forehead. "It's amazing. It really is. If I hadn't seen it, if I hadn't seen you disappear…"

"Then you wouldn't have believed it," Maya finished.

"That's right. How did you get the book?"

Maya told him everything—about the man who didn't smile, Mary Parsons, the League of Librarians, the Great Library, and APO. "The book told me to come back and tell you, but now that I've done it, I don't know what else I'm supposed to do."

"Why me?" Andy asked.

"I don't know," Maya answered. "The book doesn't really say very much. At least not to me."

"Maybe it's afraid of telling too much," Andy said slowly as he sorted his thoughts. "Maybe the not knowing is part of it, too, so you can discover things."

Maya nodded. "Maybe so. Anyway, Jennifer said that if I ever get stumped about what to do, then I should go to the 'Further Instructions' entry." She motioned with a hand. "Go ahead."

"*F* or *I*?"

"I don't know. Try *F*, and then go to *I* if that doesn't work."

Blinking, Andy turned the pages until he came to *F*, where he found the entry. "That's not how I would have done it," he muttered. "I'd have it under *I*."

"Never mind that! What does it say? Is it bolded?"

"Yes, and it says, 'Into the Forest, or What You Will.'"

"I wonder what that could mean."

"Don't know."

"Do you want to find out?"

Andy was surprised. "Me? I'm supposed to go, too?"

"Why not?" Maya asked. "Otherwise, what would be the point of coming here and telling you about the book?"

"How do we do it?"

"I'm not really sure," Maya answered. "But I have an idea. Here, give me the book, and we'll see if I'm right."

Andy passed the book to her, opened to the right place, and Maya set it on the table. "I want you to take my hand. Then I'm going to run my finger over the entry. If we're lucky, we'll both go where the book wants us to go."

Reaching across the table, Andy took Maya's hand.

"Ready?" she asked.

"Ready," Andy answered.

Maya ran her finger over the words, and there was that familiar jarring feeling. Maya automatically closed her eyes, and when she opened them, she found that she was clutching the book, which now had a plain blue leather cover but was still small enough to be tucked in a pocket. Marveling again at how the book could change, Maya quickly slid it into the pocket of her jeans and looked for Andy. He was beside her but had fallen to his knees, and he looked as though he was going to throw up.

Maya patted his back. "Wait a few minutes. You'll stop feeling so dizzy. The next time it won't be so bad. You'll know what to expect."

Nodding, Andy swallowed and then swallowed again. "I wish I had some orange soda to give you," Maya said, remembering how kind Andy had been on her first visit to the South End.

"I'll be all right," Andy said, trying to get up.

"Here," Maya said, "take my hand." Later, Andy would say that he really hadn't needed her help, and it did seem to Maya that Andy pretty much got up on his own, but he gratefully took the small, outstretched hand, and when he stood, his legs were a little shaky.

Nevertheless, Andy was the first to notice where they were. "Look, Maya, look!"

Maya turned from Andy and saw that, as the book had suggested, they were in a forest. But it was like no forest Maya had ever been to, either in Maine or in upstate New York, on hikes with her parents. There were giant ferns, fallen trees, and some underbrush, but what caught Maya's attention were the massive trees, tall and dark, that went high into the sky. They filled the forest, and their trunks were so large that Maya knew she wouldn't even be able to wrap her arms around them. She didn't think her father would have been able to, either, even though he was a tall man. Sunlight shone through the trees, needles, and branches, illuminating the spaces in between so that the forest seemed to be filled with a golden, shimmering light.

"If only my mother could see this," Maya said, noticing the contrast between the bright sun and the branches, the shapes and the colors, and for the first time, Maya got a sense of how her mother saw the world.

"It's like being in church," Andy said in a hushed voice.

Maya agreed and was about to ask Andy which way he thought they should go, when they heard a man singing.

When that I was and a little tiny boy,
 With hey, ho, the wind and the rain;
A foolish thing was but a toy,
 For the rain it raineth every day.
But when I came to man's estate,
 With hey, ho, the wind and the rain;
'Gainst knaves and thieves men shut the gates,
 For the rain it raineth every day.
But when I came, alas! to wive,
 With hey, ho, the wind and the rain;
By swaggering could I never thrive,
 For the rain it raineth every day.
But when I came unto my beds,
 With hey, ho, the wind and the rain;
With toss-pots still had drunken heads,
 For the rain it raineth every day.
A great while ago the world begun,
 With hey, ho, the wind and the rain;
But that's all one our play is done.
 And we'll strive to please you every day.

"I've heard that song before," Maya said. "But where?"

The voice was coming closer, and a lean, bald man with a large, sharp nose was coming toward them. As the man got closer, Maya could see that his dark eyes were sharp, too.

"Feste?" Maya asked, remembering the song, and at the same time also recalling that she had seen his image when she had been flipping through the book. It had been giving her previews, it seemed.

"From *Twelfth Night?*" Andy asked.

By now the man was not far away, and he said, "I might be Feste, but I'm not from twelfth night nor any other night for that matter. My mother tells me I was born in the morning."

Maya sighed and shook her head while Andy gave a sharp laugh. The man grinned. "And who might you two be?"

"We might be anyone," Maya shot back. "We might be a prince and princess on the run from an evil guardian."

Feste laughed out loud. "You have a lively wit, but it's my guess you're not royalty."

"You're right," Maya said, smiling a little. "I'm Maya and this is Andy."

Feste gave a little bow. "Pleased to meet you. You're not from around here, are you?"

"No, we're not," Andy answered, looking around. "This is the most beautiful place I've ever seen."

"So you like the Forest of Arden?" Feste asked.

"Arden?" Maya and Andy said together. "But that's from a different story," Maya added.

Feste stopped smiling, and his eyes had that sharp look again. "It's my guess you're from a different story, too."

Maya glanced at Andy. He gave a slight nod, and Maya's own intuition told her that Feste, despite his bad jokes, could be trusted. "We can't tell you everything, and there's a lot we don't know. But we are from a different story, a different land. We were sent here for some reason, but we don't know why, and we don't really know what to do next."

"I see," Feste said, and it really did seem as though he understood, at least a little. "You'd better come with me to my cottage. You don't want to be wandering around the forest by yourselves. Especially at night."

Again, Maya looked at Andy, and again there was the nod. "Thank you so much," she said.

"You are most welcome. You two came at the right time." He pointed to a large pack that was on his back. "I've been outside the forest, and I brought back supplies. We'll have plenty to eat. But we'd best get going. We still have a bit of a walk. I'll sing you a song as we go along." Bending a little, he asked, "Maya, could you reach in and grab my squeezebox? It should be right on top." Maya did as she was told and passed him the squeezebox.

"Where should I begin?" Feste asked, playing a little tune that was both sweet and sad. He glanced at the squeezebox as though it were playing on its own and was telling him something. "Yes, I suppose that is a good place to start.

Feste sang:
Once there were two brothers, very close in age,
Owen was the first with Humphrey just behind.
Their father was Duke Warwick, good and fair and kind.
But! The ways of the world are harsh,
And men want more than they should.
Too often the innocent are fooled
And mistake bad intentions for good.
Alas good Duke Warwick died far too soon,
While both sons were not yet men.
As our laws do clearly state, Owen was now the duke.
But! The ways of the world are harsh,
And men want more than they should.
Too often the innocent are fooled
And mistake bad intentions for good.
Now, Humphrey was quite unhappy with his lot
As most younger brothers unsurprisingly are.
And as he was born under a dark star
He began to lay his plans.

While gentle Owen studied
Humphrey persuaded his father's men
That bookish Owen was too weak
Then sly Humphrey showed again and again
That he was indeed strong and firm and bold.
And against Owen he turned the men cold.
They drove the unfortunate duke
Far, far from his own good court
Into this wild Forest of Arden
With only a few friends for support.
But! The ways of the world are harsh,
And men want more than they should.
Too often the innocent are fooled
And mistake bad intentions for good.

"So Owen is hiding from Humphrey in this forest?" Maya asked when the song was done.

"Aye," Feste replied.

"And you're on Owen's side?" Andy asked.

"I'm on no one's side," Feste answered. "Which means I can come and go as I please, from the Forest of Arden to town to the duke's court, and no one hinders my movements."

Maya said, "It seems to me that song says otherwise."

Feste grinned. "Ah, but it's just a song written and sung by a fool for those who might want to listen."

Shaking her head, Maya smiled and thought, "It's all mixed up. It's a combination of *Twelfth Night* and *As You Like It* and maybe even some of *The Tempest*. God only knows what else we'll find."

9: Sir John Oldcastle

Feste, Andy, and Maya walked for a couple of hours until they came to a small stone cottage in a clearing next to a stream. Along the way, Feste sometimes sang, sometimes asked questions, and sometimes answered Maya's and Andy's questions. In a roundabout way, Maya and Andy learned that six years ago, Lord Owen, along with some of his men, their wives, and a few servants, had escaped to a hunting lodge deep in the forest and that the forest had "special qualities," as Feste put it.

"What do you mean by special?" Andy asked.

"Well, the Forest of Arden decides who comes in and who stays out."

Maya looked suspiciously at the trees. "How does it do that?"

Feste laughed. "Not by any direct means. After all, the trees can't move. They're rooted to the earth."

Later, Andy would say to Maya, "You were thinking of *Lord of the Rings* and Ents, weren't you?"

"Yes, I was," Maya would reply.

But no, that was a different story, as Feste might have said. In his story, the trees didn't move or block anyone's path, but anytime someone, say, Duke Humphrey or his men, tried to come into the forest, they would become so confused that within a half hour they would be wandering in circles until they were back where they had started.

"Just outside the forest." Feste glanced at Maya and Andy. "And no matter how many times they tried, it always ended the same."

"And what about Lord Owen?" Andy asked.

"Oh, he did just fine. Found his way right to the hunting lodge. And so did that fat knight, Sir John Oldcastle, even though he's a bigger fool than I am. I expect you could get three Festes out of one John Oldcastle."

Andy laughed, and Maya asked sharply, "Feste, did you have to say that?"

"Why, yes, I did, Miss Maya. Any more questions?"

Maya sighed. "No, at least not about that. But back to the forest. How did it confuse Duke Humphrey and his men?"

For a moment, the sly, impudent look was gone, and Feste looked serious, almost reverential. "This forest is alive, Maya. These trees have thoughts, feelings. They can suggest. Listen." He stopped and put his hand on a large maple tree.

Andy and Maya stopped, too, and listened as the leaves and branches moved, swaying, rustling, whispering, it seemed. Maya got a sense of safety, that as long as she was in this forest, she was all right. Andy had closed his eyes, and when he opened them, Maya could tell that he had heard the same thing. Maya sighed again, but this time it was from relief. Even if Chet somehow managed to find his way to wherever they were, Maya knew he could not get her or the book as long as they were in this forest.

"How?" Andy asked, putting his own hand on the tree.

Feste shrugged, and the old impudent look was back. "I'm a fool, Andy, not a wise man. I cannot tell you how things came to be, only how things are. But this I do know. The forest is made of many, many trees, but in the center is a special old one, an oak, that has been there longer than anyone can remember." Feste whistled and jumped and played a little tune on his squeezebox.

And if you think it's hard to get into the forest,
Then try to find that tree.
O, yes!
Try to find that tree.
Count to one, count to three,
Count until you have to pee.
But you'll never find that tree.

Maya opened her mouth to make a tart comment about Feste's rhyming choice, but he stopped playing and wagged a finger at her. "Not a word from you, Miss Maya. Not a word. We men have to have our fun. Don't we, Andy?"

Andy grinned. "That's right."

Maya shook her head and then looked away so that they wouldn't see that she was grinning, too.

Feste's cottage had a fireplace on the back wall, two beds along each side wall, a table with benches, a cupboard for food, and next to that a shelf with a lute, puppets, a flute, the skull of some small animal, and a few leather-bound books. To one side was a ladder leading to a loft.

Feste set his pack and his squeezebox on the table. "Miss Maya, you will be sleeping in the loft." He motioned to one of the beds along the wall. "Andy, you'll sleep down here with me. Both of you will need a change of clothes. Even visitors from faraway places aren't dressed as strangely as you two are. And Maya, since you're dressed like a boy, how about if you stay that way? It will make things easier. You'll be able to move around more freely."

"All right," Maya said.

"Good," Feste said. "What do you think about cutting your hair?"

Maya put her hand on her ponytail. "It's taken me forever to get it this long."

Feste gave her a stern look. "That really wasn't a question."

Maya grimaced. "Go ahead and cut it, then. It will grow back. In three or four years."

"Oh, stop complaining. You're safe here. Isn't that worth a haircut?"

Maya thought about Chet Addington and Mary Parsons and APO. "Yes, it is," she said soberly.

Feste had gone to a chest at the end of his bed and was about to open it, but he stopped and regarded Maya. "You're running from something very bad, aren't you?" Maya nodded, and Feste turned to Andy. "And what about you?"

"I'm with her." Andy looked intently at Maya, who blushed just a little.

"Good," Feste said, pointing at Andy. "See that it stays that way." Opening the chest, Feste pulled out several pairs of shirts and trousers before he found some that he thought would fit Maya and Andy.

"Why do you have all these extra clothes?" Maya asked. "And beds?"

"Well," Feste answered, "nowadays, you never know who might need a change of clothes and a place to stay for a while." Shaking his head, he looked away. "Let's just say that even though Duke Humphrey is only a young man, he rules with a hard hand, like an old tyrant. Many have fled into this forest and have settled around Lord Owen. And woe be to Duke Humphrey if they ever revolt." Feste turned to Andy. "Remember, boy, that there is a difference between a firm but fair ruler and one that is harsh and cruel."

"I will remember," Andy said seriously, taking the clothes Feste passed him.

Feste clapped Andy on the shoulder. "I believe you." Then he passed clothes to Maya. "Up into the loft with you, and when you come down, we'll make a boy of you."

Two hours later, the three sat at the table. Feste had cooked sausage and eggs in a cast iron pan over the fire and served them with thick slices of dark bread and creamy butter.

For drink they had ale, which made Maya grimace and Andy pucker his mouth. Feste laughed. "You'd better get used to this. It's what we drink here."

"What about tea?" Maya asked.

"Oh, we have that, too, but we don't drink it with our evening meal."

Maya's hair was short, cut just below her ears, and it curled around the edges. Although there was no mirror in Feste's cottage, Maya had no doubt that as long as she was in this forest, she was going to have a series of bad hair days.

But Feste tipped his head to one side and smiled at her. "I must say, Maya, you make a very fetching boy. You can be as saucy as you want, and nobody will mind. It helps to be slim and good-looking. Still, you'd better watch what you say around Lord Owen. He might be the gentle one, but he is still a duke, and the rightful one at that."

Maya put a hand to her curling hair. "Do you think we'll meet him?"

"I do. We'll be going to the lodge tomorrow. I have a message for Lord Owen, and I have a feeling he's going to want us to stay there for a while. We'd better come up with a boy's name. Maya isn't common around here, but it sounds like a girl's name."

"What about Cesario?" Maya blurted out, before she really had time to think about it. The name from *Twelfth Night*—the one Viola had chosen for her "boy's name"—seemed right, somehow.

Feste said, "That's not common around here, either, but it's a good name, and it has the ring of a gentleman."

Later, Andy would tease her. "Cesario, huh? No Tom or Harry for you. Those names are much too common."

So Cesario it was. Maya, Andy, and Feste had just finished eating when they heard a crashing outside and a deep voice bellow, "Feste! Feste! Back at last! For God's sake you'd better have something for me to drink. Why in creation you stay in this little hut when you could be staying at the lodge is beyond comprehension. To go two miles through the dark woods to visit a friend, now that's dedication." There was another voice, a softer one, just a murmur. "Quiet, you! Or you can sit outside and let the mosquitoes bite you."

"Well," Feste said, rising from the table to get more ale and mugs, "in a few minutes you will be meeting Sir John Oldcastle and his sidekick, Harry Newton."

Maya and Andy turned expectantly toward the door, but they nevertheless jumped when it opened with a crash and banged into the wall. A huge man stood in the doorway, and at first his bulk was so imposing that Maya could hardly take in any other detail. Then she noticed the red face, the thick white hair, the bright hazel eyes, and the large, expressive mouth. Carrying a lantern, he stomped into the cottage, and his face was sweating.

Sir John wiped his forehead. "A seat, a seat! I need to sit down."

Behind him came a slight man with ginger-colored hair, light brown eyes, and an amused look that suggested that even though he had seen and heard it all from this large, sweating man, he still found it humorous.

"Sit down, sit down," said Feste. "You know you don't need to be invited."

At the head of the table was a large chair—"Especially for Sir John," Feste would say later. "That much flesh needs its own space."—and Sir John, surprisingly light on his feet for such a big man, made his way to the chair and sat down. Feste gestured to a spot beside Maya, and Harry slid in beside her.

It wasn't until Sir John had taken a grateful drink of ale that he turned his attention to Maya and Andy. "Well," he said, squinting speculatively at them, "two new ones."

Feste replied, "I found them wandering in the forest."

"They must be all right, then," Sir John said.

"That's what I thought. Otherwise, they wouldn't be here. Sir John and Harry, meet Cesario and Andy."

There were curt nods of acknowledgement, and Sir John said, "You'll be bringing them to the lodge to meet Sir Owen." It wasn't a question.

Feste said, "I'll take them tomorrow."

Sir John looked at Maya and then at Andy. "Good. They're too young to stay with a wanderer like you and too young to be on their own." The flush was gone from his face and his expression was sympathetic, almost soft. "Lord Owen will look after you," he said directly to Maya and Andy. "He knows what it's like to be on the run. And you are on the run, aren't you?"

"Of course they are," Harry said, regarding Maya. "Else they wouldn't be here."

Maya nodded. "We're hiding from someone, and we hope he doesn't find us."

"Not in this forest, he won't," said Harry.

Maya shivered. "This man has a way of finding what he's looking for."

Nobody said anything for a while. Harry fidgeted beside Maya, Sir John shook his head and took a drink of ale, Andy looked down at the table, and Feste stared into the fire.

Then Sir John said briskly, "You're as safe here as it's possible to be. In fact, it's so safe that it's positively boring. But tonight we have a fire, ale, and good company. What more can we ask for?"

"A few heads to crack?" Harry suggested.

Sir John laughed. "Aye! And one in particular I'm thinking of." But then his mood changed so quickly that Maya wasn't ready when the big fist slammed down on the table, and Sir John's face was red again. "Lord Owen won't move against that brother of his. Instead, we wait in this forest, for what I don't know. 'Strike back,' I implore. 'Humphrey's my brother,' says Lord Owen. 'He would kill you if he could,' say I but, 'He's my brother,' Lord Owen keeps repeating."

Feste drummed a little tune on the table and chanted, "A brother with a lot of men, a brother with a lot of weapons. A brother who isn't afraid to kill, and a brother who doesn't take it lightly. Who do you trust? Oh, who do you trust?"

Harry snorted. "Well sung, Feste!"

Sir John's anger passed as suddenly as it had come, and the flush left his face. "You're both probably right. But still, it's hard to just wait here and watch as Duke Humphrey destroys everything his father worked to build."

Feste's hands were still. "That one knows how to gain power, but he doesn't know how to rule."

Sir John said, "If we can ever get our Lord Owen back to his rightful place, then we'll have a good duke, a good leader."

"Where does Duke Humphrey stay?" Andy asked.

"Mostly in the duchy's principal city, Caxton, which is also the name of the duchy. But sometimes Duke Humphrey and his men come to Greendale, just outside the forest."

Feste grimaced. "When they want to flush out Lord Owen."

"Duke Humphrey comes for something else, too," Harry put in.

Sir John pursed his lips. "The fair Lady Celia. Well, he won't get her."

"She's in love with Lord Owen," Harry explained. "And before he was driven into the forest, they had an..."

"Understanding," Feste finished.

Maya sighed. "It just keeps getting more complicated, doesn't it?"

"That's the way of the world," Feste said.

"Does it have to be?"

Feste shrugged. "As far as I can tell. At least in this land."

"In other lands, too," Andy said.

The talk turned back to Lord Owen, Lady Celia, Duke Humphrey, and other names that Maya had never heard. She tried to pay attention, but her eyes kept closing, and she slumped on the bench.

"We are losing young Cesario," Maya heard Sir John say, and then she felt a hand on her shoulder.

"Go to bed," Harry said gently. "Sir John will be here for a while. He's barely gotten started."

"Harry's right," Feste added. "Go on up to bed."

Sir John raised his cup. "And we'll see you on the morrow."

Maya stumbled a little as she got up from the table and made her way to the ladder. Maybe it was the ale, but she couldn't remember the last time she had been so tired. Up the ladder Maya went, settling gratefully on the first bed she came to. She didn't care that the mattress was straw, that the blankets were rough, or that the bed didn't have a pillow. Soon Maya was asleep, even though Sir John was, in a loud voice, singing a song about love, with Harry and Feste coming in as the chorus.

In her sleep, Maya heard a different song, one without words, without instruments, more a high-pitched trill but beautiful nonetheless.

"And old," Maya would remember later. "Very old."

Images came to her, of a massive tree with branches that seemed to spread out and envelop the entire forest. Beneath the tree sat an enormous toad with a glittering red stone that appeared to be affixed to its forehead. As the toad's throat swelled into a bubble, Maya realized this was where the song was coming from. And all night long, Maya heard the song in her dreams.

10: Lord Owen

The next day, on the way to the lodge, Maya wondered what the "gentle" duke would be like. "Gentle compared to what?" Maya asked herself as she followed Feste and Andy along a narrow but well-used path. "Duke Humphrey? Chet Addington?"

The book, along with her cell phone, was in the pocket of the brown trousers she was now wearing. Maya also wore a brown waistcoat but darker than her trousers. Feste had given her a leather cap, and her curls bounced around it as she walked. If Maya could have looked down on herself, then she would have seen a petite, jaunty figure going along that path.

In truth, Maya was beginning to enjoy the adventure. The book, their return ticket, was in her pocket, and she felt safe in the forest. As she walked, Maya listened to the murmuring trees, and it didn't seem too far-fetched to imagine that they were discussing her and Andy in tones that were, well, soothing.

Every so often, Feste would look back and wink at Maya in between singing little songs and telling jokes with terrible puns.

"Terrible to you," Andy might have said.

For his part, Andy was dressed similarly to Maya but in a deep green, and even though the color was darker than illustrations she had seen. Maya couldn't help but think of Robin Hood.

"Robin Hood?" Andy would ask later, more than a little exasperated. "Robin Hood wore tights and a tunic and a weird pointed hat."

"You're thinking of Mel Brooks," Maya had answered with a laugh. "Or you will be when you see *Men in Tights.*"

Andy was, of course, thinking about the old movie with Errol Flynn, and what Andy was wearing didn't remotely resemble the Robin Hood of that film. Still, there was something about the way Andy moved—graceful yet serious and with a purpose—that put Maya in mind of the version of the story that depicted Robin Hood as a nobleman who took to the woods to escape tyranny and who would eventually bring some kind of justice to everyday people.

Like Feste's cottage, the hunting lodge was made of stone, and it was in a huge clearing that had a pasture, gardens, and smaller outbuildings. The lodge was massively bigger than Feste's cottage, and with its graceful, symmetrical lines, it gave Maya the impression of calm and order.

When Feste and Andy weren't looking, Maya took out her cell phone and snapped a quick picture of the lodge. They turned around just in time for her to get a picture of them, too.

"What is that?" Feste asked.

"Oh, it's just something from my land." Maya quickly put the phone back into her pocket. She wasn't sure if she should say anything about technology that wasn't from Feste's and Andy's time, and she changed the subject. "The lodge is built of stone, just like your cottage."

Feste raised his eyebrows but didn't press her for more information about her cell phone. "We don't use wood in this forest for building. And we use only fallen trees for our fires or for smaller projects like doors. If we didn't, we'd be out quicker than you can say Sir John Oldcastle."

Maya nodded. "Are all the forests in your land like this forest?"

They had come to the massive front door, and Feste stopped. "No, the Forest of Arden is special. But all forests, all trees, have something. Don't you think?"

"I've never really been in a forest, only in woods that weren't that deep," Andy said, and on seeing Feste's shocked look, he added, "I live in town, and I don't get out much."

Feste looked at Maya, who said, "I never thought about it before. But I will from now on."

"So will I," Andy said.

Feste made a funny face. "Good children! Oh, how you two learn!" Then under his breath. "What you two will learn."

Maya was about to ask him what he meant by that, but the big door swung open, and a small bald man stood before them.

"Well, well, Feste. Back at last. Lord Owen is eager to see you. Each night, Sir John and Harry have gone to your cottage to see if you've returned, and each night they've come back early, looking glum. But last night was different. Sir John and Harry came home very late. So we all knew. Feste was back."

Feste laughed. "Yes, Elwyn, I'm back. Was it really that long?"

"Over two months," came a low but firm voice. "And there are newcomers with you, I see." A tall, slender man with gray eyes and dark curly hair stood behind Elwyn.

Feste bowed. "Good, my lord. This is Andy and young Cesario. On my way back, I found them wandering in the forest. They stayed with me last night, but I thought it best to bring them to you."

Andy and Maya followed Feste's example and bowed.

Lord Owen smiled. "Of course. Come in, come in. Have you eaten?"

Feste replied, "Not so long ago that our stomachs are grumbling, but not so recently that they wouldn't object to a little something."

"Always hungry, aren't you Feste?"

"Always, my lord. It takes a lot to keep me going."

Lord Owen stopped smiling. "I am sure of that. Come with me. Elwyn, have Cook fix us a tray. And then, Feste, we need to talk."

They walked into a big hall with a huge stone fireplace and four long tables with benches. A row of windows at one end overlooked a broad field leading down to a river, and Maya could see men, women, and some children working in big gardens stretched across the field.

They followed Lord Owen to a small parlor off the Great Hall. This room had padded benches along the wall as well as a round table in the middle with padded chairs around it. Lord Owen motioned for them to sit down in the chairs around the table, and it wasn't long before a young girl came in, carrying a tray with strawberries, cream, a tart, a dark spice cake, and a big pot of tea.

As the girl set the tray on the table, Feste said, "I see things continue to go well here."

At first Lord Owen didn't answer. The tea was poured, the cake was served, and as Maya watched Lord Owen, who looked at her and smiled, she thought, "He's so handsome! He's nothing like Chet. And he can't be like Duke Humphrey, I'm sure."

The girl left, and finally, between bites of cake, Lord Owen answered, "Yes, for now we're doing well. The crops are growing, the cows are giving enough milk, and the hens are laying enough eggs. But for how long, Feste? Each month, more and more people come into the forest." There was a hard edge to his voice. "Driven by my little brother. If too many come, the lodge won't be able to support them. We can't clear more land."

"Out of the question," Feste agreed.

"We've been here for almost six years. It's time to do something, yet..." Lord Owen stopped, looking at Maya and Andy.

"My lord," Feste said, "these two have come from a distant land and are wise beyond their years. I think they should hear what we have to say to each other." Lord Owen looked doubtful. "Have I ever led you wrong?"

There was a gleam in the gray eyes. "There was that time…"

Feste held up his hand. "My lord, I know what you are about to say. That was a long time ago, and it was mostly because of that foolish Sir John, who convinced us to dress like women and sing bawdy songs at your father's birthday celebration. How were we to know that the duke of Itan didn't have much of a sense of humor and would stomp out in disgust and then refuse to negotiate a peace treaty with your father?"

"How indeed?" Lord Owen asked, and Maya could see he was trying not to smile. "Well, my father smoothed things over, the way he always did. And lucky for us my father had a forgiving nature as well as a sense of humor. But, come, Feste, Sir John has said the idea was yours."

Maya and Andy looked to Feste, who replied, "My lord, would you trust his version more than mine?"

Lord Owen stopped smiling. "No, I wouldn't. Sir John means well, but he's rash, and he doesn't always see things as clearly as he should."

"Well, my lord," Feste said.

"All right! Let Andy and Cesario stay. But they seem too young to be involved in all this."

"They are," Feste admitted, looking at Maya and Andy. "But it can't be helped."

Maya got the strangest feeling, right then, that Feste knew a great deal more than he had let on. She shifted, feeling the book in her pocket. Could he even know about the book? It didn't seem possible, yet he had accepted their story without question and without surprise, first bringing them to his cottage and then to Lord Owen. True, the forest had allowed them to stay, but there seemed more to it than that. Maya had meant to consult the book about Feste, but last night she had been too tired, and this morning she hadn't had the chance. Maya had barely woken up when she heard Feste calling her down for breakfast.

Feste turned back to Lord Owen. "No doubt you want to learn what I discovered while I was away."

"That's exactly what I want to know," Lord Owen replied. "You were gone so long that we were beginning to worry."

Feste shrugged. "It took that long to find out what Humphrey has planned. None who knew would speak. They didn't dare, no matter how many drinks I bought them. But at last Molly overheard a conversation. You know how it is with some people. They just don't see servants."

"What would have become of us without Molly?" Lord Owen asked.

"The cook at Caxton," Feste explained to Maya and Andy. "Not only is she a good cook, but she is also good at helping people escape and listening for bits of information. And as soon as she told me what Humphrey was planning, off I went, to return to the forest."

Lord Owen shook his head. "I don't know why my brother lets you come and go as you please. I wouldn't if I were him."

Feste grinned. "Your brother is not as smart as you are, my lord."

"That's why I'm hiding in the Forest of Arden and Humphrey is now Duke of Caxton."

"He has a different gift, if you want to call it that. Humphrey has the ability to sway men, to persuade them to follow him. But begging your pardon, my lord, he is vain and shallow. He surrounds himself with men who are the same way. All except for one." Feste stopped for a moment. "A new man whose name is Julian. And aside from the incredible malice that he bears, he's very hard to read."

"Will he complicate things?" Lord Owen asked.

"I expect so. In fact, I expect it was he who came up with the plan of action that Humphrey has decided on."

"And what is that?"

Feste looked away, unable to speak, and Maya and Andy leaned forward. Lord Owen stared intently at Feste, but still he didn't say anything.

"Tell me, Feste," Lord Owen commanded. "Whatever it is, we will have to deal with it."

Feste's normally mobile face was still and grim. "Humphrey plans to burn down the Forest of Arden, to destroy it along with you."

There was a silence. "He wouldn't dare," Lord Owen said at last. "Our family, for centuries, has sworn to protect this forest."

"Yes, my lord, but the way Humphrey sees it, the forest has chosen sides—you against him. He feels as though he no longer has to honor the family vow."

Lord Owen put a hand to his forehead. "I can't believe it."

"Believe it, my lord. Molly overheard Captain Bourgoin and Lieutenant Reed discussing it. They are two of his most trusted officers."

"When?" Maya asked. "When does Duke Humphrey plan to do this?"

"In two months, during the dry season," Feste answered. "He wants to make sure the job is done."

Lord Owen said, "That would be the time to do it."

"You will have to strike first, my lord. You have no choice. During the dry season, the fire couldn't easily be stopped."

"You are right." Lord Owen shook his head. "But whom do I have to lead, Feste? Twenty or thirty men and mostly farmers, tradesmen, merchants, and scholars. Maybe I should just turn myself in."

Feste's eyes glittered. "Good idea, my lord. That way Humphrey can finish what he's started. He can completely ruin Caxton and its holdings. From all corners of Albion, men and women used to come to Caxton to see its cathedral and library. To study at its university. To trade. Not anymore they don't. In the past six years, Humphrey has squeezed it until it's nearly dead. The prison is full, the university and library are closed, and the people will be hungry if he doesn't soon release all the farmers he's impressed into his militia."

"Yet it is so peaceful here," Lord Owen said, his voice wistful, and Maya realized that if Lord Owen had a choice, then it would be to stay in the forest and study and to oversee the running of the lodge. Maya understood that this was why Humphrey, more aggressive, had been able to take Caxton away from Lord Owen.

"It's not peaceful out there," Feste replied. "In Caxton, women don't dare leave their homes unless a man is with them."

Lord Owen looked unbearably sad. "Who would have guessed it? Humphrey was always hot tempered and strong willed, but not like this. If only our parents had lived longer. They might have been able to guide Humphrey better than I have."

Feste shrugged. "My lord, we must deal with things as they are."

"Yes, we must." Lord Owen stood, and his voice was firm. "We'll set up an area today and begin training tomorrow. Tonight, at evening meal, we'll tell those who live and work around the lodge and then ask that the word be spread to the cottages in the forest."

Feste nodded. "You'll also pick up men from the towns outside the forest. You won't even have to ask. They'll just join us. Even so, we will have to plan carefully. We will be outnumbered." Feste then turned to Maya and Andy. "Would you two mind stepping outside for just a moment? There is a matter I want to discuss with Lord Owen."

"All right," Andy replied, standing, and Maya stood as well. "We'll be waiting in the Great Hall."

11: Another Book

Maya followed Andy to the huge windows overlooking the field. The field workers were taking a break, not far from the lodge, under big trees off to one side away from the fields. A large table, set with food, stretched under the green canopy of leaves, and all around it men, women, and children sat on benches, stood, and even lounged on the ground some distance from the table. They all seemed to be at ease, and Maya could hear voices and laughter.

"They won't look like that when they hear what Duke Humphrey has planned," Andy said.

"No, they won't."

"He has to be stopped," Andy said, his voice intense. "This place is too beautiful. He can't burn it down."

"Who burn what down?" A loud voice behind them asked.

"Oh, no," Maya thought. "Sir John."

And Sir John it was, eating a big piece of bread with honey. Although Maya knew that it wouldn't be long before everyone at the lodge learned what Duke Humphrey had planned, she felt strangely reluctant to tell Sir John.

Andy, however, had no such misgivings. "Sir John!"

A huge sticky hand came down on Andy's shoulder. "Andy, my lad!" Then in a mock serious voice accompanied by a bow. "And young Cesario." This was followed by a loud whisper. "I don't think your friend likes me very much."

Maya stared coolly at Sir John. "That's not true. I just feel like you can't really be trusted. Not that you'd do something bad on purpose. It would just happen."

Looking horrified, Andy was about to say something cutting to Maya, when Sir John's laughter stopped him. "You have my number, young Cesario. Has Feste been telling tales?"

"Only one," Maya said. "But even before that I knew."

"Well, Andy," Sir John said with a wink, "if we go on any adventures, we'd better leave young sober-sides behind."

"Andy won't be going on any adventures with you," came Maya's tart reply. "He's with me."

Andy no longer looked horrified. Instead, he looked so angry that for a moment Maya thought he might actually hit her. But Andy took a deep breath, and Maya waited for the rush of hard words. They never came. Again, Andy was cut off by Sir John's laughter. "Andy, you have a small but fierce defender. The boy has spunk. I like that. But, come, what were you two discussing?"

Now it was Sir John's turn to be interrupted. "Cesario! Andy!" Feste called from the parlor doorway. "You can come back now."

"You'll find out soon enough," Maya said with a sad shrug, and she began walking toward the parlor.

"I'm sorry," Andy said to Sir John before he hurried to catch up with Maya. This time Sir John didn't laugh but instead watched thoughtfully as Maya and Andy walked across the Great Hall.

"That was so not cool," Andy whispered fiercely. "I can't believe you said what you did."

"Don't be so stupid," Maya whispered back, which only made Andy angrier.

"Who do you think you are? My mother? Remember, I'm older than you are. Don't ever talk to me that way again."

"Then act your age, and stop acting like a baby."

By this time, Maya and Andy were so angry that they would have marched away from each other in different directions if Feste hadn't been waiting for them. With his arms folded across his chest and one foot tapping the floor, Feste rolled his eyes as they came nearer. "This is no time for quarreling. Lord Owen and I have something important to tell you, something that I think you'll find very interesting."

Both Maya and Andy rushed into the parlor, neither of them in the mood to listen either to Feste or to Lord Owen. Lord Owen, who was sitting at the table, frowned when he saw their red faces, but Feste shook his head, and Lord Owen didn't say anything.

Feste pointed to the chairs. "Sit down, sit down! And listen carefully to what we have to say. Not many people know what we are about to tell you, and certainly none so young. But unless I'm mistaken, you'll understand exactly what we're talking about."

Maya and Andy sat down. They were listening intently; somehow, their fight didn't seem as important anymore.

"There," said Feste, smiling. "I knew that would get your attention."

"You have a Book of Everything, don't you?" Maya blurted out before Feste or Lord Owen could say anything else.

"See?" Feste said to Lord Owen. "I told you they would know."

Lord Owen shook his head. "It hardly seems possible. You're both so young. Especially you, Cesario."

"If I'm not mistaken," Feste said, "and I'm usually not, it's young Cesario who has a book. Am I right?" Maya nodded.

"But how?" Andy asked. "How did you know?"

"I can see things that other people can't."

"The way I can," Maya thought with a start.

"Tell us about your book," Andy said.

Lord Owen spoke, "It's been around longer than anyone can remember. As you guessed, it's called the Book of Everything, and indeed in it, there does seem to be everything. Except the words change over time, and they change depending on who has the book. It has come from a place called the Great Library, and for years, the book has stayed in Caxton, first with my father and then with me."

"Did it ever travel around?" Maya asked.

"Once it did, but not recently," Lord Owen answered. "Not in my father's time or my time. Other duchies are not as stable as Caxton is. Or was. And across the sea, on the mainland, it's just as bad. The book wanted to stay in one place."

Maya frowned. "Where is the book now?"

There was a brief silence, and Lord Owen answered, "Humphrey has it."

"I was afraid of that," Maya said. "Didn't the book warn you about him?"

Lord Owen looked weary. "Yes, but I thought the book must have been mistaken. I couldn't believe my own brother would plot against me. By the time I realized, it was too late."

Lord Owen stopped, and Feste continued, "Lord Owen and some of his men just barely escaped, and it was the book that saved them."

Lord Owen stood and went by the windows. "Humphrey was so busy going through the book, trying to see what he should do next, that we had time to escape. And we had help from some of the other servants as well as Molly."

"They hid you and then helped you get out," Feste put in.

"I won't forget them," Lord Owen said quietly. "If I ever regain Caxton."

"So the book didn't help Duke Humphrey?" Maya asked.

Feste smiled. "No, the book decides how much it wants to divulge. The past six years have been frustrating for Duke Humphrey, who wanted that book so much. Whenever he tries to discover what Lord Owen is up to or whose side I'm on, all he gets is general information. Such as, Owen of Caxton, brother to Humphrey, son of Thomas. The rightful duke."

"I bet he doesn't like that last part," Andy said with a slight smile.

Feste laughed. "Indeed, he does not. And when Humphrey looks up my name, he usually just sees a silly song that I've made up. No, the book hasn't done him any good at all. It doesn't even let him hear its voice. He threatens to destroy the book, but he won't. He keeps hoping."

Turning from the window and coming back to the table, Lord Owen sat down. "Cesario, may we see your book? We'll give it back. We promise."

Maya nodded. "I know you will." Reaching into her pocket, she took out the book and put it on the table.

"Small just like you," Feste said.

Andy touched the book. "It changes. It used to have a blue cloth cover with flowers. Now it's leather. But still blue."

As they all stared at the book, it slowly began to grow until it was so big that Lord Owen had to use both hands to pick it up. Turning the pages, he stopped periodically to read, and he seemed to be listening as well, and after several minutes, he handed the book to Feste. "Go ahead and take a look. But you are right. Humphrey is planning to burn down the forest, and our book is in danger. And we need to start planning our strategy."

Frowning, Feste also looked through the book, occasionally glancing up, and he, too, seemed to be listening. At one point he was plainly startled. "I can't see everything," he would say later. "No one can." With some reluctance, he pushed the book toward Maya. "It wants to stay with you."

Lord Owen rubbed his face. "And we've learned what happens when we ignore a book's advice."

He looked so sad that for the first time, Maya could see past Lord Owen's good looks and his dignity, to someone who was bitterly disappointed with both himself and his brother.

The book was small again, and Maya put it in her pocket. "Nobody wants to think that a brother or a father is working against the family. But sometimes it happens. Andy and I know a little about this, don't we?"

"Yeah," Andy answered. "Not this bad, but still."

Feste and Lord Owen stared at Maya and Andy. "That's the reason why they have the book, my lord."

"I guess it is." Lord Owen sat very still, his back straight, his mouth firm, and Maya knew that he would train the men in the forest and lead them to battle, even though he didn't want to, even though he still loved his brother.

Maya, blinking back tears, stood and cleared her throat. "My lord, I know I am small, but I will help you any way I can.'

Andy stood as well. "And I will, too, my lord."

Lord Owen's mouth twitched, but he didn't smile. "I thank you both. Cesario, you might be wise beyond your years, but you are too young to fight. Stay by Feste's side and do what you can to help him."

"Yes, my lord," Maya answered.

"And, Andy, I have no right to ask this of you, but if you will join me and my men, then I would be honored. Sir John will teach you how to fight. What say you?"

"I would be honored, my lord," Andy replied.

Maya was about to protest, but Andy stopped her with a look.

"Cesario," Feste said, "at times Sir John is rash, but he knows how to use a sword. He taught Lord Owen and," there was a slight pause, "Duke Humphrey."

"Sir John has been loyal," Lord Owen added. "He could have easily gone with Humphrey. It would have been better for him if he had done so. But he came with me."

"Yes, my lord," Maya said, but still there was that flicker of doubt, that Sir John would do something he shouldn't and that Andy would be involved.

Feste looked at Maya. "We'll keep an eye on Sir John. I see what you see, even more so, but there's nothing definite planned. And I'll have a word with Sir John. He usually listens to me."

Maya sighed. "All right." She felt a little better, but not much.

12: Plans Are Made

As the sun began to set, sending slanting shadows across the gardens, the workers put away their hoes, buckets, and the small carts they used for carrying away weeds and rocks. A well stood by the edge of the field, and faces and hands were scrubbed. Even so, when the men, women, and children were all seated at the long tables in the Great Hall, Maya could smell sweat and dirt and the outdoors. But somehow it was a good smell, one that reminded Maya of Pépère Roland after a long summer's day spent outside. Maya looked at the tan faces, arms, and hands of the men, women, and children. Everyone was waiting for the big platters of food that would soon be coming from the kitchen, platters that would be delivered by workers who would also be sweating, but from a different kind of labor—kitchen work.

Maya and Andy sat at the head table with Feste, Sir John, and other men and women who stared curiously at them. Maya guessed that she and Andy, as young newcomers, should be sitting at another table, but the book had given them a status they ordinarily wouldn't have had. Still, the looks Maya and

Andy received were not hostile, and, again, Maya got a sense of calm and order and the security that came with these things.

"Lord Owen is a good leader, isn't he?" Maya asked Feste.

"Yes, he is," came the answer. "Just like his father was. He's not flashy, like Humphrey, but he knows how things should go."

"He has good ideas," Andy said.

"He does," Feste replied and would have said more except that right then Lord Owen, with two of his men, came to the head table and sat down. Within minutes came the platters of food—peas, lettuce, radishes, and broccoli from the gardens, round loaves of dark and light bread, butter, and chicken so tender and succulent that it fell from the bone.

There was some talking, but mostly everyone concentrated on the food. Even the children were fairly quiet, and not one had to be reminded to clean his or her plate. After working and playing outside all day, the children were hungry, and they tackled their food with the same gusto as the adults did.

Smiling wistfully, Maya watched them and thought, "If only things could just stay this way. Everything seems so good."

Sir John might have mentioned that without taverns and plays, the nights were very long, too long. Lord Owen might have spoken about the lack of libraries and schools. Even Feste, who loved the Forest of Arden so much, would have admitted that it was a fine thing to juggle and sing on market day, with children shouting and laughing as they followed him. But Maya's thoughts went no further than herself, and she felt unbearably sad that these laughing men would have to leave the forest to fight Humphrey. Maya could picture women waiting anxiously for news of their husbands. She imagined empty places in homes where children were suddenly without fathers. Maya no longer felt safe, and she wanted to go back to East Vassalboro, but she knew who would be waiting for her there. Maya also knew that she and Andy hadn't even begun to accomplish what the book had intended when it sent them here. But what did the book intend? Maya vowed to take a closer look that night, when she was safely in bed. Perhaps then she would get at least some idea of why they were here and what they were supposed to do.

When the last tart was finished, when there was no more cream in the pitchers, and cheeks were flushed with ale, Lord Owen stood and faced the people. Now that the food was gone, the murmuring had become a loud chatter, but as soon as Lord Owen stood, the room became quiet.

He looked around the room. "Six years ago, I came to this forest, and gradually, you all joined me here. Not all who tried to enter this forest were allowed in, but you were, and I know that means I can trust you. For the past six years, our lives have been quiet but good. We've grown our food, but we haven't harmed the forest." Lord Owen stared gravely at the upturned faces. "Outside the forest, it has not been so good." Heads nodded, even the children's. "Newcomers have brought tales of repression and brutality. Feste and those who venture outside to trade and learn the news have confirmed what the newcomers have said."

Pausing, Lord Owen rubbed his face. "You all know what happened. I don't have to tell you. You also know that over the past six years, my brother, Humphrey has tried many times to get into the forest, but he has failed. Well, he has come up with a plan, and if he carries through with it, he will not fail."

The relaxed, happy looks were gone. Everyone waited, even the children, to hear about Duke Humphrey's plan.

"In two months' time, during the height of the dry season, Humphrey means to burn down the forest, and, in so doing, either kill me or flush me out."

At first, the shock of this news was so great that nobody could respond. Burn down the Forest of Arden, the forest that had so long been protected by the various dukes of Caxton? It was unthinkable, and if anyone other than Lord Owen had made a similar announcement, then nobody would have believed it. But the people trusted Lord Owen. They knew he would not lie or even exaggerate about something as serious as this.

Not surprisingly, Sir John was the first to respond. Leaping to his feet, he bellowed, "This time Humphrey has gone too far." He glanced swiftly at Lord Owen. "Begging your pardon, my lord. I know he is your brother. But to burn down the Forest of Arden! We must march on him before he does this."

A great cry rose from the men in the hall, with shouts of "Sir John is right" and "We are with you, my lord" and "To burn down the forest!" Lord Owen held up a hand, and gradually the hall became quiet. Sir John, with a triumphant nod, sat down.

"Sir John is right, and I thank you all. Tomorrow, we will set up a practice area to train those who wish to join me. This, unfortunately, will mean more work for the rest of you."

A young woman, with curly brown hair and a baby in her lap, called out, "Don't you worry about us, my lord. We'll be glad to do our part, too." The other women, young and old, raised their voices in support.

"Thank you, Meg. Thanks to you all," Lord Owen said, smiling just a little. "But some men will be chosen to help you with the gardens and the harvest. Without food, what would become of us?" He paused. "And if we are successful, why, then, the food can come right along with us."

"It will be needed," Feste put in so quietly that Maya was the only one who heard him.

A massive man with dark red hair and a beard rose from his place beside Lord Owen. "My lord, many in Greendale will join with us as soon as we leave the forest. I know they will."

"And so will Thorndike," someone called.

"So will Oakton!" And on it went until everyone's town had been pledged.

The red-haired man sat down, and then Feste stood. The crowd became quiet, knowing he was the one who had most recently been "outside," as the area beyond the forest had come to be called.

"Aye," Feste said, looking around the room. "Many will join us. Not all who are outside were turned away by the forest. Many stayed because they had to for some reason, or because they didn't dare make the journey, which has become extremely dangerous. Some have even stayed to help Lord Owen, when the time comes. But make no mistake—outside, it is harsh, even in Greendale, which is so close to our forest. Soldiers patrol the land and kill anyone who looks like they might be coming to the forest. People are afraid, and rightly so. I do not like to mention this, my lord, but I must. Even if we pick up men along the way, we will be outnumbered. Humphrey has turned Caxton into a sort of military city, and he is using the university as barracks to house the men he has pulled from the countryside. No expense has been spared, and all resources are going toward Caxton."

Sitting down, Feste glanced at Sir John, who looked back with narrowed eyes before calling out, "We might be outnumbered, but we can't just wait to be burned down."

"No, we can't," Lord Owen said evenly. "And in the next few days we'll come up with a plan that takes Humphrey's numbers into account. We'll tell you as soon as we do. We will keep you informed." Then he sat down.

Women and men nodded. Slowly, they began to move around, stopping to talk in groups. Lord Owen stayed at the head table, listening to the advice that came from his men, the workers, and even a few of the children. He paid attention to them all and managed not to smile when the children offered their suggestions.

A young boy with white, sun-bleached hair stood before Lord Owen. "Begging your pardon, my lord, but it's hard to fight a bully who's bigger and stronger. If you fight head-on, you'll probably get your nose smashed." Lord Owen, who was bent toward the child, nodded.

"Davy!" a woman's voice called. "Don't be bothering Lord Owen. Come along, now. It's time to go home."

Lord Owen placed a hand on Davy's shoulder. "Thank you. I'll keep that in mind. Now you'd best go along with your mother."

Smiling, Davy ran off to join his family, and Lord Owen

looked at Feste and Maya, who were sitting nearby. Almost everyone else at the head table had moved to the end of the hall by the windows, where the deep blue of twilight shimmered. Benches had been pulled away from tables, and Sir John was expounding on some point, his fists pumping the air. Beside him, Andy sat watching and listening with that quiet intensity he had.

"Now they all know," Lord Owen said simply, motioning for Maya and Feste to come closer. Sir Broderick, the large man with the red hair and beard, already sat nearby.

"Indeed they do," Feste replied as he and Maya moved closer to Lord Owen.

"But how will we stop Duke Humphrey and his men?" Sir Broderick asked. "What are the odds, Feste?"

"I would say they outnumber us two to one."

"That little boy is right," Maya said. "You can't attack head-on with numbers like that. You'll be smashed flat."

Sir Broderick stared curiously at Maya, and Feste said quickly, "Sir Broderick, this is young Cesario. He comes from a far-off land and is wise beyond his years."

Maya nodded. "It's our educational system. They start us young and encourage us to speak our minds and think for ourselves."

Feste turned his head and made a sound that was something between a cough and a laugh, and even Lord Owen grinned. "Watch out, Broderick, for young Cesario. He's already scolded Sir John, and he does seem to know a thing or two."

Sir Broderick replied dryly, "If we ever retake Caxton, then maybe we should keep that educational system in mind."

"Maybe so," Lord Owen answered. "But it seems to me that Davy and Cesario are right. Sir John might be eager to fight, but a direct march on Caxton would be suicidal."

"Greendale has a barracks." Feste reached for a bowl with some peas in it, leftover from the evening meal.

"Aye," Sir Broderick said. "And a good-sized one. They want to be ready should we ever come out."

"True, but they don't have hundreds of men. Fifty or so instead." Feste placed a handful of peas on the table. "This is the city of Caxton, about five days' march from the lodge." Feste placed smaller piles of peas on the table. "Here are the towns supporting Caxton—Glenridge, Oakton, Newfield, Thorndike, and lastly, Greendale." Feste marched his fingers between Greendale and Thorndike. "One road connects these two towns, a road with plenty of woods for cover."

"We could probably take the barracks in Greendale," Lord Owen said. "But as soon as Humphrey got word, he'd send troops from Thorndike to attack Greendale."

Maya stared at the peas. "Humphrey's men would have to be funneled down that one road?"

"That's right," Feste replied.

"Well, then." Maya said. "You could hide in the woods and pick off Humphrey's men. Just like during the Revolutionary War."

"What war?" Feste, Lord Owen, and Sir Broderick asked together.

Maya shook her head. "A war in my land. But that strategy worked."

Sir Broderick cleared his throat. "Seems cowardly."

Sir Owen frowned. "Yes, it does."

"What choice do we have?" Feste asked. "When we are so outnumbered?"

There was a brief silence. "He has a point," Sir Broderick said, and Lord Owen nodded thoughtfully.

"Once Thorndike is taken, men will join your side," Feste said. "And unlike many of the men in Humphrey's militia, the men will be with us because they want to be. Our side will still be outnumbered, but when Humphrey marches on you from Caxton, your odds will be better."

Lord Owen said, "You're right. The plan of ambushing the men from Thorndike is our best option. Tomorrow, we'll begin training."

"Sir John won't like the idea of ambushing the men from Thorndike," Maya said, glancing at the big man. "He'll want to fight them head-on and march all the way to Caxton."

"Sir John will follow orders," Lord Owen said. "He always does, even though he might complain."

Maya didn't say anything. She looked at Feste, who also remained silent. Later, he would say, "You can't control everything," and Maya would agree. But what she couldn't control right now was her worry.

"And one other thing," Lord Owen said. "This plan might be a good one, but keep in mind what we'll be doing. We'll be killing men from our duchy. Our own men." Lord Owen closed his eyes and then opened them. "If this should work, then the killing stops as soon as possible, and all are pardoned."

Sir Broderick and Feste nodded, and Maya thought about what it would be like to kill men who had been with you for most of your life.

"Civil war," Maya said softly, but Feste heard her, and he looked sad, tired, and even a little old.

13: The Voice of the Book

By the time everyone left the Great Hall, it was late. Lamps had been blown out, tables cleared and washed, and floors swept. Maya and Andy followed Feste as he led them up the broad staircase that went from the Great Hall to the second floor. There was a long hall, with many doors on either side, and at the end was another staircase, short and steep, that went to an attic, of sorts, but one that was clean and tidy. It had two beds, two washstands with basins of water, and shelves to store things. Off that room was a smaller room, with one bed.

Feste gestured toward the little room. "For you, Miss Maya."

"Thank you," Maya said, and even though this room was much starker than her room in East Vassalboro, they somehow had a similar feel.

Feste rummaged in his pack and found a clean white shirt, which he passed to her. "Something to sleep in." Then he passed her a change of clothes. "Can't have you wearing the same thing every day."

Maya's arms were full, and she turned toward the small room.

"Maya?" Feste called.

Maya stopped. "Yes, Feste?"

"Sometime soon—I don't know exactly when—there will be choices for you to make, some bigger than others. Remember, you can say no."

Maya frowned. "What do you mean?"

Feste shook his head. "I can't say anymore. I shouldn't have said this much. Just remember, you can say no."

"All right, Feste," Maya replied.

As Maya went into her room, Feste had one last bit of advice. "Keep the book with you at all times. Don't leave the room without it."

"I will, Feste." Maya yawned, shutting the door. She, too, had a washstand with a basin of water, and after washing, she slipped into the shirt that Feste had given her.

A candle flickered on a nightstand. Maya got into bed and opened the Book of Everything, hoping to get an idea as to what she and Andy should do next.

Maya had a feeling that the book wouldn't send her anywhere else soon, that it would be safe to run her finger over the entries so that they would expand. And she was right.

The first bolded entry Maya came to was *Albion*. She learned that Albion was on a planet called Ilyria and that the world was not very technologically advanced. Maya also learned that Albion was a large island, long ruled by warring dukes who paid no attention to a series of weak and ineffectual kings. For too many years, the dukes had feuded among themselves, but in between the fighting there had been periods of peace. Recently, Lord Owen's father had helped keep the peace. With his skills of persuasion and his firmness of character, he had managed to stop the dukes from fighting each other. He had even convinced them to support the king. But then Lord Owen's father had died. Owen, when he was duke, had had some success in keeping the dukes from fighting, but now that Humphrey was duke, and Owen was in exile, all that had changed. Albion was on the verge of a civil war partly instigated by Humphrey's actions. And Humphrey?

"He wants to be king, of course," Maya whispered. "Why stop with Caxton?"

"Very good," she heard a soft voice say. With a start, Maya realized that what she had heard was the voice of the book, a voice that was reasoned and assured.

"I heard you talk!" Maya said.

"That's right," the book replied. "But you can only hear me when I'm open."

"Can everyone who reads you hear your voice?"

"Eventually, with most people, if we want them to. But with you it has happened sooner than it usually does." The book did not feel the need to mention that there were a few people who could hear, even if the books didn't want them to.

"So that's what Feste meant about Humphrey not hearing the book's voice. And why has it happened sooner with me?"

"That's for you to find out. Andy is right. It's not good to be told too much too soon. But one thing I can say, which you already know. You can see more than most people, and that is part of the reason."

"Right," Maya muttered, and she had the strong feeling that at times, the book could be quite maddening.

"But there is something else you should know. Cinnial sent a book to this world, and we can certainly see the results—the strife and the lies."

"Cinnial? Just who is this Cinnial, anyway?"

There was a brief silence, and Maya got the feeling that the book was considering how much information it should share. "Cinnial was a senior apprentice at the Great Library. But he couldn't pass the test to become one of the librarians who makes Books of Everything, and when he found this out, it made him bitter. He convinced a few of the other senior apprentices who had failed that they had been treated unfairly, and they stole their apprentice books along with a console used to make new books. Then, they left the Great Library, but because they had figured out how to shield their books and them-selves from us, we don't know exactly where they went." The book's tone was rueful. "They had taken us completely by surprise. We were so focused on making books and collecting information that we didn't know what was going on until it was too late. Take note, Maya! This can happen to anyone. In time, Cinnial and his apprentices began to make more books, and their goal seems to be to bring one to each world that has a Book of Everything. They work slowly, because they don't have a big staff like the Great Library does, and since they are not connected to the Great Library, their books are incomplete. But even so, Cinnial can do enough damage with his books. And the more information he gathers, the worse it gets. One day he might even be able to steal a Book of Everything, and then another and another."

Maya swallowed. "What would happen then?"

"On world after world, the bad ideas would eventually over-come the good ideas. Not temporarily, but for good. Facts wouldn't matter. Facts would be what Cinnial wanted them to be, and if our books were gone, then there would be nothing to counterbalance the lies."

"But so far no Book of Everything has been captured?" Maya asked quickly, wanting reassurance. "Right?"

"So far," came the answer. "But Cinnial is getting closer. We know that Cinnial has sent a book to this world. Although Cinnial's books can block much, they can't block everything. There's always a little ripple of energy around the books, ours and theirs, when they move from place to place. The ripple can be hard to spot, but the Great Library is very vigilant, now that we know what Cinnial is up to. A while back, there were a few ripples in Ilyria and most recently, in Albion. It is likely that whoever has Cinnial's book will be trying to steal Ilyria's Book of Everything. And since Humphrey has Ilyria's Book of Everything, there is no telling what will happen."

Maya's stomach felt queasy. It was bad enough to have to worry about one Book of Everything. Now she had to worry about two.

"I am sorry." The book's tone sounded truly regretful. "I'm sorry you even had to get involved. But on that train, Mary Parsons could see that you were the one who could help, even though she didn't have me to guide her. Your abilities just blazed forth, which is a good thing because I was paralyzed. Fortunately, Chet was so intent on Mary that he didn't notice you. Nobody sees everything all the time, not even Chet."

"Is there anything else I need to know right off?"

"Two more things. First, tonight you will be called to make a choice that will change your life even more. However, you can say no, and we will find another way."

"But?"

"It will be more difficult, and the possibility of failure will be greater."

"Some choice."

"But you do have one."

"What's the second thing?"

"Keep me with you at all times, no matter what happens tonight. I only see possibilities, but someone at the lodge would very much like to have me if he knew about me."

"Sir John?"

"Yes, and if he did manage to steal me, I would guide him as best I could. But with Sir John it wouldn't be easy."

"It wouldn't be easy to guide him," Maya agreed. "But how would he find out about you? Not from Feste or Lord Owen?"

"There is someone else who knows about me."

"Andy! Would he tell?"

"It's a possibility. He looks up to Sir John."

Maya muttered, "I knew it. I knew Sir John would cause trouble." She sighed. "All right, then. I'll be careful. But why am I here? What am I supposed to do?"

"Save the Book of Everything on this world, and, in the process, save me as well."

"How am I going to do that?"

"By helping Lord Owen defeat Duke Humphrey."

"You want me to fight?" Maya felt her throat close in panic.

"No, something equally as dangerous. I want you to keep your eyes open. Soon you will be leaving this forest, and what you learn will not only help this world but your world, too."

"Will Feste be with me?"

There was a slight hesitation, one so slight that Maya didn't notice it. "Yes, now that's enough for tonight. You need to get some rest. Put me on the shelf under the nightstand, but leave me open. When I'm closed, I can't communicate with you."

Maya had more questions, but she did as the book had instructed. She felt too tired to argue, and settling into bed, Maya shut her eyes. She heard a song, faint but beautiful and soothing, one that tugged on her consciousness, making her even drowsier.

"Sleep," the book's gentle song instructed. "Sleep, sleep."

Maya slept curled within the melody until she was woken by another song that pushed against the book's song until it gradually took over. Maya recognized the second song. It was the one she had heard the night before, at Feste's cottage. But this time it had words that pulled at her.

"Follow me," the song said.

Maya slowly opened her eyes. "Book? What should I do?"

"Follow the song. Then you will have an important choice to make."

Maya sat up in bed. On the nightstand, the candle was still burning, but it was very low. Everything was night-still, and from the next room, Maya could hear Feste snoring, and Andy, too, even though his snores were softer.

Shivering, Maya took off the white shirt and put on the clothes she had worn that day.

"Don't forget to put me in your pocket."

Nodding, Maya reached for the book, closed it, and put it into her pocket. The song from the forest was tugging at her now, pulling her toward the door, which Maya opened, and then she tiptoed past Feste and Andy. Down the attic stairs she went, across the long hall, and down the second set of stairs.

Not sure where to go, Maya stood in the Great Hall. Luminous moonlight shone in through the long windows at the end of the hall, and the song led Maya along the row until she came to a door at the very end. Maya put her hand on the latch, lifted it, and pushed. The door easily swung open, and Maya stepped into a night that was aglow with the soft pale light of the moon.

The song guided Maya across the field along the edge of the gardens. The night's dew wet her shoes, mosquitoes whined around her head, and small animals crept in the shadows, taking care not to come out into the open. An owl flew by, a large, dark silhouette in the moonlight, and smaller silhouettes, bats, swooped and dove, hunting insects. Enveloped by the light of the moon, surrounded by night sounds, and urged on by the song, Maya came to the edge of the field, where the grass stopped, and the forest began.

"Come," the song beckoned. "She is calling you."

And Maya vanished into the forest.

14: To Have Both Eyes Peeled

How long did Maya walk through the forest? Later, it would become such a blurred memory that she had no way of knowing. Sometimes, in her recollections, it seemed to Maya that she walked for two or three nights, which she knew couldn't be true because she was back in bed by dawn. Or at least that's what Feste would tell her later. At other times, Maya had the impression that the song carried her swiftly through the forest, speeding her along through giant ferns and around underbrush. The deeper into the forest Maya went, the louder the song grew, and it became obvious that the song was many voices twined together, guided by one that was stronger, richer, and fuller than the rest.

Even though the book was in her pocket and even though it had urged her to follow the song, Maya was afraid. She couldn't help it, and she was annoyed with herself for feeling that way.

Later, she would remark somewhat tartly to the book, "You might be good, but you sure have a way of getting people into scary situations." The book, diplomatically, would refrain from answering.

Finally, Maya came to a big clearing. The song was very loud, and in the moonlight Maya could see where the song was coming from—hundreds and hundreds of toads, on rocks, on fallen logs, on the ground. At the edge of the clearing was a huge, dark oak tree with branches as big as the trunks of some trees. The branches spread out in a giant canopy of leaves, and this was the tree Maya had dreamed about the night before. Beneath the tree sat the enormous toad with the glittering red stone on its head. The strong voice, loud and insistent, came from the large toad.

As soon as Maya stepped into the clearing, the song stopped, letting go of her, and Maya stumbled, nearly falling to the ground.

"Welcome, Maya," the enormous toad said. "Our song has brought you here, but you must come the rest of the way freely, by your own choice."

Swallowing, Maya whispered, "Who are you?"

"I am the Toad Queen," came the stern reply. "The Old One and I sit at the heart of this forest, and it gives us our power and our energy."

"Why did you call me?" Maya asked, her voice still low.

But the Toad Queen heard her. "If you want to know, come closer. If not, turn around, and our song will guide you safely back to the lodge."

Maya was afraid, but she was also curious. She remembered what Feste and the book had said about choices and that the choice she made tonight would affect everything that followed. What could the choice be? Maya had to find out.

"Will you come?" the Toad Queen asked.

"Yes." Maya began walking toward the Toad Queen. Little toads leaped out of her way, but Maya still stepped carefully, not wanting to crush any of them.

The journey across the clearing seemed nearly as long as the journey through the forest, but finally Maya stood before the Toad Queen, who was as big as a dog, and not a small one.

The Toad Queen impassively regarded Maya, and there was neither sympathy nor malice in the huge amber eyes. Maya felt small before this massive creature who sat completely still, confident and serene. In the face of such majesty, Maya couldn't help but bow, and the smaller toads trilled approvingly. The Toad Queen's mouth rippled with what might have been a smile, but it was soon gone.

The Toad Queen's voice was surprisingly gentle. "Maya, you of course know you can see things that most cannot."

Maya nodded.

"It is because of this that you have the book. It is also because of this that you are here before me. Now, you have an important choice to make. Do you want to stay as you are, or do you want to be able to see even more?"

"How much more?"

"Not everything. Even with my help that isn't possible. But enough to see past a lot of the barriers that creatures put up."

Maya licked dry lips. "And this seeing will help save the two books?"

"Yes."

"What will you do? And will it hurt?"

"I will peel both your eyes. And it will hurt very much. But more important, once it is done, it is done. You can never go back to the way you were before, and you will be different from most of your kind."

"I already am. That's why the book came to me."

"True," the Toad Queen agreed, "but not the way you will be if you have your eyes peeled. You will see a lot more, but much of the time it will make you feel alone and apart."

"The book said if I refuse, then there would be another way."

"There are a number of ways, but the chances of success are not good."

Maya remembered what the book had said would happen if Cinnial managed to steal a Book of Everything. She thought about how lies were sometimes stronger than the truth, about how lies often won. Even though she was only fifteen, Maya knew enough about her world—about men such as Hitler and

Stalin—to realize how close a battle it was, even with the help of a Book of Everything. Without Maya's help, this beautiful green forest, older than she could even imagine, would be burned, and its power would not be strong enough to stop the flames. On Earth there were problems just as big—Maya had often heard her parents discussing climate change, and they worried about what things would be like for Maya and her generation. Maya knew she had to help, even if it hurt, even if it made her feel alone.

"I'll do it," Maya heard herself say, as if from a distance.

"You are sure?" the Toad Queen asked.

"Yes," Maya answered.

"You are a brave child," the Toad Queen said, and the small toads leaped and chirped in approval. "I've never peeled the eyes of one so young. After I've done it, you won't be able to see anything. But our voices will guide you back to the lodge. I don't know how long you won't be able to see. It's different for everyone. Feste will help you. He will know what to do. I peeled his eyes many years ago, but he still remembers. It's not something one easily forgets. Now, for the final time I will ask you. Are you sure you want to go through with this?"

Maya trembled but, "I'm sure."

"All right, then. Come closer."

Maya stepped toward the Toad Queen, who raised her front leg. On each toe was a glistening claw, and the toes on her right leg were folded shut over something. The Toad Queen opened them, and three acorns shimmered in her grip.

"These are a present from the Old One. He doesn't usually give these away, but he thinks you will need them. They will take you wherever you want to go, but you can only use them each once, and the acorns can only transport one person at a time."

Taking the acorns, Maya bowed toward the tree. "Thank you." As she put the acorns in her jacket pocket, Maya heard a deep creaking of branches.

The Toad Queen said, "The Old One accepts your thanks and warns you to be careful."

"I will," Maya said.

"Good. Are you ready?"

"I'm ready."

Then, moving faster than Maya could have imagined, the Toad Queen's foot shot forward. A gleaming claw raked across one eye and then the other.

Maya screamed. The burning, oozing pain was terrible, and crying, she put both hands to her eyes.

"Do not touch them," the Toad Queen commanded. "It will do no good, and it might do some harm."

"I can't help it. They hurt so much." Weeping, Maya dropped to her knees.

"Do not touch them!" The Toad Queen's voice had such force that Maya's arms dropped to her side. Her hands twitched—what she wanted to do most was dig at the awful pain—but her arms stayed down.

The Toad Queen began to sing, and she was joined by the other toads. The song nudged Maya to her feet, lifted her across the clearing, and carried her in a swoon through the forest. Maya didn't feel the ferns or the underbrush. All she could feel was the burning that came and went as she lapsed in and out of consciousness. Maya was vaguely aware when she left the forest and passed by the big gardens by the lodge. In the gray dawn, the song carried her to the back of the lodge, where Feste was waiting. Someone else was there, too—Lord Owen.

As the song slid Maya into Feste's arms, where Maya fell and then collapsed, Lord Owen exclaimed, "Feste! She looks terrible!"

"She will heal," Feste replied, holding Maya close.

Swirling around Feste, the song clamored insistently. Feste said, "I'll take good care of her. There is no need to worry." There was a clucking chime. "Yes, I know she's young. That just means that she'll heal faster. Now go back to the ones that sent you here. They'll be wanting their voices back." Maya dimly heard the song scold Feste before it moved across her in a comforting wave of sound and hurried back into the forest.

Feste carried Maya into the lodge.

"Shall I take her?" Lord Owen asked.

"No, she's very light."

As they moved across the Great Hall, Lord Owen said, "If I had known what it would do to her, I would have stopped her. She is too young for this."

"Begging your pardon, my lord, but she is almost a young woman. She is small for her age. She will heal. My eyes did and quite quickly, too. They don't look like hers now, do they?"

"No, they don't."

"She had a choice, my lord. Even before her eyes were peeled, she saw enough to understand what would happen if Cinnial's side gets the two books."

They had stopped in the Great Hall by the stairway, but they knew they couldn't stay there long. The cook and her assistants would soon be getting up.

"Not much of a choice," Lord Owen murmured, placing a hand against Maya's cheek. She didn't move. "Poor child! Feste, take her to her room before anyone catches sight of her. I'll have a breakfast tray sent to you, and I'll be up later on to see how she's doing."

With a nod, Feste carefully climbed the stairs to the second floor and started down the long hall. All the doors were closed except for one, which was opened just a crack.

"Sir John," Feste said softly but fiercely, "if you tell anyone about this or even think about creeping to the attic rooms, then I will throttle you myself, if Lord Owen doesn't get to you first. I swear I will."

"Don't worry, Fool," came Sir John's reply. "I wasn't planning on doing either of those things."

If Feste hadn't been so distracted by Maya's bleeding eyes, then he might have thought to ask Sir John what his plans were. But a curt, "Good!" was all the answer Feste gave, and soon he was going up the narrow stairs to the third floor.

Sir John closed his door. "Good, indeed," he muttered to himself. "Well, well. As usual, they've gone behind my back and made plans." He went back to the big, canopied bed in the middle of the room, climbed the little steps leading up to it, and sat on the edge of the bed.

Sir John's eyes were narrow as he remembered all the times they had kept plans from him. True, he sometimes said things he shouldn't. He didn't mean to; the words just came out before he had a chance to stop them. But this didn't happen often. Or at least not every time, and Feste had no reason to plot behind his back. Sir John had noticed the conversation last night at the head table after Lord Owen had made his announcement. Sir John had seen Feste and young Cesario, who was a smaller version of Feste, talking to Lord Owen. They were trying to persuade Lord Owen not to march on Caxton. Sir John was sure of it. Instead, they would dither and wait until it was too late, until the Forest of Arden was burned, and everyone was either in exile or dead. And neither state appealed to Sir John.

"I won't let them do it!" Sir John's big fist came down on a massive thigh. "If they won't take action, then I will. I'll show them who is right."

In Sir John's calmer moments, he had to admit that it was Feste who was right most of the time. It galled Sir John, but it was the truth. But Sir John was not in one of his calmer moments. The lodge was all well and good for a week or two of hunting, playing cards, and drinking, but they had been here too long. Sir John felt so restless that he could hardly stand it. The country life, with its quiet days and even quieter nights, was not for him, and it had been too long since he had slept in his own bed in his own Rose Cottage in Caxton. Sir John reflected on how that damned fool Feste just loved living in the forest, and even Lord Owen seemed content to oversee the lodge and the gardens as well as the workers and the field hands.

Sir John shook his head. At times, Lord Owen acted more like a country squire than a duke. And he always had been one to need a nudge. Hadn't Sir John warned Lord Owen about Humphrey? But Lord Owen hadn't listened, and look what had happened. This time around, Sir John would give Lord Owen the nudge he needed. Sir John wasn't sure how he was going to do this, but he did know that he should move soon. With young Cesario so obviously indisposed, Feste would not be able to keep track of as much as he usually did. Sir John sensed that something big, something important, was being kept from him, and he knew just who would give him some answers.

15: Stolen

As Feste carried Maya into her room, Andy woke up, and he scrambled out of bed to see what had happened to her. Feste put Maya on the bed and removed her waistcoat. When Andy looked at her blood-smeared face and even bloodier eyes, he put a hand to his mouth and ran from the room. As soon as Andy was done throwing up in the chamber pot, he reluctantly came back to find Feste wrapping long bandages over Maya's eyes and winding the strips around her head.

Feste glanced at Andy. "She'll be all right. I promise you."

"What happened to her? How can she be all right when she looks like that?" Andy's voice, normally deep, was shrill.

Feste gently washed off the blood from Maya's cheeks. "Maya agreed to have her eyes peeled, and when she heals, what she sees will help both our world and yours." He touched her cheek gently. "She's very brave."

At first Andy couldn't say anything. His stomach still felt queasy, and he sat heavily on a chair by the bed. "Did you do this to her?" Andy finally asked, his voice a low, fierce whisper.

"No," Feste answered. "I don't have the ability to peel eyes."

"Then who did?"

"The Toad Queen." Feste gently slid the Book of Everything from the pocket of Maya's trousers and put it in the pocket of his own trousers. Then he pulled up the blankets and tenderly tucked them under her chin.

"Who is the Toad Queen?"

"Look, right now I have to tend to Maya. Go down to breakfast, and when you come back, I'll tell you about the Toad Queen."

But just then Maya began to whimper, and Feste said, "Damn it! I forgot to get something for the pain. Andy, before you go to breakfast, could you go to the apothecary's cottage and get a packet of sleeping powder for Maya?"

"Where is the cottage?"

"It's the one closest to the lodge, in the back by the gardens, on your left."

"All right." Andy stood.

"Hurry, then! And don't tell anyone about this. The less everyone knows, the better. Do you promise?"

Andy's shoulders twitched. "Yeah, yeah, I promise. Who would I tell?"

By now Maya was weeping, and Feste took her in his arms. "Just go!"

Andy ran down the stairs and across the long hall. As he passed by one of the rooms, the door opened quickly, and Sir John came out of the room.

"Andy, my lad! Where are you going in such a hurry?" The large man jogged alongside Andy.

Later, Andy would say, "I had to tell him something. He wouldn't go away."

"My friend isn't well," Andy blurted out. "Feste sent me to the apothecary's to get some sleeping powder."

"Ah," Sir John said. "Shall I show you where the cottage is?"

"Yes," Andy said gratefully. Somehow, he always felt better when Sir John was around. The large man had such vitality that Andy felt energized when he was with him. Sometimes, Andy had dark moods, when all he wanted was to be by himself, shut away in his room until the mood passed. But Andy could sense that when he was with Sir John, the dark moods wouldn't come. It was as though Sir John had his own corona, which radiated out from him in a large circle, warming everyone it touched.

"Burning is more like it," Maya might have said, but Andy pushed that thought away.

Sir John easily kept pace with Andy, but as they left the lodge, Sir John, stopped. "I always get the feeling that Feste is keeping something from me. Do you ever get that feeling?"

Andy stopped, too, and his face was flushed. "Feste certainly kept this from me. And he knew what was going to happen."

Sir John patted Andy's shoulder. "That's how Feste is. He's a good man—I'm not saying he isn't—but he thinks he's smarter than everyone else."

"He should have told me! Maya—I mean Cesario—and I are together."

A slight jerk of the head was the only indication Sir John gave that he had noticed Andy's slip. But Andy hardly realized that he had given away Maya's secret. Instead, his thoughts were turned toward Maya's bloody eyes and Feste's duplicity.

"He's planning something," Sir John said.

"And he's got the book now. I saw him put it in his pocket."

"The book?" Sir John asked casually, trying to keep his rush of excitement from showing.

"Our Book of Everything! And who knows what Feste will do with it?"

"A second one!" Sir John muttered under his breath. Louder, he said, "Feste's got something planned, my boy. You can count on it. And you can bet it doesn't include us." Sir John stood in the shadow of the lodge, safe from the view of the third-floor window. "The cottage is there." Sir John pointed toward the one nearest the lodge. "You'd best go by yourself. Feste might see us together, and you know how he is."

"I sure do," Andy said bitterly.

"You might ask the apothecary for two packets," Sir John suggested casually. "Your friend is pretty bad, I gather. It might be good to have a back-up."

"I'll do that," Andy said.

But when Andy returned to Maya's room, he handed only one packet to Feste.

Maya was still weeping. Hardly even noticing Andy was there, Feste poured a small amount of the packet into a cup and then added water from the pitcher on the washstand. Feste tenderly put his arm under Maya's shoulders and lifted her slightly. With his other hand, he brought the cup to Maya's lips. "Drink this, Maya. It will make you sleep. When you wake up, you won't feel so bad."

"I can't, Feste. I feel terrible."

"Yes, you can. Open your mouth just a little and take a few sips."

"It hurts so much."

"I know. I know." Feste's voice was gentle. "Drink, Maya."

Maya opened her mouth, took one small drink and then another. "A little more," Feste said. After a few more sips, he said, "All right. That's enough." Gradually Maya stopped crying, and then she sighed as her body began to relax. Soon she was asleep.

Andy's own eyes were wet, and he impatiently brushed his tears away. "I hope this is worth it all."

"So do I," Feste said, as he slid his arm from Maya's shoulders.

There was a knock on the door of the room Feste and Andy had slept in. "Would you go see who that is?" Feste asked.

When Andy returned, he was carrying a tray with a plate of buttered toast and a mug of tea. "Lord Owen had this sent for you."

"Aye, he said he would." Feste moved the pitcher of water to the floor. "Here, set the tray on the stand." Feste licked dry lips. "I'm glad to see that mug of tea. I'm so thirsty."

Andy did as he was told, taking care to focus his attention on Maya rather than on the mug. "She looks really bad."

Feste drank some tea and then replied, "I know she does."

"She'll get better?"

"Yes, her eyes will heal. The day will soon come when you won't be able to tell. Nobody will. Except Maya, of course." Feste yawned and rubbed his eyes. "I'm tired. I didn't get much sleep last night. I kept waking up, listening for her to leave. And once she was gone, I got up and waited."

Feste finished the tea and put the mug back on the tray. His eyes fluttered shut, and his head jerked up as he tried to keep his eyes open. But they closed again. "I'm too tired," he said in a low voice. "Much too tired." Once more, his eyes opened briefly, and he glared balefully at Andy. But soon Feste's eyes were shut, and he was sleeping just as soundly as Maya.

Andy waited for a few minutes, then a few minutes more. When Feste began to snore, Andy reached into the pocket of Feste's trousers and grabbed the book. The book came out hard, as though it didn't want to leave the pocket, and Andy had to pull with such force that he ripped Feste's trousers. With the book in hand, Andy waited anxiously for Feste to wake up, waiting for the onslaught of harsh words.

"And I would have deserved them," Andy would say later.

But Feste slept on, and Andy bolted from the room.

16: New Plans

Maya slept deeply for what seemed like a long time. But Feste was right—when Maya woke up, she did feel better, much better. In fact, her eyes hardly hurt at all, and Maya reached up to remove the bandages.

"No," a voice said, "leave the bandages alone until Feste can have a look."

"Lord Owen?"

"Yes, I'm right here."

"Where's Feste?"

There was a slight hesitation. "He's in bed." But there was an edge to Lord Owen's voice that, along with the pause, made Maya think something was wrong.

"Is Feste all right?" Maya tried to sit up, but Lord Owen's firm hand guided her back down.

"Feste is all right. He's beginning to wake up now."

"Lord Owen, please tell me what happened." Maya's voice was calm. There was a hint of authority in her voice, an authority that hadn't been there even as recently as a day ago and that would deepen over time.

Lord Owen sounded sad and weary. "After all you've been through, there's no reason not to tell you. Andy and Sir John put some sleeping powder in Feste's tea, right after you came back from the Toad Queen. After the sleeping powder took effect, I presume it was Andy who stole your Book of Everything. In his note, Sir John didn't mention who actually took it. But Feste never would have let Sir John come near you, so it must have been Andy who literally ripped it out of Feste's pocket."

"I knew something like this would happen! Sir John left a note? That means he's gone?" Then came a horrible thought. "Is Andy gone, too?"

"Oh, yes. There was a note. Andy and Sir John are both gone. And Harry Newton as well. Where they are heading I can only imagine. Sir John was vague about the details. He probably hasn't worked it out himself. He's a great one for making up things as he goes along. Worse yet, by the time we realized something was wrong, they had been gone for hours and hours. Sir John can move fast when he wants to. Don't let his bulk fool you."

"They've left the forest, haven't they?" Maya asked. "With the book?"

"That is most certainly the case. Sir John, in his note, only said that it was long past time to show Humphrey a thing or two. Sir John told me not to worry, that he had something very powerful to help him. The word *very* was underlined several times, and so was *powerful*. He was referring to the book, of course."

If the situation hadn't been so grave, then Maya would have laughed. Instead, she sighed and said, "What an idiot that man is. And Andy isn't much better."

"There's hope for Andy, at least. He's young. But Sir John is past hope." Lord Owen's voice was hard.

"It couldn't get much worse, could it?" Maya asked, putting a hand to her forehead.

"No, it really couldn't."

"I'm going to kill him," came a voice from the other room. It was Feste, and he didn't sound as though he was joking.

"My brother might get to Sir John first."

"What a thought," Feste replied. Maya heard him get out of bed and walk slowly across the room.

"How are you?" Lord Owen asked.

"Still groggy. They gave me too much. It doesn't take a lot."

"They wanted you to sleep soundly," Lord Owen said.

"They got their wish." Swaying slightly, Feste came and stood by Maya's bed.

"Here, sit down." Lord Owen rose from the chair.

Feste didn't argue, and he sat down, putting a hand on Maya's arm. "Maya, how are you feeling?"

"Actually, pretty good. Can we take the bandages off?"

Feste rubbed his face. "Give me a few minutes, and I'll take a look." He turned to Lord Owen. "You sent some men after Harry, Sir John, and Andy?"

"Yes, a few, with Broderick in charge. I told them to find those three and bring them back, even if it meant leaving the forest. And I told them to send word as soon as they found Sir John, Harry, and Andy. So far, we haven't heard anything."

"How do they send word?" Maya asked, thinking of the cell phone in her trousers.

"We use pigeons, of course," Lord Owen replied. "That's not how it's done on your world?"

"No," Maya said. "We have other ways." She still felt reluctant to talk about Earth's technology, and she quickly changed the subject. "Where do you think Sir John went? And what will he do?"

Lord Owen said, "It is my guess that Sir John went to Greendale to find allies. Most of the town is on our side, but since they are so close to the forest, they feel no need to join us here. Even though there is a fairly large barracks in Greendale now, the town's people know that they can escape quickly if they have to do so. I expect Sir John will try to convince the town's people to help him take the barracks. Sir John can be very convincing, and he isn't above telling a few lies to advance his cause. With Sir John leading the way, the town will attack the barracks. If they succeed, it will be on to Thorndike. But by then Humphrey will have gotten word and will send his troops against Sir John."

"And most likely they'll be crushed," Feste said. "Sir John and Andy will either be killed or taken prisoner. Then, Humphrey will have two books."

"Which means whoever Cinnial sent will have the chance to steal two books," Maya finished. "He was the man you couldn't quite read in Caxton, wasn't he?"

"I suspect so," Feste replied. "Julian was able to hide a lot from me, more than most people can."

There was a long silence as Maya, Lord Owen, and Feste thought about all that had happened, and how Sir John had drastically changed things.

"Do you think Sir Broderick will be able to persuade Sir John to come back?" Maya asked anxiously.

"I don't know," Lord Owen replied. "It all depends on Sir John's mood. Sometimes he can be reasoned with, but sometimes he can't. Truthfully, my hopes are not high. But we have to try."

"Feste," Maya said, "please take a look at my eyes and see how they are doing. I can't just stay like this with Andy and the book gone."

Feste nodded, and leaning over, he began to remove the bandages. Maya's eyes were closed, and she opened them as soon as he took off the last bandage.

"There!" Feste said with a smile. "What did I tell you?"

Lord Owen bent toward Maya for a better look. "I never would have believed it after seeing her this morning. There's a bit of red, but not much."

Feste patted Maya's cheek. "In a few days, that will be gone too. How do you feel, Maya?"

Maya blinked at the two men as impressions and images came to her. The strongest was Lord Owen's rage over what Sir John had done. No matter how things turned out, this time Lord Owen wouldn't easily forgive Sir John, as he had so often in the past. Feste, too, was angry with Sir John, but he was smiling down affectionately at Maya, and she realized he thought of her as the child he had never had but had always wanted. Maya even got an impression of a dark-haired woman, little and quick, who was now gone from Feste's life.

"I feel fine," Maya said, closing her eyes to get away from the images. "But I keep seeing things about both of you, things I wouldn't have seen before. Will it always be like this?"

"You'll learn to control it," Feste said. "To just look on the surface most of the time and to only look deeper when you want to. But you will always see more than you did before, and sometimes you will see things you shouldn't. You'll learn the art of keeping your own council."

Nodding, Maya opened her eyes, and as she did, there was a knock on the door.

"Yes?" Lord Owen asked.

"A message for you, my lord."

Lord Owen hurried from the room. There was a silence followed by some swearing. Lord Owen strode back into the room. "It's from Sir John. He's taken Broderick and the other men as captives. Temporarily, of course." Lord Owen crushed the note. "The barracks haven't been taken, but Sir John is soon going to lead the town into battle. That fool is going to ruin everything."

"I didn't think he would go this far," Feste said, and Maya remembered what the book had said about Cinnial and how his plot at the Great Library had gone undetected. She understood that even with peeled eyes, with the ability to really see, emotions could get in the way. Feste was fond of Sir John. They had a long history together. And she also got the sense Feste would have an easier time forgiving Sir John than Lord Owen would.

"We will have to march immediately," Lord Owen said. "Even though we are not ready. We have to get that book back."

Maya didn't have to look very deep to get images of slaughter and defeat. "Let Feste and I go first. Feste is the one closest to Sir John. He might be able to talk Sir John into coming back to the forest."

Lord Owen shook his head. "By the time you get to Greendale, Sir John will have attacked the barracks. By then it will be too late."

"I have something that will get us there fast," Maya said. "Feste, will you give me my jacket?" Feste handed the jacket to Maya, and she reached into a pocket, retrieving two of the gleaming acorns and leaving the remaining one in the pocket.

"The Toad Queen gave me these acorns. They are from the Old One, and they will take us to Greendale. Lord Owen, please let Feste and I go and try to get Sir John to come back with us."

"You should rest a day or two more," Lord Owen said. "I will go with Feste."

"No, my lord," Feste replied, staring at Maya. "Let Maya come with me. I don't know exactly why, but I get the feeling that she should. In the meantime, begin preparations to march on Greendale. We'll send word as soon as we know whether we can persuade Sir John to stop what he has started."

Lord Owen shook his head. "I'm the one who should go." But in the end, he agreed and left Feste and Maya so that they could get ready.

Servants brought water for washing, and they also brought food as well. Once Maya and Feste were dressed, they ate quickly. They hardly spoke to each other; they didn't really need to. Each one had a sense of what the other's actions would be, and they moved efficiently, almost as a unit.

Maya did have one question. "How long has Lord Owen known I am Maya and not Cesario?"

"I told him the day we came here. I knew your secret would be safe with Lord Owen. Are you ready to go?"

Maya answered, "I'm ready."

Feste and Maya each held an acorn. "Take us to Sir John in Greendale."

17: Captured

Sir John had set up headquarters in a large sleeping chamber over the public room in the Golden Toad Tavern. The big man's face was red, flushed by his own success and by too much ale. All around Greendale, men who could be trusted had been told of his arrival and his plans, and they were more than ready to help him take the barracks. For nearly six years, they had chafed under what was, in fact, an occupying force sent to Greendale because of its proximity to the forest and because most of the town remained loyal to Lord Owen. As soon as it became truly dark, about fifty men would join Sir John, and they would storm the barracks, taking Humphrey's men by surprise. Sir John laughed and drank some more ale.

Andy sat next to Sir John, but he wasn't laughing. Now that they were in Greendale, Andy wasn't so sure they had done the right thing by stealing the book and leaving the lodge. They had consulted the book several times, and each time it said the same thing—"Go back to the forest; go back to the lodge. You are in grave danger here."

But Sir John had dismissed the book's advice. "What a worrywart! I can't see what the use of it is. Things are going just as they ought. We hid in the woods and came into town at dusk. Nobody saw us." Then he closed the book and didn't consult it again.

Sir John was not wrong. Nobody had actually seen the three enter the tavern from the back and go up to the big room. They had stayed hidden in the room while Oakley, the tavern owner, sent word around Greendale that Sir John was in town, and he had plans that came directly from Lord Owen.

"A lie," Andy thought, imagining what Lord Owen's reaction had been when he had found Sir John's note.

What Sir John, Harry, and Andy didn't know was that Simon, the tavern's stable boy, was keeping watch, as he had been instructed to do if anything out of the ordinary seemed to be happening. Five days earlier, Simon had been approached by the lieutenant of the barracks, and a little silver was all it took to make Simon a spy. The boy lived on the edge of town, in a small cottage with his mother. They both worked hard, but there never seemed to be enough money for the things they needed. When he took the silver, Simon told himself that he didn't care who was duke—Lord Humphrey or Lord Owen. It was all the same to him. He and his mother would still be poor, regardless of who ruled, and the silver meant that Simon could buy more food for the two of them.

In the darkening night, in between feeding the horses and cleaning out the stalls, Simon watched but didn't see anything that he could directly report. But then luck was with him. When Simon was finished for the day, he went around back to the Golden Toad's kitchen, to get a drink of milk before walking home. If Bridget, the cook, was in a good mood, she would give Simon a cookie or a small piece of cake, which, in truth, he wanted much more than the milk. As he approached the back door, Simon saw three men quickly make their way through the kitchen, but not quickly enough. Simon caught a glimpse of a massive back and bright red hair.

"Who's that?" Simon asked, coming into the kitchen.

"Oh, no one special," Bridget said briskly. She handed Simon a cup of milk, but no cookie or cake. "Here, drink up and be gone. Maisie is sick, which means there's no one to help me. And there's a lot going on tonight."

But Simon wasn't fooled. He knew that the big man was Sir Broderick, whose estate overlooked the town of Greendale. He also knew that for the past six years, Sir Broderick had been in the forest with Lord Owen. The captain of the barracks and his family now lived in Sir Broderick's big house.

Something was going on. But how to find out what it was?

However, luck was with him again. From the public room, Oakley was yelling for Bridget to hurry up with the food.

"All right, all right!" Bridget hollered back. She was also Oakley's wife, and grabbing a tray full of plates loaded with food, Bridget hurried into the great room.

Simon didn't hesitate. He slipped up the backstairs that led to the tavern's sleeping chambers. Loud voices guided him down the hall, to one particular door, where Simon, trembling just a little, stopped and listened long enough to understand what was being planned.

Luck was with him for the third time. Not only did Simon manage to leave before Andy was sent to the kitchen for a pitcher of ale to soothe tempers, but Bridget was in the public room with another tray of food when Simon peeked into the kitchen.

Holding his breath, Simon ran through the empty kitchen. Quietly leaving the tavern, Simon slowly made his way to the barracks. Along the way, he hid in the shadows of buildings and stood very still when anybody passed by. Nobody noticed him. A short time after he reached the barracks, a pigeon left the rooftop and disappeared quickly into the ever-darkening night.

Meanwhile, in the big chamber, nobody knew that Simon had heard Sir John's plans for attacking the barracks.

"A drink!" Sir John cried. "We could all use a drink!"

While Sir Broderick and the other two men, Timothy and Duncan, briefly conferred with each other about whether they should have a drink, Sir John pressed something into Andy's hand. Sir Broderick decided a drink couldn't hurt, and he would say later, "I even thought it might calm Sir John down enough so that he would just come with us. What a fool I was!"

Andy quickly put the packet into his pocket, and Sir Broderick, Timothy, and Duncan had been so intent upon their own conversation that they didn't notice the exchange. A little later, as Andy sprinkled the last of the sleeping powder into three of the mugs—taking care to keep track of where they were on the tray—he knew that he shouldn't be doing this. As much as he hated to admit it, he was beginning to think that Maya had been right not to trust Sir John's judgment.

"Why does she always have to be so right?" Andy thought bitterly as he picked up the tray from a table in the hall not far from the big room.

Andy realized he had a choice. He could empty the mugs and refill them with clean ale. But it seemed to Andy that things had gone too far—the town was alerted, and they were ready to strike the barracks. How could they just cancel the attack? And maybe, just maybe, if things worked out as they should, Feste, Lord Owen and, especially, Maya would forgive him for what he had done.

And so it was, a half hour later, that Sir Broderick and his men were asleep in a smaller sleeping chamber directly off the big room.

Sir John said, "They won't sleep all night. There wasn't enough powder for that. But they'll sleep for five hours or so. More than enough time for us to take the barracks. Then, what can they say? We will be triumphant!"

Harry scowled. "There's a lot they can say." He, too, was beginning to have second thoughts. Taking the barracks was a bold plan—an important step in overthrowing Duke Humphrey. But drugging Lord Owen's most trusted advisor was quite another thing, especially when Lord Owen had specifically ordered them all to return to the forest.

"Posh!" Sir John shook his head. "They will be grateful that I gave Lord Owen a boot in the right direction."

"You'll be the one getting a boot," came a familiar voice. "If Lord Owen doesn't send you into exile, you'll be lucky."

Harry, Sir John, and Andy all jumped. Feste and Maya stood before them, and they weren't smiling.

Sir John bellowed, "How in God's name did you get here?"

"Never mind that," came Feste's cool answer. "Now call off your plans and come back to the lodge with us."

Sir John snorted. "The town is on our side. Taking the barracks will be easy. You know we have to do it."

"Yes, but not now. We need more time to train and plan. And the book shouldn't be out of the forest. There are larger forces at work here, Sir John. Forces that are even larger than you."

"No! I won't call off the plan! We'll catch them all by surprise. Duke Humphrey won't expect this."

"I can't argue with that," Feste replied, and Maya marveled at his patience with Sir John, who had such a mixture of emotions that Maya had a hard time sorting them out—love for Caxton and its holdings, real affection for Lord Owen and Feste mingled with exasperation, impatience, and resentment at being thwarted in his plans.

Andy hardly dared look at Maya. By now, he was so sorry for his part in Sir John's plans that he couldn't look anyone in the eye. But he did glance quickly at Maya, at her drawn, tired face, at her eyes that had just a tinge of red, and he was surprised by what else he saw—a glimmer of sympathy.

"Where are Sir Broderick and the others?" Feste asked.

"In the next room sleeping," Sir John said.

Feste shook his head. "You drugged them, too?"

"What do you mean by 'too'?" An astonished Harry turned to Sir John. "You drugged Feste, didn't you? He never told you that he went along with your plans but that he had to stay with Cesario, who was ill."

"So many lies," Feste said. "For shame, Sir John, to treat us all like this."

Anger came upon Sir John so quickly that he barely had time to realize what he was doing. His big hand, clenched into a fist, shot out and hit Feste square in the face, between his eyes. Feste fell to the floor, and "No!" Maya screamed, crouching by his side. But Feste was unconscious, and a dark, ugly bruise began to spread across his face.

Sir John stared at his fist as though it weren't a part of his body. "Didn't mean to do that."

Maya stood, and her face was pale with worry. "But you did it anyway, didn't you? Sir John, it's time you started thinking before you act."

"Be quiet!" Sir John said roughly, his eyes bright. "Or you'll be on the floor beside Feste."

As Andy moved toward Maya, she said, "You're bluffing. You wouldn't hit someone so small. Even you wouldn't go that far."

"You're right." Sir John's hand was unclenched. "But that doesn't mean I won't stow you in the next room with Sir Broderick and the others." Moving quickly, Sir John caught Maya and covered her mouth with his hand. "Get me some strips of sheet so I can bind her," he ordered Harry.

In a daze, Harry used his knife to cut off strips of sheet from the big bed in the room. Maya's hands and feet were bound. Gagged as well, Maya struggled and tried to scream, but it was no use. Soon she and an unconscious Feste, also gagged and bound, were in the room with the slumbering Sir Broderick and his men. But before Sir John had carried her into the room, Maya had felt a hand on her back—Andy's hand—and with that touch he told her that he would free her as soon as he could.

18: Julian

Simon hid in a ditch across the street and watched as Sir John and men from town attacked the barracks. The boy had mixed feelings as he listened to the battle. On the one hand, there was the silver he had earned, but on the other hand, he couldn't help but root for the townsmen who were taking back their town, which was also, as he was beginning to realize, his town. However, thanks to Simon, the men in the barracks were armed and ready, which meant that taking it was more difficult than Sir John had anticipated. Both he and Harry were slightly wounded, and some of the men from town had been killed. In the end they won—the men from Greendale fought fiercely to retake their town, and the captain of the barracks was among the dead. But, "It wasn't supposed to go this way," Sir John kept muttering to himself.

The only reason that Andy hadn't been either hurt or killed was that Sir John had told him to stay in the public room so that Andy could keep an eye out for any suspicious comings and goings. Andy thought, "Sir John knows I can't fight. If we had stayed at the lodge, the way we should have, then he could have taught me."

Instead, he was left behind in a room that was nearly empty except for an old man with long gray hair who had slipped in just after Sir John had led the men to the barracks. The old man seemed to be dozing in a corner, and a broad, floppy hat pulled down low hid his face. He looked so shaky and frail that Andy decided he wasn't worth worrying about. Andy's main concern was the book in his pocket, which he touched from time to time. Sir John had given it to him before leaving. Even Sir John knew better than to bring it with him into battle. Andy was also worried about the prisoners upstairs, especially Feste, who had not regained consciousness and seemed badly hurt.

Sir John had told Andy not to do anything with the prisoners upstairs, to wait until the barracks was taken. "Then I'll free them myself," Sir John had said. "And let things fall where they fall."

"But I'm not waiting," Andy said to himself. As he turned to go upstairs, he heard someone ask, "Waiting for what?"

Andy spun around. The voice came from the old man in the corner. His hat wasn't pulled quite so far down, and he sat a little straighter.

"A friend is waiting for me upstairs. I'd better go," Andy said, his hand on his pocket.

The old man stared at Andy's hand. "Indeed you'd better. A lot going on in Greendale right now, isn't there?"

"You got that right," Andy said, half to himself and half to the old man.

"You involved in any of it?"

"More than you can know."

"In over your head?" The man's voice was sympathetic, and Andy had the strongest impulse to tell him all that had happened, from the first time he saw Maya in the South End to being in Greendale with Sir John.

"It's a long story," Andy said, resisting the impulse.

"They always are. But I'm not going anywhere for a while. Surely your friend can wait a little longer."

"No, not really," Andy replied.

The old man's voice was an odd combination of compelling and soothing, and if it hadn't been for his recent experience with Sir John, Andy might very well have told him everything. But after all that had happened, Andy was wary.

The old man's voice was a little more insistent. "Sit down just for a bit and tell me what you can."

Andy found himself sitting down, but he stayed on the edge of his seat. He looked at his hands. "I've done a lot of things I shouldn't."

"Ashamed, are you?"

"Yeah, I've betrayed a friend, and now I have to make things right." Andy squirmed, as if to stand.

"Stay for a while longer," the old man said, and Andy did as he was told. He had the strangest feeling that the old man's voice was actually keeping him in his chair. "And how did you betray your friend?"

"I worked against her while she was sick. I even stole something from her."

The old man shook his head. "That's not how you keep friends."

Andy's face was red. "No, it isn't."

"But maybe your friend was in the wrong, and you were in the right. Look how things have progressed."

"No, she was right, and I was wrong. She can see things that others can't see. Just like Feste."

"Can she indeed?" The old man tried to keep his voice neutral, but Andy could hear a sharp spark of interest that the man couldn't conceal, so sharp that Andy almost felt as though he were being poked. Andy stood quickly.

Andy blinked. "I'd better go see my friend."

There was a quick hiss that came from the old man. "I guess you'd better. Perhaps I'll see you later."

But Andy left the room before the old man could say anything else. Tipping his hat back, the old man sat up very straight. "Well," he said, with a slight smile. "Well, well." He began to rise from the chair, but just then Oakley, the innkeeper, came into the room to see if there was anything the man wanted. Later, the old man would say, "That three or four minutes made all the difference. But then, they often do."

Gagged and with her hands and feet tied, Maya sat on the floor next to Feste, who was still unconscious. The room was dark, lit only by a pale gleam of moonlight. Could Feste be dead? It seemed as though he had been unconscious for a long time. And he was so still. Maya struggled to free herself, but Sir John had bound her tightly, and the knots wouldn't budge. Exhausted, Maya closed her eyes. Sir Broderick and his men had been placed on the two beds, and Maya could hear the men snoring. Then, she heard footsteps in the next room.

The door opened, and a voice called, "Maya?"

It was Andy. He came quickly into the room, found her sitting on the floor, and untied the gag. Using a knife that Sir John had given him—"You should never be without one, my boy"—Andy cut the strips of sheet that bound her hands and feet.

"Andy," Maya whispered.

"Maya, I'm so sorry!"

If they had been in a brighter room, then Maya would have been able to see the tears in Andy's eyes. But Maya did not need to be in a brighter room to sense how sincere Andy's shame and regret were. Because of this, she couldn't be angry with him, the way she would have been two days ago.

"I know," Maya said, rubbing her wrists. Then she touched Andy's shoulder. "I know."

Andy was blinking. "I'll untie Feste." Andy cut the knots, but Feste didn't move, and when Andy removed the gag, it was wet with blood. Touching Feste's face, Andy felt more blood.

"I think Sir John might have really hurt Feste," Andy said. "There is blood all over his face."

Maya knelt beside Feste placing a hand on his chest. She felt a flicker of life, but it was faint. "Andy! What are we going to do?"

"I have the book," Andy said, standing. "Let's go into the other room, where the lamps are lit. Maybe the book will know what to do. If only we had listened to it earlier. None of this would have happened."

"Never mind that!" Maya cried, with a touch of her old impatience. "Let's go!"

They rushed into the other room. But as soon as Andy took the book from his pocket and opened it, a voice said, "This is certainly my lucky day."

A man leaned against the doorway, watching them. It was the old man from the public room, except he really wasn't old. His face was smooth and still, and his hair, which came to his shoulders, was not gray but instead a very light blond. There was no shakiness now. Instead, there was such a fierce vitality, combined with a glittering malice, that Maya could hardly breathe.

Trying to catch her breath, Maya reached for the book, but the man struck first. With astonishing speed, he moved from the doorway to Andy's side and grabbed the book from his hand.

"You'll get nothing from me, Julian," the book said, but there was despair in its voice. The book could see Julian, now that he was in Julian's hand, but it was too late.

"I wouldn't be so sure of that," Julian said. "There is someone who knows quite a lot about how to get information from a book of everything."

"Cinnial," the book said.

"That's right, Cinnial. And that's where you will go as soon as I have the other book." Maya could feel the pride and ambition in Julian as he thought about presenting not one but two books to Cinnial. "Humphrey has been quite obstinate when it comes to the book," Julian continued pleasantly, as though discussing the weather. "Amazingly so."

"But you need him, don't you?" Maya asked. "Otherwise, you would just torture him until he told you where the book was hidden. Then you would kill him."

Julian gave Maya a sharp look, and Maya had the uncomfortable feeling that he could see as much of her, if not more, as she could see of him. "That's right. What could be better than pitting brother against brother? Albion is ripe for falling." With a black-gloved hand, he touched Maya's face, and she pulled away from him. "Humphrey has a Book of Everything—I know he does—but there didn't seem to be any hurry to get it from him. There would have been plenty of time after we burned that damned forest." Here Julian's lips curled, but his voice stayed even. "Then, we could have killed Owen, tortured Humphrey, and gotten the book. Meanwhile, there would be civil war and chaos in the duchy of Caxton. With any luck, it would spread throughout Albion and then to the rest of Ilyria."

"You had it all planned, didn't you?" the book asked.

Julian squeezed the book. "As a matter of fact, I did. But then you came along, and these two as well." He jerked his head toward Maya and Andy

"Is he talking to the book?" Andy whispered, and Maya nodded. In a rush, she understood that Julian could hear the book even though it didn't want him to.

Julian's attention was on Earth's Book of Everything. "My own book warned that something big was happening. It couldn't tell me exactly what, of course. You and your people have the shielding thing down. You learned it from us, didn't you? But you can't shield yourself completely. There is always a bit of a ripple, which my book caught coming from the Forest of Arden. If that fat fool hadn't acted when he did, why, you all might still be safe in the forest. We should give Sir John an award." He turned to Andy. "And you, too. You played your part, didn't you?"

Andy was pale, but he didn't look away. "Yes, and I'll always be sorry for what I did. Always."

Julian smiled, but it was more like a grimace. "Why waste your time with regret, especially when you don't have much time left?" He snapped shut the Book of Everything, and Maya heard a faint, "Help me, Maya!" before the book disappeared into one of Julian's pockets.

"You won't be helping anyone anytime soon," Julian said to Maya. "In fact, you won't even be able to help yourself." Julian took something out of another pocket, and it looked like a knife's handle. He pushed a button on the side, and with a high-pitched whine, a very thin, gleaming blade popped up. Julian took a step toward Maya. "I'm tempted to spare you and bring you back to Caxton with me and then to Cinnial. You're young to have what you have. It would be interesting to see how it develops, to see if it can be guided."

"I'd never go to your side," Maya cried, even though she was terrified.

"Don't be so sure." Julian's voice was thoughtful. "I'm not so sure." As Julian hesitated, considering Maya, Andy sprang at Julian, and "Now!" urged a voice inside Maya. Using her best Ariel leap, one she had practiced over and over when she was in *The Tempest*, she, too, sprang at Julian. In a rare moment of being caught off-guard, Julian dropped the knife and staggered backward. As quick as a cat, Maya grabbed the knife and heard it hum with pleasure as she turned toward Julian. He and Andy had fallen to the floor, and Julian's hands were around Andy's throat, squeezing hard.

Maya immediately realized that the knife's job was to stab and slash and that it didn't matter whom the victim was. The knife responded to whoever was holding it, and if allowed, it would guide her to just the right spot to do the most damage.

Maya sprang again, but Julian and Andy rolled to one side, and instead of stabbing Julian in the middle of the back, Maya hit his shoulder. The knife slid in easily, smoothly, as if there were no skin, muscle, or bone. Screaming, Julian let go of Andy, and he immediately reached into a pocket in his trousers. Out came a small, black book, and when Julian opened it, Maya heard a crisp, sly voice ask, "To Mortmain?"

"No, to Caxton. I need to go there first."

"Right!"

Before Julian disappeared, he said to Maya, "I'll get you." He glared at Andy. "And you, too." Then he was gone.

19: The Last Acorn

For a while, Maya just stood there holding the bloody knife. The Book of Everything was really gone this time, and Maya felt worse than she ever had in her life, even worse than when her father had left. Her eyes stung with tears, and she wanted to throw herself down on the floor and weep. But she heard a sound that was something between a choke and a cough.

"Andy!" Maya rushed over to him. He was lying on the floor, but his eyes were open, and he was breathing in great ragged gasps.

Maya touched his face. "Are you all right?"

Andy nodded. After a few minutes, he was able to sit up, and Maya patted him on the back. "He almost had me," Andy said at last.

"I know."

"If you hadn't grabbed the knife and stabbed him..."

"I know."

The knife was still in Maya's hand. It was quiet now, but Maya sensed the knife was waiting for the next opportunity to stab, and it felt strangely warm. And dangerous. Shuddering,

Maya thought about what this knife could do if someone like Julian was using it, and she pushed the button on the side to retract the blade. She put the knife in the pocket of her trousers, and through the cloth, she could still feel a slight warmth.

"Maya, what are we going to do now? Julian has our Book of Everything. How are we going to get it back?"

"I don't know." Maya sat down next to Andy. It all seemed so hopeless that she didn't have the slightest idea what they should do next.

A woman's voice called, "Feste? Maya? Andy?" They heard footsteps coming down the hall.

"Feste!" Maya scrambled to her feet. How could she have forgotten him?

A young woman came into the room. She was slender, not tall but not short, had brown eyes, a firm mouth, and blonde hair with a hint of red. The woman looked as though she was used to giving orders and then having them obeyed.

"Lady Celia?" Maya asked, remembering how Feste, Harry, and Sir John had spoken of her that first night in the cottage, a night that seemed distant now.

"Yes," she answered. "And you must be Maya and Andy."

Maya nodded. "But how did you know about us?"

"I've received several messages from Owen. The first came when I was visiting my aunt in Thorndike, and I returned to Greendale as soon as I could, just before the barracks was attacked. Owen asked me to try to find you, to see if you were all right. So here I am. But where's Feste?"

Maya bit her lip. "Feste is in the other room. He's hurt. I think he might be dying if he isn't dead already."

Lady Celia grabbed a lamp, and Maya and Andy followed her into the room. Feste was lying on the floor, and his breathing was quick and shallow. From the beds, there were slight noises as Sir Broderick, Timothy, and Duncan struggled to wake up.

Lady Celia knelt by Feste's side. "How?" she asked, looking up at Andy and Maya.

"Sir John," Andy answered. "He lost his temper and hit Feste in the face."

"We need to bring him to my house," Lady Celia said.

Oakley was summoned, servants were fetched, a stretcher was found, and Feste was carried, as gently as possible, out of the tavern to a small side street, not far away, to a large L-shaped house. An hour later, as the fighting at the barracks wound down, Feste lay in one of Lady Celia's best guest bedchambers. The town's doctor had been called, and he hurried to New Place—the name of Lady Celia's house—knowing he would soon be needed at the barracks once the fighting stopped.

The doctor tended Feste. Maya, Andy, Lady Celia, and a still groggy Sir Broderick, Timothy, and Duncan sat in her parlor and waited. Sir Broderick was furious, but he was too tired to do much about it.

"I've half a mind to give you a good thrashing," he said to Andy. "Even if you are nearly a man."

Ashamed, Andy looked away, and Lady Celia replied, "Andy doesn't need a thrashing. He knows what he has done. He's had a hard lesson—and it's not over yet—but he's learned."

"Yeah," was all Andy could say. Despite the shame, there was a dignity about him, and Maya had the strangest feeling that she had seen him before, in her own time.

Sir Broderick regarded Andy. He was still frowning, but, "I guess you're right. Sir John really made a mess this time."

"Oh, it's more than a mess," Maya said in a soft voice.

But everyone heard her, and Sir Broderick asked, "And just how did you and Feste get here so fast?"

Everyone waited—including Andy—and Maya was not sure what to say. How much should she tell them? About her Book of Everything? About her eyes being peeled? About the acorns? Maya could see a lot, but the Toad Queen had been right: she couldn't see everything. Maya wished Feste were there to do the explaining. Instead, he was mortally hurt and upstairs with a doctor who probably couldn't do anything to help him.

Maya decided to be frank. "I'm not sure how much I should say. I know you can all be trusted, but still…"

Lady Celia came to her rescue. "We don't need to know everything. Just enough to make some sense of what's going on. You're a bit like Feste, aren't you?"

"Yes," Maya answered. "We can both see things."

"I'm not surprised," Sir Broderick replied. "Right from the start, I could tell there was something different about you. And you and Feste seemed to have quite a bit in common."

Maya smiled just a little. "But I don't make bad puns the way he does."

"Of course you don't," Lady Celia said, looking at Maya, who knew that here was someone who would be an ally. "Go ahead, Maya. Tell us as much as you think you should."

Maya began slowly, carefully choosing her words. "This is bigger than you all think. It goes way beyond Albion."

"Duke Humphrey is getting outside help," Lady Celia said.

Maya nodded. "There's a man named Julian who is advising Duke Humphrey. This man is very powerful. And his power doesn't come from this world. Even if Sir John hadn't done what he did, Julian and Duke Humphrey would have been hard to go up against. But it's worse now. Julian stole something important from Andy and me. A special book that helps us. Honestly, it doesn't look good for either Lord Owen or for the Forest of Arden."

"We have a special book, too," Lady Celia murmured.

"Ours is a lot like yours," Maya said.

Then the room was quiet. Maya could sense the various reactions: Lady Celia's alarm and her concern for Lord Owen, whom she loved deeply; Sir Broderick's own concern, which was mingled with anger and desperation as he tried to come up with some kind of new plan; Timothy and Duncan, whose feelings were akin to Sir Broderick's; and Andy's shame, which was strengthening into a resolve to make things right.

"But there's one thing you should all know," Maya said. "Andy attacked Julian, who was going to kill him and take me with him. If Andy hadn't done this, then everything that we've gone through would have been for nothing. Andy and I were sent to help you. I know we are young, but we were chosen. I'm sorry I can't tell you more."

The room was still quiet. "Some help, but he's brave, at least," Timothy finally said.

"Aye, and still young," Duncan put in.

Sir Broderick rubbed his tired face. "And we know how persuasive Sir John can be. He's pulled tricks on all of us at one time or another."

"I'm sorry," Andy said.

"Let's deal with what's at hand," Lady Celia said. "I'm going to go up and see what the doctor has to say about Feste."

Maya asked, "May I come, too?"

"Of course," Lady Celia answered.

The doctor was just getting ready to leave when Maya and Lady Celia came in. He was a young man, lean and sinewy, with sandy blond hair. Maya only had to glance at him to know there was nothing he could do for Feste. Rushing to the bed while Lady Celia spoke to the doctor, Maya took one of Feste's still hands and held it in her own.

"Don't leave me," Maya said. "I need you. I can't do this on my own."

Feste's spirit flickered restlessly in his body. It was ready to leave, but it had been waiting for Maya. "Yes, you can," came the firm reply. "But you'll need help that you can't get here."

"Help from where?" Maya asked.

"From where it all began. You still have an acorn left."

Maya patted her pocket. "Yes."

"Then use it. I'm not sure if it will take you that far. You might have to help it along. But you can do it. You have it in you. Your vision is even stronger than mine was at your age."

Maya was crying. "Oh, Feste!"

But Feste's spirit had left his body. It hovered over the bed before rushing over to Maya, brushing against her wet cheek.

"Goodbye, Maya. I love you, child."

Maya covered her face with her hands, and she felt a pat on

her shoulder. It felt so much like Lily's touch that Maya stopped crying to see whose hand was on her shoulder. It was Lady Celia's, and her own face was shiny with tears.

"He's gone," Lady Celia said with a sigh. "How we shall miss him. Not only was he a good friend, but he also did more for this duchy, for all of Albion, than anyone will ever know." She placed her hand on Feste's pale forehead. "He'll be buried in the forest, which he loved so much."

"We'll have to tell Lord Owen," Maya said, thinking of how close the two men had been.

"He'll be here by noon tomorrow," Lady Celia replied. "It's time. He's bringing most of the able-bodied men with him, and they'll start marching at dawn for Greendale. It's sooner than we would have liked. But what can we do? Sir John has taken the barracks, and Humphrey soon will be sending troops to Greendale."

Wiping her eyes, Lady Celia found a handkerchief, and blew her nose. Her shoulders were set, and she held her head high, but Maya could see how discouraged Lady Celia was, that she was expecting slaughter and defeat.

Maya knew these were probable outcomes. But she also knew that she had to follow Feste's last instructions.

"Lady Celia," Maya said, "I have to leave, and I don't know how long I'll be gone."

Lady Celia looked bewildered. "But where will you be going?"

"I can't really say. If and when I come back, then I can tell you more. But before he died, Feste told me that I needed to go someplace else for help. And he's right. We need help badly."

"Will Andy go, too?"

"No, just me. Can you look after him if I'm gone for a while?"

Lady Celia was about to answer when they heard a commotion on the stairs. Voices were raised—Sir Broderick's, Timothy's, and Duncan's—and a voice louder than them all—Sir John's. There was a loud scuffle followed by the thumping of heavy footsteps up the stairs. The door opened with a bang, and Sir John's large body filled the doorway. One of his arms was bandaged, but he didn't look seriously hurt.

"Feste!" Sir John called, stepping into the room.

"Feste is dead," Lady Celia answered.

Sir John stopped. Maya could see that he was stunned, that part of him didn't believe Lady Celia, but as he stared at Feste's too-still body, Sir John knew it was true. His friend was dead.

"Oh, Feste."

There was such loneliness and despair coming from him that despite all Sir John had done, Maya felt sorry for him. Before her eyes had been peeled, Maya would have felt nothing but rage toward Sir John. But seeing changed things, and Maya was beginning to get a sense of how complicated it all was.

Sir John staggered toward the bed. Sir Broderick had come into the room and looked from Feste to Lady Celia, who nodded. Closing his eyes, Sir Broderick turned away.

Lady Celia and Maya said nothing as Sir John went to the bed and stood, staring down at Feste. There were tears on Sir John's face. "I didn't mean to hit you so hard. I didn't."

Maya put her small hand on Sir John's big one. "His spirit is gone. He can't hear you."

Sir John's voice was fierce. "Go ahead and say it! I deserve it. From both of you, but especially from Maya."

Lady Celia swallowed. "Sir John, we don't have to tell you what you have done. Tomorrow, you will have to face Owen. Until then, there's nothing much either of us can say."

"Except for one thing," Maya said. "Feste would have forgiven you."

Recriminations and accusations could not have had a harder effect. Sir John sat down on the chair by the bed and wept.

"We'll leave you with him for a while," Lady Celia said. "Come on, Maya."

They left the room, and the last image Maya had was of Sir John hunched over Feste's dead body. A little later, Maya stood in a bedchamber not far from where Feste lay. At Maya's request, Lady Celia had brought her there immediately. Maya knew that she had to follow Feste's instructions right away and that if she spoke about it to Andy, then she might lose her nerve. In her hand, she held the last glittering acorn.

Maya had no doubt where Feste wanted her to go, but would the acorn really take her there? Could it? To Maya, the destination seemed way beyond reach, and she had the feeling that even the Book of Everything would have balked at the request she was about to make. What hope did an acorn have, even one with special powers? But Feste had been right. Maya needed help, as did Lord Owen, Lady Celia, Sir Broderick, Andy, the Forest of Arden, Caxton, and Albion. And Earth.

"All right, then." Maya clutched the acorn, which seemed to pulse a little in her hand. Encouraged, Maya said, "Take me to the Great Library."

The acorn hesitated and then there was a surge as Maya was propelled through various times and places, none of which looked familiar to her. Faster and faster, she hurtled through vast distances, and Maya's heart pounded painfully. Something pulled at her, something strong, dark, and insistent, and Maya felt that if it didn't stop she would soon break apart and fly into a thousand pieces to be scattered across the universe.

"No, no, no! Leave me alone!" Maya's thoughts cried, and she joined her own stubborn will with the acorn's energy. There was another surge as something even stronger and more insistent pulled her away from the force that was trying to break her apart. Maya had the strangest sensation of being guided by a strong and unfathomable energy that stretched in every direction.

Maya stopped fighting, knowing she was safe. Finally, after what seemed like a long time, everything was very still. Opening her eyes, Maya stumbled against a row of books on a long shelf. In a daze, Maya looked around. Shelves with books went all the way to the ceiling and stretched along the four walls of a small room. Maya, with a shaky laugh, fell to her knees. She had made it to the Great Library.

Then she heard a voice. "Who are you and how in heaven's name did you get here?"

20: An Unexpected Visitor

A woman sat at a long table not far from where Maya had landed. Books were piled all around her as well as various small tablets with circuitry, and there was also something that looked like a console with a center section in which a small book was nestled.

The woman stood. She was dressed in a white shirt and black pants, very crisply ironed, and her blonde hair was pulled back in a bun. "Who are you?" she asked again, and her voice was as crisp as her clothes.

Maya also stood, knowing how rumpled and disheveled she must look. Her legs were unsteady, and she swayed a little. "My name is Maya." She held out her hand, showing the woman the acorn, which was now dark and shriveled. "This is how I got here."

The woman looked from Maya to the acorn. "That must have taken quite a bit of effort."

"Yes," Maya answered, rubbing her face. "Yes, it did. I almost didn't make it. It felt like something was trying to pull me apart, but then it seemed like something else helped me. Not the acorn. Something stronger." She put the acorn in her pocket.

For a moment, the woman looked startled, but she soon regained her composure. "Sit down. You look exhausted. No surprise there. I'll go make some tea. But first the director will have to be told about you."

There were chairs around the table, and Maya gratefully sat down across from the woman, who pushed a small button on a box on the side of the table.

"Yes, Elspeth?" a woman asked, her voice calm and assured.

"Could you tell Sydda that I have an unexpected visitor and that he should come here as soon as he is able?"

"Someone from the Great Library?"

"No, someone from outside."

There was a pause. "I see. He's not in his office, but I'll call him. Immediately."

"Thank you," Elspeth said. "Please tell him that the visitor doesn't look dangerous."

"I'll do that." There was relief in the calm voice. "Thank you, Elspeth."

As Maya listened to the conversation, she looked at the array that was on the table. Despite her exhaustion, she was fascinated with what she saw. "Are you making a Book of Everything?"

Elspeth shook her head. "No, I'm still a senior apprentice. This is a practice book. But if all goes well, my next one will be a Book of Everything."

"It's complicated, isn't it?"

"Oh, yes. It's taken me years to get this far. And it will take me years to make a Book of Everything." Frowning, she regarded Maya. "Really, I'm the one who should be asking the questions, but it seems pointless to start until Sydda gets here. Otherwise, you'll just have to repeat yourself."

Just then there came a ringing sound, very much like a phone, and Maya waited for Elspeth to tend to whatever was making the noise.

But with raised eyebrows Elspeth said, "I believe that sound is coming from one of the pockets in your trousers."

Maya started. It was her cell phone. Reaching into her pocket, she pulled it out and answered it. "Hello?" she asked tentatively.

"Maya?" a familiar voice asked. "What's going on? Are you all right?"

Blinking, Maya turned to Elspeth. "It's my father. I can't believe my cell phone works here."

"Everything works here," Elspeth replied and then added gently. "You'd better talk to him."

"Maya? Who are you talking to?" her father asked.

"A new friend," Maya answered.

From Elspeth there was a hint of a smile. "Good quick thinking," she would say later.

"Oh," her father said. "So you're all right?"

How could Maya answer that question? She had had her eyes peeled. She had nearly been killed. And she was in a place called the Great Library, a place that was as close to heaven as Maya could imagine. Then, a terrible thought came to her. What if she had died, and she would never see her parents again?

"Dad, can you hold on for a moment?" Without waiting for an answer, Maya put her father on hold and turned to Elspeth. "Am I dead?"

Trying not to smile, Elspeth shook her head. "No, you're very much alive. Otherwise, you wouldn't be able to talk to your father."

Maya felt nearly as relieved as Scrooge had felt when he woke up in his own bed after having been visited by the spirits.

"Dad?" Maya said. "I'm fine."

"You sound, well, different."

"It's just me," Maya replied, even though she had a strong hunch that she had changed so much in such a short time that her parents, grandparents, and friends were bound to notice. But that was a few problems away. First she had to get back to Albion, rescue the two books, get back to Earth, face the man who didn't smile, and probably do something else, even though Maya wasn't sure what that might be.

"I'm glad to hear that," her father said. "I just thought I'd call back in case something was the matter. You hung up so fast."

"Everything is fine here," Maya said truthfully, and Elspeth smiled again.

"Hope to see you soon, Maya."

"I'd like to see you, too." Maya was sincere. After all that had happened, Maya was confident that she could face Inga Peterson and her children.

"Let's make plans."

"All right."

"Goodbye, Maya."

"Goodbye, Dad."

"And Maya? Continue with your story. It's a good one."

"Thanks, Dad."

Maya hung up, and Elspeth asked, "Parent troubles?"

"Yeah, but somehow they don't seem as big anymore."

"That's one thing about getting involved with a Book of Everything and the Great Library. They put things in perspective. Now, I'll go make some tea. Sydda should be here soon."

Elspeth left, and Maya, feeling incredibly weary, lay her head on the table and closed her eyes. She must have dozed because when a chiming voice asked, "Who are you, and why are you in Elspeth's office?" Maya sat up with a jerk and gave a slight screech.

Maya's screech was met by an answering screech, and a young woman jumped back. She had been standing a short distance away from Maya, and she had a mass of long, blonde curls held together by a bright pink ribbon. She wore a dress the same color as her ribbon, and the dress billowed to just above her ankles. Then there were the boots, an eye-popping shade of green. The color of the clothes seemed to set the woman in motion, even though she was standing still, but the most striking thing about her was her size. Maya guessed that the woman was about three feet tall. "Just like a hobbit," Maya thought.

The woman quickly regained her composure and asked sharply, "Are you supposed to be here? Does Elspeth know about you?" There was a fierce look on the small face as the woman took in Maya's curly hair, roughly cut; the cap, which had somehow managed to stay on her head despite the distance she had traveled; the trousers; the jacket.

Just then, Elspeth, carrying a tray with a huge pot of tea, came into the room, and the woman spun around so fast that her dress was a pink blur. "Elspeth!"

"Hello, Alani." Elspeth set the tray on the table. "What are you doing here?"

"You told me to come at 2:00 so that you could show me a little of how the console works."

"Yes, yes, of course. With all the excitement of our un-expected visitor, I forgot. Maya, this is Alani, a junior apprentice. Alani, this is Maya." Frowning, Elspeth regarded Maya. "I don't really know what you are, but I expect we'll find out soon."

There was a slight bob of the curly head, and Alani asked, "Did you come here on your own?" Maya nodded, digging in her pocket for the acorn, and finding it, she held it for Alani to see.

Alani stared at the blackened acorn in the palm of Maya's hand. "That little thing brought you here?" She turned to Elspeth. "What's Sydda going to make of this? A teenager, a rather grubby one, coming on her own to the Great Library." She whirled to face Maya. "Did someone send you here?"

"In a way. But he's dead now," Maya answered sadly.

The expression changed on Alani's small face, and shaking her head, she made sympathetic clucking sounds. Maya got a sense of a mercurial personality, not quite under control, and a very strong will that was working on it.

"It seems like death always brings us here," Alani said.

Elspeth reached for the teapot. "Not always."

"But you have to admit that it's true a lot of the time."

Elspeth was still. "There is a great battle going on. And Cinnial's gaining ground."

"He's clever, that one." Alani's hands were in a fist. "He always knows how to work on our weaknesses. Always prodding. Always offering. But never afraid to kill if he doesn't like the answer he gets."

An image came to Maya of a beautiful little family dressed in bright clothes stained dark with blood. Everyone was dead, all stabbed, and their skin was dark with streaks. With a sharp intake of breath, Maya put her hand on the pocket with the knife.

"What did you see?" Alani asked sharply. "You can see, can't you?"

"Yes," Maya answered. "I saw what must be your family. All dead. I'm so sorry."

Alani nodded. There were tears in her eyes, but all she said was, "You'll do."

"Indeed she will," a lilting voice said. A slight man, not tall but not as short as Alani, had come into the room. He wore a yellow robe, and he had white hair, cropped short, but his face was so smooth and dark that it was hard to tell if he was young or old.

Elspeth stood and gave a slight bow. "Sydda."

Alani made a little whirling motion with her hand and also said his name. Maya began to scramble from her chair, but Sydda said, "Oh, sit down, sit down. I could certainly use a seat myself. This place is so big I feel as though I've been walking for miles." He laughed, and despite all that she had been through, Maya smiled, feeling that maybe things weren't so hopeless after all.

"Sydda's laugh is like that," Elspeth would say later.

Glancing at the tea tray, Sydda said, "I see there is tea but only three cups. Alani, why don't you fetch another cup?"

"Yes, yes, of course!" And with a flurry of pink and green, Alani was gone, closing the door behind her with a slam.

As they all sat down, Maya said, "Alani has a lot of energy."

Sydda smiled, and there was a dimple in his cheek. "Alani has energy enough for all three of us."

Elspeth said, "I'm sorry Alani was here. I had told her to meet me at 2:00 so that we could go over the console."

"It doesn't really matter," Sydda said mildly, looking at Maya. "If I'm right about our visitor, then what she has to say will be of importance to us all, and soon everyone at the Great Library will have to be filled in."

As Maya considered Sydda, she knew that despite his smooth face, he was very, very old. Sydda was still regarding Maya, and from him came a feeling of great tranquility mixed with knowledge, both of which were reflected in his brown eyes, kindly yet shrewd.

"You've come a long way," Sydda said. "You're Maya, aren't you?" Maya nodded. "I've known for some time that you might be coming, but I couldn't really be sure. It was highly improbable, especially for someone so young. Of course for a while, that worked in your favor. Nobody on Cinnial's side really knew about you." Sydda laughed again. "And they don't have the Great Library to keep them up-to-date. They have to guess about a lot of things, and they are often wrong."

"This is how I got here," Maya replied, showing him the acorn. Then she repeated what she had told Elspeth. "But something tried to pull me apart, and something, not the acorn, stopped it and helped me get here."

"Well, well," said Sydda, and even he looked a little startled. "Very interesting, indeed. But let's have some tea first. I believe I hear the sound of small feet running down the hall."

The door swung open, and Alani, slightly out of breath, stood in the doorway. She held a cup.

When the tea was poured and the cookies—chocolate-covered shortbread—were passed around, Sydda sighed. "No matter what the circumstances or what my age is, tea always tastes so good."

"Yes," Maya answered. She had taken a great gulp of tea,

then another, and now her cup was nearly empty. She had already eaten one cookie and was working on her second when Elspeth poured more tea into Maya's cup.

"You'd better get started with your story," Sydda said. "If I'm not mistaken, it's quite a long one."

Maya took another sip of tea and started where it all began, on Earth, on the train between New York and Boston. Later, Maya would realize that the story had started much, much earlier—with her father leaving; with her quiet mother who was afraid of flying; with her grandparents living in Maine. But Maya had to start somewhere, and the train was where everything seemed to come together.

Sydda and Elspeth listened quietly while Alani fidgeted beside them. "No questions until the end," Sydda had insisted, and Alani would never go against his wishes.

By the time Maya was finished, the tea and cookies were long gone. Elspeth and Sydda both stared intently at Maya, and Alani had stopped fidgeting.

"What is she going to do now?" Alani asked. "Do you know, Sydda?"

"Not exactly," Sydda answered. "There are several possibilities. Some are good, and others are not so good."

"We can't give her another Book of Everything," Elspeth said. "Even though that would be the best thing to do. They take so long to make, and there are too many places that don't have them yet. Plus, we need some books for the recruiters."

"We have to do something!" Alani exclaimed.

"That we do," Sydda replied.

"But what?" Elspeth asked.

"We could give her an apprentice's book," Sydda said.

Elspeth looked shocked. "That's never been done, not since Cinnial and his accomplices…"

Sydda cut her off. "I know."

"Will an apprentice's book be enough to help?" Alani asked.

Sydda said, "I'm not going to deny that it won't be as good as a Book of Everything. However, I'm afraid we really don't have much of a choice. That said, some of the apprentice books are very good, and any one of them would be a great help. But I will have to call a meeting and put it before the board. This is too big of a decision for me to make on my own. Maya, you will have to come speak before the board members."

Maya nodded.

"Now, you must have some questions." Sydda laughed. "I'm sure I don't have time to answer them all, but I could answer a few, anyway."

Maya had so many questions that she almost didn't know where to start, and for a while she was silent, but she finally asked, "How does the Great Library work?"

"Everything in our universe is connected. To use one of your own planet's terms, it's like a giant web, and the Great Library is in the middle of it, in the hub, so to speak, and everything flows through us. We collect the information, store it, and then use it to make Books of Everything. The Books of Everything, in turn, are hypersensitive to this giant web, and they can travel along the various paths to the various worlds. Also, some people are born with an extreme sensitivity to this interconnectedness. I was and so were Elspeth and Alani. And, of course, you were."

"But people don't always use it for good, do they?"

"No, I expect Chet has this sensitivity, and Julian most certainly does." Sydda looked pensive. "Cinnial took some of the best with him when he left the Great Library."

"Have you always been the director?"

Sydda shook his head and then laughed. "I'm old, but I'm not that old. There have been others before me. But I've been here for a long time."

"How come we all speak the same language?"

"We don't, but when you come into contact with a Book of Everything, it connects you to the web's common language, which means you can understand everyone, and they can understand you. Very handy! I'm terrible at learning languages."

The next question Maya asked in a low voice. "When I was coming here, what was trying to pull me apart, and what helped me?"

Sydda was quiet for a few moments as he considered the question. "You were caught between Chaos and Time. A very tricky place to be." Sydda wasn't laughing now. "Many people wouldn't have survived the struggle."

"I don't understand," Maya said, shivering as she remembered how she felt as though she was going to be torn into a thousand pieces.

"Think of Time as an arrow," Sydda replied. "In our universe, at the beginning of all things, Time was set on its course, and onward it flew, sure and powerful. But at the beginning something else was set in motion, and that something was Chaos, constantly trying to knock Time off its track. Now, Time is more powerful than Chaos, but Chaos is persistent. Sometimes it strikes head-on, sometimes it hides and feints, but it is always there, always waiting, and now and then, it succeeds in diverting Time from its course. Never for very long, but even a little is enough to cause trouble, and there has been lots of trouble on the various worlds. But so far, Time has always managed to regain its course, and order is restored."

"So far," Maya repeated. "And Cinnial?"

"He has aligned himself with Chaos," Sydda said quietly. "While we at the Great Library are on the side of Time."

"A great battle," Maya murmured, remembering what Elspeth had said.

"And you are now part of it," Sydda said sadly. "There is one more thing you must know. Nobody, not even those of us who have been at the Great Library for a long time, truly understands all the aspects of Time and Chaos. Even as we choose sides, Time and Chaos remain mysterious."

Maya was silent, and Sydda asked gently, "Do you have any more questions?"

Maya shook her head. "No, that's enough for now." Her shoulders drooped. Maya felt weary again, and combined with her weariness was the ache she felt over Feste's death, an ache that would be with her for quite a while.

"Would you like to rest?" Sydda asked.

"Yes," Maya answered, "I would."

21: Around the Great Library

"Maya," a voice said, "it is time to return to us. You have slept long enough, and there is much to do. I'm sorry, child, but that's the way it has turned out."

Maya woke with a start and sat straight up in bed. For a moment, she thought that Feste was talking to her, and her heart began to beat fast. But then she saw that Sydda was sitting next to her, and they were in a small, bright room with white walls.

Sydda shook his head sympathetically. "No, not Feste."

The ache, which had been gone while Maya slept, came back. "Feste's dead."

"That's right."

Maya felt tears on her cheeks. "I can't stand it, Sydda."

"Yes, you can, Maya. You know you can." He might have added, "You must." But Sydda knew better than to say this to someone who was grieving yet still had so much to do. Instead, he let Maya cry until she could cry no more, handing her a huge handkerchief so that she could wipe her face and nose.

"Why does it have to be like this?" Maya asked, when she could speak again.

"We live in a sad universe, one with too much greed, pride, and suffering. Not enough compassion. It's that way every-where, Maya, not just on Earth or on Ilyria."

Oddly enough, this stark but truthful answer made her feel calmer. Another adult might have tried to smooth things over, to make the situation seem better than it was, but not Sydda. And Maya could see that while he might not tell her the whole truth, which she knew she wasn't ready for anyway, Sydda's replies would always be honest but kind.

Maya sighed. "How long have I been sleeping?"

"Two days."

"Have you been here the whole time?"

"No, sometimes Elspeth sat with you. Other times Alani. We took turns." Sydda smiled. "It seems you now have quite a defender with Alani. She is on your side, and when Alani decides to be on someone's side, she is a loyal friend."

"I could use a loyal friend," Maya said, smiling just a little.

"You sound as old as I am," Sydda replied, laughing.

"I feel that way right now."

"I expect you do. You will never be the way you were before you had your eyes peeled, Maya. That girl is gone."

"I know. The Toad Queen told me it would be like this, but I didn't know exactly what she meant."

"How could you? But tell me, would you have chosen dif-ferently if you had known?"

"No," Maya answered carefully. "It seemed there was no choice."

"There was a choice," Sydda replied. "Some things are fixed in time, but others are not. Your path wasn't completely fixed. No one's is. I know. It seems incredible, given what has happened. Time likes to have various possibilities, to keep options open, and having your eyes peeled was one of the options."

"Sydda, was I meant to get the book and meet Andy?"

Sydda shook his head. "No, you were not. There is a third element that I didn't tell you about, and that element is Chance. Chance works with Time, and because of Chance, you were on that particular train when Mary needed help. Time fixes the big events but leaves the details to Chance."

Maya was silent as she thought about this.

Sydda patted Maya's arm. "So much to learn and think about! But right now you need to eat and then be up and about. Perhaps Alani could show you around the Great Library. I've scheduled a board meeting after lunch. We must convince them that you need an apprentice book to take with you back to Albion."

"Will they agree?"

"I expect so, even though the board will no doubt have what seems like an endless discussion about it." He winked at her. "Remember, we're on Time's side."

An hour or so later, Maya had eaten—Alani had brought a tray to her room—and she was wearing clean clothes—black pants and a white shirt like Elspeth's.

"I suggested a skirt like mine," Alani said. "But Elspeth thought you would be more comfortable in trousers."

Despite Alani's quicksilver personality, or maybe because of it, Maya could see that the tiny woman's feelings were easily hurt. "Your skirt is really pretty," Maya said slowly. "But where I come from, our clothes are more like Elspeth's."

Alani sighed. "That's what Elspeth said." Then she brightened. "But never mind! Sydda said I could show you around the Great Library. Where should we begin? Inside or out? You can't see it all of course. It's much too big, and I'm not allowed to go beyond the third floor." But Alani, with her elbows tucked close to her side and her feet pointing outward, ready to sprint, looked as though she was going to try to show Maya as much as she possibly could. "Let's start inside, since we're already here."

What followed next was a whirlwind tour with Alani being both a whirl and a wind, as Maya would put it later. "Please slow down," Maya had to plead from time to time. Alani would say, "Sorry!" and slow down for a while. But soon enough, Maya would be hurrying to keep pace with the tiny woman, and if Maya hadn't been so sad or so tired, then it would have made her laugh.

In this way, starting from the third floor where the senior apprentices lived—Maya had stayed in an empty room not far from Elspeth's—Maya saw that floor's classrooms, offices, small kitchen, and two comfortable parlors, both of which had soft chairs, TVs, and board games.

"TVs?" Maya asked as they raced out of the senior apprentices' parlor to take a look at that floor's stacks. "I can't believe you have TVs here."

"We have everything here," Alani said, echoing Elspeth's comment about how everything worked at the Great Library.

"What do you watch?"

"Oh, lots of things from the various planets that know how to make shows and movies. From your planet, one of our favorites is *Doctor Who*. There sure are a lot of episodes."

"Yes," Maya agreed, remembering how she used to watch it week after week with her father.

The senior apprentices' stacks, in a huge bright room with bookshelves that went from the floor to the ceiling, had ladders that seemed to move on their own accord, across and up and down. Maya wanted to try one of the ladders and take a look at some of the books, but Alani hurried her on to the second floor, the junior apprentices' floor, which was very much like the third floor. Along with the stacks, parlors, and kitchen, there were classrooms and small bedchambers. They stopped briefly by Alani's room, which had bright cloth wall hangings, a collection of shells, a big vase of flowers, and a tumble of books on her small desk.

"I'm not very tidy, I'm afraid. Not like Elspeth."

Maya smiled and shook her head. "I'm not, either."

Both the second and third floors were large rectangles whose inner sides ran along an open space with big windows, and when Maya looked out one of the windows, she gazed down on a crown of leaves at the top of some big trees. Bright-colored birds flew among the branches, and when Maya looked up, she saw that the trees were enclosed by walls with windows that went up for many, many stories.

"Is that a courtyard?" Maya asked.

"Yes. Impressive, isn't it?"

"I've never seen anything like it."

Alani smiled. "Neither had I, until I came here. But let's go! There is plenty more to see."

Along the way, Maya met each floor's head librarian as well as various assistants and apprentices, junior and senior. Maya could tell by the speculative looks she got that word had already spread about her arrival. But no one asked her any questions.

"Sydda is going to speak at the noonday meal," Alani said. "He'll introduce you. Today, everybody is to eat in the Great Hall." Alani lowered her voice. "I've heard that even the retirees are going to come down, and they hardly ever leave their floors." Alani stopped, her smile bright and proud. "And Sydda let me show you around. He said I had earned it after sitting up with you for two nights in a row."

Maya put her hand on Alani's arm. "Thank you."

Alani blushed. "Oh, well, we small ones have to stick together. Even though you're bigger than I am, you're small for your kind, aren't you?"

Maya made a face. "I'm short, and I guess I always will be."

"There's nothing wrong with being short," Alani exclaimed with such vehemence that Maya laughed again, and Alani laughed with her.

Down to the ground floor they went, with its Great Hall full of long tables and chairs that would seat over a hundred people, enough room for everyone at the Great Library. The room was lit from two sides—one wall with windows overlooked the outside, and Maya caught a glimpse of blue water. The other wall overlooked the courtyard, and the light that came in was cool and green.

"Let's go to the courtyard," Maya said. "Please!"

"All right, all right," Alani said. "But you have to meet Alexander and his assistants, Ichabod, Ebenezer, and Mortimer."

The courtyard was warm but not stuffy—a slight breeze came from somewhere—and Maya sat on a bench under a large oak tree. Tall ferns grew in clumps throughout the courtyard, and moss-covered rocks lined small streams that wound through the courtyard. In the center was a rippling pool that seemed to feed the streams, which in turn fed the pool. Maya couldn't figure out how it all worked, but then again, pretty much all of the Great Library was a mystery to her. The only reason she could manage to accept any of it was because of her experience with the Book of Everything, which had completely changed the way Maya thought about not only Earth but the universe as well.

Bird song filled the courtyard. Maya sighed, and then she sighed again, but not because she was tired or unhappy but rather because being in the courtyard made her feel safe and relaxed. There was something about the feel of the place that reminded Maya of the Forest of Arden.

Alani sat beside Maya on the bench, and her feet didn't touch the ground. "I like it here, too." Alani was still, and she reminded Maya of a hummingbird at rest. "But you want to see more, don't you?"

Maya smiled, no longer tired. She was still sad, but her grief didn't feel overwhelming, the way it had earlier. "Yes," Maya replied, "I want to see more."

Before the midday meal began, Alani was able to introduce Maya to the steward, her husband, and their two children. Most important—at least to Alani—Maya met Alexander, the head librarian of the main floor. Alexander was a grave young man, short, slender, and dark, and as soon as Maya saw Alani and Alexander together, she could tell they were in love. She could feel it radiate forth from them, and she could also see it in their faces.

Alexander's assistants, Ichabod, Ebenezer, and Mortimer, were all so old that it looked as if they might crumble at any moment and blow away. "They could retire if they wanted to," Alani would say later. "But they don't want to." Despite their age and apparent fragility, each man had a fierce vitality, and their sharp, old eyes seemed to take in as much as Maya's young ones did.

All three men sat at the information desk, and Maya, Alexander, and Alani stood in front of them.

"Well," said Ichabod to Maya, "you've come a long way."

"And have lost something very dear," Mortimer murmured.

"But you still have a long way to go," Ebenezer added.

"You can see, too," Maya said.

"Yes," the three men answered at once.

"Did the Toad Queen peel your eyes?" Maya asked.

"No," came the answer, from Ichabod. "There are other ways of having your eyes peeled."

Alexander smiled. "Let's just say that children from the mainland don't get away with too much."

"Children?" Maya asked, blinking. "Mainland?"

"Why, yes," Mortimer answered in his soft voice. "This is a library. Everybody is welcome. At least on the first floor."

Maya looked around the enormous room. Along with bookshelves with many, many books, there were tables, couches, and chairs, and few of the seats were empty. Men and women, young and old, sat hunched over books, and Maya could hear the sound of children's voices coming from a side room.

"You had better take her outside," said a familiar voice. "So she can see how it is." Sydda had come out of a door in the center of the room.

"His office," Alani whispered to Maya.

Alexander nodded, and the three old men said together "Take her outside."

22: The Board's Decision

"Is the Great Library on an island?" Maya asked, squinting in the bright sun and seeing water all around.

"Yes," Alani answered. "Are you surprised? I know I was."

"I am surprised. And I didn't expect the Great Library to look like a castle, either."

Maya and Alani had just walked through the main entrance. Behind them was the Great Library, looking indeed like a castle. It had white stone walls, four towers, turrets, and a black roof.

"I thought it would be more modern," Maya said.

Alani shrugged. "Even though it looks new on the inside, the Great Library is very old."

In front of them, a narrow road led to a small village, whose buildings were also made of white stone, and there were inns, shops, houses, and streets, all built on a hill and slanting toward the ocean.

"Who lives in the village?" Maya asked.

"The shopkeepers, people who help take care of the Great Library, although some workers live at the Great Library, too.

And some of the junior and senior librarians."

"Junior and senior librarians?" Maya asked.

"Yes, the ones who decide to get married."

Maya stared at Alani. "Do many get married?"

Alani plucked at her sash, a bright purple. "Not many, but some. The ones who fall in love and who don't work on books of everything. There are lots of other jobs that need doing. Not everyone can work on books." Alani's voice was quiet. "Only a few are chosen each time from the senior apprentices. But first there are prelims, for the junior apprentices. Then, junior apprentices who pass the prelims work on practice books, which are the finals."

"And Alexander?"

Alani said, "He didn't pass the prelims. But he has other talents. He's the youngest person ever to be head librarian of the main floor stacks. Sydda wanted someone young but level-headed to work with people from the mainland. Someone polite and gentle but firm. That's Alexander!"

Maya frowned. "It must be hard to pass those prelims."

"Very hard! Not only do you have to gather information for the book, but you also have to have something else, a kind of intuition, which you give to the book. Without that intuition, the facts would just be so much data. The books have to act as guides on the various planets. Does that make any sense?"

"A little," Maya replied. "But it seems as though it should have been all set before you got here so that you wouldn't have to bother with prelims and finals."

Alani repeated what Sydda had said. "Not all things are set. Time likes to keep its options open. And then there is Chance."

"You and Sydda talk about Time and Chance as though they are alive."

"I think they are, in a way."

Maya was silent for a moment and then asked, "People who work on Books of Everything can't get married?"

Alani shook her head. "Not while they're working on books. It takes too much effort. And when they stop working on books, well, all they usually want is quiet and rest." Then she grinned. "Except for Mortimer, Ichabod, and Ebenezer. But as Sydda likes to say, they are in a category of their own."

Maya looked beyond the village to a sandbar that went to the mainland, which was some distance away. From somewhere within the Great Library came a loud chiming.

"That's to let the patrons know the tide is coming in. If they want to walk back to the mainland, now is the time to do it. Once the tide is in, you can only get back and forth by boat. Until the tide goes out again. Would you like to see what's behind the Great Library?"

"Sure," Maya answered.

A big stone terrace with chairs and tables overlooked a broad expanse of land edged by a small forest. Long, wide gardens stretched nearly to the forest, and again Maya thought of the lodge and the Forest of Arden. There were people sitting on the terrace as well as working in the gardens.

Alani asked, "Would you like to sit out here until the noonday meal?"

Maya nodded, and they found an empty table by the edge of the terrace. Maya could feel people looking at her as discreetly as possible, and she tried not to stare back. There were short people, tall people, slim people, and heavier people. Some had dark skin, some were very pale, and some had skin with hues of blue and green and red.

"I've never seen so many different kinds of people," Maya whispered.

"They come from all over the universe," Alani whispered back. "There's a lot of variation."

Maya considered this but then asked, "What about you? What will you do if you pass the prelims?"

Alani's small face was serious. "If I pass the prelims, then I will work on an apprentice book. It is my duty to try."

A loud chiming bell rang.

"Time to eat," said Alani, rising, and everyone else started getting up, too. Even the people who worked in the fields looked as though they were gathering their tools so they could be put away before the meal.

"Are you ready to be introduced?" Alani asked, smiling just a little.

Maya nodded. "And I'm ready for the board meeting, too, even though I've never been to one before. But I do have one more question."

"Just one?"

"Well, no, but just one for now. Who works in the gardens?"

"We all do," Alani answered. "Even Sydda." Then she made her voice sound like Sydda's. "It is important to work with your hands as well as your head."

Maya laughed, knowing that was just how Sydda would have said it. Alani laughed, too, and they went inside the Great Hall for the noonday meal.

The food was both familiar and unfamiliar. There were round orange vegetables that tasted like peas; dark purple vegetables, cut in rounds, that tasted like carrots; and various kinds of lettuce—one was yellow with a slight buttery flavor. There was a long red tuber with purple flesh that was a cross between a sweet potato and a regular one. Maya ate a little of everything and even took seconds of the flaky, fragrant fish, served whole on a platter.

She remembered a time, not long ago, when she hardly ate anything. That time was gone. Maya knew she had to eat, that she needed to be strong for what lay ahead, which in all likelihood would be as arduous as what had come before. "Well," she thought, "maybe not quite as hard as coming to the Great Library." That had nearly killed her. Maya really couldn't begin to imagine what lay ahead, but in the meantime, there were oddly colored vegetables and a dessert that actually looked and tasted like chocolate cake.

Maya sat at the end of a long table with Alani, Alexander, Elspeth, Mortimer, Ichabod, and Ebenezer. The room was full of people, and extra tables had been brought in so that everyone could have a seat. The steward and some of the kitchen staff circled the room as they made sure everything went smoothly.

Sydda sat at a table in front of the room, with men and women who looked as old as Mortimer, Ichabod, and Ebenezer.

"That's where we should be," Mortimer murmured.

Ichabod laughed. "With the old folks?"

"Mortimer's right," Ebenezer said. "We're all as old as dirt, after all. Just like they are."

"Maybe even older than some of them," Mortimer put in. "But we're still not ready to sit with the retirees. We might not ever be."

Just then, Sydda stood and beckoned for Maya to come to the front of the room to stand on a dais by some long windows. With her shoulders back and her head high, Maya joined Sydda, and everyone was quiet as Sydda held up his hand.

"By now, most of you know about our unexpected guest. Well, she wasn't totally unexpected. A few of us knew that she might be coming. But we weren't sure, and I suspect neither was Time. But here she is, and her name is Maya. She is from Earth, a little planet on the far edge of a distant galaxy. Don't be fooled by her size. She's escaped two very dangerous men—Chet, who is from her own planet." Sydda paused. "Then Julian, whom you all know about. And she escaped Chaos." A loud murmur, something like a gasp, filled the room, and Sydda held up his hand again. Soon it was quiet, and he told Maya's story. Hearing someone else tell it—especially Sydda, who presented it so calmly and clearly—Maya could hardly believe how much had happened to her in such a short time. But the people in the Great Hall just listened and nodded, and Maya understood that almost everyone there had come from a long distance and had had adventures, too. While their lives might not have been quite as eventful as hers, they were all at the Great Library for a reason.

"So now," Sydda concluded, "Maya needs our help if she is going to retrieve both Books of Everything. If she fails, well, I don't have to tell you what will happen if she fails. Cinnial will have two books, and the Great Library will be in dreadful danger. This afternoon, right after noonday meal, there will be a board meeting where we decide the best way to help Maya." Sydda turned to Maya. "Would you like to add anything?"

What could Maya say to all these people from various worlds who had chosen to work at the Great Library? "I see, at least a little, how things are," Maya began slowly. "I'll do my best to get both books back." An image came to Maya of Anne Hunter, and pausing, she remembered what the librarian had said. Maya continued, "On Earth, where I come from, my town's librarian told me 'Facts do matter, and with facts come knowledge.' We can't let Chet and Julian's side win. If they do, then facts won't matter at all."

From one of the tables came clapping—Maya was pretty sure that Alani had been the first to start in—and soon everyone in the room was clapping, too. As Maya blushed, Sydda turned to her and said, "Very nicely put. Now on to the board meeting."

Twelve people—six men and six women—sat at a table in a conference room directly off the Great Hall. The board members had eaten lunch in the Great Hall; they had all heard Sydda speak. Most of the men and women appeared neither young nor old except for two—a pale, frail woman who looked as though she should be a retiree (she wasn't), and a boy who looked as though he were still in grade school (he wasn't).

Before the meeting started, Sydda asked the board members to introduce themselves, and as they did, Maya caught flashes of where they had come from and things that had happened to them. But try as she might, she couldn't remember any of their names. Too many impressions were coming from them until Maya thought firmly, "Stop!" Surprisingly, the impressions did stop. The room was now just a room full of people.

Glancing at her, Sydda nodded slightly, as though in approval of her ability to control the flow of impressions. Maya heard a faint "Very good" come from Sydda, even though he didn't say anything out loud.

Then, the president of the board, a small man with dark,

curly hair, called the meeting to order. Although his face was serious, there was a slight twinkle about him that Maya liked. Sitting beside the president of the board, a tall, blue man was ready to take notes on what looked like an electronic notepad. The president began, "I call this special meeting to order at the director's request. Sydda, we all heard you tell Maya's story. We understand how serious the situation is. I'm assuming you have some kind of plan in mind. Why don't you tell us what it is?"

Sydda bowed his head. "Thank you, Galen, for coming directly to the point." Some of the board members shifted slightly in their seats, and Maya could tell by their expressions that a few of them thought that Galen had come to the point a little too quickly—especially one woman with a sharp nose, straight-cut hair, and light green skin.

But Sydda continued, "I, too, will come right to the point. My suggestion is that we let Maya choose one of the apprentices' books to take back with her to Albion. I also want to suggest that we send someone from the Great Library to go with her. I know this is breaking precedent. But the library's Book of Everything also agrees this is the best thing to do. You all, of course, are welcome to verify this for yourselves."

The woman with the pointed nose and green skin frowned and spoke up, her voice crisp and high pitched. "Surely the book offered a few other suggestions. It usually does. Send an apprentice book with a teenager? Very risky. Too risky, if you ask me."

"Yes, Margoe," Sydda answered calmly. "It is risky. And you are right. The book did offer other suggestions—all of them as risky as this one."

"Why do you think this is the best thing to do?" asked a plump man with a fringe of black hair.

Sydda hesitated. "Call it intuition, Jonah. As I mentioned in the Great Hall, Maya eluded Chet, overcame Julian, and made it to the Great Library. Some of it was because of Chance, but part of it was something else. Call it intuition again, this time Maya's intuition. And most important, she has had her eyes peeled."

The room was quiet, and Maya could tell everyone was

shocked. Finally, Astrid, the very old woman, spoke, "But, Sydda. She's so young."

Sydda nodded. "She is young, but not as young as she looks. And it was her book's recommendation for Maya to have her eyes peeled."

"That book should have known better," Margoe said.

"I had a choice," Maya said quickly. "I could have said no. But I could imagine what it would be like if Cinnial got a book of everything. If the Forest of Arden, with the Old One and the Toad Queen, was burned down. If Earth didn't have a book of everything. I know I'm young, but I'm not a child. I'm a teenager. And I had to try and help."

Again the room was quiet, and some members of the board were smiling in admiration. But not Margoe. "Sydda, the girl is brave, but I still don't like your plan. Not one bit. We have no right to send a teenager into such a dangerous situation. And with an apprentice's book! We should send someone else. That was one of our book's suggestions, wasn't it?"

Sydda leaned forward. "It was. But what Maya will see and has seen will help her both on Ilyria and on Earth. No one from the Great Library can replicate her experience, which, in the end, might very well be what tips things in our favor."

Galen asked, "Maya, what do you think about this? Do you want to go back to Albion, or do you want us to send someone else?"

Maya answered slowly, "Ever since I can remember, I could see things that other people couldn't see. Sometimes I knew what was going to happen before it even happened. Now I understand why, at least a little. Sydda has told me about the Great Library, how it is connected to all things, and how some people have an extreme sensitivity to this connection. Sydda also told me a little about Time and Chance and Chaos. I want to go back to Albion. I want to help."

Heads nodded, and a woman with gray eyes said, "This might be true. But Margoe is right. You are too young."

"But I've come so far!" Maya exclaimed, with some of her

old impatience. "And I was right about Chet, I was right about getting my eyes peeled, and I was right about Sir John."

There were several minutes of silence as the twelve trustees regarded her. Maya flushed but would not look down.

Sydda was the first to laugh, and the trustees soon joined in. Seth, the trustee who looked as though he were still in grade school, laughed the loudest. Even sharp, austere Margoe was grinning.

"I suppose you will always be somewhat impatient," Sydda would say later. "But that's not necessarily a bad thing. Sometimes, a little impatience, if applied correctly, can get things moving."

"Astrid," Sydda said when he was done laughing, "you are the eldest board member. You are even older than I am."

"It is good of you to remind me of this," Astrid said, and her wrinkled but elegant face crinkled even more as she smiled.

"I meant it as a compliment, of course," Sydda said quickly.

"Of course," came the equally quick answer. "And what do I think? It seems to me we should go along with your plan. In the many, many years you have been the director, you have never led us in the wrong direction."

"There is always a first time," Margoe snapped, no longer grinning.

"Yes, there is," Astrid answered serenely. "Nobody, not even Sydda, is incapable of making mistakes. But I think we should trust his judgment about this. And I think we should trust Maya's."

Sydda nodded in thanks. "Seth? As the youngest on the board, what is your perspective?"

Seth didn't answer right away and finally said, "I agree with you and Astrid, but I think Margoe has a point, too. As the youngest on the board, I just don't have the experience that everyone else has." Maya started to speak, but Seth held up his hand. "But I do think we should go along with Sydda's plan. One reason Maya got as far as she did is because she is so young. Chet never suspected her, and even Julian was caught off guard."

"All right, all right," Margoe said, her voice more than a little grumpy. "And who are we going to send with her?"

"Elspeth," Sydda replied.

There was a long, long silence, and even Margoe was too astonished to make a sharp retort. All the board members' thoughts and impressions were blocked from Maya, and she realized that earlier, when the meeting first began, they had been sharing exactly what they wanted to share. And what were they thinking about Elspeth that they didn't want her to know?

Astrid was the first to speak, and Maya could tell she was carefully choosing her words. "But Elspeth is still just a senior apprentice. Surely, Sydda, someone with more experience should be sent to make up for Maya's youth."

"The acorn brought Maya to Elspeth," Sydda said simply. "I believe there is a reason for this."

"Coincidence, surely!" Jonah exclaimed.

"Is it?" Sydda asked. "What makes you so certain? The acorn, guided by Time, could have taken Maya anywhere in the Great Library. To any of you. To me. But it didn't. It brought her to Elspeth."

Galen frowned. "Have you asked Elspeth yet?"

"Of course not. I wouldn't without the board's approval."

There were more questions, more discussion, some grumbling, but in the end, when the vote was put forth and seconded, Sydda's motions were unanimously approved—Maya would get to choose an apprentice's book to take with her to Albion, and Elspeth would be asked to go with Maya.

Margoe had the last word. "But I don't like any of this. Not one bit."

And who, really, could argue with her?

23: Maya's Choice

Maya lay in bed in the little room not far from Elspeth's. A window by the bed was open, and Maya could hear the swish and churn of the ocean as the tide came in. In the distance came the call of a foghorn.

"It sounds like the Maine coast," Maya thought.

For the first time since coming to the Great Library, Maya was alone, and she was so keyed up she couldn't sleep. In the morning, she would be brought to the room where the apprentices' books were kept—behind locked doors not far from Sydda's chambers. After what Cinnial had done, the director wanted the apprentices' books close by and under lock and key.

"How will I know which book to choose?" Maya wondered. "There are hundreds of them."

In between worrying about which book to pick, images of the evening meal, held on the terrace, came to Maya.

"We need a picnic!" Sydda had proclaimed. "To help send you on your way."

"A picnic," Maya thought, smiling. She could hardly believe that Sydda would want to plan a picnic when things were so serious.

That's exactly the time to have a picnic," Sydda had said. "And besides, things are always serious."

Again, the food had been familiar and unfamiliar—sweet, savory, wildly colored, and with spices that Maya had never tasted. But in honor of Maya, there had been something like barbecued chicken—the moist white and dark meat of some kind of bird, grilled and brushed with a tangy sauce.

Maya had met many of the junior apprentices—Alani's friends—and even though they were all older than Maya, they were so friendly and welcoming that Maya was completely at ease with them. All of the junior apprentices, in varying degrees, had a sensitivity to the web that connected the Great Library to everything else, and they could see things that most people could not. With a slight shiver, Maya realized she felt more at home with Alani and her friends than she had ever felt with her classmates on Earth.

"Except for Leah and Danielle," Maya thought loyally, and she suddenly wondered what they were doing. Had they sent her any messages? Her phone was on a little table by her bed, and Maya reached for it.

There were several messages from both girls.

"What are you doing?" Danielle asked. "Haven't heard from you. Are you bored?"

Leah's asked the same thing and added, "Big excitement on the island. The pres is coming for a vacation. Security everywhere. Dad grumbles but our family has been invited to a party with the pres next week. Dad's thrilled out of his mind. I'm going, too."

Maya texted back, and almost everything she wrote was completely untrue. "Not much going on in East Vassalboro. Everything is the same." Just for a touch of honesty, she wrote, "I met a boy with dark blue eyes."

Andy. What was he doing? Was he angry with her for leaving? Did he still feel guilty for what he had done? When would she see him again? Then, an unwelcome thought, with many implications: Would she see him again?

Turning off her phone, Maya set it back on the small table, and she tried to go to sleep. Instead, Maya thrashed from one side of the small bed to the other and kept turning her pillow to its cool side until there wasn't a cool side anymore.

There was a soft knock on her door. "Maya?" a voice called just as softly. It was Elspeth. "May I come in?"

"Yes," Maya answered, sitting up slightly.

The door opened, and Elspeth slipped into the room. With her blonde hair down and her white robe, Elspeth looked more like a princess than a senior apprentice.

She sat on the edge of Maya's bed. "I thought you might be worried and that you might like some company."

"Thank you," Maya said, feeling both relieved to have Elspeth's calming presence and a little foolish for wanting it.

Maya lay back down, and Elspeth rubbed Maya's back, just the way Lily had done when Maya was small and had had a bad dream.

"This all feels like a bad dream," Maya said, then added quickly. "Not the Great Library, but Chet and Julian and the stolen books."

"I know just what you mean," Elspeth replied. "I'm feeling a little worried myself. Three days ago, I thought I'd soon find out whether my apprentice book passed the finals. That with some luck, I might soon be working on a Book of Everything." Elspeth stopped rubbing Maya's back. "Instead, I'll be going to Albion with you tomorrow."

"I'm sorry, Elspeth."

"Don't be. None of this is your fault." Elspeth began rubbing Maya's back again, and as she did, she sang a song. Elspeth's voice was as high and as perfect as a flute's. Maya only vaguely understood the words—something about a proud old family who lived by the sea and who sent someone every fifty years to the Great Library. The song mingled with the sound of the waves outside, and within five minutes, Maya fell asleep.

The next morning, after breakfast, Maya stood in the middle of the room where the apprentices' books were shelved.

"Be firm with those ladders," Sydda had warned. "They sometimes can get out of hand. Especially with someone as young as you are."

"How do they work?"

"Basically, just give a command, and with any luck, the ladder will go in the direction you want. Remember, be firm."

"Can't you stay?" Maya asked anxiously.

"No, you must choose on your own with no help from anyone."

"Is there any kind of shelving order?"

Sydda had laughed. "Of course there is. This is a library Good luck, Maya. And remember, be firm with the ladders."

Then he had left, and Maya was alone, dressed in the clothes she had worn when she had traveled from Albion to the Great Library. As soon as she made her choice, she and Elspeth would go to Caxton, where the wounded Julian had taken Earth's Book of Everything.

Like all the other rooms with books in the Great Library, the shelves went so high that it made Maya a little dizzy to think about going to the top. Six ladders hovered near her by the lower shelves, but across the room, one blue ladder stood by itself, as though it were sulking. Or biding its time.

Each ladder was a different color, and this would be Maya's first choice: Which color should she pick? Red had always been Maya's color, so she went over to the red ladder and stepped on the bottom rung. The other ladders made various sounds that ranged from snarls of disappointment to huffy sighs.

The red ladder quivered as Maya stepped onto it, and before she had time to say anything, the ladder shot straight up. Screaming, Maya nearly fell off the ladder, and she frantically grabbed the sides. Her hat did fall to the floor, and Maya's curls blew around her face.

As the red ladder went up, down, and sideways, Maya soon realized the other ladders were in sharp pursuit. A green one was gaining on them, and when it got too close, the red ladder lunged sideways, knocking it back. Again Maya screamed and nearly fell. With a satisfied snort, the red ladder continued to career around the room, knocking away any ladders that came too close.

Sydda had told Maya to be firm, but all she could do was cling to the red ladder and try not to be sick. Her stomach felt so queasy from all the motion that if it didn't stop soon, Maya knew she was going to throw up.

"Stop!" Maya finally cried. "That's enough! I'm here to choose a book. Not to play stupid games with a bunch of ladders."

With what sounded like a shriek, the red ladder began to buck like an angry pony. Fortunately, it was close to the floor because Maya fell with a thud. The room became very quiet, and Maya was angrier than she had been in a long time. Jumping up, she stamped her foot and glared at the ladders, which were arrayed sheepishly around her.

The red one nudged her leg, but Maya kicked it away. "Don't touch me! Don't even come near me. What is the matter with you? This is serious. I have to pick the right book, and that's hard enough. I don't need trouble from all of you."

There was an embarrassed but sad silence, and then Maya understood. The ladders were bored. Hardly anyone came into this locked room. The apprentices' books were seldom used for reference, and Sydda had strict control over the few who came to look at them. Maya was the first new guest in a long time.

"All right," Maya said crisply. "Each one of you go to a section that you think I should see. You'll all have a turn." Maya retrieved her hat, put it on, and then shook her finger at the ladders. "But no more fooling around! I need to find a book."

The ladders sprang to attention, and with a slight clatter, they went to various places around the room, and Maya noticed these sections had books, some plain and some with patterns, that were the same color as the ladders. The blue ladder seemed to nod in approval and went to a spot across the room, to shelves with blue books.

Maya chose the green ladder. "Now go slow! I don't want to fall again."

The green ladder did as it was told. As it moved, Maya placed her hand on the spines of the various books. From some books she felt nothing, but from others she felt a little tingle. There were numbers on each book, and along with being shelved by color, they were also shelved in chronological order, with the oldest book having the lowest numbers. Maya guessed correctly that this would be the case with each colored section.

Not sure whether oldest or youngest would be best, Maya picked a book from each section, and she let her intuition guide her. Maya even got on the red ladder again. Last was the blue ladder, and there were several that Maya could have chosen, but her hand kept coming back to one with a plain blue cover. There was something about it that seemed familiar, and she finally picked that one.

Seven books were arrayed on a table in the middle of the room. One by one, Maya opened them and listened to their in-experienced but eager voices. Somehow, they knew why she was there, and each book desperately wanted to be chosen.

"After what Cinnial and his accomplices did," the Green Book explained, "it will be a way to redeem the apprentices' books."

"I suppose it will," Maya said slowly. But which book should she choose?

The Green Book was the most understanding, and Maya was tempted to go with that one. But, in truth, they all had dif-ferent qualities that Maya admired. The brown one was down-to-earth and practical; the red one was full of boisterous energy; the White Book was bright and focused; the Black Book was moody but deep. The Purple Book had such authority that Maya hesitated in front of it for a long time. Maybe a book with authority would be just what she needed.

The Blue Book was the last book, and as soon as Maya opened it, she knew what her choice would be. The book, calm yet assured, sounded so much like Earth's Book of Everything that Maya was immediately drawn to it.

"I'm sorry," Maya said to the others, who were very disappointed. "I know you'd all be good. But for some reason, the Blue Book seems like the best one."

"I'm not surprised," the Brown Book said. "After all, Earth's book and the one you picked were made by the same person."

"I didn't want to tell you," the Blue Book said to Maya. "I wanted you to make your own choice."

"That was very proper of you," the Purple Book remarked. "The rest of us are grateful. Good luck to both of you. We all know how much is at stake."

The other books echoed what the Purple Book had said, and Maya regretfully put them back on the shelves. She returned to the Blue Book, still open, on the table.

"Are you ready?" she asked.

"I am ready," came the answer.

Picking up the book, Maya closed it, and it became small enough to fit in the pocket of her trousers.

"Let's go," Maya said.

Sydda was waiting for Maya in his own private parlor not far from his bedchamber. To Maya's surprise, Ebenezer, Mortimer, and Ichabod were there as well as a slim young man wearing a broad hat. Then Maya realized that the young man wasn't a man at all.

"Elspeth?" Maya cried.

Elspeth took off her hat and gave a bow. The long, golden hair had been cut so that it came just below Elspeth's ears.

"Your beautiful hair!"

Elspeth shrugged. "It will grow back. I read a bit about Albion last night, and in Albion it is better for two traveling alone to be male rather than female."

Sydda nodded. "That's right. When it comes to women, Albion—indeed all of Ilyria—is behind the times." Sydda sighed. "Well, these things can't be rushed. We can guide, but planets must evolve in their own way."

"If they don't destroy themselves first," Ebenezer put in.

"They don't always," Ichabod said. "Many of them learn. That's why we send books."

"But it is usually touch and go," Mortimer added. "You have to admit it."

"Now, now," Sydda interrupted. "We're here to see Elspeth and Maya off and encourage them." Sydda shook his finger at the three old men. "No more pessimistic pronouncements." Then he laughed, and Ebenezer, Ichabod, and Mortimer laughed with him. But when Sydda turned to Elspeth, his face was serious. "Have you chosen a new name?"

"On Albion, I'll be Sebastian." Elspeth grinned at Maya. "It seemed like an appropriate name to go with Cesario. They're both from *Twelfth Night,* after all."

"Oh, you're a clever one," Ichabod said. "It's a pity no one in Albion has ever heard about Shakespeare."

"You have gifts for Elspeth and Maya to help them get the books back," Sydda reminded the three old men before they went off on another tangent.

"So we do," said Ebenezer. "I'll go first, and my gift is for Maya." Reaching into his pocket, he pulled out an old silver coin so tarnished that Maya couldn't see any markings on it.

As Maya took the coin, Ebenezer told her, "This is a lucky coin. I've had it for a long time. It was given to me by Chance, and it's gotten me out of a lot of tight spots. You don't really have to do anything. Just keep it in your pocket, and if there is a choice, well, the odds will be in your favor. There's no razzle-dazzle, or anything like that. Just a slight nudge in the right direction, which, even with Time on your side, you will certainly need. But don't lose it! It's extremely bad luck to lose a lucky coin. And when you are done with it, I want it back."

"Thank you, Ebenezer." Maya put the cool little coin in the pocket of her vest.

"That is quite a gift," Sydda said. "Fortunately the library has a couple of other lucky coins."

"I wouldn't have given it otherwise," Ebenezer replied.

At first Maya thought they were joking, but then she got a sense that both men were serious, that the lucky coins somehow helped protect the library.

Ichabod went next, handing Elspeth a small black case. She opened it, and inside was a pair of golden glasses attached to a chain. "Since you have not had your eyes peeled, these glasses will help you see. But take care not to wear them too long. They are strong, and it will not be the same as having your eyes peeled. If you wear them longer than ten minutes, then you might lose your vision. Forever."

Elspeth took the case and put it in the pocket of her waistcoat. "Thank you, Ichabod. I'll be careful."

Mortimer handed a small paper packet to Maya. "Inside this packet is a little mint that when eaten will take a person's memory away. Not forever, but for a long time."

"For Julian, perhaps" Elspeth murmured as Maya took the packet from Mortimer.

"Yes," Mortimer replied. "But getting Julian to eat the mint will not be easy. After all, he isn't likely to just take candy from you."

"Still," Sydda said, "it would be very useful if Julian were to forget what it was he wanted to do—from burning down the forest to taking two Books of Everything to Cinnial." Then, turning to Elspeth, Sydda leaned forward slightly until his forehead touched hers. "Good luck, Elspeth. I know you have given up a great deal to go to Albion. I also know what a challenge it will be for you."

"Thank you, Sydda." Elspeth smiled just a little. "Sometimes plans have to be changed."

Sydda patted Elspeth on the shoulder and turned to Maya. Just as he had done with Elspeth, he touched his forehead to Maya's. "You are a brave young woman. You will always be welcome at the Great Library, and the way will always be open to you." He lowered his voice to a whisper. "I took the knife from the pocket of your trousers. It only has one purpose, and it is very dangerous." Maya nodded. She had noticed it was gone, and she had been relieved not to have it anymore.

"Good!" Sydda said in a louder voice. "Now it is time for you two to be off. We'll be keeping track of your progress, of course."

Maya took the Blue Book from her jacket pocket and opened it.

"Are you ready?" the book asked.

"Ready," Elspeth and Maya said together, grasping hands.

"Take us to Caxton while Julian is still wounded from when I stabbed him," Maya said, but as she did, a small brightly clad figure bolted into the room, grabbing Maya's arm just before she and Elspeth disappeared.

"Alani!" Sydda, Ichabod, Mortimer, and Ebenezer all cried at once. But it was too late. The three were gone to Caxton.

24: On the Road

With the sun just starting to rise and the sky slowly turning from gray to blue, Andy trudged out of Greendale, on the only road out of town. He had the clothes he was wearing, the knife Sir John had given him, and a rucksack stuffed with food stolen from Lady Celia's kitchen. For that matter, the rucksack had been stolen, too, from a hook on the wall near the kitchen's back door. Andy had gotten up while it was still dark, before the cook and her helpers had risen to start the morning meal. Then, while most of Greendale was still asleep, Andy had left town.

Never had Andy felt so low, not even when his father had left. Andy had known it was not his fault that his father had gone away, and although it put him in a dark, sad mood, he had not felt guilty about it. But now, Andy felt such guilt over what he had done that it made him feel sick to his stomach, and even though he hadn't eaten since the night before, he did not touch the food in his pack. He just wasn't hungry.

Lord Owen and his men had arrived in Greendale the day before and had set up headquarters in Sir Broderick's reclaimed manor. As soon as Sir Broderick and Lady Celia had finished telling Lord Owen all that had happened—the taking of the barracks, the theft of Earth's Book of Everything, Feste's death, and Maya's disappearance—Andy had been summoned.

Andy knew he had it coming, and he knew he deserved it, but he was so shaken by Lord Owen's hard face and cold words that he could hardly reply. Andy just bowed his head and closed his eyes while the miserable guilt settled in his stomach. Finally, there was a silence. Looking up, Andy saw that while Lord Owen's face wasn't exactly soft, it wasn't quite as hard as it had been.

"Andy," Lord Owen said, "you, Harry, and Sir John did a monstrous thing. I can see that you know this and are sorry for it. Nevertheless, if you were from this world, I would banish you from Caxton. But you are not from this world. For you, banishment would not be appropriate. When and if Maya returns, and when and if your world's book is recovered, then she will want to take you back with her. Therefore, I am placing you under house arrest, of sorts, with Lady Celia. Go there and stay with her until you receive further notice."

"Yes, my lord," Andy answered, too miserable either to argue or to plead his case.

When Andy came out of the study, Sir John and Harry were sitting on a bench in the hall, waiting to be called in.

Pale and drawn, Harry didn't say anything, but Sir John asked, "Well, Andy, my boy?"

"I'm to go stay with Lady Celia," Andy managed to reply.

"Ah," Sir John said. "Yes, of course." The man's shoulders were hunched, and Sir John looked so sad and dejected that Andy felt a little sorry for him.

"Even though I shouldn't," Andy thought angrily. "If it hadn't been for Sir John, none of this would have happened."

But even as he finished thinking this, Andy knew that without his help, Sir John never would have gotten as far as he had. "You're the one that stole the Book of Everything," the clear, honest part of Andy put in. "It's just as much your fault as it is his."

"Sir John!" Lord Owen called, his voice cold and terrible. "Come in here."

Squaring his shoulders, Sir John stood and took a deep breath. All his bravado, all the boisterous energy were gone. "Here I go, Andy."

Sighing, Harry raised his eyebrows but remained silent.

Andy left quickly, not wanting to hear any of what Lord Owen would have to say to Sir John and Harry. Across the broad fields he ran, back to Greendale, to New Place, Lady Celia's house, to his room on the second floor, where he lay, hardly moving, on his bed.

Never had he felt so alone. When Andy's father had left, there had been plenty of people around to help fill the empty space—his mother, his grandparents, his aunts, his uncles, his cousins, and his friends. They all lived close by. Whenever he felt lonely, he could just walk to one of their apartments, where he was always welcomed.

With Maya gone, there was nobody in Greendale who knew him. He was on a different planet, in a different time, and if Andy hadn't felt so miserable and guilty, then he would have been overwhelmed by the panic that hovered just around the edges.

The sun began to set, and the bright afternoon light faded to a gentle glow. Slowly, as the shadows of twilight began to move in, the air became cooler, and the light in the room became dim. A servant came, knocked on the door, and told him it was time for evening meal. Andy did not move. How could he eat?

He must have fallen asleep because a sharp rap on the door made him jump. "Andy? May I come in?" It was Lady Celia, and her voice was so firm that her question wasn't a question at all.

Sitting up quickly, Andy smoothed his hair and rubbed his face. "Come in."

The door opened, and Lady Celia entered, carrying a tray. "I guess Lord Owen got his message across."

"Yeah, he did," Andy replied.

Lady Celia set the tray on a table by the bed. "It seems you will be staying at New Place for a while." Andy nodded, and Lady Celia continued, "If you are to stay in my house, then you must eat. Everybody in this household eats regularly, and I won't have any exceptions."

Lady Celia sat on a chair by the bed, and Andy understood she would not go away until he ate, which he dutifully did. Later, he could not say what the food was, whether it was hot or cold, or if it tasted good. But he ate enough to satisfy Lady Celia.

Taking the tray, she said, "We'll talk tomorrow, when you've had a chance to calm down."

As Lady Celia left the room, Andy knew he wasn't going to calm down. Not until he had somehow managed to set things right, to make up for what he had done. He couldn't bring Feste back, and Andy closed his burning eyes as he thought about the slim man's death. But the Book of Everything was another matter. Andy had stolen it, and with this action he had set things in motion so that Julian, in turn, could steal the book. Andy thought, "I need to try to get that book back."

"To Caxton!" Julian had cried before he disappeared, and Andy had heard enough to know that Caxton was the principal city in Duke Humphrey's duchy.

"And that's where I'll go," Andy thought, rising from the bed to stare out the window as night settled on Greendale. He would try to get the book back and bring it to Lord Owen, whom he had promised to serve. "Maybe," Andy thought, "Maya will be back by then. Maybe she will forgive me."

So now Andy was on the road. He had little food, no money, and only a vague notion of where he was going. Andy also had no idea how he would get the book, but he knew deep inside that he was doing the right thing.

"Julian might kill me," Andy said to himself. Even so, there was a part of Andy that believed he would somehow get to Caxton and do some good.

The sun rose, casting a glow on the trees. Birds began to sing, and the undergrowth rustled with the stirrings of small animals that had hidden in burrows, crevices, and hollow trees for the night. Andy walked on, half listening to the sounds and half rehashing all that had gone on during the past two days. Distracted, it took him a while to realize that someone was behind him in the woods, to his right, tracking him. There wasn't much sound to give it away, only the occasional soft crunch of leaves and pine needles, but even so Andy could sense that he was being followed.

Shivering, Andy wondered if maybe he had been wrong in thinking he would make it to Caxton. Instead, maybe it would end right now for him, on the road out of Greendale.

But Andy was not ready to give up when he had just barely started. Up ahead, the road curved sharply as it went downhill. Andy sprinted—he was a fast runner—and rounding the curve, he bolted into the bushes on the left-hand side of the road and hid behind a large boulder. If he peered around the edge, he could just see the road. With his hand on his knife, Andy waited, thinking, "Come on, where are you?"

But Andy was patient—he always had been—and eventually a slight figure crept cautiously around the corner. He was a boy of about eleven or twelve, with red hair. Andy wondered if the boy could possibly be alone. The boy hesitated, looking around, but nobody joined him. It seemed he was alone. A fierce look came over the boy's face, and he clenched his hands into fists.

"I know you are out there somewhere waiting to jump me!" the boy yelled defiantly, his voice surprisingly deep and husky for one so slender. "You can't run that fast."

Reluctantly, Andy grinned. The boy reminded him of an orange cat he'd once had, so feisty that every night the cat got into a fight with some other cat in the neighborhood. By the time the cat had turned two, he had the scarred and battered ears of an old-timer.

Moving quietly through the bushes, Andy made his way around the rock. The boy's back was to him, and Andy slipped out of the forest onto the road.

"Who are you?" Andy asked. "And why are you following me?"

The boy jumped straight up and whirled around to face Andy. The boy's hands were still clenched into fists, and Andy braced himself for a charge. Instead, the boy took in Andy's height and cool expression, and gradually the fists unclenched.

"My name is Simon Forster," the boy said. "I saw you leave town before the sun was up."

Andy folded his arms across his chest. "Do you usually follow everyone who leaves town?"

Simon shrugged. "Not many people leave Greendale alone before the sun's really up. I was just curious, that's all."

"Were you?" Andy asked, staring intently at Simon. "Or is there something else?

Simon shifted uneasily, not the first child to be unsettled by those deep, blue eyes. "You're Andy, aren't you?" Andy nodded, and Simon continued, "I'd heard about you, about how you'd done something wrong and that Lord Owen ordered you to stay with Lady Celia."

"Where did you hear that?"

"At the tavern. Walter, the head groom, told me."

"How did you know I was that person?"

"I know everyone in Greendale, but I didn't know you. I figured you must be the one Walter had told me about." Simon hesitated. "And now you're giving Lord Owen the slip?"

"No, I'm going to try to make up for what I did."

An odd look came over Simon's face. "You're not running away?"

"I'm not running away," Andy answered shortly. "Now you'd better head back to Greendale. I need to move on."

The boy looked down the road in the direction of Greendale. "I'm not going back."

"Why not?" Andy asked.

"I did something wrong, too. It'll only be a matter of time before everyone finds out."

"Like what?" Andy couldn't imagine what the boy could have done that would make him want to leave town all by himself. "It can't be that bad."

"Oh, yes it is!" Simon cried.

"What did you do?"

But Simon looked away, his face a stubborn red, and Andy knew that neither stern words nor stern looks would make the boy talk.

Andy sighed. "What are you going to do?"

Simon turned back, and Andy noticed that Simon's eyes were nearly as deep a blue as his own.

"I want to go with you," Simon said.

"No way!"

"I'll just follow you. You can't make me go back."

Andy shook his head, but he knew that what Simon said was true. Still, he had to try to talk Simon out of following him. "Look, Simon, I don't know what you did, but I know what it's like to feel bad about something. I understand. I really do. But you can't come with me. Where I'm going is dangerous." He lowered his voice. "I might not make it back. Go home, Simon, where it's safe."

Andy could see that his words moved Simon, but the boy shook his head. "I can't go back. Don't you see? When they find out what I did, I'll be in big trouble."

Andy stared at Simon, and Simon stared at Andy. Neither blinked for a long time, then Simon looked away. "I can't go back," the boy repeated in a soft voice.

"All right," Andy said.

"All right?" Simon asked, looking hopeful. "I can come with you?"

"Yeah, even though you should go home. You're a damned fool, Simon, to want to come with me."

Simon didn't say anything.

"You hungry?" Andy asked, wondering how long the food in his rucksack would feed two people.

"Aye," Simon answered.

"Then let's move off the road and find a place to eat. But we have to make this food last a long time. I don't have any money, and I'm not good at hunting."

Simon just smiled.

25: Simon's Story

As it turned out, Simon knew how to raid birds' nests, snare rabbits, and catch fish with a line and hook he carried in his own rucksack.

"You're pretty handy," Andy said, as they made a fire. For their breakfast, Simon had caught two large fish from a nearby stream, had started the fire, and had two sticks with pointed ends to cook the fish. Simon and Andy had made the fire quite a distance from the road, far enough so that they wouldn't be seen or heard. The trees were thick around them, and the underbrush provided even more of a screen.

"I've had to be," Simon replied. "My father died when I was little. My mother helps clean one of the big houses in the village, but she doesn't earn much. The woods are full of things to eat. You just have to know how to find and catch them."

Impressed, Andy nodded. He was smart. He knew he was. He had always done well at school, so well that he expected to be at the top of his graduating class, if he ever made it back to Earth. Somehow, when he read, things just came to him. He could make connections between books in ways that most of his classmates could not. But in the forest, with Simon, Andy had the feeling that he wasn't very smart at all, that Simon would be feeding him, when it should have been the other way around.

"What about your mother?" Andy asked suddenly. "Won't she miss you?"

"She doesn't know I've left," Simon said grimly, picturing her stricken expression when she realized he was gone.

"Why did you run away? What happened?" Andy asked, staring into the fire and at the sizzling fish. He thought that if he didn't look directly at Simon, then the boy would feel less threatened and be more inclined to tell his story.

There was such a long silence that Andy decided Simon wasn't going to tell him. But Andy didn't press Simon. Instead, he kept staring at those fish, which were beginning to smell good.

Finally, in a low voice, Simon began to talk about Addie, his mother, about how she was as thin and as wiry as he was, and how from her, Simon had gotten his red hair. Addie was hot-tempered and sometimes slapped him, but Simon was quick to tell Andy that his mother worked hard to take care of him, that it hadn't been easy when his father died. Simon described how after his father's death, his mother's small face had taken on a pinched look, and how her laughter, once more frequent than her slaps, just seemed to disappear.

With the money Addie made cleaning, they had managed to get by. But lately school fees had taken up a lot of her small salary. One night Simon watched as his mother wearily sat at their table and divided a small pile of coins into different stacks. Simon knew that the biggest stack was for school fees, which meant there wouldn't be enough for tea, flour, molasses, sugar, or cornmeal, things they couldn't hunt or grow or forage. Or bread from the bakery in town—Simon's mother certainly didn't have time to make bread anymore.

Since Duke Humphrey had taken over, none of the towns received any money for their schools, the way they had when Lord Owen was duke. Now, the townspeople had to pay for everything. The mayor—who was Oakley, also the owner of the Golden Toad—tried to keep the fees as low as possible.

"But what can we do?" Oakley had asked. "We have to pay the teachers, one for the girls' grammar school and one for the boys'. We have to get school supplies." So each student was charged, and some students had to drop out.

But not Simon. "I don't have to go to school," Simon said, sitting across from his mother. "If I didn't, I'd have more time to work at the Golden Toad, more time to chop wood and lay in a supply for winter. More time to hunt. I can read. I can do sums. What more do I need to know?"

Simon's mother paused, her hand hovering over the largest pile of coins. "I want you to finish school. You'll never be able to go to university, but at least you'll have finished grammar school. The first in our family. We all had to drop out and work." Simon's mother rubbed her eyes. "Always so many children to feed. Mama just kept having them."

"But Mama!"

"No!" Addie said firmly, raising her hand. Simon thought she might slap him, even though she seldom did anymore now that he was older. But instead his mother placed her rough little hand over his bigger one. "I want you to go to school."

Simon didn't know what to say so he remained silent, embarrassed that his mother was holding his hand, but he didn't pull away. Somehow, he just couldn't bring himself to do so.

In the weeks that followed, when there was no tea or bread, Simon brooded about all the money that went for his schooling. He brooded about it while he cleaned the stables at the Golden Toad after school. He brooded about it when he hunted and fished, and he brooded about it when he occasionally allowed himself the rare treat of standing in front of Greendale's small bakery, with its shelves of bread, rolls, and tarts so that he could close his eyes and take in the warm, yeasty smell. In truth, Simon had enough to eat, but he never had as much as he wanted, and he never felt really full. Besides, there was something about bread, soft and chewy on the inside, crunchy on the outside, and intensely satisfying.

Then there were those funny round chocolate cakes, the ones with the white filling between two layers, which he only had as a special treat on his birthday and on holidays. They fit right in the palm of his hand, and Simon was obsessed with them. He daydreamed about them in odd, spare moments when he wasn't working or at school. They were often in his mind at night before he fell asleep.

"Whoopie pies?" Andy asked.

"No," Simon said, poking a fish, which was nearly done. "We call them palm cakes."

After school, on nice days, many of the boys and girls went to the bakery to get a palm cake. Sitting on the green that separated the boys' school and the girls' school, the children would lick the white filling and nibble on the chocolate cake. Most days, Simon would hurry away from them, not looking back, as he went to the Golden Toad and to his job at the stables. But one day he stopped on the edge of the green, not far from the tavern, and watched as the children ate their palm cakes.

Simon felt a flush of anger. Why should school cost so much? Why shouldn't he have a palm cake after school like everyone else? The flush stung his cheeks and made his eyes water, and Simon turned his head.

"Those palm cakes certainly look good," a crisp voice beside him said. "I think Greendale has the best around."

Simon jumped. Beside him stood a tall, slim man with light brown hair, a large nose, and a small, almost prim, mouth. Simon recognized the man. He was Lieutenant Osborne, the second in command at the barracks, and his horse stayed in the stable at the Golden Toad. Simon just nodded and tried to slip by Lieutenant Osborne, but a hand on Simon's shoulder stopped him.

"Too bad you can't have one like the others do."

"There's not enough money," Simon said gruffly. "School costs too much."

"Yes, indeed. Very expensive. Well, we live in hard times. We all must pay more. We must support Duke

Humphrey against those rebels who want to see Lord Owen return."

Simon barely remembered what it had been like when Lord Owen was duke. He knew that most of the village supported Lord Owen, but he and his mother, on the edge of town, were too busy working to worry very much about who was in charge far away in Caxton. But Simon nodded, wanting to get away from Lieutenant Osborne.

Lieutenant Osborne smiled. "I'll see you later. Maybe I'll come by to check on my horse."

"We take good care of your horse!" Simon exclaimed. "We take good care of all the horses."

"Glad to hear it." With a soft whistle, Lieutenant Osborne turned away and headed toward the tavern.

Later that day, when Simon was nearly done with the horses, he heard that whistle again, and when he looked up, there was Lieutenant Osborne. Walter, the head groom, had gone to the tavern for his before-supper pint, and Simon and Lieutenant Osborne were alone.

Reaching into his pocket, Lieutenant Osborne pulled out something small and round and wrapped in paper. He handed it to Simon, who knew just what it was. Simon's mouth began to water, but he didn't take the palm cake.

"This is for you," Lieutenant Osborne said. "Take it. You know what it is."

"Why?" Simon asked. He stood by a small, gray dappled mare, and for support, he put his hand on her warm flank. The mare whinnied softly. Horses liked Simon just as much as he liked them.

"You look as though you could use a treat," Lieutenant Osborne said offhandedly. "However, if you don't want it, I'll eat it."

But Simon did want it, and it was all he could do to stop himself from snatching the palm cake from the lieutenant's hand. Still, Simon hesitated, sensing there was more to the offer than a palm cake.

Lieutenant Osborne continued, "Look, I'm going to level with you. We could use a lad like you, someone with sharp eyes who can be on the lookout for anything unusual." Lieutenant Osborne's free hand went into the pocket of his trousers, and when it came out, he had a palm full of silver coins. Enough, Simon realized, to pay for his school fees for the upcoming year, with plenty left over for bread, tea, cornmeal, and maybe even a palm cake or two.

With that money, he and his mother wouldn't have to struggle so much. They could eat more and worry less, and maybe that pinched look on his mother's face would go away. Without saying a word, Simon took both the silver and the palm cake.

"So you became a spy," Andy said, still staring into the fire.

There was a slight hesitation. "Aye."

The fish were done. Andy and Simon began to eat, and for a while neither boy said anything.

Andy spoke first. "You spied on your own town!" Andy knew that he shouldn't have said this, that by stealing the Book of Everything from Feste, what he had done was just as bad, if not worse. But somehow the words just came out before Andy could stop them.

Andy expected an angry retort from Simon, but instead Simon sighed. "My own town."

"Did your mother know?"

Simon shook his head. "I never told her how I earned the extra money. But I think she guessed that it wasn't from anything good. She kept asking me where it came from, and I told her it was from tips I got at the stables. But she knew it was too much."

"So what did you do?"

"A couple of nights ago, when I was working late, I saw Sir Broderick and two men go up the backstairs in the tavern. Sir Broderick is the squire of the village, and I hadn't seen him since Duke Humphrey took over. I knew something big was happening, and I was able to sneak upstairs without anyone knowing it. Some of the voices were loud, and I overheard the plans."

Andy shook his head. "We never guessed anyone was

listening. And then you went to the barracks and told Lieutenant Osborne about the attack?" Simon nodded. "But Greendale won. You don't have to feel too bad."

"No thanks to me," Simon said. "And someone found out. Maybe I wasn't careful enough. Maybe someone saw me go to the barracks. I don't know."

Nobody had seen Simon go to the barracks. Instead, it was his obsession with palm cakes that had given him away. Simon went from having a palm cake on his birthday and holidays to having one every day. Chester, the baker, noticed, and he in turn mentioned it to Walter, who was his friend.

"Has the boy been stealing money?" Chester asked. "I know he and his mum are too poor to afford palm cakes every day."

"I don't think so," Walter said slowly. "I've never known him to steal anything, and he's been working at the stables for nearly a year."

"You might want to say something to him. I'm not the only one who has noticed. Greendale's a small place."

But deliberate and taciturn, Walter said nothing. He watched, and he noted how every day Lieutenant Osborne seemed to visit his horse just when Walter left for his pint, when Simon was alone in the stables. "Oh, Simon boy," Walter said to himself. "What have you done?"

Then time suddenly seemed to speed up, giving Walter little opportunity to consider how he should approach Simon. With remarkable stealth for one so large, Sir John had crept into the village and had stayed right in the center of town, in a chamber over the public room.

"But nobody saw them come in," Walter would tell Chester. "I'm sure of it." Walter had been in the Golden Toad that evening, and the soldiers were boisterous and relaxed, just the way they always were. There was no hint of watchfulness or tension. Walter would add, "Those soldiers didn't know that Sir John was in the room above them, planning to take over the town. They found out later."

While soldiers drank and gambled in the tavern, a few men

from town went around to the back of the Golden Toad and up the narrow side stairs that led from the kitchen to the upstairs hall and the chamber where Sir John was staying. There was a quick conference, and plans were made. The men left as quietly as they had come, to gather in a barn on the outskirts of town, where other men would join them, and they wouldn't be seen. Late at night, after the soldiers had returned to the barracks, Sir John and the men had attacked. Walter had been with them, and so had Chester.

"Except the soldiers were all ready. They must have found out when they went back to the barracks," Chester said the day after the battle. He and Walter were sitting on a bench behind the bakery, and they were smoking their pipes on their midmorning break.

"Someone told them," Walter said, and Chester nodded.

Chester put his hand on Walter's shoulder. "I know you like the boy. He works hard, and so does his mum. Let's face it, Duke Humphrey hasn't exactly made things easy for them. Not for any of us."

Walter shook his head. "No, he's not a quarter of the man that Lord Owen is."

"Right now, with Lord Owen back, Feste dead, and the barracks taken, there is a lot of hullabaloo. But sooner or later, someone's going to put it together."

"The captain was killed, but Lieutenant Osborne wasn't," Walter said slowly.

"So Lieutenant Osborne's the one who got to our Simon?"

"He did," Walter replied.

"Lieutenant Osborne will talk, you know he will. Lord Owen is a just man, but no matter what happens, it's bound to go hard on Simon. The whole town will turn against him."

"You'll keep it to yourself?" Walter asked. "You'll let me take care of it?"

"Aye," said Chester. "I will."

"You always were soft on Addie, weren't you?" Walter asked

"That I was. Addie was a real spitfire in her younger days. And that smile! Don't see her smiling much anymore."

"Not much for her to smile about," Walter said, and then added. "I used to fancy her myself."

"Did you? You never let on."

"I knew I didn't have a chance with her."

Chester nodded. "Well, we both have good wives."

"That we do."

On the day after the battle, Simon had stayed home from school. He pretended he didn't feel well, not so sick that his mother had to stay with him but sick enough not to go to school. In fact, Simon really didn't feel well. His stomach was jumpy and nervous, and his head ached. He dozed in his room until midafternoon, not even getting up to eat the food his mother had left for him on the table in the little room that served as both kitchen and parlor.

When Simon did get up, he dressed quickly and ate even faster, hardly even tasting the food. He decided to go to his job at the stables. Then he could at least find out what was going on as well as earn a little money.

Walter was waiting for Simon at the stables, and the look on Walter's face was grim. "So, you decided to show up."

Simon let out a deep breath. Walter knew.

Walter came right to the point. "What you did was just plain wrong, Simon. Lord Owen is the rightful duke. You should be working for him, not against him."

Simon nodded miserably. Before he had taken the silver, Simon had hardly ever thought about either Lord Owen or Duke Humphrey, but he was certainly thinking about them now.

Walter said, "I'm not the only one who knows what you did. Chester does, too."

Simon sat down heavily on a small stool by one of the stalls. If Chester knew, then it wouldn't be long before everyone else did as well. Simon swallowed, and then he swallowed again.

Looking at the boy, Walter's expression went from being grim to being sad. "Why did you do it?"

"We needed the money," Simon said, his voice barely above a whisper.

"There are good ways to earn money, and bad ways."

"I know."

"You aren't the only one who did wrong," Walter said, a little less severely. "There's Andy, the boy who came with Sir John, and he's in trouble, too. Lord Owen has put him under house arrest at Lady Celia's. And Sir John and Harry Newton. They stole something and then pretended they had orders from Lord Owen. We weren't supposed to attack so soon. Lord Owen has banished Sir John and Harry."

"What am I going to do?" Simon asked, and he began to tremble.

Reaching into his pocket, Walter pulled out a pouch. "Here's a bit of money. Your back pay, as it were. Get out of town early tomorrow morning, before the sun is up. Make your way to Caxton. Nobody will know you there." Simon nodded. "Stay off the road. You'll have to follow it, of course, but don't be too visible. We all expect that in the next day or so, Humphrey will order the barracks in Thorndike to retake Greendale. We have people in Thorndike we can trust and who will let us know. Our pigeons can go faster than their men." Simon flushed, thinking of his own betrayal of Greendale, but Walter continued calmly, "You're good in the woods. You know how to be quiet and how to hide. They won't catch you. You'll want to go the indirect way to Caxton, through Oakton rather than through Glenridge. It's less built up, and there will be more trees for cover. The other way, through Newfield, is farming country. It's where we get our wheat. No trees that way. You got that?"

"Aye," Simon answered. "What if Greendale doesn't fall?"

"Then Humphrey will be sending more men." Walter paused. "He might even come himself. So stay hidden! There's no telling what can happen when men are on the march."

Simon shuddered, thinking of making this long journey alone. "What about my mother?"

"Do you really want her coming with you, lad?" Walter asked softly. "Do you want to put her in that kind of danger because of what you did?"

Simon shook his head slowly. He would leave while his mother was still asleep.

"That's what I thought. I'll talk to her tomorrow." Walter pulled two more things out of his pocket, a letter and a map, which he handed to Simon. "The map will help you get to Caxton. I'll go over it with you in a few minutes. When you get to Caxton, go to the Barking Dog Tavern in town. I know the head groom. I've written a letter of recommendation for you. Despite what you've done, you're a good lad, and you've got a way with horses."

Simon took the letter. "Thank you, Walter."

"And Simon, next time, think before you take money. Keep your wits sharp. You're still young, but you're old enough to know better. You're twelve, after all."

Simon stared at the dirt floor. "I will. I promise."

Walter didn't say anything, but Simon felt Walter's big hand come down on his head and give it a gentle pat. Simon didn't say anything, either. Instead he looked around at the place he had come to love, the fragrant—some would say smelly—stables with the horses—alert, bright, warm, snorting, stamping, chewing, and, yes, messing. Simon was fond of them all, and he didn't care who their owners were.

And then there was Walter, who moved so quietly and patiently among the horses that they never shied away from him or kicked him. If one of them became nervous, Walter would put his hand on the horse's back, and soon the horse would be still.

"Walter has a calming effect on horses," Oakley often said, and Simon desperately wished he, too, could have that same calming effect on horses. But he didn't. Not yet.

Then, after taking in the stables, Simon left to go home and get ready for his journey to Caxton. His head was down, his shoulders were hunched, and he didn't look back.

26: Off the Road

At Simon's insistence, they stayed off the road, but as they moved through the underbrush, they kept the road in view. The going was slower, but Simon said, "Walter thinks that any day now the barracks at Thorndike will attack Greendale, so that Duke Humphrey can take the town back."

"Walter's probably right. How will Greendale know the soldiers are coming? Will they be sending out scouts?" Andy asked, thinking of books he had read.

"Someone from Thorndike will send a message with a pigeon," Simon answered. "I've been looking out for it, but I haven't seen it. Course, in the woods like this, it would be easy to miss."

"Pigeons," Andy thought. "They're even better than scouts." Despite what had happened, despite what he was going through, Andy was beginning to love this wild, green world that was so far from the hot pavement and the tenement buildings in the South End.

Then a long silence followed as each boy was absorbed with his own thoughts. But late morning, Simon stopped, cocking his head to one side to listen. "Do you hear anything?" he whispered.

Andy was about to say no, but then he closed his eyes and listened more closely. Yes, he did hear something, and it sounded like soldiers marching. Nodding, Andy opened his eyes, and Simon pointed to a thicket of bushes a little farther into the woods. He and Andy hurried to them, and if they peered through the branches, they could watch the road but remain hidden. Soon men came marching down the road, and Andy counted them as they passed. By his reckoning, there were at least a hundred. With their leather armor and their swords, the soldiers looked formidable to Andy, and this would be one of the many times when he would wish that he had stayed in the Forest of Arden long enough for Sir John to show him how to use a sword. Beside him, Simon looked grim.

They stayed hidden until the soldiers were well past them, and even when Andy and Simon began moving, they didn't talk, staying deeper in the woods than they had before seeing the soldiers. They pushed through tall ferns with spider webs. Occasionally, a small snake would dart by their feet, disappearing without a sound into the underbrush. The day became warm, and Andy's back was sweaty under his rucksack.

Finally, when it was well past noon, Andy said, "Let's stop for some bread and cheese. It's been a long time since we've had those fish." He was still young enough to feel hungry much of the time, just the way Simon did, and they had been walking for quite a while.

"I wonder how it's going," Simon said, as they sat down.

"Don't know," Andy replied, taking out a loaf of bread. He tore off a big chunk before handing the loaf to Simon. An image came to him of Maya, Feste, Sir Broderick, and Lord Owen at the long table on that first night he and Maya had stayed at the lodge in the Forest of Arden. So much had happened that it seemed like months had passed rather than days. Andy remembered that while Sir John had been expounding on his plans to take Greendale and then move on to Caxton, at another table Maya, Feste, Lord Owen, and Sir Broderick had been planning something on their own. They just hadn't been as loud about it as Sir John had been.

Andy took a drink of water from a water skin Simon had brought and had set between them. "I think Lord Owen has a plan."

"You do?" Simon asked hopefully.

"Yeah," Andy replied. "And even though Maya is gone and Feste is dead and we attacked too soon, I bet Lord Owen is going to follow the plan."

"What kind of plan could they have?" Simon asked. "Won't they just march and attack the men from Thorndike?"

Andy, who knew his history as well if not better than Maya, shook his head. "No, I don't think they will just march and attack. From what I heard when I was with Lord Owen, Humphrey's men outnumber his men by a lot. So Lord Owen has to be careful, even if his men are evenly matched with Thorndike's men. Lord Owen can't send for reinforcements. I bet you anything that as soon as Greendale gets word, Lord Owen and his men are going to hide in the woods and attack the soldiers from Thorndike when they don't expect it."

Simon nearly choked on his bread. "That's not how it's done here."

"It is where I come from."

"Where do you come from? And who is Maya?"

"It's a long story. When we stop for the night, I'll tell you."

Soon they were done with their meal and were ready to make their way through the forest again. Looking back the way they had come, Simon said, "I wish..." Then he stopped.

But Simon didn't have to finish for Andy to know what he meant. "Yeah," Andy said. "Me, too. I'd like to be in Greendale with Lord Owen. But I have to go to Caxton. I have to try to make up for what I did."

Simon stared at him, and Andy could see the admiration on the boy's face. "I'm no hero, Simon. Don't look up to me. What I did was just as bad as what you did."

Simon didn't say anything, and his face became unreadable. But as they walked, when Andy wasn't looking, Simon sneaked glances at him. He did admire Andy. Andy was brave to leave when he had been commanded to stay at Lady Celia's, brave to strike out for a place where he didn't know anyone, with no one to help him.

Simon thought, "At least I have the letter and some money. And I'm just running away. He's trying to make things better."

Even though it occurred to Simon that Andy probably wouldn't have lasted until midmorning without him, that Andy would have stuck to the road and therefore probably would have been captured, it didn't take the shine away from what Andy was doing. In truth, it made Simon admire Andy even more.

"He is brave," Simon thought stubbornly. "Even though he won't admit it."

As the sun was starting to set, they came to Thorndike, and they crouched in some bushes on a slight rise above the village. From a distance Thorndike looked much like Greendale, only somewhat bigger and, somehow, a little shabbier. There was a main street with a tavern, where some of the shutters were broken; a green that needed scything; some shops, a few of which were boarded up; and clusters of dingy houses on side streets. The barracks was on the edge of town, and all was quiet. Nobody was on the street, and the village had a deserted look.

"It looks like everyone left town," Andy said.

Simon shook his head. "I bet some of the men who stayed behind are getting together to plan how to help Lord Owen. They are probably on the other side of town, where we can't see them. I hope there is no one here to give them away," Simon ended in a low voice.

Andy felt a pang of sympathy for Simon. Andy knew that no matter what Simon did, he would never forget how he had betrayed his town, but all Andy said was, "Come on, let's go."

Simon said, "If I'm going to try to catch some fish or set my snares, we should stop now so that I can do it before it gets too dark to see."

"Sure," Andy replied, wondering how a snare was set.

"And let's go deeper into the woods to make our camp. We don't know who is going to be on the road tonight."

"Right," Andy said.

As the setting sun filled the forest with a soft golden light, Simon took out a knife and made small marks on the trees as they went farther and farther away from the road. The boy was as alert as ever, but Andy could tell by the droop of his shoulders that Simon was exhausted. Andy was just as tired, and when they came to a clearing with a bed of pine needles and not many rocks, Andy said, "Let's make camp here for the night."

"Maybe while I'm gone, you could get wood for a fire," Simon suggested, his voice tentative, as though he didn't want to tell Andy what to do but decided he should anyway. "But just get fallen branches that seem dry."

Andy wasn't sure whether he should be irritated or amused. "I do know that much, Simon." But Simon was gone, leaving Andy by himself to gather wood. Nearby, but unseen, a bird sang, its clear notes going up and down. The song had an ethereal quality, as though some hidden, magical creature were playing the panpipes.

By the time it was dark, Simon had started a small fire with the wood Andy had found. Simon had caught two more fish which were sizzling over the fire, and he had set out his snares Simon had also gathered what looked like strawberries, which he had put in a small clean but faded cloth that he had taken from his pack.

"A feast," Andy said, his stomach rumbling as he held a stick with a fish over the fire. Simon smiled, but he kept glancing at the woods around them, and in the dim light, Andy could tell the boy was worried about something.

"What is it, Simon?" Andy asked.

"The forest is getting thinner," Simon said. "Pretty soon, we might not be able to hide as well."

"The forest is getting thinner?" Andy asked, somewhat incredulously. There were trees all around them, and to Andy, who had grown up in a tight neighborhood with few trees, it seemed as though they were in the middle of a vast forest. But when he looked closer, Andy saw that Simon was right. The forest around Greendale had a wilder, more overgrown look than this forest did. The trees were farther apart, and when Andy put his free hand out, he felt a stump where someone had recently cut down a tree. Also, and he hadn't noticed this before, the trees here seemed more like normal trees. Andy didn't feel safely enveloped by the forest, the way he had when he was in the middle of the Forest of Arden. Whatever made the Forest of Arden special seemed to be disappearing as they headed south to Caxton.

"There are stumps everywhere" Simon said. "They're cutting the forest down." Later, they would learn it was on Duke Humphrey's orders. To carry out his plans he needed money, and one way he could get more money was to sell Caxton's fine wood to other parts of Albion.

"We'll just have to move far enough away from the road so that we can't be seen," Andy said, and although Simon nodded, he still looked worried.

After the fish and the berries had been eaten, and a bit more of the bread—both Simon and Andy were still hungry and couldn't resist taking just a little more to go with the fish—Simon said, "Tell me about Maya. Tell me how you both came here."

Andy hesitated as he wondered how much he should say. Should he mention the book? Andy thought of Maya, small and dark haired, who so often followed her intuition and who was so often right, and he found himself smiling. Andy was drawn to her pretty face and lively mind, even though she was younger than he was. Quite simply, he missed her, and not only because she seemed to have an intuitive sense of what to do.

"Not long ago," Andy began, "I met a girl named Maya, and she wasn't like anyone I've ever known. She just appeared in my neighborhood one day, as though brought by magic."

"Was she?" Simon stared intently at Andy.

"In a way," Andy answered. "Look, Simon, I can't tell you everything, but I'm going to tell you a lot. But only if you promise to keep it to yourself. Do you promise?"

"I promise," Simon said solemnly.

"Shake on it?"

Without hesitation, Simon shook on it.

So Andy told Simon about Maya and the Book of Everything. He didn't go into great detail about the book, only that it had magical qualities, which included the ability to whisk readers from world to world. He told Simon about the Forest of Arden and Sir John and Lord Owen and Feste. He told about Maya having her eyes peeled. And, in a low voice, Andy told how he and Sir John had schemed to get the Book of Everything away from Feste and Maya. After that, Andy's story galloped to a finish, ending with Feste's death, Julian's theft and injury, the fall of the barracks, and Maya's disappearance.

Simon's eyes were wide. "Where did she go?"

"I don't know."

"Will she come back, do you think?"

Andy was about to say that, again, he didn't know, but a part of him felt certain that Maya wouldn't leave him here all by himself. "Yeah, I think she will. Or at least she'll try."

"And you're going to try to take the book back from Julian, who's staying in the castle at Caxton?" Simon asked.

"That's my plan."

"I don't see how you are going to do it. Steal the book from someone like Julian?" Simon's normally husky voice ended in a squeak.

Somehow, that ending squeak struck Andy as being funny, and he began to laugh. Then something broke between Andy and Simon, and they were both laughing so hard that tears streamed down their faces. They laughed until their eyes burned; they laughed until they could laugh no more, and they both lay back, gasping for breath. Andy felt light-headed but better than he had in a while, and he could tell that Simon felt better, too.

The next morning, Simon rose early to check his snares and found he had caught a rabbit.

Bringing it back to where they had camped, Simon began to skin it, and Andy watched with a horrible fascination.

Something rose in Andy's throat, and he swallowed frantically, afraid that he was going to be sick. All the meat he had ever eaten had come from the neighborhood market, behind a glass case, where Lee, the owner of the store, would take out as much as you wanted, weigh it, and neatly wrap it in white paper. Andy knew that meat came from animals. Of course he did. But he had never pictured the blood and the sinew and the shape of the actual animal as it was skinned and cut up.

"What's the matter?" Simon asked, his voice a little sharp. "Haven't you ever seen a skinned animal?" Andy shook his head. Simon stared at Andy as though he couldn't quite believe it. "I don't like doing this, but we have to eat."

"I know," Andy replied.

Soon the rabbit was on a spit, and while it cooked, Andy and Simon studied the map. While it was true that all roads led to Caxton, Andy could see that there was only one direct route, which passed through Glenridge and went straight to Caxton. Then, there were the indirect routes—the roads that went to Oakton, to the west of Caxton, and to Newfield, to the east. With his finger, Simon traced an invisible line from Thorndike to Oakton to Caxton.

"It'll add another day if we take that route," Andy said.

"Aye," Simon agreed. "But Walter told me not to go through Glenridge, and I think we should do what he said. I bet all the trees will be chopped down around Glenridge. And he said it was all fields in Newfield."

Andy frowned at the map. "I want to get there as soon as I can. We're almost out of bread, and the cheese is all gone."

Simon stared at Andy. "If the soldiers get you, then you won't be getting your book back. We don't have to have bread and cheese. We can get by on two meals."

Andy didn't say anything as he considered the upturned, freckled face and Simon's intense expression, but he knew Simon was right. This, in turn, made Andy think of Maya, who had been right about so many things, and of Sir John, who had not.

"Time to start listening to those who are right," Andy thought, even though he felt certain that Simon would go whichever way Andy chose. "O.K.," Andy said out loud. "We'll go through Oakton." And Simon sighed with relief.

"You really trust Walter, don't you?" Andy asked.

"Without him, I wouldn't have known to leave Greendale until it was too late. He gave me that map. He gave me a letter for the head groom at the Barking Dog in Caxton." Simon hesitated. "He gave me money."

"Did he?" Andy tried not to smile. "So you have money for more bread. You were planning on sharing some with me? Weren't you?" Andy teased.

But Simon answered earnestly, "Aye, I would share bread with you. But I'm not sure how safe it will be to get some in Oakton. I'm afraid someone will notice we're from away."

Andy remembered Simon's story about the palm cakes and how he and his mother didn't have enough money for bread. "Bread means a lot to Simon," Andy thought, both embarrassed and moved that the boy would share some with him.

Simon looked away, also embarrassed, and asked gruffly, "You shared yours with me, didn't you?"

For breakfast, Simon and Andy had the rabbit and half a loaf of bread. "Only half a loaf left," Andy thought as he ate, trying not to picture the earlier scene of Simon skinning the rabbit. Then, a little uneasily, Andy realized that it was a good thing Simon was with him and not just because he could hunt and fish. After seeing the marching soldiers yesterday, Andy understood how dangerous it was to be outside the forest and outside Greendale.

"I never would have gotten this far without Simon," Andy thought. "What a weird stroke of luck it was to meet him."

After their breakfast, Simon and Andy headed back toward the road. The two walked until the sun was high in the sky, and Simon figured they were halfway to Oakton. As Simon had feared, the trees were much thinner than they had been between Greendale and Thorndike, and Andy and Simon had to leave quite a distance between themselves and the road, which seemed to flicker between the trees as they walked. However, there were still enough trees to prevent them from easily being seen, which was fortunate because just as they were getting ready to find a place to have their noonday meal, they heard the sound of marching feet. Again, Andy and Simon hid in the bushes as the soldiers went by. This time there were only ten of them.

"They're patrolling," Simon whispered. "Walter said that all day long, soldiers go up and down all the roads between the villages and Caxton."

"A police state," Andy whispered back, shaking his head as he thought about how hard it was to get to Caxton, of how they had to hide and watch out for soldiers.

"What's that?"

"It's when a ruler doesn't let citizens move around freely," Andy said. "When he tries to control every part of a person's life with forces, some secret and some open."

There was a long silence as Simon considered this. "I don't really remember when Lord Owen was duke, but I've heard how different it was when he was in Caxton, how people could go where they wanted to."

There was a gleam in Andy's eyes. "We have to help get Lord Owen back to where he belongs."

Simon stared at Andy. "Won't getting the book away from Julian be hard enough?"

"Yeah, it will be hard, but we have to try to help Lord Owen, too."

"How?"

"Don't know. But let's think about it, O.K.?"

"O.K.," Simon said slowly, and Andy grinned to hear Simon use a word that was clearly unfamiliar to him.

Andy remembered that night at the lodge, when Lord Owen had told the people how Humphrey planned to burn down the Forest of Arden. And Andy remembered what Feste had said about those who had not come to the Forest of Arden: "Some stayed so they could help us when the time is right."

"There's a resistance. And we'll join it," Andy said, a little grandly.

"What?"

"We'll join the ones who are against Duke Humphrey. I bet you there are some in Caxton who are on Lord Owen's side."

"Aye," Simon replied. "Walter told me there are some in every town, including Caxton."

"Well, then," Andy said, and his blue eyes gleamed even brighter.

Something stirred in Simon, something akin to hope. Part of him was afraid, but another part of him wanted to join the resistings, or whatever Andy had called it. If he did, and somehow Lord Owen became duke again, then Simon thought that maybe he could go back to Greendale and live with his mother and work with Walter again. Maybe the people in town would forgive him for what he had done. Then another thought came to Simon. If Maya didn't come back, then maybe Andy could come live with him in Greendale. Simon had always wanted an older brother, someone who was just like Andy—calm, smart, and patient—someone who could study the situation and make plans and wasn't afraid to act. True, Andy had made his share of mistakes, but he was doing all that he could to set things right.

And even though Simon knew he was going into danger, for the first time since leaving Greendale, Simon felt as though he could breathe again.

27: The Resistings

All that day, soldiers marched up and down the road, and Simon and Andy had to be constantly alert, hiding whenever they heard the sound of marching feet. By this time, the forest by the road had become so thin that hiding was difficult. It was only Simon's sharp ears and vigilance that prevented them from getting caught, and more than once they had to make a run for it to the receding trees and bushes.

"We might as well have gone through Glenridge," Andy grumbled.

"There are quite a few trees left here," Simon said loyally, in Walter's defense. "More than around Glenridge, I bet."

"Maybe," came Andy's short reply.

Simon didn't say anything, but he wondered how long it had been since Walter had been out of Greendale. He couldn't remember ever seeing Walter leave town. "I bet it has been a long time," Simon thought. Maybe before they had started chopping down the trees. Simon shifted uneasily under his rucksack. What else didn't Walter know?

When the sun began to set, Andy and Simon left the side

of the road and went far into the woods to make camp, and Simon made his little slashes on the trees. They followed their routine from the previous night. While Simon foraged for food and set his snares, Andy collected wood for the fire. Andy even laid it so well that when Simon came back with some kind of bird he had downed with a slingshot, he looked at the pile of wood, arranged a stick or two out of habit, but pretty much left it as Andy had laid it.

"I'm learning," Andy said, and Simon smiled.

Then came a chopped head and a flurry of feathers. Yet again, Andy's stomach heaved, but not as violently as the night before. Andy supposed that if he stayed in this world long enough, he might eventually have a strong enough stomach so that he could skin a rabbit or pluck a bird. Simon had also brought back some mushrooms and some little tubers, which he sliced thin. The bird on the spit began to sizzle, and fat dripped into a frying pan Simon had placed beneath it. When the bird was nearly done, Simon used his handkerchief to move the pan. After draining some of the fat, Simon fried the mushrooms and tubers in the remaining fat. Never had a meal tasted so strange or so good, and Andy wished they had some bread left so they could sop up the browned bits and the fat in the frying pan.

But their bread was gone—they had eaten the last of it for their noonday meal—and this meant that tomorrow they would have to stop midday so that Simon could hunt. Or they would just have to wait until evening and only have two meals that day.

Andy's mother didn't earn a lot of money, but she had always made enough to buy plenty of food, treats as well as vegetables and meat. Andy had never had a hungry day in his life, and he didn't much like the idea of skipping a meal.

Andy wondered if he could convince Simon to go into Oakton so they could buy some bread. He glanced at Simon, stretched out by the fire, and the boy, as always, was alert but also relaxed. Andy decided he would try. Bread was not the only thing he was interested in. Simon had said there were men in every town who were on Lord Owen's side. Perhaps he could connect with some of them, which might, in turn, help him when he got to Caxton.

Andy decided to begin with flattery. "That sure was a good meal."

"Aye," came the reply. "I was lucky to get that bird. Could have used a bit of salt, though. And pepper, as well, for that matter."

"Those mushrooms and white things were good, too."

"They're called groundnuts."

"Groundnuts," Andy repeated. "I've never had anything like them."

Simon didn't respond, and Andy wondered what Simon would think of some of the things he and his mother ate—Spam, bread so spongy that a slice could be rolled into a firm ball, and creamed-style corn. This brought him back to bread.

"Simon," Andy began, "we ate the last of the bread today."

"I know."

"What do you think about going into Oakton, very early, to get some from a bakery? Oakton must have a bakery, if Greendale has one."

"Aye, I expect Oakton has a bakery."

"Well, what do you think?"

"I'm afraid we'll get caught." Simon was still lying by the fire, but he no longer looked relaxed. "Oakton is bigger than Greendale, but the baker will know we're from away."

"We can make up a story so that the baker will be on our side."

"What kind of story?"

"The truth, kind of. That we're on our way to a job at the Barking Dog that Walter's arranged for you."

"Why would I leave my village?"

"Because you'll make more money at the Barking Dog, and there's more room for advancement," came Andy's prompt reply. "Then, you'll have more money to help your poor widowed mother."

"What about you?"

"I'm an older cousin, and I'm going with you so that you won't have to travel alone."

"That is a good story," Simon admitted slowly.

"And there's some truth to it. We just don't have to tell the whole of it."

"Do we really want bread that much? Soldiers might catch us and either make us join them or take us prisoners. Then what would we do?"

Andy paused. "It's not just the bread. I'm hoping we can meet some of those men who are on Lord Owen's side. They might know people in Caxton who can help us, and the baker would be a good person to start with."

"How would you do that? You can't just come right out and ask."

"No, of course not. But there are ways of leading a conversation that can give you an idea of how a person is leaning."

And Andy, actually, was quite good at this. When a friend's father had been running for state representative, Andy had worked on the campaign. In the South End, Andy had gone door to door to hand out fliers and to talk about his friend's father. Andy's dark good looks, his friendliness, and his ability to make small talk had gotten him into the homes of some of the crankiest old men and women in the neighborhood. While Andy had talked, he had listened, too, and had learned quite a bit. His friend's father had won, and he claimed it was because of the votes he had gotten from the South End.

"It would be dangerous," Simon said.

"My whole plan is dangerous," Andy replied. "And I could really use some help when I get to Caxton. You got me this far, and without you, I would have been caught. But in Caxton, I'll need a different kind of help. That's why I need to join the resistance."

Simon was silent as he considered what Andy had said. He realized Andy was right. While Simon could keep Andy safely hidden in the forest and hunt and forage for food, Simon knew he would not be as useful when they got to Caxton, where he didn't know anybody.

"All right," Simon said. "But we go before the sun rises, before the soldiers are on patrol. The baker will be at the bakery. Bakers get up early."

Simon was right. The baker was not only up, but with a long paddle, he was pulling hot loaves of bread from a brick oven. Andy and Simon had gotten up early, followed the road while keeping a safe distance from it, and had crept around the back of the buildings on the main street. The houses and shops were in even worse repair than they had been in Thorndike, and the whole town had a hunched, gray look, as though the buildings hadn't been tended in years. But baking bread smells good no matter where it is baked, in a prosperous town or in a poor one, and Andy and Simon had followed its tantalizing smell to the bakery.

The baker was a young man, lean and muscular, with dark curly hair and slight lines that crinkled around his eyes. He glanced at Andy and Simon as they stood in the doorway.

"You two are up and about early," said the baker.

"Aye," Andy said, adopting one of Simon's words. "We're on our way to Caxton."

The baker paused. "Are you?" He raised his eyebrows. "An exciting place to be right now. Where are you from?"

"Greendale," Andy said.

The baker carefully removed the last of the bread and set the loaves on racks to cool. "Greendale," he repeated, staring hard at Andy and Simon. "Now that's an exciting place, too, from what I've heard."

Andy had been ready with the story about the Barking Dog and Simon's poor widowed mother, ready to nudge Simon into telling it, but something about the baker's expression and his careful questioning led Andy to believe that they could speak frankly.

"Aye," Andy said again. "Lord Owen has taken Greendale."

The baker's voice was soft. "Now why would two boys be out and about when a great battle is brewing?"

"Something was stolen, and we need to get it back."

"And it's in Caxton?"

"It's a book, an important one."

The baker and Andy sized each other up, and the baker nodded. Then he turned to Simon. "Do you speak?"

"Aye, I speak," Simon answered gruffly.

The baker grinned. "Just wondering. You two hungry?" Both Andy and Simon nodded emphatically. "How about some warm bread and butter and some hot tea?"

"Sounds great," Andy said.

"I can pay," Simon put in.

The baker shook his head. "For two lads from Greendale, breakfast is on me."

Andy and Simon exchanged guilty looks, but they followed the baker into a small back room that had a table, a few chairs, and a small fireplace with a kettle of simmering water. From a cupboard, the baker took out three mugs and three plates. Soon the mugs were filled with hot tea, and there were thick slabs of buttered bread on each plate.

Andy had never really liked tea, but in that little back room behind the bakery, Andy thought it was the best drink he had ever tasted, and from then on, tea was what he drank in the morning, if he could get it, and during the rest of the day as well. As for the bread and butter—Andy and Simon went through four slices before they finally sighed and pushed their plates aside.

The baker, who had eaten only two slices, gave them a stern look. "Now that your stomachs are full, let's talk a little about your plans. But first things first, I'm Guy LaPlante. And you are?"

"Andy Murphy" and "Simon Forster" came the two replies.

"There, we have names," Guy said, smiling just a little. But the smile was soon gone. "Do you have any idea how dangerous it is out here?"

"Of course we do!" Simon retorted. "There are soldiers every-where, and so many trees have been chopped down that it's hard to hide."

Guy stared intently at Andy and Simon. "If you think it's bad here, just wait until you get closer to Caxton. Everyone is supposed to have papers now, from the mayors of their towns, giving them permission to travel. At Caxton, there are guards at the city gate, checking everyone's papers. And if you don't have them, then the guards will find out why, and their methods aren't gentle."

"See?" Andy said to Simon. "I told you it was becoming a police state."

Guy gave Andy and Simon a quizzical look, and shrugging, Simon shook his head. "You're not from Albion, are you?" Guy asked Andy. "You have an accent. And the way you talk is different."

"No, I'm not from around here. I'm from away." Very far away, Andy might have added, but he didn't.

"And neither of you have papers, do you?" Both Andy and Simon shook their heads.

"We didn't know we needed papers," Simon replied gravely.

"No, I suppose you didn't," Guy said. "It's a recent decree that came out a few days ago, around the same time that Greendale was taken. Humphrey isn't taking any chances as he gets ready to go into battle against Lord Owen."

"You're on Lord Owen's side, aren't you?" Andy asked, desperately hoping he hadn't misread the baker. But he had to know for sure.

"Aye," Guy answered. "I'm for Lord Owen. The duchy of Caxton used to be the most prosperous one in Albion. Then Humphrey took over, and he takes, but he doesn't give back. There's no money for school or roads or even a fire department. Every town is on its own. We get nothing from Caxton anymore, the way we did when Lord Owen was duke."

"That's why school is so expensive," Simon put in.

Guy nodded. "All Humphrey cares about is building an army. That's where the money goes, and he's draining the duchy dry, chopping down its best trees. Rumor has it that after Humphrey defeats Lord Owen, he plans to take all of Albion And what about you two? Whose side are you on?"

"Lord Owen's," Andy answered.

"Both of you?" Guy asked.

"Both of us," Andy replied. "And we need to get to Caxton."

"Have you been listening to me?" Guy asked. "It's a miracle you got this far. You'll never make it to Caxton."

"I have to try. If we get that book back, then it will be a big help to Lord Owen," Andy said with that quiet dignity he had.

"The book is magic," Simon added.

"Magic," Guy muttered, rubbing his face. "All right. I'm going to bring you someplace where you can get some help. It'll take us a while. I'll get my wife to run the bakery. Lucky for us she's a quick thinker who doesn't need to ask too many questions before she gets the point. She'll cover for me and will tell the customers I'm sick."

"Thank you," Andy said.

Guy shook his head. "You're welcome, but don't be too grateful. You're not in Caxton yet."

Guy's wife had shining auburn hair, and she understood the situation just as quickly as Guy had predicted.

"Be careful," she said before they left, giving Guy a quick kiss.

"I'll be careful. I always am."

"Thank you," Andy said to Guy's wife, who nodded but didn't smile.

It was still early enough so that few people in town were up. Nevertheless, Guy was cautious, leading Andy and Simon through back streets that brought them to the edge of town, to a farmhouse with a big barn. To Andy's surprise, Guy took them into the barn, where a large man with blond hair was milking cows. He was about the same age as Guy, and he looked up from his milking.

"Good morning, Guy," he said cordially.

"Good morning, Eben," Guy said.

"You taking these boys to the hideout?" Eben asked, as casually as if he were asking Guy how much milk he wanted to bring home to his wife.

"I am," Guy replied.

"They're kind of young, aren't they?"

Guy shook his head. "You could say that."

"I just did."

"We can't help how old we are," Andy said.

"I guess you can't." Eben turned to Guy. "You sure this is a good idea?"

"No," came the answer. "But if I don't take them to the hideout, then they'll just go off by themselves to Caxton. They're looking for a book that was stolen."

"A magic book," Simon added quickly.

Eben scratched his head. "A magic book. Well, I guess they should go to the hideout."

"That's what I thought," Guy said.

Eben stopped milking, patting the cow on her side. He moved the bucket of milk out of kicking range. "All right, then."

He and Guy walked to a stall that was filled with harnesses, yokes, pails, rakes, and shovels. At the back, on the wall, in the upper-left-hand corner was a large hook with a harness hanging from it. Removing the harness, Eben pulled on the hook, and the wall swung open to reveal stairs going down into darkness.

"I don't know what the situation is at the hideout," Eben said. "I haven't seen anyone for a day or so, but I expect things are happening fast now that Greendale and Thorndike have fallen. As far as I know, everyone is still there. But they'll be making their move soon."

Andy and Simon looked at each other. "Thorndike has fallen?" Andy asked.

"Aye," Eben replied. "Lord Owen and his men hid in the forest and took the soldiers from Thorndike by surprise."

Andy nodded. "That's what I expected he'd do."

Both Guy and Eben gave Andy an appraising look, but there was no more time for questions. From a bracket on the wall in the stairway, Guy took a torch and lit it.

"Be careful," Eben said. "We can't afford any mistakes. Not now."

"I know," Guy answered. "We'll be careful."

"When you come back, stop by the house if I'm not here. So you can tell me how things went."

"I will," Guy said.

With Guy in the lead holding the torch, the three went down the stairs. Behind them, the wall clicked shut, and the flickering light revealed a long darkness at the bottom of the stairs, a darkness that resolved into a tunnel.

"Where does this go?" Andy asked. The air was damp and close, and the tunnel smelled like musty dirt. The ceiling was so low that Andy had to stoop, and along with the dark, this gave him an uncomfortable, closed-in feeling.

"To the forest," Guy answered. "To the hideout, where we can gather without being seen or heard. A place to stay if Humphrey has issued a warrant for your arrest."

"How long is this tunnel?" Simon asked, putting out his hands to feel the cool earth and the wooden supports.

"Long," came Guy's answer. "But when Humphrey took over, we knew we would need it. We knew we'd have to be able to go back and forth without being seen. Especially with the woods getting chopped down. That Humphrey's a great one for taking our wood."

Enveloped by the glow of the torch, they walked, and Andy lost track of time. He couldn't wait to get out of the tunnel, and it seemed to him as though they would never reach the end. But eventually, the tunnel began sloping upward, and they came to a large opening that was covered with branches. Guy pushed them aside, and they stepped out into the middle of a forest, not quite as deep and wild as the Forest of Arden, but deep enough so that few of the trees had been chopped down.

"This is better," Simon said, as he and Andy helped Guy

cover the hole. He shook his head. "Not like the forest between Thorndike and Oakton."

"Aye," Guy replied. "Humphrey hasn't got this far. Not yet."

They walked for a while longer, until the sun was overhead, but it wasn't yet noon. Both Andy and Simon were hungry again, and each boy wondered silently what kind of food would be at the hideout. Finally they came to a clearing with a huge log building that had a massive stone chimney. The windows not only had shutters, but glass as well.

"Here's the hideout," Guy said.

Andy whistled. "That's some hideout."

Pleased, Guy grinned. "A lot of us worked on it, and we even smuggled in glass for the windows. Good thing, too, because some of the men have been living here for four years."

"It's a little like the lodge in the Forest of Arden," Andy said. "Except it's not made of stone."

"In a way it is. But not as big. From what I've heard, there's a real community at the lodge now."

"Yeah," Andy replied. "Lord Owen knows how to run things."

"Let's hope Lord Owen can return to running things," said Guy.

As they approached the hideout, two men with bows and arrows came from behind trees. Their arrows were drawn, but they were pointed downward, and Andy knew that if he and Simon hadn't been with Guy, then they would have been in serious trouble. "Of course," Andy thought, "without Guy, we never would have known how to get here."

"Sion. Ifan." Guy nodded to the men. "Is Rhys in?"

Sion, who was tall with ginger-colored hair, said, "He just got back from Thorndike, but he's in, all right. In the thick of plans." He shook his head. "If we pull this off, well, it will be one for the books."

"It's a bold one," Ifan put in. He was shorter than Sion.

"A new plan?" Guy asked.

"Aye," Sion answered. "Two of Rhys's friends have joined us."

"How did they get here? Eben didn't mention anybody new."

"They met Rhys in Thorndike and came the back way with him." He nodded at Andy and Simon. "Aren't you two a little young to be coming here?"

Simon flushed. "We might be young, but we made it to Oakton from Greendale, and the soldiers didn't catch us."

"Not an easy thing to do right now," Guy put in.

"No, it isn't," Sion answered, his voice serious. "Well, go on in. They'll be happy to see you. We're always happy to see the one that makes our bread."

Grinning, Guy led the way to the log house, with Andy and Simon right behind him. The day was warm, and all the windows were open. Laughter and a booming voice came from inside, a voice so loud and familiar that Andy could hardly believe what he was hearing. But when Guy opened the door, Andy saw an enormous woman wearing a white bonnet and a green dress with enough material for three normal-sized women. Lifting her dress to reveal a white slip, flicking her head from side to side, the woman was prancing back and forth in front of a group of men, who were sitting around a large table. The men were laughing. Guy began to laugh, too, and Simon joined him.

But Andy didn't laugh. He just stared at the large figure, not wanting to believe what he was seeing. "Holy shit!" he finally said under his breath.

Glancing in Andy's direction, the woman stopped prancing. "Andy, my boy! You've found us. Come in, come in!"

28: At the Hideout

"Sir John," Andy said, and there came a rush of feelings so contradictory that Andy wasn't sure whether he wanted to punch the big man in the stomach, hug him, or run back out the door.

"You know this person?" Guy asked, and beside him Simon stirred uneasily.

"I know him all right. I was with him in the Forest of Arden, and I was with him in Greendale."

"A man," Guy said. "Of course."

Andy saw Harry Newton sitting at the table. Harry was looking at Andy, and shrugging, he rolled his eyes.

Andy thought, "What now? What is Sir John planning? He never gives up."

Aloud, Andy said in a cool voice, "Hello, Sir John."

"You're quite the resourceful one to find a way to this hideout," Sir John replied jovially, but there was a sharp undertone to his voice as he regarded Andy's stiff figure.

A short man with dark curly hair stood up. He had a thick powerful body and an expressive face.

"Rhys," Guy said, "I've brought two boys who are intent on

getting to Caxton. I figured you'd be able either to help them or stop them."

Both Andy and Simon stared reproachfully at Guy, and the room became very quiet.

Rhys frowned, but his voice was not unfriendly. "Their names? And why do they want to go to Caxton?"

"Andy Murphy and Simon Forster," Guy said, pointing to each boy. "They say a magic book was stolen from them, a book that might help Lord Owen. They want to get it back."

Sir John looked intently at Andy, but for once he didn't say anything. Rhys's eyes were narrow. "A magic book, you say?"

"No, that's what they say," Guy replied.

Rhys grinned reluctantly. "And you believed them?"

Guy hesitated. "We've all heard stories of a special book that's been in Caxton for years and years. A book that can guide and provide much information. As far as we know, Humphrey has it, and the book is still in Caxton."

"The book I'm after is not the same book, but it's similar," Andy said. "It comes from my land, and it was stolen from me by a man named Julian, who's with Humphrey in Caxton."

Suddenly the room wasn't quiet anymore as everyone began to talk at once. But all Rhys had to do was hold up his hand, and everyone was quiet again.

"We know who Julian is," Rhys said. "When he came to Caxton, things got even worse than they were when it was just Humphrey. He's smarter than Humphrey and more dangerous."

"He is dangerous," Andy agreed. "But he's also wounded."

Again there was excited chatter, and again Rhys held up his hand.

"And how do you know this?"

"Because I was with him in Greendale when it happened," Andy replied. "Julian has his own book, which helps him travel in an instant from place to place."

Rhys nodded slowly. "That would explain why nobody in Caxton has seen him these past few days. Usually, wherever Humphrey goes, Julian goes too." Rhys was smiling. "Aside from Greendale and Thorndike going back to Lord Owen, that is the best news I've heard in a long time. Guy, you did the right thing bringing them here."

"I couldn't just let them go on their own to Caxton."

"No, you couldn't." Rhys looked sternly at Andy and Simon. "I'm not promising anything, but I will consider how you might get safely to Caxton."

Andy was about to argue, but Guy squeezed his arm, and Andy remained silent. Men from the table began getting up, and Rhys motioned for Guy to join him. Andy was about to follow Guy when he felt a big hand on his shoulder.

"Andy, my boy," Sir John said softly. "We need to talk."

"Yeah, we do," Andy said, shrugging away from the hand.

"We'll go upstairs," Sir John said. "Everyone's down here. We'll have some privacy." He motioned toward Simon. "What about this one?"

"Simon pretty much knows about everything that's happened," Andy replied.

"He might as well come, too." Sir John's expression was sympathetic. "It won't be much fun for him to stay down here alone."

Andy felt himself softening toward Sir John. But by the time they had climbed the stairs and entered a large loft with so many wooden cots that it looked like a barracks, Andy felt resentful as he thought about Sir John prancing in the green dress. They made their way to a cot that must have been Sir John's because the big man sat down on it. Andy and Simon settled on the floor beside the cot as Sir John removed the white bonnet and laid it on the bed.

"What were you doing down there?" Andy asked. "Have you forgotten what happened so soon that you could put on a woman's dress and prance like an idiot?"

Simon gasped, and even Sir John was taken aback by what Andy had said. But instead of bellowing, the way Andy expected he would, Sir John leaned forward and said in an intense, soft voice, "I will never forget what happened in Greendale. Not for as long as I live. I am not dressed like a woman for the fun of it. It is part of a plan Rhys and I have devised."

Andy swallowed. "Do Rhys and his men know what happened in Greendale?"

Sir John shook his head. "They don't know the whole story. I've only told them bits and bobs."

"They don't know we've been exiled," a voice behind them said. It was Harry, and he sat on a cot across from Sir John. "They don't know how Feste died, and they don't know how we stole the book, disobeyed orders, and took Greendale when we weren't supposed to." He sighed, and there were lines of fatigue on his face.

Sir John said, "It's been too chaotic for word to spread and a good thing, too. Otherwise when Harry and I met up with Rhys in Thorndike, he never would have taken us here."

"And why did you want to come here?" Andy asked.

"Why do you want to go to Caxton?" Sir John countered.

Andy plucked at his trousers. "What I did was wrong, and I want to get that book back."

Eyes glittering, Sir John stared at Andy. "Do you think you're the only one with a conscience? Do you think you're the only one who wants to set things right? One was like a brother and the other was like a son. One is dead by my own hand. The other is gone from me. He will never forgive me."

Andy sighed. "All right. But why did you have to look like you were having so much fun?"

Sir John wiped his eyes and smiled just a little. "Things are pretty serious around here, and in the upcoming week, they're going to get even more serious. It seemed to me the men could all use a laugh. Even got one from old Harry, who hasn't done much laughing lately."

Smiling, Harry shook his head.

"What's the plan, then?" Andy asked. "Are you going to try to get into Caxton dressed like a woman?"

Sir John nodded. "That sums it up neatly."

"What are you going to do when you're there?"

Sir John leaned forward and so did Harry, as though they were afraid someone from Caxton was going to hear them. "Soon, Humphrey will be marching on Thorndike and Greendale, to try to take back the two towns. He'll leave some men behind, of course, but most will go with him."

"A perfect time for us to strike," Harry put in. "Sir John and I will get in first. We'll be driving a cart where Rhys and a few of the men can hide under a false bottom. We have a place where we can stay in Caxton. Meanwhile, the rest of Rhys's men will be waiting in a deserted barn just outside town."

Sir John said, "Come nighttime, when the bell strikes twelve, we'll take the two gates, the town's and the castle's, and let in Rhys's men. With any luck, and with help from those in Caxton who are on Lord Owen's side, we'll take Caxton for Lord Owen."

"With a lot of luck," Andy replied. "But it's a good plan. Humphrey will be divided. That's the time to attack."

"That's what I thought." Sir John modestly smoothed the wrinkles from his gown. Then he looked at Simon, who had been silent the whole time. "And where do you fit into the scheme of things? Are you guilty of something, too?" It was meant as a joke, but Simon's face turned red, and he looked down at his hands.

"Ah," Sir John said, waiting for Simon to speak. But Simon remained silent. "Can you at least tell me why you were headed to Caxton?"

"To get a job in the stables at the Barking Dog," Simon answered. "I have a letter from Walter, the head groom at the Golden Toad, in Greendale. He's recommended me."

Sir John's expression became sober, and Harry shook his head. "Sorry to have to tell you this, Simon, but the owner of the Barking Dog is dead, and so is the head groom. Humphrey found out there was going to be a meeting there, with men who are loyal to Lord Owen. Humphrey had them all executed."

Simon put a hand to his face. "But what am I going to do now?"

Andy patted Simon on the shoulder. "You'll stay with me If we can get the book, well, then you won't have anything to worry about."

Simon's expression was solemn. "Walter didn't know."

"No way he could have, really," Sir John said. "It happened right before Greendale was taken. We just heard about it ourselves from Rhys."

"I bet Julian had something to do with this," Andy replied.

"I expect you're right," a voice said. "Julian has been behind a lot of things." It was Rhys, who had come up to the loft, and Guy was beside him.

"But Julian is wounded," Harry said. "This means there is no better time for our plan."

Guy said, "Chance is favoring us right now. Let's just hope it continues to favor us." He looked at Andy and Simon. "I'll be off now. You're in good hands with Rhys and his men."

Andy stood, and Simon did as well. They walked over to where Guy and Rhys were standing. Andy held out his hand, and Guy shook it. "Thank you, Guy, for everything you've done to help us."

Simon held out his own hand. "If you hadn't helped us, we would have been caught."

"And tortured," Rhys added grimly.

Guy shook Simon's hand. "Well, none of that happened. Glad you two came to the bakery first. Stop by anytime." To Rhys, he said, "I'll let you know as soon as Humphrey and his men are past Oakton."

"We'll be waiting," Rhys replied.

With a wave of his hand, Guy left, going lightly down the stairs. Rhys turned to Andy and Simon. "You boys sure you still want to go to Caxton? It would be safer to stay here."

"I'm sure," Andy replied, and Simon nodded.

"All right, then. Sir John, how would you like to have two grandsons? And Harry, that would mean you have two sons."

Sir John laughed. "Nothing would please me more."

"Good. I'll have Carwyn get their papers ready tonight. He's good. So far, no one has got caught using his papers. But now it's time to eat. There is bean stew and cornbread and strawberry crumble. You two hungry?"

Andy and Simon nodded, and Sir John said, "Of course they're hungry. Am I right, Andy, my boy?"

"Yeah," Andy said, smiling. "You're right." He felt the big man's hand come down on his back and give him several affectionate thumps.

29: Reunion

A wagon pulled by two large brown horses went down a road that a day earlier had been crowded with marching soldiers. A large woman with a white bonnet and a green dress sat in the front of the wagon, and beside her sat a younger man holding the reins. The wagon was tall and open, and in the back, sitting among wooden boxes, kegs, and baskets were two boys, one tall with dark hair and the other smaller with red hair.

"No patrols on the road today," the woman said.

"The soldiers have either made camp outside Thorndike or have been left behind to guard the city."

The woman glanced behind her in the wagon. "It's a pity. If we had known for sure, well, it would have been a much more comfortable ride for some of us."

"Aye," the man replied, "but better safe than sorry. We're not far from Caxton."

The big woman fidgeted. "You two back there still have your papers?"

"Yeah," said the taller, dark-haired boy—Andy. "You've probably asked me twenty times. The answer is always the same."

The woman—Sir John—was about to say something when suddenly they came across three travelers on foot—a fair, slender young man, a dark-haired boy, and another small boy with short blond curls and dressed in such bright clothes that he looked like a tiny clown. They were grouped by the side of the road, and they were arguing.

"You must go back," the fair young man said sternly.

"I want to go with you two," the little boy said, trembling. "Please don't bring me back."

The older boy—who seemed to be consulting a small, blue book—spoke, "Why can't you be more definite? And where in the world are we?"

"You're on the road to Caxton," Sir John said pleasantly. The wagon had come to a stop. "You're about a mile away, but when you go around the bend and to the top of the hill, you'll see our fair city."

Jumping, the three looked at Sir John. They had been so engrossed in their argument that they hadn't noticed the wagon.

"Lord almighty," Sir John said. "Is that who I think it is?"

"Maya!" Andy called, jumping up and springing from the wagon.

"Andy!" came the reply, for it was indeed Maya.

They ran to each other, and Andy grabbed Maya, hugging her fiercely. And then, to everyone's surprise, especially Maya's, Andy kissed her on the lips. Maya did not pull away.

From the wagon, Sir John hooted. "That's some greeting, Andy, my boy."

Beside him, Harry chuckled.

In the back of the wagon, Simon stood stiffly. "Maya," he whispered.

From somewhere deep within the wagon came a muffled banging. "What's going on out there?"

Andy and Maya pulled away from each other, but he held onto her arms. "You came back," he said, his face bright with joy.

Maya smiled. "Did you think I'd leave you here?" She had

the strangest feeling in her stomach, a feeling she had never had before.

"No, but I was afraid you might not be able to come back."

The fair young man—Elspeth—and the small brightly clad boy—Alani—had moved closer to Maya and Andy. In the wagon, Harry was pushing aside some baskets and boxes to reveal a small panel. He pulled it open, and out came Rhys and three other men.

Quick introductions were made, and as Maya's real name was known, Elspeth decided to go by her real name.

Rhys shook his head. "A man dressed like a woman, and women dressed like men. We live in strange times."

"We live in dangerous times," Elspeth replied. "And Caxton is at the center of things."

"And why exactly are you going to Caxton?" Rhys asked.

Elspeth glanced over at Maya, who was looking down at the book. "It's all right to tell them," Maya said. "We're all on the same side."

"Another book?" asked Sir John.

"An Apprentice Book," Maya said.

Elspeth said to Rhys, "An important book was stolen from Maya and Andy, and I am here to help them get it back." She frowned at Alani, who was fidgeting by her side. "And so is Alani."

"That's why I was going to Caxton," Andy said. "To get the book back."

Sir John smiled. "Let them ride with us! We can all be related. When we get to Caxton, we can talk more, but we shouldn't stay by the side of the road too long. The soldiers don't seem to be patrolling anymore, but you never know."

"What about papers?" Rhys asked. "To get into the city?"

"Actually, Maya and I have papers," Elspeth answered. "We knew we would need them."

"But I don't," Alani said a little sheepishly.

"There's no more room in the hidden compartment," Rhys said. "Even for one as small as you."

"Is there a blanket in the wagon?" Maya asked.

"Aye," Harry answered.

"Alani can ride in the wagon with us," Maya said. "When we get to the city, she can hide under the blanket."

Rhys rubbed his face. "The guards usually search the wagon, and there will be trouble if they find her. I don't want our plans ruined."

"And your plans are to take Caxton?" Maya asked. "With Sir John in disguise to smuggle you in?"

"That's right," Rhys answered.

As Maya looked at the book, her hand went to the left pocket of her trousers. "I don't think we'll get caught. In fact, I think Chance will be on our side."

"Are you sure about that?" Rhys's stare was cool and stern.

Maya did not look away. "As sure as a person can be. And the Apprentice Book is sure, too."

Rhys smiled just a little at the slight, confident girl who was dressed like a boy. Then he shrugged. "Let's go to Caxton."

Simon, who had been silent the whole time, had seen Maya's hand go to her trouser pocket. "She's got something in there, and I'm going to find out what it is," Simon said to himself.

And Maya, who usually saw so much, did not catch this flicker of resolve from Simon. She could tell that he resented her, but Maya's focus was not on Simon. It was on Alani and Rhys, and, most of all, Andy.

"No one can keep track of everything all the time," Feste might have said, and before the night was over, Maya would find out how true this was.

Soon, the wagon was on the road again. Rhys and his men were hidden under the false bottom while Elspeth, Maya, and Alani sat in back with Andy and Simon. A blanket was folded by Alani's feet, and she had her hand on it, ready to whisk it over herself should the need arise.

"Where did you go when you left me in Greendale?" Andy asked Maya in a low voice.

"To the Great Library. Elspeth and Alani come from there."

"The Great Library," Andy whispered.

"Oh, Andy, it really is amazing. It's bigger on the inside than it is on the outside, and there are floors and floors of books. Everything is clean and quiet. Peaceful. And in the middle of the building is a courtyard that feels like the outdoors."

"That must be something to see," Andy said.

"It is!"

Elspeth listened but didn't say anything. Simon's expression was so grim and quiet that it made Elspeth uneasy. Reaching into a pocket in her waistcoat, Elspeth pulled out a small black case and removed a pair of glasses. She put them on and looked at Simon. Yes, she could see now. Elspeth caught impressions of a lonely boy who had worked too hard for too much of his young life, a boy who didn't have quite enough to eat. She saw how Simon had come to regard Andy as a cross between a father and a brother and how Maya was a threat to him.

"He knows she'll take Andy away," Elspeth thought.

Her eyes began to burn, just a little. Mindful of the instructions she had received, Elspeth took off the glasses, put them back in the little black case, and put the case in the pocket of her waistcoat.

A shout from Sir John interrupted Elspeth's thoughts and Andy and Maya's conversation.

"Caxton! At last! After all those years in the forest." There was a long pause. "What has Humphrey done?"

Harry stopped the wagon at the top of a large hill that overlooked the city. Beside the big man, Harry sat tense and still, as though he could hardly believe what he saw. Elspeth, Alani, Maya, Simon, and Andy all stood up for a better view. They saw a walled city with a small castle whose towers rose above the wall. But the countryside around Caxton had been stripped clear of its trees, and left behind were ragged stumps and big piles of brush. Worse yet, on the open land, where crops should have been growing to feed the city, fields lay fallow and ragged, not by plan to give the land a chance to rest, but rather by neglect.

Harry was the first to recover. "We'd been warned. Rhys's men, after all, are hiding in a deserted barn. What kind of place has deserted barns? Now, let's see if we can get in."

Quickly, Alani pulled the blanket over herself while Elspeth, Andy, Maya, and Simon settled back into the wagon. Down the hill it went, toward Caxton, which had once been one of the loveliest cities in Albion.

30: The Chimes at Midnight

At the city gate, the guards looked bemused rather than hostile or intimidating. Sir John had recovered from the shock of seeing masses of tree stumps and abandoned fields, and he had thrown himself into his role as the sister of the fictional Edith, who was dreadfully sick and needed good care and good food.

"Her name is Edith Pargeter." Sir John spoke in a high-pitched voice that reminded Maya of Hyacinth from the old British sitcom *Keeping Up Appearances*. Maya bit her lip to keep from laughing.

Sir John said, "Poor lamb, she is so ill. She wrote and told me not to come, what with all the hullabaloo going on right now. 'Stay home, sister,' Edith wrote, 'until the fighting is over.' But I said to my son Cedric here, 'I will not stay home, not with poor Edith being so sick.' And you know what this dear boy said?"

The guards shook their heads. Both men felt that any response would not only be unnecessary but also futile.

"Why this dear boy said, 'I'll take you to Auntie. Didn't she come tend you last winter when you were so sick with the grippe that you could barely raise your head for a sip of broth?'"

If the guards thought that Matilda Green—Sir John's nom de guerre—had made a very robust recovery, they kept it to themselves. There was just the slightest of smirks as they stared in amazement at the large figure in the green dress and the white bonnet.

Sir John glanced back into the wagon. "Then, of course, the rest of them wanted to come, the two cousins as well as my grandsons. Well, I couldn't very well deny them, could I? After all that dear Edith has done for us. When my poor husband, Cedric the elder, died, Edith would send us money from time to time, money that she had earned herself. Never was a better hand for making lace. Surely you've seen some of her work? It's the best in Caxton."

As the guards shook their heads, Maya marveled at Sir John's inventiveness. She could almost picture Edith, as spare in build as Sir John was large, and quiet and industrious rather than boisterous.

"The poor lamb hasn't been making lace lately, has she?" Sir John directed this toward the back of the wagon, and a dutiful chorus of "No!" was the response.

"No, indeed." Sir John sighed. "So here we come, despite all the commotion going on around us. We've brought lots of good things to eat, to help our Edith regain her strength."

The guards gave a cursory glance at the baskets and boxes, but they did not search the wagon. "Do you have papers?" one of them asked.

"We surely do," came the trilling reply. "Come on everyone, hand your papers over so that these young men can take a look at them."

A flutter of papers passed from hand to hand to the guards. Again there was a cursory glance, and then the papers were handed back.

"Everything looks all right to me," said the shorter and eldest of the two.

"They look all right to me, too," said the other. "We'd better open the gate so that this woman can see her sister."

"Bless you, bless you!" Sir John cried as the gate slowly began to open.

The wagon rolled into the city, and the gate closed behind them. When they were well inside the city, Elspeth leaned forward and said in a soft voice, "That was quite a performance." The big man inclined his head but did not turn around.

Maya whispered to Andy, "It's good to have Chance on our side." Andy nodded absently, not really knowing what she meant.

But Simon, with his sharp ears, had heard what Maya said. "She's got something lucky," Simon thought. This made him want to see even more what Maya had in her pocket. Not steal it. Not exactly. Simon just wanted to take a look at it. That's what he would say later, and it was mostly true.

Harry drove the wagon up High Street, dirty and littered with trash, and the rotting smells were horrendous. From underneath the blanket, Alani choked and gagged, and the others did the same. All the shops seemed to be closed, and except for a few pigs rooting in the trash, the normally bustling streets were nearly deserted.

"Didn't used to be like this," Harry said grimly.

"We'll get it cleaned up, by God," Sir John added.

Harry drove the wagon to the castle's gates, and Sir John told a different tale. This time, he was Molly's cousin Edwina, come to stay with Molly to get away from the fighting in the countryside, and various children and other cousins had come as well. Again, there was a bemused look and a cursory glance at the papers before the guards waved Harry into the castle's courtyard.

"Two for two," Sir John said triumphantly when they were far enough away so that he couldn't be heard, and Maya got the impression that Sir John was sorry there wasn't a third story to tell.

Harry drove the wagon around to the side of the castle and stopped the wagon in front of a green door. Out stepped a woman with copper-colored curls, a white cap, and a striped apron over her brown dress. While it might not be true, as some people unkindly suggested, that the woman was as large as Sir John, she was quite big.

"Ah, Molly Beston," Sir John said. "It's been a long time."

"Sir John," Molly replied with a laugh, taking in the bonnet and the green dress. "That's quite a disguise."

"You should have seen him at the city gate," Harry said. "For a moment, I almost believed he was my mother."

Molly laughed again, but she glanced up at the windows in the tall walls above them. Everything seemed quiet.

"Everyone's having their supper right now," Molly said. "But you never know. Come in, come in, before someone sees you."

Elspeth, Alani, Maya, Andy, and Simon quickly jumped from the wagon, and Harry climbed in back, quietly opening the panel so that Rhys and his men could get out. Just as quietly, they crawled from their hiding place, slipped out the back of the wagon, and followed the others into Molly's parlor.

A while later, Molly's son, Jem, drove the wagon to the castle's stables where the horses could be fed, watered, and brushed.

"Our cousins have come to stay with us until the fighting is over," Jem told the stable boys. "They brought some supplies with them."

No questions were asked. The three stable boys could easily understand why Cook's cousins might prefer the safety of Caxton to what was going on outside the walls in the countryside.

"Don't blame them," said one of the stable boys. "I wouldn't want to be out there while Duke Humphrey shows his brother a thing or two."

The other stable boys were silent, and Jem just nodded. They all knew better than to make comments about Duke Humphrey to someone who was still loyal to him. "Besides," Jem thought, "he'll find out soon enough."

On the other side of the castle, in a room high above the courtyard, a pale man with white hair shivered beneath the blankets. All day, indeed for the past week, servants had kept a fire going even though it was summer. Still, Julian was cold, sick with fever from the wound that his own knife had given him.

Julian wondered how this had happened. How had he lost control? As soon as he had felt the sting of the knife, Julian knew he was in trouble, for not only did the knife cut, but it also poisoned. Most people, without the proper medicine and care, would have been dead by now. But Julian was not most people.

After coming back wounded from Greendale, before he was too weak to leave his bed, Julian had hidden Earth's Book of Everything in a niche in a wall that was covered by a tapestry. After putting his own black book beneath his pillow, Julian had called for the servants to fetch a physician to take care of his wound, even though Julian was fairly certain there wasn't much that could be done for him on this miserable, backward planet.

The physician, as inept as Julian expected he would be, came and wrapped the wound. As soon as the physician and the servants left, Julian reached under his pillow for his book and opened it.

Right away, the book began to nag and carp. "What are we still doing here? You said we'd return to Mortmain after gathering some things in Caxton. We need to go back now so that you can be taken care of. There is nothing more that can be done in Caxton. It's out of your hands now. Owen has taken Greendale, and the odds are in his favor for Thorndike, which means Humphrey will soon attack Owen and his men. And then who knows what will happen?"

By now, Julian was very weak, and he placed the book, opened, on the stand beside his bed. "I'm not going back just yet. I'm staying here."

The book swore at Julian and told him what a fool he was.

"You've got one book. That's enough. Pick me up right now so that we can return to Mortmain!"

Although Julian stared dully at his book, he didn't follow its instructions. Return now, when he was so weak? When he only had one book? No, that was not how Julian envisioned his return. He wanted to go back strong and well with both books, Earth's and Ilyria's. Julian knew having two books would redeem his status so much that he would once again become Cinnial's trusted confidant and adviser. After what Julian had done on the last planet, one book would not be sufficient; it would take two books to get back into Cinnial's good graces.

Julian assumed that Cinnial had sent him to this backward planet because he didn't think Julian would be able to accomplish much. Julian was wrong about this, but he would only find out much later what Cinnial's true intention had been.

On Ilyria, there were no networks of communication, no trackers, travel was primitive, and the people hardly knew enough to wash their hands, never mind their whole bodies. Usually, when society was at this stage, one of Cinnial's books would be sent to the planet and left with someone who seemed suitable, someone who would be receptive to Cinnial's ideas. Then, when the situation looked promising, when societies were more advanced and in chaos, Cinnial often sent someone to try to steal that planet's Book of Everything.

Julian believed that Cinnial expected him to spend many more years, if not decades, on Ilyria before begging to come home. Well, Julian would not beg. He would return in triumph with two Books of Everything.

"Do you know what your problem is?" Julian's book asked bitterly.

"I do," Julian answered. "But you're going to tell me anyway." Julian's voice was barely above a whisper, but his book heard the answer clearly.

"You like to toy with people. You toy and toy, and then you strike. When you do, there's a spectacular bloody mess, but it doesn't always work in your favor, does it? We've known for quite a while that the cook, Molly Beston, has been plotting against you and Humphrey, but it amused you to keep her off guard, to keep her wondering. You should have gone after her when it became clear what she was up to. Now you're in no condition to go after anyone, and it looks as though Owen's side has a good chance of winning. I don't know why Cinnial has put up with you for so long."

Julian's lips curled. "When I recover, I'm going to rip your cover to shreds. Then we'll see how long you last."

"No, you won't. You're nothing without me."

"Enough!" Julian reached over and snapped shut the book. Why he didn't put the book back under his pillow, he couldn't say. It was what he should have done, and it wouldn't be long before Julian would find out why. Instead, the book, mute and closed, stayed on the stand.

Time passed. A day? Two days? Servants came and went, and one in particular, Eli Prenderhook, stayed with him longer than the rest. They bathed him and lit the candles when it was dark. One afternoon, Julian opened his eyes to find Humphrey's sharp face peering down at him.

"What the hell happened to you?" Humphrey asked. "How could you get yourself injured right now? Owen has taken both Greendale and Thorndike."

"If I were stronger, I'd snap your neck," Julian thought. But all he could do was lie there and grimace.

Humphrey continued, "You're no use to me like this. You'll have to stay behind when we march tomorrow."

"Wait," Julian whispered. "In a couple of weeks I'll be better. I can come with you and advise you." His bleary eyes tried to focus on Humphrey's face, tried to will him into staying.

"I can't wait," Humphrey said. "Owen has taken two towns. If I don't move immediately, then he might regain Caxton."

Julian knew there was some truth to this, but Humphrey's idea of success was different from Julian's. "My book can help us discover Owen's plans and defeat him. Your book won't tell you anything useful."

"Yes," Humphrey said, staring at the book on the stand. Then in one quick movement, Humphrey snatched the book and put it in one of his pockets. Fear and rage gave Julian the energy to sit up and grab at Humphrey, but with a strong arm, the young man pushed Julian down. "You're not going anywhere."

"That book is mine! It won't help you."

"Are you sure about that?" Humphrey asked. "I'm not. If I win, then I'll return it to you. If not, well, here you are. In Caxton."

Humphrey left an astonished, angry Julian, so weak now he could hardly raise his head. Julian slept, and when he awoke, Eli was sitting by his side. Eli, in his early teens, was slim and had sandy blond hair. Right from the start, Julian had liked the sly, slightly malicious look on the boy's face and had known that Eli was one of his kind. Julian realized that Eli was keeping a death watch over him, and Julian also realized that if something wasn't done soon, then he might indeed die.

"Eli," Julian whispered.

Eli leaned closer to hear what Julian was saying. "Aye, master?"

"Do you know anyone who can heal and who might know things that the damned physician does not?"

"Like an old witchy woman?"

"Something like that."

"Aye, there's one that lives on the edge of the city, and she comes and goes as she pleases. Nobody stops her. They don't dare."

"Go get her," Julian said. "I have gold. I'll make it worth your while and hers, too."

Eli smiled. "Aye, master."

"And, Eli, if I don't make it, there is something I want you to do for me." Eli nodded, looking grave. "Behind the tapestry with the castle, there is a niche with a book hidden in it. Take the book and hide it where no one will find it. Will you do that?"

"Aye, master," Eli said again. "You can count on me. But it won't come to that. The old witchy woman will heal you. I'll be back as soon as I can."

Eli sprinted out of the room, and Julian dozed fitfully, waking as the bell began to chime at midnight and then falling into unconsciousness as the poison finally took hold.

Earlier in the evening, in Molly's cozy parlor, everyone from the wagon had found a seat—extra chairs had been brought in—and Molly was busy serving egg sandwiches from a huge platter. Plans had been discussed, and the group going after the book had decided to wait until the twelfth hour, when Rhys, his men, and Sir John would be taking the castle gate. At the same time, men positioned in the city would take the outer gate.

"The commotion will work in our favor," Elspeth said. "And we're lucky that Julian's own book is gone. This means our Apprentice Book can see him clearly."

"The Apprentice Book told you this?" Rhys asked Elspeth.

"Yes."

"It doesn't know who took Julian's book?"

"No, but we think it's Humphrey. The Apprentice Book can't find him, even though it should be easy. By all accounts, he's with his army. Julian's book must be shielding Humphrey."

"Aye," Rhys said. "Humphrey's been spotted by our people. You and the book must be right."

Then the talk turned to food, and Sir John said, "Molly, my girl, no one can make an egg sandwich like you can. You just have the knack."

There were nods of agreement and appreciative grunts as the sandwiches were gratefully eaten. Grinning, Molly shook her head. "I can't believe you made it into the city. I was sure you'd be captured."

"Have a little faith, Molly," Sir John said, taking a mug of ale from Jem, who had a tray full of mugs.

Molly laughed sadly. "Faith. Have you seen what's happened to Caxton?"

"Aye." Sir John's voice was quiet. "Lord Owen will put things right."

"I hope so," Molly said, stopping in front of Maya, who helped herself to an egg sandwich. As Maya leaned forward, a small hand reached into her pocket and removed a coin. Nobody noticed. They were too absorbed by their egg sandwiches and by Molly.

"Humphrey never suspected you were working against him?" asked Rhys.

"No, and he never knew I was the one who helped Lord Owen escape in the first place." Frowning, Molly set the platter on a round table conveniently near Sir John. "But that Julian knew. I swear I could see it in his eyes every time he looked at me. I kept waiting to be thrown into prison, but the guards never came. I never could figure out why."

Maya said, "I think Julian likes to keep people off guard. Then, when they least expect it, he gets them."

Alani stared at Maya. "That's just what happened to my family. They kept waiting to be arrested, and when it didn't happen, they relaxed. Then they were murdered."

Elspeth said, "Julian will soon be wishing he hadn't waited. But we're certainly glad he did."

"Molly, why are the fields all around Caxton so ragged? Where are the gardens to support the city?" Sir John asked.

Molly sighed. "Duke Humphrey has pulled all the boys and men from their farms and has conscripted them into his army. This spring, there were no crops planted around the city, and I understand it's that way throughout much of the duchy. I don't know what's going to happen this winter. But Humphrey doesn't care about that. All he can think about is having enough men to defeat his own brother, and he figures he can make enough money selling wood to support his troops," Molly ended angrily.

"And where are the remaining troops housed right now?" Rhys asked.

"As far as I know, they are bunked down in the university, which has been closed and turned into a sort of military academy. Am I right, Jem?"

Jem nodded. "Humphrey has taken most of the men with him, but the ones that are left behind are staying at the university."

"How many would you say are left?" Rhys asked.

Jem rubbed his chin. "Maybe twenty-five or thirty. He didn't dare leave any more behind."

"How many men will be joining you?" Elspeth asked Rhys.

"Fifty, maybe more."

"And at least that many from Caxton," Molly added.

"Aye," Jem said. "And some right from the castle. We can help you take the castle's gate."

Rhys smiled. "You know, this just might work."

"Of course it will work," Sir John said, reaching for another egg sandwich.

There was more talk, and plans were rehashed. The egg sandwiches were eaten, and a platter of little cakes followed.

"Here's to our success," Sir John said, raising his mug.

The other mugs were raised. "To our success!"

Just then, the bell began to ring the eleventh hour, and Rhys stood. "We'd better start getting ready for the midnight chimes." He went to Elspeth and took her hand in his. "Good luck getting the book back."

Elspeth gave Rhys's hand a squeeze. "And good luck to you."

31: Lost and Found

Maya wasn't exactly sure how it had happened, but somehow she had gotten separated from the others. First, Maya had given the Apprentice Book to Elspeth so that she could see where they needed to go in the castle to get to Julian's chamber. Then, Maya felt something in her shoe, a small rock that dug painfully into her foot. Crouching to one side of the dark hallway, Maya removed her shoe and shook out the pebble. By the time the shoe was back on her foot, everyone was gone, and, alarmed, Maya stood quickly. As she did, she twisted her ankle, and Maya had to bite her lip to keep from crying out.

For the past year or two, Maya had had an annoying tendency to twist and sprain her ankles, and this certainly felt like a sprain to her. If it was, Maya knew it would be at least a week, maybe even more, until she would be able to walk normally. Why did this have to happen now?

Limping slowly, Maya came to the end of the hall. Was she supposed to go upstairs and turn right or turn right and go upstairs? Maya reasoned that as slow as she was, the group could have gone either way and be out of sight by now. Maya con-

sidered the stairway and the right turn. She just couldn't remember. With a sigh, Maya turned right, hoping it was the
direction she should take. She also hoped everyone in the castle
would be in bed and asleep.

"Some lucky coin," Maya thought, reaching into her pocket
as she hobbled down the hallway. But there was nothing in her
pocket. Maya stopped. Of course. She had lost her lucky coin,
and that was why her luck had changed. By now, her ankle hurt
so much that Maya didn't think she'd be able to make it to the
end of the hall, much less up the stairs to Julian's chamber.
Deeply discouraged, Maya sat down to rest, and all she could
think about was her throbbing ankle.

Looking up from her ankle, Maya saw a light coming
down the hall in her direction. Maya couldn't run, and there
really wasn't anywhere to hide unless she went into one of the
rooms. Maya brought her knees to her chest and scrunched
down, trying to make herself as small as possible, but as the
torch and its light came closer, Maya realized there was no way
she could escape being seen.

So Maya stood slowly to face whoever was holding the
torch. It turned out to be a boy, taller than Maya, and when he
came to where she was standing, he stopped to stare at her. Maya
stared back, seeing slyness and maliciousness in this boy, and she
knew without a doubt that he would not be on her side.

"Who are you?" the boy asked. "I've never seen you before."

"Do you know everyone in this castle?" Maya asked, holding
her head high.

The boy grinned, but it was not a friendly grin. "Pretty
much. I make it my business to know. You are a stranger." Grabbing her arm, he squeezed it hard. "Who are you?"

Maya tried to pull away. "Let me go. I have as much right
to be here as you do."

"I don't think so." The boy took out a knife, pressing it to
her side.

"Are you two going to stand there squabbling all night?" a
low voice asked.

An old woman stood beside the boy. Her face was so wrinkled that it seemed to Maya that the woman must be as old as Ebenezer, Mortimer, and Ichabod. She was small enough so that Maya could look right into her bright, dark eyes, and the woman smelled of herbs and the outdoors.

Andy stopped suddenly. "Maya's gone!"

They had been rushing up the stairs, and Andy had turned to say something to Maya, except she wasn't there. The others stopped, too.

Elspeth opened the Apprentice Book. "Where is Maya? What? She twisted her ankle and is on the floor below us?"

"Is she talking to the book?" Simon asked.

"Yeah," Andy answered. "You can do that with Books of Everything if you're really good."

Elspeth frowned at the book. "Simon took Maya's lucky coin? Why didn't you mention this sooner? Yes, I know you are an Apprentice Book and that you can't keep track of things as well as a Book of Everything. But still!" Elspeth turned to Simon. "Did you take Maya's lucky coin?"

"Aye," Simon answered hoarsely as Andy, Alani, and Elspeth all stared at him.

"Stupid boy!" Alani exclaimed. "Where is it?"

Simon reached into his pocket, found the coin, and took it out for everyone to see.

"That explains why Maya's not with us, why she twisted her ankle," Elspeth said.

Simon shook his head. "I don't understand."

"Bad luck comes if a lucky coin is lost or stolen," Elspeth explained patiently.

Simon looked down at his feet. "I'm sorry. I didn't know. I just wanted to see what she had in her pocket."

"Did you plan to give it back?" Andy asked.

"Aye, but I didn't have a chance."

Alani grabbed Simon's arm, and her face had such a fierce expression that Simon expected to feel a stinging slap on his cheek. Instead, she shook Simon's arm. "Give the coin to me. I'll return it to Maya and bring her to Julian's room. I'm faster than all of you."

Seeing Elspeth's frown, Alani added quickly, "And I'm strong, too. Maya can lean on me if she needs to."

Elspeth consulted the book. "All right. But be careful. Maya is not alone, but the book thinks you'll be able to handle the situation." Then she told Alani where Julian's room was.

Simon dropped the coin into Alani's waiting hand, and she was gone, a bright flash in the flickering light of the torches in the stairwell.

Andy was impressed. "Wow! She can really move, can't she?"

"Oh, yes," Elspeth answered with a slight smile. "Alani can run like the wind. And she can kick pretty hard, too. We had to work on that when she first came to the Great Library."

Maya heard the rapid-fire patter of Alani's feet before she saw her, and suddenly Alani was by Maya's side, pressing the coin into her hand.

"Alani," Maya said gratefully, and all at once it seemed as though her ankle didn't hurt quite so much. Maybe she hadn't sprained it after all. Maybe she had just twisted it.

Laughing, the boy pointed at Alani. "Who is that? Your fool?"

Alani's little foot shot out, kicking the boy in the stomach. He let out a startled "Oomph!" and dropped the knife, which was retrieved by a small hand.

The old woman laughed. "There, Eli, you've lost your knife." Her keen gaze took in Alani and Maya. "We're all going to the same place, I think. Shall we continue?"

Eli's face was red. "They can't come with us."

"I don't see how you're going to stop them," the woman said. "After all, one of them now has your knife."

"I could call for someone to take them away," Eli said.

The woman stared severely at Eli. "Yes, you could, but meanwhile your master lies dying. I think we'd all better move along."

Eli looked stubborn, but "All right," he said. "Don't try anything. I will be watching."

The old woman laughed again as they began walking down the hall. "Eli, it would be best not to say anything. Just come along."

Maya could tell that Eli would have liked to have said a great deal more. But with Alani pressing his own knife at his side, he followed the old woman's advice.

"Do you need to lean on me?" Alani asked Maya.

"No," Maya replied. "My ankle doesn't feel too bad now. It only hurts a little."

"Why are you going to see my master?" Eli burst out, unable to remain silent for too long.

Maya considered Eli and decided to tell him the truth. "He stole something from me, and I've come to get it back."

From Eli's silence, Maya could tell he knew exactly what she was referring to. By now, they had reached the stairway, and they all went up until they came to the next hallway.

"Second door on the right," Alani said crisply.

"How did you know that?" Eli asked.

"We have our resources," came the quick reply.

"Shall we go in?" the old woman asked, opening the door.

Elspeth, Andy, and Simon were standing by the bed, staring down at a pale figure. They looked up as Maya, Alani, Eli, and the old woman came into the room.

"Who are they?" Elspeth asked.

"Are you all right?" Andy asked Maya, going over to her and taking her hand. Maya nodded.

The old woman answered, "I am Evangeline, and I am here to heal this man, if I can. The boy with the knife at his side is

Eli, the man's servant. Perhaps you could lower the knife? Eli is certainly outnumbered here." This was directed at Alani, who followed the old woman's suggestion. Evangeline said to the others, "Later you can tell me your names, but first things first."

Slowly, but with assurance, Evangeline went to the side of the bed, lifted the covers, and saw the bandages. "His wound is on his back?" Julian was lying on his side, and his chest and back were wrapped.

"Yes," Maya answered quickly before Eli could respond. "On his shoulder."

"Oho! And how do you know this? According to young Eli, you are a stranger here."

There was a slight pause. "Because I stabbed him. He was going to kill Andy. We were in Greendale."

"Well, well." Evangeline looked at Andy and Elspeth. "Help me turn him onto his stomach."

Gently, Andy and Elspeth did as they were instructed, and Julian moaned horribly. From a large, brown leather pouch that hung by her side, Evangeline removed a small pair of silver scissors and snipped at the dressing. Everyone except for Evangeline gasped when they saw the wound, red and bloody at the shoulder where the knife had gone in, and the black lines that streaked down his back.

Evangeline glanced at Maya. "That was some knife. Do you still have it?" Maya shook her head. "Where did you get it?" Maya pointed at Julian.

Evangeline touched Julian's shoulder, and he shivered but remained unconscious. "You are not a good man, are you?"

"He is a great man!" Eli retorted. "Greater than anyone here."

"No," Evangeline replied, "not greater than anyone here. But certainly he is a very powerful man. Most would have succumbed to the poison by now. I shall try to heal him, of course. That is what I do." Digging into her pouch, she removed a small jar and opened it. After dipping her fingers into the jar, Evangeline spread a smooth white paste onto Julian's wound and down his back as well. A strong smell, sharp but not unpleasant, filled the room.

"If we are lucky, this will draw out the poison," Evangeline said. "I should have been called sooner." She gave Eli a stern look. "You should not have let this great man suffer."

"I am just a servant," Eli answered sullenly. "It is not my place to suggest."

"H-m-m-m," Evangeline said. Then she turned to the others. "And who might the rest of you be?"

When Elspeth introduced herself as Sebastian and Maya as Cesario, Evangeline raised her eyebrows but made no comment. Smiling just a little, Elspeth introduced Andy, Alani, and Simon as well. There was a brief silence in the room, and outside the castle, in the courtyard below, came the faint sound of men yelling and the clashing of swords.

"What is that?" Eli asked, starting.

"A rebellion," Evangeline answered. "And even though I am on the edge of things and try to remain neutral, I think it is high time for a rebellion. Ah, look! The black lines have receded just a little." Everyone peered at Julian's back as Evangeline spread more of the pungent cream onto the wound.

"What do you mean?" Eli asked angrily. "Duke Humphrey is our master."

Evangeline pursed her lips. "But he was not always the master here, was he? Humphrey forced out his own brother, Owen, the rightful duke. Some men should not be rulers. Not ever." She gave Julian's back a light pat, which nonetheless made him moan. "Sorry," she added. "And you, Cesario? You have come for something this man stole?"

"Yes," Maya replied. "A book." She watched Eli and saw him glance quickly at a tapestry on the wall. Just as quickly, he looked away, and Maya said, "I think I know where it is."

Going over to the tapestry, Maya pulled it back to reveal a small niche that contained several pouches and the Book of Everything, now as small as an address book, and a deep, deep shade of blue that was almost black.

"There you are!" Maya reached for the book.

"No!" Eli shouted, and Alani raised the knife, pointing it at him.

"Put the book back," came a low, ragged voice. One of Julian's eyes was open, and he stared balefully at Maya.

"No, Julian," Maya replied, looking older than her fifteen years. "I will not put the book back. It doesn't belong to you."

"You're quite the one, aren't you?" Julian asked, his lips curled in a grimace.

"She certainly is," Evangeline said, and to Maya's embarrassment, everyone except for Eli nodded.

Maya stared down at the book, now a lighter shade of blue. It had grown just enough to fit perfectly in her back pocket, and tenderly, Maya opened it.

"Maya!" the book exclaimed. "You made it!"

"Of course I did," Maya said, glancing quickly at Andy and then back to the book. "I couldn't leave you with Julian."

"I'll come after you," Julian said. "I'll get it back."

Looking down at Julian's back, Evangeline scolded, "The salve is starting to draw the poison out. Now, am I healing you just to have you make ugly threats? No, I am not. And you are not out of the woods yet. Young Eli here will have to apply this salve every hour until the black lines are completely gone. Understand?"

Eli snatched the jar away from Evangeline. "Yes!"

"Julian?" Evangeline asked.

"Of course I understand!"

"Good. I will also mix up something for you to sleep. It will help the healing."

"It seems like all I've been doing is sleeping," Julian muttered crossly.

"He will recover," the Book of Everything said quietly to Maya. "And if he does, then he will go on to cause great harm on this planet."

Julian heard the book, and there was a cold smile on his face.

In turn, Maya frowned at Julian. Despite all the cruel and vicious acts Julian had committed—flashes of them came to Maya as she regarded him—she felt sorry for him. He looked so weak and defenseless, too worn out, even, to block Maya's inquiring eyes from seeing. She saw how he and Cinnial had had a falling out and how Julian was here against his will. Then one flash came to Maya that made her gasp, and she looked inadvertently at Alani. Ever sensitive to what others were doing, Alani saw the look and stepped closer to the bed to peer at Julian. At the same time, Elspeth took out her small gold glasses and also peered down at Julian. She, too, gasped at what she saw.

Frowning, Julian considered Alani. "The bright clothes, the small stature. You come from Copernia, don't you?"

"Yes, my father was the prime minister, but he was murdered along with the rest of my family. I am the eldest child, and I was away at school." Suddenly her eyes became wide. "It was you! You killed them with that awful knife. They wouldn't let me see the bodies, but I heard they went completely black." She trembled, tightly clutching Eli's knife. "I should kill you for what you did." Alani raised the hand with the knife, but Evangeline caught her arm, and the old woman's grip was surprisingly strong.

"No, child, not like this. A murder for the murders he committed? And what would that do to you?"

Alani was crying. "He deserves it." But she lowered her knife.

Elspeth removed her glasses, putting them back in their case in the pocket of her waistcoat. "He does deserve it, Alani. He is monstrous. And even though I hate to admit it, he is also my kinsman. But Evangeline is right about a murder for a murder."

Julian's attention was now on Elspeth. "So you come from the House of Jortensen. I can see it—the fair skin and hair."

"Wow!" Andy said to Simon. "This is getting really weird." Simon, with his mouth slightly open, just nodded.

With a slight smirk, Julian asked Elspeth, "And you and Eli's witchy woman are my protectors?"

"Oh, I wouldn't say that," Elspeth replied. "You don't have your book, do you?" Closing his eyes, Julian clenched his fists. "Humphrey took it with him, didn't he? And guess where we are going next?"

"Don't count on getting my book from him," Julian snapped, opening his eyes.

Elspeth leaned forward, her voice soft. "Not only do I plan on getting your book, but I'm also going to get this planet's Book of Everything and give it to Lord Owen. And you? Well, you'll be on this planet for quite a while, until Cinnial turns his attention to it and you. And he has a lot of things competing for his attention right now, doesn't he? There's a lot going on in the universe."

Julian grimaced, and even though he was weak, his hand shot out, grabbing Elspeth by the throat. Gasping, Elspeth dropped the Apprentice Book and pulled away from Julian. Quickly, she retrieved the Apprentice Book.

Maya knew what she should do even though Earth's Book of Everything had remained silent, as had the Apprentice Book, which Elspeth held slightly open. Neither book dared say anything; they were afraid Julian would overhear them. Quietly stepping back, Maya reached into her pocket and closed her hand around a little white envelope. Slowly and carefully, she passed the envelope to Evangeline, who took it without comment and just as slowly and carefully slid the envelope into her bag. Nobody saw the exchange. They were all looking at Julian and Elspeth.

With the mint safely in her bag, Evangeline stepped forward. "Now, now! Enough recriminations and attempted stranglings. Cesario, you have retrieved what is yours, and I think it is time for all of you to leave." She cocked her head to one side. "Unless I am very much mistaken, the battle for Caxton is nearly over, won for Lord Owen." Evangeline smiled down at Julian. "But I will stay a little longer to give you a sleeping draught as well as a nice peppermint lozenge that will help with the pain."

Julian, weak from exertion, just nodded, and Eli cried, "I will stay with my master."

"Of course you will," Evangeline said. "For quite a while, in fact."

As Maya, Elspeth, Alani, Andy, and Simon started to leave, Evangeline put her hand on Maya's head. "May your vision continue to be true and strong. May it guide you well."

As Maya felt the warm blessing settle over her, she understood that not only was Evangeline like her—sensitive to the interconnectedness of all things—but also that her eyes had been peeled. And just as Sydda had done before Maya left the Great Library, Maya touched her forehead to Evangeline's.

"Thank you," Maya said. "Thank you very much."

32: Owen and Humphrey Fight

"By God, you should have seen it!" Sir John exclaimed. They were all back in Molly's parlor, and this time platters of buttered toast and mugs of tea were being passed around.

"They came in from all over the countryside to help take back Caxton. There were so many on our side that it was hardly a battle. Over in a couple of hours."

"Where are Humphrey's men?" Andy asked.

"Either dead or in prison," Rhys answered. "Lord Owen can deal with the ones who are in prison when he returns."

"Humphrey still isn't defeated," Elspeth reminded him. "It isn't over yet."

"I know, but because so many men came to our side, in the morning we're going to march for Thorndike and attack from the rear. We're ready for this to end. Every year, it has gotten worse and worse. There is no money for our schools, no money for the services the duke used to provide. Humphrey has taken most of the young men from the farms right before harvest time. Unless they return soon, it is going to be a lean winter." Rhys shook his head. "And what about you? Did you find your book?"

Elspeth smiled. "We found it."

Alani fidgeted. "And we found out that Julian killed my family."

"I am very sorry," Rhys said. "Lord Owen will deal with Julian, too."

Andy, who was sitting next to Sir John, asked quietly, "Will you be marching with Rhys and the men?"

Sir John shook his head and answered just as quietly, "No, Andy, my boy. I will be moving on. Best that way."

But Rhys had heard the exchange. "You're not coming with us, Sir John? Why not?"

Sir John took a deep breath. "Because I've been banished."

Rhys stared in astonishment at the big man. "Banished? And all this time you acted as though you were doing just what Lord Owen had ordered."

Sir John's voice was low. "Looks can be deceiving."

For a while, nobody said anything. "What in the world did you do?" Molly finally asked.

Sir John swallowed. "I'd rather not say. But Lord Owen was right to banish me. I deserved it."

"And me as well," Harry added.

"Both of you!" Rhys exclaimed. He turned to Andy. "And what about you?"

"I wasn't banished," Andy said. "But I was put under house arrest."

Rhys pointed to Simon. "And him? Was he in on it, too?"

"No," Sir John answered before Simon could say anything. "He's just a lad. What could he do?"

Simon felt a surge of affection for the big man. Someday, Simon knew he would have to come clean about what he had done. But not now. Unlike Sir John and Andy, he just wasn't ready.

"You might as well tell us what happened," Rhys said to Sir John. "I would rather hear it from you than from someone else."

So Sir John told him, starting with the theft of Earth's Book of Everything and ending with Feste's death. Andy filled in with the details about Julian, and when they were done, there was a long, long silence. Molly sniffed and used her apron to wipe her eyes. She had known Feste for many years and liked him very well.

Maya's gaze went from Sir John to Rhys. She was a little unsure of how to read his stony looks. Rhys, too, could keep things hidden when he wanted, and Maya was beginning to understand that while she could see a lot because she had had her eyes peeled, some people, even if they weren't directly connected to the Great Library, would be able to block her.

And much to Maya's surprise, as she considered Sir John, she actually felt sorry for him. She missed Feste, of course, so keenly that there was still an ache, but Maya had to admit that Sir John's vitality and his ability to recover from his mistakes—however terrible—were beginning to win her over. Most men, after doing what Sir John had done, would have hurried into exile without a second thought. But not Sir John. In his own boisterous way he had rushed in to help retake Caxton, which he clearly loved. While he might not exactly have saved the day, Sir John certainly had been instrumental in getting Rhys and his men into Caxton, and now the city was being held for Lord Owen.

Maya said, "Sir John, let's face it. We haven't always gotten along. But, not only were you brave smuggling us into Caxton, but you were also a good actor."

Sir John smiled just a little. "That is high praise coming from you."

Maya smiled, too. "Stay in Caxton a while longer. If we defeat Humphrey, then I'll ask Lord Owen to pardon both you and Harry."

"Do they deserve it?" Rhys asked sharply.

"I think they do," Maya replied, meeting his stare. "Without Sir John and Harry's help, Caxton wouldn't have been as easy to take. Admit it, hardly anyone could have pulled off what Sir John did with those guards."

"You are quite the little miss," Rhys said, but the look on

his face wasn't as stony, and his dark eyes even had what might be called a slight twinkle in them.

"That's what a lot of people seem to think," Maya said a little ruefully. "Sometimes, when he's mad at me, my father calls me a pain in the ass."

Everyone started laughing, and Maya laughed, too, even though, for the first time, she understood her father's point of view. She never took anything meekly, and she didn't back down easily. Her mother could somehow quietly guide Maya in the direction she wanted Maya to go. But Maya's father was more fiery. When he was upset, he bellowed, and Maya bellowed back. "We're a lot alike," Maya thought and realized with a slight pang that aside from her mother, there was no one she loved as much.

"Aye, then," Rhys said, when the laughter had stopped. "What are your plans?"

Elspeth looked at Maya and Alani. "I think we should leave immediately. First to get Lord Owen, and then to confront Humphrey. I am hoping we can convince Humphrey that he is so outnumbered he should surrender, and we can avoid a battle."

"Good luck," Molly muttered. "He's another one that doesn't give up easily. Unfortunately, he doesn't use it for good."

"I know," Elspeth said. "But we have to try."

"We should still carry on with our plans," Rhys stated.

"Yes," Elspeth answered. "Both books agree that there are no guarantees with Humphrey, especially now that he has Julian's book. We might need you and your men."

"Will you sleep before you go?" Molly asked.

"No," Elspeth said. "We should leave now, before dawn, before any battles begin."

"Lord Owen might be asleep himself," Molly said.

"Then we will have to wake him." There was no hesitation in Elspeth's voice, and Maya caught a glimpse of the firm resolve that was just beneath her calm exterior. As Mémère

Celine would have put it, the iron hand in the velvet glove. Elspeth turned to Andy. "Will you come or will you stay?"

Andy frowned. "I'd like to come with you, but Lord Owen is going to be really mad at me for not staying with Lady Celia. I think you would have an easier time with him if I wasn't there to tick him off."

"All right." Elspeth stood. "We should be going. One way or another, we will return to let you know what happened and so that you and Maya can return to your own planet. Rhys, again, good luck. I hope you and your men don't have to fight, but it's good knowing you'll be coming."

Rhys also stood. "Thank you. And I am glad you are on our side. You would make a formidable commander. Do they allow women in such roles where you come from?"

Elspeth laughed. "Yes and no. At the Great Library, men and women are equal, but we really don't have commanders, as such. We gather information, and we make books. That is our job."

Rhys inclined his head. "Should they ever need one, they will know where to look."

Elspeth flushed, just a little. "Thank you, Rhys. Now, Alani and Maya. Are you ready to go?"

"Ready," they both replied together.

As it turned out, Lord Owen was not asleep. He and his men had pitched tents in a big field outside of Thorndike, and sitting at a table in his tent, he stared at battle plans, reviewing over and over what the strategy should be. After a while, Lord Owen's thoughts ranged from one subject to another. He remembered when Humphrey had been born and how he couldn't wait for Humphrey to grow old enough to play with him. Lord Owen recalled the games they had played on their wooden stick horses. There were battles, adventures, escapes from evil wizards, and near misses with fire-breathing dragons. Lord Owen smiled as he thought about the zest and the energy of their make-believe games. His smile went away as he remembered something else—how Humphrey always wanted to lead, always wanted to win. And Humphrey had been so persistent, so intense, that Lord Owen had often let him have his way.

"Too often?" Lord Owen asked aloud, at the same time knowing that his childish self never could have foreseen what Humphrey would become.

"Lord Owen?" a voice asked.

Lord Owen jumped, looking up from his papers. Standing in front of him were a slim, blond man, a very small boy dressed in bright-colored clothes, and Maya.

Lord Owen stood quickly. "Maya! You are back!"

Maya laughed. "Everyone has been so surprised when they see me."

"The odds were not exactly in your favor," Lord Owen replied.

Maya was serious. "No, they weren't. But here I am, and I've brought two people from the Great Library to help us. This is Elspeth and Alani. Like me, they decided it would be best to travel as men in this world."

"I see," Lord Owen said. "I am pleased to meet you." He motioned to several chairs on the other side of the table. "Will you sit down?"

They all sat down, and Elspeth leaned forward a little. "We have some news. Tonight, there was a battle at Caxton, and it was retaken for you. Have you gotten word of this?"

Lord Owen looked a little dazed. "No, not yet. That is good news indeed. Who led the men?"

"Rhys did, and men joined him from all over the countryside. It was an easy battle. Not many were killed."

"Ah, Rhys. A good man to have on your side."

"And not so good to have against you," Elspeth finished. "Come morning, Rhys and his men will be marching to attack Humphrey from the rear. They won't get here for a couple of days, but they are coming."

Lord Owen was very still. "But you did not come here just to tell me this. A pigeon with a message could have been sent, and I expect soon one will be."

Elspeth nodded. "We came for another reason. We have two books, now. We retrieved Earth's Book of Everything from Julian, and we also have an Apprentice Book to help us." Elspeth took out the Apprentice Book from her pocket, and Maya did the same with Earth's Book of Everything.

Again, Lord Owen looked a little dazed. "Go on."

"That is the good news," Elspeth said. "The bad news is that Humphrey not only has your world's Book of Everything, but he also took Julian's book, which functions much the way a Book of Everything does, except that it doesn't have as much information available to it, and its mission is a little darker."

"A lot darker," Alani put in.

"A lot darker," Elspeth agreed.

"Will it advise him?" Lord Owen asked.

"There's a good chance of it." Elspeth hesitated and then went on. "As I'm sure you've discovered, the Books of Everything have their own intelligence, which they, in turn, use to decide what kind of information to give and how much guidance to provide. Julian's book will want to return to Julian, and it will do its best to guide Humphrey in that direction, even if it's in a roundabout way."

"Will the book know about our battle plans?" Lord Owen asked.

"I don't know," Elspeth answered. "It's a possibility."

"But you've come with your own plan."

"Yes. Our books will take us to Humphrey's tent. I think we should go and try to convince him to abandon his plans. You've taken Greendale and Thorndike, and Rhys has taken Caxton. Humphrey is caught in between."

"When Humphrey has decided to do something, he doesn't give up easily."

"So I've heard," Elspeth replied. "But we have to try. Think whom you'll be killing if you go into battle with Humphrey."

Lord Owen said grimly, "I can think of nothing else. Men and boys who are from this duchy and who were once under me."

"We have the books, and we can make a quick escape if we need to."

Lord Owen stood. "Which we probably will, knowing Humphrey. But you are right. It is worth a try."

Elspeth also stood. "Let's go."

Barely five miles away, in another open field, Humphrey also sat at a table in his tent. Both books, the black one and the green one, were open in front of him. Although Humphrey couldn't hear the voices of the books—not yet—he sensed they were arguing, and he caught traces of it in the writing. He had turned to *O*, in each book, in an attempt to discover what Owen had planned. His Book of Everything gave a stern warning: "Don't go against Owen. He is your own brother, and these are your people. Don't pit them against each other."

The Black Book came back with the written rejoinder: "Ignore that cowardly Green Book. Your forces outnumber Owen's, two to one." The Black Book didn't tell Humphrey about what was happening in Caxton. It felt too many details would distract the volatile man, who needed to focus on the battle before him. If Owen was defeated, then Caxton and Rhys could be taken care of later.

The Green Book: "Don't listen to that Black Book. It has its own agenda, and it doesn't involve you or Albion."

Humphrey's lips curled as he regarded the Green Book. "And you don't have your own agenda?"

"Of course it does!" the Black Book hurriedly put in. "It wants Lord Owen to win. It has never wanted you to be the duke."

Humphrey struggled to control the anger that was always there, waiting. "You're right. This book has always preferred Owen to me." He snapped shut the Green Book and pushed it away. Later he would deal with it and perhaps destroy it. But not now. There was too much to consider before the sun rose, and he and his men moved against Owen and his men.

Humphrey turned to the Black Book. "What do you suggest?"

He read the warning—"Watch out! They are here!"—and looked up to see his own brother standing in front of him along with a young blond man and two boys, one of them quite small.

Putting the Black Book in the pocket of his trousers, Humphrey stood quickly, very much aware that his sword was in its scabbard, leaning against the foot of his cot, and it was not within easy reach. Humphrey tried to keep his tone cool. "I could have you all arrested."

"No, you couldn't," the blond man replied with a calmness that Humphrey envied. "We have two books, and we can be out of here before your men have a chance to respond. You will hear us out."

"What do you want? Surrender?" Humphrey asked. "Remember who has the most men."

This time Owen spoke, and he had a firmness that Humphrey had never seen before. "You don't have as much of an advantage as you think you do. Rhys has taken Caxton for me, and men from all over the duchy have joined him. As soon as the sun rises, he will be marching from Caxton."

"You are lying!"

Owen shook his head. "No, I am not. When have I ever lied to you?"

"You are wrong, then. You just want me to leave so that you can be duke again, and you won't have to fight."

Owen smiled sadly. "There is certainly some truth to what you have said, but I am not wrong. Caxton has fallen, and Rhys and his men are coming."

The two brothers stared at each other. One breathing hard, and the other, waiting. Fascinated, Maya stared at Humphrey and Owen. While their looks were similar, their demeanor and their attitudes were so different that it was difficult to believe they had come from the same parents. Humphrey was as tense as a cat, ready to spring, and Owen stood braced for the attack.

"You never really wanted to be duke," Humphrey said. "All you wanted to do was stay in the library and read your books. You are no leader."

"That might have been true once," Owen replied. "But it is no longer true. I am the rightful duke."

"And why should you be the rightful duke?" Humphrey retorted. "Because you were born first? That gives you the right? While those of us who were born second just have to accept our fate? No, I will not accept it! I am a better duke than you are. I am with my men always, in the front, leading. I do not hang back."

The arrogance in Humphrey's voice goaded Maya to speak when she knew she shouldn't interfere with the two brothers. "Men might follow you, Humphrey, but you're a terrible leader. You don't think about what's good for your people or the land. You just think about yourself."

Humphrey bellowed, "Who are you to talk to me that way?"

"Never mind!" Maya snapped back, facing his angry stare.

With a yell, Humphrey scrambled over the table and sprang for Maya, but Lord Owen was just as quick, and his body deflected Humphrey's. Both men fell to the ground, and they began to pummel each other.

"No!" Maya cried, rushing toward the fighting men, but Elspeth held her back.

"You must let Lord Owen fight his own battle," Elspeth said. "At least for a little while."

"But it's my fault," Maya said, stricken. "I made Humphrey mad."

"Humphrey was angry as soon as he noticed us. Even I could see that, and surely you could, too."

The two men rolled on the damp ground. Lord Owen's nose was bleeding, and Humphrey had a black eye. Sometimes it looked as though Humphrey had the upper hand, but then Lord Owen would break free from his grip, and he would be on top.

"My lord!" a voice outside the tent called. "Are you all right?"

And here Elspeth did something so astonishing that both Maya and Alani just gaped at her. In a voice low and sultry, she said, "He's not alone, and we don't wish to be disturbed."

"Excuse me, my lord," came the hasty reply, and Elspeth winked at Alani and Maya.

"She sure is full of surprises," Maya thought, and her estimation of Elspeth, already high, rose even higher.

For five minutes or so, the two brothers fought, and by the end they were both bloodied and bruised and out of breath. Humphrey was fiercer and more wiry, but Lord Owen was larger and just as determined. In the end, Lord Owen had Humphrey pinned to the ground, and the two men stared angrily at each other.

"Give up, Humphrey," Lord Owen said, breathing raggedly. "You have lost."

"Never!" Humphrey literally spat out the words, and spittle flew onto Lord Owen's face.

But Lord Owen didn't flinch. "You have no choice. Elspeth will take you away, and with you gone, your men will follow me."

Humphrey twisted his head to look at Elspeth, who waved the closed Apprentice Book at him, and all of a sudden he went limp. "All right, I give up." His words came out hoarsely, as though they were being squeezed from his throat.

"If I let you go, do you promise not to attack any of us in here?" Lord Owen asked.

"I promise!"

"And you will turn over your men to me?"

Humphrey grimaced but, "Yes, yes!"

Later, Lord Owen would say ruefully, "I should have asked him different questions."

And Elspeth would reply, "We should have had our books open. They might have been able to warn us."

However, Lord Owen did not ask different questions, and Earth's Book of Everything and the Apprentice Book were shut. Elspeth and Maya were too intent on what the brothers were doing to consult with the books. Lord Owen slowly released Humphrey and stood. For a moment, Humphrey was still, and the look he gave Owen was so full of hatred that Maya almost felt it as a physical blow.

Then Humphrey leaped to his feet. "You've won for now, but don't think this is over." Before anybody could stop him, Humphrey pulled the Black Book from the pocket of his trousers, and opening it, he ordered, "Take me away from here!"

Maya heard the book's sly voice. "Your wish is my command."

And Humphrey and the book disappeared.

33: Reckonings

As the sun began to rise, casting a glow in the dawn sky, Lord Owen left the tent and stood surveying Humphrey's men—his men, now, if he could persuade them to lay down their arms. Inside the tent, Elspeth, Alani, and Maya were waiting, just in case something went wrong. All the books had agreed that Lord Owen—now the duke—would almost certainly persuade the men to pledge their allegiance to him, that most of them would return to their trades or their family farms.

"But you never know," the Green Book had said. "There is always a chance that something will go wrong at the last minute. Who knows where Humphrey and that book went? They are shielded from us."

"Then there are the officers," Earth's book had put in. "They will be difficult to convince."

"Yes," Elspeth had replied. "We might have to show them a thing or two." Duke Owen agreed, and plans were made.

As Duke Owen continued to look over the encampment, he gathered his thoughts. The Green Book was in the pocket of his trousers, at the ready should he need it. All around, fires were burning, and breakfast was being prepared before what was supposed to be the big battle.

One of the officers, Captain Bourgoin, came over to where Duke Owen stood, and at first he thought he was approaching Humphrey. But then as he got closer, he stopped and stared in astonishment. "You! How did you get here? And where is Duke Humphrey?"

"Humphrey's gone." Duke Owen's hand rested on his sword.

Captain Bourgoin's hand was on his own sword. "Where?"

Duke Owen said, "I don't know. We fought and I won and Humphrey... left."

"He left?" Captain Bourgoin asked with a scowl.

"He left," Duke Owen replied firmly, standing tall. "And I will tell you no more. Now gather the other officers and bring them to the tent. I wish to speak with all of you."

There was such authority in Duke Owen's voice that Captain Bourgoin said, "Yes, my lord!" and went to gather the officers.

Soon three men—Captain Bourgoin, Lieutenant Reed, and Sergeant Smyth—were sitting in front of Duke Owen. Elspeth, Alani, and Maya stood by the duke, and the officers stared at them and at Duke Owen. The expressions on their faces were both hard and confused. Not long ago, they had been in the middle of rousing the men for battle. Now they were sitting in front of the man they were supposed to be fighting, and their lord had somehow "left," as Captain Bourgoin had incredulously informed them. But it must be true. Why else would Lord Owen be there rather than Duke Humphrey?

"As I told Captain Bourgoin," Duke Owen began, "Humphrey has left, and before he did, he agreed to turn his men over to me."

"Do you have any proof of this?" Captain Bourgoin asked.

Elspeth removed the little gold glasses from their case and put them on, and Maya also stared intently at all three men.

Duke Owen sat very straight. "You have my word. You have known me long enough to know what that is worth."

Captain Bourgoin nodded slightly, but his expression did not change.

Duke Owen continued, "My men have taken Greendale and Thorndike. You know that. What you don't know is that Rhys Gruffyd, who was joined by men from Caxton and Oakton, has taken Caxton and very soon will be marching to join my forces."

The three men sitting in front of him were silent, blinking rapidly as they tried to adjust to the new and unwelcome turn of events. Captain Bourgoin spoke, "My lord, your word has always been good. I freely admit this, even though I sided with Duke Humphrey. But what's to stop us from taking all of you as hostages? There are only four of you, after all." He did not need to add that two of the three standing by the duke were rather small.

As Elspeth put away her glasses, Duke Owen gave a slight nod, and Alani, with Earth's Book of Everything held slightly open, moved so fast that there was no time for Captain Bourgoin or the other two officers to react. She raced around the table, grabbed Captain Bourgoin's arm, and said, "Take us to Rhys." Then the two disappeared.

Lieutenant Reed and Sergeant Smyth leaped to their feet and drew their swords. "Where did they go?" Lieutenant Reed demanded.

"They went to see Rhys Gruffyd," Duke Owen answered. "But don't worry. They'll soon be back."

Just as the duke finished speaking, Alani and Captain Bourgoin returned. Alani joined Elspeth and Maya while Captain Bourgoin, his face white, fell to his knees and wrapped his arms around his stomach. Quickly sheathing his sword, Lieutenant Reed helped Captain Bourgoin into a chair.

"As you see," Duke Owen said, "we could be gone in seconds. You would not be able to take us as hostages. And Captain Bourgoin, did you see Rhys Gruffyd?"

Swallowing, the captain nodded. "He and his men are just outside of Caxton, and they are headed our way."

Sergeant Smyth said, "Well, I guess the jig is over for us, then. Our lord is gone, and we're caught like rats between terriers, some of which can disappear without so much as a by your leave."

"Shut your stupid mouth," Lieutenant Reed snapped.

"I'm only telling the truth," Sergeant Smyth replied.

"You've always had a way with words, haven't you?" Lieutenant Reed asked.

Sergeant Smyth remained unruffled. "I take particular pride in assessing the situation and telling it like it is, especially to myself."

"You're such an idiot!" Lieutenant Reed said.

"Enough you two!" Captain Bourgoin commanded. His face was still pale, and he turned to Duke Owen. "What do you want us to do?"

"I would like you to gather all the men so that I can address them," Duke Owen said. "I intend to pardon all who are willing to lay down their arms so that they can return to their farms or their trades."

"And what about us?" Captain Bourgoin asked.

"I should take you as prisoners and have you executed," Duke Owen replied coolly. "The three of you helped my brother overthrow me. Then, you assisted him with his cruel and repressive plans. But if you will stand by me when I speak to the men, then I will allow you and your families to leave the Duchy of Caxton, as long as you sign a pledge never to return and never to work against me again."

"Sounds reasonable to me," Sergeant Smyth said. "It sure beats execution."

Even Lieutenant Reed couldn't argue with this, and in the end, all three men signed the papers that Duke Owen had hastily but neatly drawn up in prose that was simple and clear.

When the men had gone, Duke Owen turned to Maya and Elspeth. "Well?"

Maya replied, "I get the feeling that Captain Bourgoin and Sergeant Smyth will keep their word."

"But for different reasons," Elspeth added. "With Captain Bourgoin, it will be because he is honor bound to do so."

"Yes," Duke Owen said. "Long before I was overthrown, Captain Bourgoin had pledged himself to Humphrey."

Elspeth continued, "But with Sergeant Smyth, it will be because other opportunities will come along, and there will be no reason for him to return."

"And Lieutenant Reed?"

Both Elspeth and Maya shook their heads, and Alani said, "Even I could see what a snake that man is."

Duke Owen rubbed his face. "No doubt you're right. On the other hand, if Lieutenant Reed comes back, then I'm sure I'll have bigger things to worry about. Well, I have given my word that these three men and their families may leave safely, and I plan to keep it."

"But you must always be on guard," Elspeth said. "And expect that one day, your brother and Lieutenant Reed might return."

"I know," Duke Owen said. "I have learned my lesson with Humphrey."

Half an hour later, all the men had been gathered from their tents, and they stood before Duke Owen. Again, Elspeth, Alani, and Maya stayed in Humphrey's tent and had their books ready, should events take an unexpected turn. With her hand on Maya's arm, Alani waited, her small body poised for action.

An unsmiling Captain Bourgoin and Lieutenant Reed and a reasonably cheerful Sergeant Smyth stood by Duke Owen. The men were quiet as they stared in amazement at Duke Owen.

Duke Owen said, "I know you did not expect to see me here before you. Indeed, I did not expect to be before you like this, without a battle and without a lot of blood spilled. But I can't say I am sorry that it has turned out this way. I did not wish to kill any of you." The men stayed silent, but they shifted uneasily, and their leather armor creaked in the still and humid morning air. "I will be brief. My brother, your lord, has left, and before he did, he agreed to release you from your duty to him. If you lay down your arms and promise to serve me, then you will all be pardoned. Captain Bourgoin, Lieutenant Reed, and Sergeant Smyth are here to verify this."

Captain Bourgoin and Lieutenant Reed nodded, and Sergeant Smyth called out, "You can trust Duke Owen to keep his word." This earned him a glare from Captain Bourgoin and Lieutenant Reed, but Sergeant Smyth ignored them.

Duke Owen could see that although the men were still at attention, some of the tension was gone. "During the years I was in exile in the Forest of Arden, I heard tales of how it was outside, of how first the University of Caxton was closed and then the library. Of how the towns stopped getting money for their schools. Of how many of you were taken from your farms or from your trades against your will. Well, it is over. As soon as it is possible, we will open the university and the library. As soon as we can, towns will get money for their schools. Go back to your farms, go back to your trades, and let us restore Caxton to what it was before this all started."

The men's faces, golden in the sun, were upturned toward the duke, who stood on a small hill. There was a slight murmur as the men whispered to each other, and Maya, unable to resist any longer, poked her head through an opening in the tent so that she could see what was going on.

One of the men, young, tall, and broad, started it. Drawing his sword and holding it flat in both hands, he approached Duke Owen and laid the sword before him. "My lord," the man said, "I lay down my arms and gratefully accept your pardon."

Duke Owen nodded. "Your name and occupation?"

"Will Durent, apprentice blacksmith from Newfield."

"Will Durent, apprentice blacksmith from Newfield, go back to your town and to your trade."

Will bowed, and before he could take his leave, men were hurrying to get in line behind him. Most were like him and had been conscripted into Humphrey's forces. Some, however, had served freely, drawn by Humphrey's brash energy and charisma, but seeing that their lord really was gone and that these blacksmiths, farmers, coopers, and farriers were eager to lay down their arms and return to their homes and their work, they, too, fell quickly into line.

Alani and Elspeth were peeking with Maya, and Elspeth sighed with relief. "It's turned out the way it should. At least for now. And that's all we can really ask."

Maya cried softly as she thought about how happy Feste would have been if he had lived to see Duke Owen returned to his rightful place, and Alani cried in sympathy with Maya. Elspeth put one hand on each of their heads and let them cry.

When Duke Owen returned to Humphrey's tent, he was weary but happy. "They are gathering their things so that they can leave. I need to return to my men and tell them what has happened. Will you three go to Rhys and tell him?"

"We will," Elspeth replied.

"But before we go, I have a favor to ask," Maya said.

"And what favor could I refuse you?" Duke Owen said, smiling. "You've done so much for us."

"You might not feel that way when you hear what I'm about to ask."

"Go on, then." Duke Owen was still smiling.

Maya told him about Sir John and Harry and how they had helped retake Caxton. She told how Andy had joined with them so that, he, too, might make up for what he had done. Maya was careful to include a description of Sir John in his gown and of how his acting had convinced the guards at both gates to let them in without searching the wagons.

Duke Owen was not smiling anymore. "What a fool that man is!"

"He is a fool sometimes," Maya agreed. "But he is also brave, and he loved Feste." Here her voice caught a little. "He didn't mean to kill him. He loves Caxton. He really does. And he loves you."

Duke Owen rubbed his face. "I suppose next you are going to ask me to pardon all three?"

"Yes."

Duke Owen was silent. Maya waited anxiously, and beside her, Elspeth and Alani waited, just as anxiously. Maya almost mentioned that the quality of mercy was not strained, but she stayed quiet as Duke Owen considered the request.

"Are they still in Caxton?" Duke Owen finally asked.

Maya nodded. "After Caxton was taken, Sir John and Harry were ready to leave, but I asked them to wait until I had talked to you. And it would mean a lot to Andy if you would forgive him before we go back."

Duke Owen's face was grave. "I will pardon all three even though what they did was so terrible that it almost brought disaster to Caxton and to your land as well. But, Maya, I am only pardoning them because you asked me to do so."

Maya smiled. "It's still a pardon. Thank you, Duke Owen. Thank you very much."

With their Books of Everything, Maya, Elspeth, and Alani returned to inform Rhys and his men there was no need to march to Thorndike, to tell Andy, Sir John, and Harry about the pardon, and to get some much-needed sleep.

"I feel as though I could sleep for days," Maya thought as she settled with a sigh into a soft bed in one of the castle's guest bedchambers. While Maya, as well as Elspeth and Alani, slept for a long time, it was a day rather than days. All three, along with Andy and Simon, were on the wall at the city gate when Duke Owen returned. The townspeople were cheering, and it seemed as though there had never been a day as sunny or as fine as that day was then.

"I'll never forget this," Maya said to Andy, who was standing beside her.

"I won't either. You're sure he's going to pardon us?"

Maya nodded. "He promised." Duke Owen had just ridden into the city, and he waved to both of them. Instead of his usual serious expression, he was smiling, buoyed by the welcome he was getting.

"See?" Maya said, as they all turned to watch him ride up High Street to the castle's gate.

An hour or so after Duke Owen had settled in and had spoken with all the servants and the steward, he called Andy, Sir John, and Harry into his office.

Duke Owen said, "I never expected it to end like this and see you three before me in Caxton."

Sir John inclined his head. "My lord, you are back where you belong."

"And I understand you and Harry and even Andy helped take Caxton for me."

"We all played our part," Sir John said gruffly. "I think you know how sorry we all are for the other part we played."

"I do. I have always known that. But it doesn't change what you did."

"No, my lord." Sir John wiped his eyes, Harry looked down at his feet, and Andy stood still, calm on the outside but trembling within.

Duke Owen's voice was less severe. "Nevertheless, I have promised Maya that I would pardon all three of you, and so I am. Consider yourself pardoned, and for God's sake, next time think before you act."

"We will!" Sir John exclaimed. "I plan to live the rest of my life at Rose Cottage, in quiet retirement. You'll never hear another peep out of me."

At this, Duke Owen actually laughed, and Harry and Andy laughed, too. "Come, John. Let's be realistic."

Sir John smiled broadly. "Well, maybe I'll get out now and again. But thank you, my lord."

"Aye," Harry said. "Thank you."

Andy said his thank-yous, but there was something else on his mind. "My lord, I would like to ask your advice about something."

"Yes?"

"It's about Maya."

Sir John clapped Andy's shoulder. "Seems like you have things well in hand."

Andy blushed. "It's not about that."

"Go on," Duke Owen said gently.

"For now, things are good for you. Your brother is gone, and you're back in Caxton. For Maya, her troubles aren't over. Back where she comes from, there is a man who is out to kill her and get the book. She's the most amazing girl I know. But she's only fifteen. How can she face this man—Chet—who has already murdered someone to get the book?"

"She needs help," Lord Owen stated.

"Yeah, she needs help. Big time. Maya said three librarians would be there to help her. But how are librarians going to defeat Chet, a vicious man who has something that will disable a Book of Everything? They're librarians. They shelve books. They don't fight."

The Green Book was open on Lord Owen's desk, and Andy could tell that Duke Owen was listening to it. Duke Owen looked from the book to Andy. "My book tells me that these librarians are tougher than they look and that they will be able to help Maya. She won't be alone."

"I want to help Maya, too."

Duke Owen shook his head. "My book has also told me about how you and Maya are from different times. You need to go back to your own time. There might be complications if your past self is in the same time as your future self."

Andy was quiet, but there was a stubborn look on his face, and Sir John spoke, "Andy, my boy, you and I learned the hard way what happens when you don't follow a Book of Everything's advice."

"And so have I," Duke Owen put in. "Had I listened, Humphrey might not have taken Caxton to begin with."

Sir John continued, "Look at the calamity we caused. Now, you don't want that to happen where you come from, do you?"

"No, I don't," Andy said slowly.

Sir John's face was serious. "So don't do anything foolish."

As much as Andy wanted to return to Maya's time and help her defeat Chet, he knew Duke Owen and Sir John were right. "I won't. I promise."

"Good," Duke Owen said. "See that you keep that promise."

"But what's going to happen with Chet?" Andy asked.

Duke Owen smiled. "The books have a plan for Chet."

"Does Maya know?"

"She knows. And Andy? You're right. She's an amazing girl."

Now it was Andy's turn to smile. But almost immediately, Andy felt a sadness and a loneliness settle on him as he thought about returning to his time and never seeing Maya again. Duke Owen nodded sympathetically, and Sir John's big hand came down on Andy's shoulder.

34: Leavings and Farewells

In the days that followed, Maya, Andy, Simon, Sir John, Harry, Elspeth, Alani, and even Rhys occasionally met at Rose Cottage, where Sir John's housekeeper, the "redoubtable Mrs. Hall," as he called her, served them tea and muffins. However, most of the time, they seemed to gravitate to Molly's parlor. Sir John wasn't surprised.

"We're near the source," he said, helping himself to a plum tart from a big platter Molly had set on the table. "Mrs. Hall is good in her own way, but there's no one that can touch Molly when it comes to cooking."

Everyone nodded, and for a while the room was quiet as plum tarts were eaten and tea was drunk. Three days had passed since Duke Owen had ridden into Caxton, and they all had had soft beds to sleep in and three meals a day, with an afternoon tea as well. Simon had never had so much to eat, and he viewed the abundance with a mixture of amazement and gratitude. As long as Simon could remember, his mother had had to ration their food, to make things last as long as possible.

They were rested and well fed, and the time, as they all knew, had come for the travelers to return to their homes.

Rhys had decided to stay and help Duke Owen restore Caxton to the way it was before Humphrey took over. "When will you all be leaving?" he asked Maya, Andy, Elspeth, and Alani.

"Alani and I will be returning to the Great Library after we finish our tea and tarts," Elspeth said. "We've already taken our leave of the duke."

"And after tea, Andy and I will be returning to our homes, too," Maya added.

"You will be missed." Rhys looked at them all, but he looked longest at Elspeth.

"And we will miss you," Elspeth replied, her cheeks flushing just a little. "Despite what Humphrey did, Caxton is a good place. With Duke Owen's guidance, it will recover."

"It's a beautiful place," Maya said, thinking of the Forest of Arden.

"It really is," Andy agreed. "The most beautiful I've ever seen."

"I wish we could all come back for a visit," Alani said in her impulsive way. "But we're lucky we got to come at all."

Elspeth laughed. "Especially you." And seeing the abashed expression on Alani's face, she added, "But your quick ways certainly came in handy."

The Apprentice Book might have said, "See? I told you Alani could be useful." But it was closed and in the pocket of Elspeth's trousers.

"What about me?" Simon asked in a small voice. "What am I going to do?"

"You can stay right in Caxton," Sir John said. "One of the castle's stable boys died during the battle, and the job is yours, if you want it. What do you say?"

"Aye!" Simon answered quickly. "I want it." Somehow, even though everything had worked out the way it should, Simon decided it would be best to stay in Caxton for a while.

Simon also shrewdly realized that Andy had been right. Simon could make more money and have more room for advancement in Caxton than in Greendale. Then, in turn, he could give more money to his mother.

"What's going to happen to Julian?" Rhys asked.

"He's going to be a permanent resident of the castle, where we can all keep track of him. Thanks to something that Evangeline gave him, his memory is gone, and right now he is not a threat," Elspeth answered. "He seems content to just sit by the window and read. Eli is attending him."

"Won't Cinnial notice that something is wrong?" Andy asked.

"Not right off. I get the feeling that there has been a schism between Julian and Cinnial." Elspeth turned to Maya. "Did you get that feeling, too?"

Maya nodded. "I did. I think Julian didn't want to be here, and Cinnial sent him as some kind of punishment."

"Ha!" Sir John protested. "A punishment! What a way to think of Albion."

"There are lots of different places in the universe, aren't there?" Rhys asked, staring intently at Elspeth.

"Indeed there are," Elspeth answered carefully. "Some are a lot like Albion. Others are not."

"I'd like to see some of them," Rhys said. "I'd like to see the Great Library."

"Not too likely," Elspeth said softly, and she looked a little wistful. "But you never know."

"Time likes to keep its options open," Maya said, thinking back to a conversation she had had with Sydda.

Elspeth laughed. "Yes, it does." And Rhys smiled at her.

When the tarts and tea were gone, Sir John stood and so did Harry. "Simon, my boy, come with us. We'll bring you to the stables and introduce you."

Simon stood and turned to Andy. "Well, goodbye." Simon tried to say this in an offhand way, but his voice caught at the end of the sentence, and the effect was ruined.

Andy put his hand on the boy's shoulder. "Goodbye, Simon. I never would have made it to Caxton without you." Simon just nodded, unable to speak.

"Let's get out of here," Sir John cried, "before we start having a blubberfest." One of his big hands steered Simon toward the door. But then he stopped, and his eyes were bright. "Goodbye to you all! Who knows what would have happened if you hadn't come along? The forest might have been burned down and Duke Owen either captured or killed. Farewell to you all, and many thanks."

With Harry adding his own farewells, the three left Molly's parlor.

Rhys shook his head. "I'll be around to keep an eye on the three of them."

"Good," Maya replied, and now it was her turn to be sad. "With Feste gone, someone will need to."

"Farewell," Rhys said. "A part of me hopes that we meet again, and a part of me doesn't. If we do, I'm sure it will be because there is trouble."

He left quickly, and Elspeth and Alani turned to Maya and Andy. "Well," Elspeth said, taking the Apprentice Book from her pocket.

"Well," Maya echoed, removing the Book of Everything from her own pocket.

Leaning forward, Elspeth kissed Maya's forehead. "Take care, Maya. You are going back to a dangerous situation. But the librarians are well equipped to help you."

"Thank you," Maya said, blinking rapidly. "Thank you for everything you've done."

"It was an adventure," Elspeth said with a smile. "I must say, I enjoyed it." She turned to Andy. "And good luck to you with the rest of your life. It seems to me that you've learned quite a few things."

"Yeah, I sure have," Andy answered.

Elspeth took out her gold glasses and put them on. "And you'll carry them forward with you." Elspeth looked as though she would have liked to have said more, but she didn't. Instead, she put her glasses away.

"Do you have the lucky coin to take back to the Great Library?" Maya asked.

Elspeth patted the front pocket of her waistcoat. "I do, and I'll be careful not to lose it."

Alani didn't say anything. Sniffing loudly, she just hugged Maya and Andy, who, in turn, hugged her back.

Finally, Elspeth and Maya opened the books.

The Book of Everything spoke to the Apprentice Book. "You did all right."

"Thank you. I was nervous. I messed up a couple of times."

"But it was nothing major," Elspeth said. "I'll be able to make a good report to both Sydda and the board."

Maya touched the Apprentice Book. "Goodbye. And thank you."

"It was my pleasure," said the Apprentice Book.

"Are we ready?" Elspeth asked, and everyone nodded. "All right, then."

Within a whirling few minutes, Maya and Andy were back in Andy's clean, tiny kitchen. "It looks exactly the same as when we left," he marveled.

"No reason why it shouldn't," Maya said. "I asked the book to bring us back pretty much the same time we left."

Andy nodded, and neither he nor Maya spoke for a while. "I'd better go," Maya finally said.

"Are you sure you'll be all right?"

"Yes, I trust the book and the librarians."

"I'd like to come with you, but I know I can't."

"No, you belong in this time, and I belong in my own."

Bending down, Andy kissed her on the lips. "Do you think we'll ever meet again?"

Maya, a little breathless, was about to say no, but then she had the strongest feeling that she would see him again. "You know, I think we will. Goodbye, Andy."

"Goodbye, Maya. I hope I do see you again."

And with that, Maya was back in her very own room under the eaves in the old farmhouse in East Vassalboro. Except for the low murmuring of the television downstairs, the house was still, and she could hear the tick, tick, tick of the old pendulum clock in the hallway. Maya turned to the book for advice, but it was silent and this could only mean one thing—Chet was nearby. She quickly pulled down the shades and took out her cell phone from the back pocket of her trousers. Turning on her phone, Maya called Anne.

"Stay where you are," Anne instructed her. "We'll take care of Chet, and we'll call you when we're ready."

"All right," Maya said, and after she hung up, she sat on the bed. Maya pictured Chet, hiding somewhere, probably in the field behind the house. She thought of the librarians, who would be stalking him. What was happening? Had they found him yet? Could the three librarians really deal with Chet?

Jumping up, Maya began to pace. She had been in the center of so much, in Albion and at the Great Library, that she couldn't stand being cooped up in her room while the librarians confronted Chet. She itched to go to the back field and help. True, Maya was still afraid of Chet, but she had had her eyes peeled, she had traveled to the Great Library, and she had faced Julian. Could Chet be any worse? Maya didn't think so.

Maya knew she should follow Anne's instructions—she really did—but after ten minutes, Maya couldn't wait any longer. She would need some kind of weapon—she just couldn't go out empty-handed.

Unlocking the desk, Maya put the Book of Everything into one of the compartments and hunted around the other compartments. Nothing. Then she opened the drawer and saw a little white-handled jackknife. Thinking of the knife that had stabbed Julian, Maya almost laughed. What good would a jackknife be against Chet? Still, it was better than nothing, and she shoved it in her pocket.

Maya bolted from her room and ran down the stairs. Her mother and grandparents were watching television, and as Maya ran down the hall to the kitchen, Mémère called out, "Where are you going, Maya?"

"To see Anne Hunter. We're working on a project." And before Mémère could say anything, Maya was out the door.

35: The Whirligig of Time

Chet was hiding in a stand of trees in the field behind the old farmhouse. Under the light of a half-moon, he was enveloped by night noises—frogs, owls, and the sound of the wind as it blew through the trees. It almost made Chet feel nostalgic for the farm he had come from, where his mother had worked and scrubbed until her hands were red.

Chet knew the girl was upstairs in the house. As he had sneaked around the backside of the house with its connected shed and barn, he had seen her outline briefly by the window as she had peered out and then had hurriedly pulled down the shades. "So close," Chet thought. The girl and the book were so close. Chet patted his pocket. The book would not be able to help her now, no matter where it had taken her or what it had shown her. After all, what could a book do with a fifteen-year-old girl? It must have been desperate, Chet decided, his lips curling.

Chet clutched his gun with its silencer. He would wait in the field until everyone went to bed and then creep inside. If he was lucky, and Chet expected he would be, then a door would remain unlocked, and he could slip in without being heard. If not, well, he would find another way. It was hot, and all the windows were open. Chet could cut through one of the screens and crawl into the house. Contented, Chet settled against a tree. Everything was in its place. There was the gun, of course, and he also had a knife hanging from his belt. The device was in one pocket, and a small flashlight was in the other.

He heard a movement through the grass, and Chet waited, still and ready. But nothing emerged from the tall grass, and Chet concluded it was just an animal, a fox, maybe. Just as he settled back against the tree, he heard another sound, a little louder than the first. Chet was certain this was no fox. It was a two-legged creature trying to be stealthy and almost succeeding. Silently, Chet moved around the tree, away from the sound. Peeking around the trunk, Chet saw a slight figure creeping toward him. Could this be Maya? Could it really be this easy? But why was she out here?

In the moonlight, Chet could see her looking from side to side, as though she was searching for someone. Then she stopped.

"Who's there?" she called softly.

Quickly and quietly, Chet struck, rushing out from behind the tree and grabbing Maya. He put the gun to her back.

She gave a little shriek, and he said, "Any more of that, and I'll shoot you."

Maya was still, and Chet asked, "Why are you out here?" There was no answer, and he shook her hard. "Tell me!"

"I was going to meet a boy," Maya blurted out. "I waited for a while, but he never came, and I was about to go back home."

"A boy." Chet was not sure whether he believed Maya, but he could picture two teenagers creeping out to a back field to be together, and the idea disgusted him. "He better not show up, or I'll shoot him."

"He isn't coming." Maya's voice was genuinely sad as she thought about Andy and how she desperately wished that he were coming to help her.

"Good," Chet said, and he abruptly changed the subject. "In Rhode Island, you got a book from a woman on the train. Where's the book?"

Maya twisted around to consider him, and Chet had the feeling that she was trying to see into him. Chet felt uneasy—who was this girl, anyway?—but he knew how to close himself away from unwanted attention, and he directed all his focus toward Maya. "If you don't answer my question, then I will break your arm."

Maya could tell he wasn't bluffing, and she realized she should have followed Anne's instructions. Maya had been looking for the librarians—she could sense they were somewhere in the field—but instead she had blundered into Chet. Maya remembered how Jennifer had said there was something about Chet that eluded the Book of Everything's attention, and Maya realized the same thing had happened to her. She hadn't known Chet was behind the tree until she was nearly on top of him.

"I've hidden the book," Maya answered, her mouth dry.

Chet leaned down until his lips were by her ear, and his breath was hot and sour. Squeezing her arm, he whispered, "Go get the book and bring it to me. If you're not back within five minutes, then I'll come looking for you and the book. And if I have to come into the house, then I will kill your mother and your grandparents. Oh, yes. I know all about them."

"Can you really just get away with killing so many people?" Maya heard herself ask. Now what had made her say that? Mouthy to the end, as her father might have said.

"I can indeed," came the whispered answer. "When you know the right people, you can get away with a lot."

"But why do you do it?" Maya was stalling for time, hoping that the librarians would find them, but a part of her really did want to know why Chet did what he did. Holding her breath, Maya waited for Chet to break her arm, but instead he answered her question.

"Why? Because someone needs to keep things in line, to keep order. To make sure the right people get the right things."

"The right people?"

"There's us, and then there's the rest of you." Chet's voice was contemptuous. "And what's good for the right people is good for the rest of you. People have forgotten how to work hard, and now they expect handouts."

"That's not true!" Maya couldn't keep the indignation out of her voice, even though Chet had a gun pressed to her back and a tight grip on her arm. "People can work hard and still be poor." Mémère Celine had said this many times, and after meeting Andy and his mother, Maya was beginning to understand what Mémère had meant.

"A little idealist," Chet said, sneering. "Where did you get that from? Your artist mother and your professor father? You've had quite the easy life, haven't you? Private school, vacations, nice clothes. You've never had to work for anything, have you?"

"I'm only fifteen."

"Ha! At fifteen I was cleaning pig and chicken shit. Fifteen is not too young to work. Ten isn't too young to work. Even five-year-olds can do chores."

"Did you have to do chores when you were five?" Maya asked, and there was sympathy in her voice.

Chet squeezed her arm. "Never mind! Now go get that book. And remember, you have five minutes."

"Five minutes," Maya repeated, wondering where those librarians could be.

Chet let go of Maya's arm, and she sprinted across the field toward the farmhouse. She had to give him the book or else her mother and grandparents would die, but how could she just hand over the book to Chet?

Maya came to the edge of the field, and there, hiding in the lilac bushes by the side of the barn, was Anne. She had not been there when Maya had come into the field.

"Maya!" Anne called sharply but softly. "What are you doing out here? I told you to stay inside."

"I know," Maya whispered back. "But I had to come out and see what was going on. I ran into Chet, and he said if I don't give him the book, then he'll shoot my mother and my grand-parents."

"Where is he?"

"In the stand of trees on that little hill."

"No," said a still voice, and around the corner of the barn came Chet. "I'm right here, following you, to make sure you're doing what you're supposed to be doing. And what do I find? An accomplice. I knew there was something not quite right about you."

"You don't know a thing about me," Maya said defiantly. "Even though you think you do."

"But I will when I'm done," Chet said. "You'll talk. Both of you will. First I'm going to start with your friend and then will come your turn. But not out here. I passed some stalls under the barn. Now move it, both of you."

Anne raised her gun. "I'm armed, too. Drop your gun."

Chet aimed his gun at Maya's head. "Can you be sure you'll get me before I get Maya?" he asked Anne.

Anne lowered her gun. "Right," Chet said. "Now give the gun to me."

Silently, Anne did as she was told.

Chet took the gun. "A tranquilizer gun? Really?"

Anne replied coolly, "We're librarians. We don't shoot to kill. And that dart would drop you in no time."

"Fools," Chet muttered, throwing the gun into the field. As the gun disappeared into the tall grass, Maya slipped her hand into her pocket and found the little knife, which she opened. Chet was so intent on the tranquilizer pistol that he didn't see Maya fiddle with the knife, remove it from her pocket, and cup it in her hand.

"All right. Into the stalls."

Chet marched Anne and Maya around the barn, away from the house, and into the low, dark cow stalls. "Where's the light?" Chet asked.

"On the wall by the door," Maya answered. The little knife was ready, and as Chet groped for the light, looking away for a few seconds, Maya sprang at him just as he flicked the switch. She moved so fast that Chet didn't have time to react before the jackknife was in his shoulder. Screaming, Chet dropped his gun. Moving just as fast as Maya, Anne grabbed the gun.

Swearing, Chet caught Maya by the shoulder, but Maya still had the jackknife, and she stabbed him again, this time in the arm. "I'm going to slit your throat," Chet said, reaching for his own knife.

"No, you are not," Anne said, pointing the gun at Chet's leg. "Let Maya go and hand over the knife."

"Do as she says," another voice commanded. It was Jennifer, and she and David were standing in the doorway. They, too, had guns, and they were pointing them at Chet. "You are outnumbered and outgunned."

"Jennifer Morgan," Chet said, loosening his grip on Maya, who pulled away from him and stumbled to Anne's side. "I should have known you were behind this."

"Chet Addington," Jennifer replied. "At last we meet. Now give us the knife."

"Tranquilizer guns," Chet sneered.

"The gun I'm holding shoots bullets," Anne reminded him. "And I will use it if I have to."

Before Chet could reply, Jennifer pulled the trigger, and a dart hit Chet in the arm. His mouth went round with surprise, and he dropped the knife. Blinking once, twice, three times, Chet fell to his knees. He turned to Maya. "Don't think this is over." Then he slumped to the floor.

"Jennifer sure can shoot," Anne would say later. "She's the best shot in the league."

David searched Chet's pockets until he found the device. David also found Chet's cell phone and the keys to his car, and he gave them to Jennifer. Anne turned to Maya. "I'll take the device away from here. Call me as soon as the book works. We don't know the device's range."

"I will," Maya said as she ran from the cow stall to the house.

"Is that you again?" Mémère asked as a little later Maya sped back downstairs with the book in her pocket.

"It's me," Maya called rather breathlessly.

"What did you say you were doing?"

Maya quickly gathered her thoughts. "Anne Hunter, some of her friends, and I are in the cow stalls going through a play we might put on."

"In the cow stalls?"

"It's a creepy space with stairs going to the shed, which means we can block out the action. Right now we've just captured the bad guy."

This almost made sense, and Mémère had no reason to be suspicious. "All right, then."

With the book in her back pocket, Maya ran to the cow stalls. She opened the Book of Everything, and it asked, "Ready?"

"So the device has to be fairly close to work," Jennifer said, and Maya was not surprised that the librarian could hear the book's voice. "That's something, anyway."

"I'm ready." Maya put her hand on Chet's arm, and the two disappeared. Within minutes, Maya was back, alone.

"All set?" Jennifer asked.

"All set," Maya replied. "But I feel a little guilty bringing Chet to Caxton."

"But the book recommended it?" David asked.

"Not only our book," Maya answered. "But Albion's and the Apprentice Book, too."

Jennifer nodded, but her face was stern. "You should have followed Anne's instructions and stayed in your room until we captured Chet. You could have been killed. And Anne, too."

Maya felt her face flush. "I know. I'm sorry. I just couldn't wait."

"It turned out all right in the end," David said.

"It did. But still." Jennifer wagged her finger at Maya. "You might be gifted, but you still have a lot to learn."

Maya's face grew even hotter, and she stared at her shoes.

Jennifer sighed, but it was more a sigh of relief than an exasperated sigh, and when Maya hopefully looked up, she saw that Jennifer's expression was not so grim.

"You have quite a bit to tell us," Jennifer said. "Can you come to the library tomorrow morning before it opens and make a report?"

"I don't think there will be any problem," Maya said, relieved that the lecture was over. "When Mémère asked me what I was doing, I told her we were rehearsing for a play. I can say we're working on the play."

"You're certainly a quick thinker." Jennifer smiled just a little. "And you're dressed as though you're going to be in a play, that's for sure."

"Maybe *Oliver Twist*," David put in, staring at her trousers, her jacket, and her vest.

"My grandparents and mother haven't seen me yet," Maya said. "They just heard me in the hallway."

David grinned. "Wait until they see your hair."

Maya wrinkled her nose. "What am I going to say?"

"I have no doubt that you'll think of something," Jennifer replied. "And what about the book?"

Maya had been holding the book, and she opened it. "I want one last night with Maya," the book said. "And then I'll go with David."

Jennifer relayed the message to David, who could not hear the book. At least not yet. "We'd best be going. We need to find Chet's car and drive it back to where he rented it, so APO won't trace the car here. We're assuming it's a rented car, since he took the train at least as far as Providence."

"Chet's car is about a mile down the road, parked where there are no houses," the book said. "And he rented the car in Boston."

The book gave Jennifer the name and address of the rental agency, which she recorded in her phone. Looking up, she asked, "David, are you ready for a trip to Boston?"

"I'm ready," came the answer.

Jennifer continued, "We can use Chet's phone to text some messages to his APO contacts. We can tell them the book was here, which they no doubt know, but that now it is gone, and Chet is on its trail."

"Where did Anne bring the device?" Maya asked.

"To her mother's in Waterville, and we'll pick it up on our way to Boston so that we can drop the device off at the league's headquarters in Concord."

"It will be a little like traveling with a pit viper," David said

"Yes, it will," Jennifer agreed, heading toward door. "But the league needs to examine it soon before APO realizes what's happened."

David followed her. "Goodbye, Maya. Can't wait to hear your story."

"Yeah," Maya said, thinking of how much she had to tell them.

"Me, too." Turning, Jennifer patted her on the shoulder. "Goodbye, Maya. You've traveled a long ways, haven't you?"

"I have." Just thinking about the distance made Maya feel tired and grimy.

"Go take a bath," Jennifer advised. "And get a good night's sleep. You don't have to worry about Chet anymore. And Maya? Good job."

"Very good job!" David added, winking at Maya.

Then they were gone, disappearing into the dark field surrounding the house.

Maya followed Jennifer's advice. She went upstairs, washed her hands, started running water in the tub with the claw feet, and went to her bedroom for her pajamas. Maya locked the book in the desk, just in case. "I'll take you out as soon as I'm done with my bath."

"Who are you talking to, Maya?" Lily stood in the doorway. "What are you wearing? And you cut your hair?"

Maya jumped. "I was just talking to myself. And, yeah, I cut my hair. I was tired of having it long. The clothes are for the play we'll be putting on."

Lily folded her arms across her chest. "Those clothes look like they've seen a lot of wear."

Maya was about to reply, but the expression on Lily's face made Maya stop. For the first time, Maya could really see her mother, not just as a mom, which is how Maya had always seen her, but as a person, and with a shock Maya realized that Lily, too, could see things that other people could not. But unlike Maya, Lily's attention was not centered on people. Instead, it was on houses and landscapes and shapes and light and color. Her mother had never spoken about it, but then again, her mother was not much of a talker.

Maya also understood that even though people were not Lily's primary concern, there were a few people who were, and Maya was one of them. Besides art, Maya was Lily's main focus, and this had been one of the reasons why Giles had left. He couldn't stand being in third place. Second place, yes, because he loved Maya, but not third place, not behind art.

"Oh, Mom!" Maya cried, knowing that she should look away, that she should not be seeing so much. But somehow, she couldn't. All this time, Maya had thought she was like her father—and in many ways she was—but Maya now realized that in one crucial, essential way, she was like her mother, even though they used their talents for different things.

"What's wrong, Maya?" her mother asked. "What's happened?"

And Maya did something she had not done for a year or so, something that was not considered cool for a fifteen-year-old girl to do. Grabbing her mother, she hugged her fiercely, smelling the spicy sent of the soap Lily liked to use.

"Can't you tell me?" Lily asked softly. "You're not hurt, are you?"

Maya just shook her head, and there were tears in her eyes. She couldn't tell her mother all that had happened. Not yet. Maybe later. But then again, maybe never. Maya felt the strange sensation of wanting to protect her mother, of not wanting her to know how strong, malicious forces were at work everywhere in the universe. Maya wanted her mother to paint and not worry and not know how many tight spots Maya had been in. And besides, would her mother even believe her?

"Tell me when you're ready, then." Lily patted Maya's back and kissed the top of her head. "You better go check the water in the tub. You don't want it to overflow. And when you're done with your bath, come downstairs. I'll make you some popcorn."

Sniffing, Maya rubbed her eyes and went to the bathroom, where the tub was indeed quite full. She returned to her bedroom, grabbed her pajamas, and undressed in the bathroom.

Never before had a bath felt so good, and never before had Maya been so eager to sit on the couch with her mother and eat a bowl of popcorn. Clean and in her pajamas, Maya went back to her room, and folding the waistcoat and the trousers, she put them on the chair by the desk. Maya removed her cell phone. Later, Maya would click through the pictures until she found the one of Feste and Andy, taken in front of the lodge in the Forest of Arden. They both looked so impossibly real and the lodge so impossibly solid, and Maya would stare at the picture for a long time.

When Maya went downstairs, her mother and grand-mother were in the kitchen making popcorn and iced tea. Her grandfather was in his recliner, and he looked at her.

"Nice haircut," he said. "Cute and curly."

"Thanks, Pépère." Maya sat on the couch.

"Time for the nightly news. Big doings in Maine right now. The president is vacationing in Bar Harbor."

"Leah texted and told me. Her family has been invited to one of the president's parties. Her father's all excited."

"It's not every day that the president invites you to a party."

"No, it isn't."

"And it's not every day that a president comes from Maine."

Maya was about to agree but found herself strangely speechless. She didn't pay much attention to politics, but she, of course, knew the president had come from Maine.

"From Waterville!" her grandmother had crowed after the last election. "I didn't know his family, but they didn't live that far from us. His last name might be Murphy, but his mother was a Bolduc. So he's part French."

"And he sure can speak a lot of languages," Pépère had put in. "I wonder how he learned so many, growing up in Waterville."

The news came on, and there was a picture of the good-looking president with his good-looking family, his wife and daughter. They were staying in a big house with gray shingles, and there were people all around.

On that lush green lawn, with his laughing daughter and smiling wife, stood none other than Andy, an adult Andy with those blue, blue eyes, and his dark hair was now speckled with gray. Maya's thoughts raced: "President Murphy! Why didn't I realize? Well, he never even told me his last name. All I knew him by was Andy, and now he's President Drew Murphy. Why couldn't the book have told me? It should have told me!"

But then Maya saw something on television that stopped her racing thoughts. Standing among a group of the president's friends and advisors was Duke Owen's brother, Humphrey, sharp and dark haired, dressed in modern clothes and with a modern haircut. He, too, was smiling, but in a lean, avid way. "Maybe I'm wrong," Maya thought desperately. "Maybe it's just someone who looks like Humphrey." But Maya wasn't wrong, and she knew it.

"It's quite something, isn't it?" Pépère asked. "All that commotion."

"Oh, yes," Maya agreed. "It certainly is."

Preview

Library Lost

Book Two in the Great Library Series

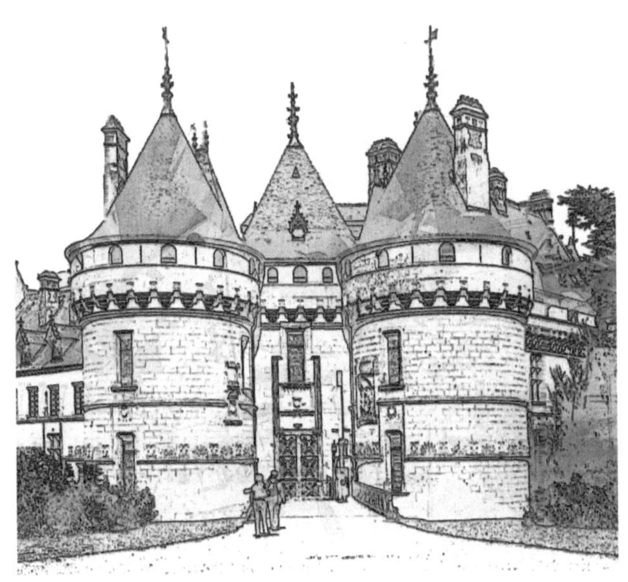

1: The Book Has Some Explaining to Do

Maya sat on the couch between her mother and her mémère. As she drank iced tea and ate the freshly popped popcorn—"No microwave for us," Mémère insisted—Maya tried not to think about Humphrey and Andy, both in Bar Harbor, about three hours from Mémère and Pépère's home in East Vassalboro. Maya just wanted to relax, to listen to Mémère's plan for the next day, which involved going shopping, and to listen to her mother's brief, soft responses.

But despite her best intentions, Maya did keep thinking about Humphrey and Andy. How long had it been since she had seen Andy? No more than three hours, Maya decided. It had been in 1976, and he had been seventeen years old. But now—as Maya had just seen on TV on the evening news—Andy was at least as old as her own father.

"And the president of the United States," Maya thought. "That book sure has some explaining to do."

But Maya was too tired and shocked to race upstairs and find out what the book had to say for itself. "The book should have told me," Maya thought wearily, resting her head against the back of the couch.

Then there was Humphrey, murderous Humphrey from Albion and the faraway planet of Ilyria. He was with Andy in Bar Harbor. "President Murphy," Maya thought, correcting herself. But why was Humphrey so close to the president of the United States? Why couldn't President Murphy see Humphrey for what he was—cruel and aggressive and ambitious—and that he was not to be trusted? But even as Maya formed this question in her mind, she knew the answer. Andy, or President Murphy, couldn't see people the way she could. That was not his talent. Instead, it seemed, winning elections was his talent.

Mémère had stopped talking and was staring curiously at Maya. "You're quiet tonight."

"I'm tired," Maya answered truthfully. Beside Maya, her mother shifted uneasily, knowing something was wrong but not knowing exactly what that something was.

"You need to get a good night's sleep so that we can have fun when we go shopping," Mémère said. "Do you want me to call my hairdresser, Dot, to find out if she has time to trim your hair tomorrow?"

Maya shook her head. On Ilyria, Feste had cut her hair, and Maya didn't want anyone else to touch it, at least not for a while.

Mémère squinted critically at Maya's hair. "It's cute, all short and curly like that, but it needs shaping."

"Not right now, Mémère," Maya said quietly but firmly, sounding more like an adult than a teenager. Maya could sense Mémère puzzling over the adult tone of voice. "Maybe in a week or two," Maya added quickly.

"All right, all right." Mémère patted Maya's leg and kissed her cheek. "I'm so glad to have you here."

After all that she had been through—going back in time, traveling to the Great Library and to Ilyria—Maya was glad to be in East Vassalboro, too, and she smiled at her grandmother, who smiled back and gave her another kiss on the cheek.

Much later that night, when the house was dark, and the only sound was the ticking of the pendulum clock in the hallway, Maya crept out of bed, went to the desk, unlocked it, and took out the Book of Everything. Maya didn't say anything until she was buried beneath the covers—hot though the night was—and even then she whispered.

"Why didn't you tell me about Andy, that he's President Murphy? Why did you have to let me see him on the evening news?"

"I'm sorry, Maya," the book replied. "I couldn't tell you when we were in Albion. You might have given too much away. Andy had to discover his path on his own, not because of something you let slip. And when we got back to Earth, there wasn't time. I was going to tell you tonight."

Maya was about to remind the book that she could keep a secret, but then Maya stopped—she knew the book was right. In Albion, she and Andy had become close, and Maya might have said something, perhaps unintentionally, perhaps not. "You could have at least told me about Humphrey," Maya whispered at last.

"Humphrey?" the Book of Everything asked, and it sounded genuinely surprised.

"Humphrey. He was right there next to President Murphy. And Humphrey looked like he was up to no good. Same as ever." The Book of Everything was quiet, and at first Maya was puzzled, but then she understood. "You didn't know, did you? That's what you meant when you told me that something I would see in Albion would help me on Earth."

"That's right. I knew something was going on, that someone with a book had come to Earth years ago, when Andy was still a senator. But I didn't know who it was."

"The books can shield themselves and whoever has them."

"They do, except when they travel, there is always a little burst of energy. But as far as we know, the only time Humphrey has traveled with the book was when he came to Earth. At the time, the feeling at the Great Library was that it was someone sent by Cinnial to help APO steal me, even though Earth is not exactly at the center of things."

Maya thought about APO—the Association for the Preservation of Order—and of how they had been after the Book of Everything for a long, long time. "But it was Humphrey, instead, with the book he stole from Julian."

"Ilyria and Earth have a connection," the book replied. "Somehow, even though I didn't know about Humphrey, I had a hunch that taking you to Ilyria would be the right thing to do."

"You'll let the Great Library know?"

"I will." The book's voice sounded amused. "I'm in constant contact with the Great Library. They have a data team, a small one, to keep track of me. And now, after your visit to the Great Library, Sydda himself will be checking in on me, from time to time."

"But what could Humphrey be doing here?"

"Who stabbed Julian?"

Maya put a hand to her face. "I did. Julian's book brought Humphrey to Earth because of me."

"And you were also instrumental in helping Owen defeat Humphrey."

Maya sighed. "So both Julian's book and Humphrey are out to get me. What am I going to do? You're supposed to go to Hartland with David tomorrow."

"I'll let the Great Library know what has happened. You won't be left to your own devices. I promise. And I have a plan."

"What is it?"

"I'm going to ask Sydda to let you use the Apprentice Book again, the same one you brought to Albion from the Great Library."

Maya was shocked. "The board will never agree to let the book go out again."

"I think they might. The situation on this planet is more critical than it ever has been. APO has developed a device that will immobilize me. The League of Librarians has captured one of the devices, but there are probably more out there. Humphrey has Julian's book, and they are plotting something that includes you." The book's voice became firm. "Other planets are having similar problems, and we Books of Everything could use the help. The Apprentice Books have been shut up for way too long. They need a purpose, too. It is time for the board to relax its policy."